DELTA G

DAVID J. CRAWFORD

Published in 2012, by Gypsy Publications
Troy, OH 45373, U.S.A.
www.GypsyPublications.com

Copyright © David Crawford, 2012

Crawford, David J.
Delta G / by David J. Crawford
ISBN 978-1938768-03-3 (paperback)

Library of Congress Control Number
2012945995

Edited by Rosemary Naulty
Cover and Book Design by Tim Rowe

Photos Courtesy of: USAF, NASA, US DOE, Franklin, R. and
Gosling, R.G., Greg Trent, Becker-Hagens, Brain/Mind Bulletin –
1987, Physiology in Fractal Dimensions, American Scientists, Vol 75,
American Journal of Orthodontics, Fibonacci Quarterly, Dec 1979

PRINTED IN THE UNITED STATES OF AMERICA

ACKNOWLEDGEMENTS

I would like to thank several people who have contributed and helped me with this effort, especially my wife, Irene, who has spent countless hours editing and supporting me in having this book come to fruition.

I am grateful to Mr. Gary Taube, a colleague and close friend, who has provided invaluable technical advice and guidance.

I would also like to thank and dedicate this book to my loving parents, Gary and Judy for raising and nurturing me to be able to follow my dreams and to use any God given tallents. Thank you both.

ABOUT THE BOOK

This science fiction novel starts with the search for an explanation as to why targeting errors were occurring with ICBM warheads along with unexplained orbital shifts in satellites and space shuttles. The investigation conducted by the Air Force leads to the discovery of new forces in nature. As it turns out, an effort has been underway for half a century to understand and harness these forces which will open the door to the secrets of the universe.

Major Dave Sheridan started his career as a young lieutenant assigned as a missile engineer working with Titan II ICBMs under the foothills of the Ozark Mountains in Arkansas. These ICBMs used a targeting algorithm that included 13 variables. One of them was the Earth's acceleration due to gravity. This value is extremely important to an ICBM targeting system that used accelerometers as part of its inertial navigation system for guidance and course changes. Certain variations in the Earth's gravity are well known, mapped, and understood depending on location. However, unexpected anomalies were encountered that could not be explained. Other strange forces of nature came into play. An investigation into targeting errors leads to discoveries of earth shattering proportion.

The search for answers takes Dave Sheridan on a twenty-five year quest from the top of the world in Greenland, to the remote deserts of the Nevada Test Site, to the tropical waters and islands off Florida's southeast coast, and finally to the Headquarters for Air Force research and development at Wright-Patterson Air Force Base in Ohio.

What was found involved the stitching of the fabric of time and space. Gravitational waves do exist as well as more bizarre torsional waves. These waves can be focused, bent, and even amplified by humans resulting in antigravity. These waves shape the universe we live in and link mind to matter.

Even more alarming is that these forces of nature are not new to the human race. This book neatly ties together several mysteries, legends, myths, and, rumors to explain the unexplainable. Nature in itself is very simple to understand once its secrets are revealed.

However, strange any of this may sound, time is related to both gravity and magnetism. Atomic clocks record time passing slightly faster in orbit than at sea level, the difference being gravity is weaker higher up. An electrical current will produce a magnetic field at right angles to it, but since there are three planes of space, where is the gravitational plane? No one, including Einstein, could ever find it. What forces really exist out there? The Delta G Program Office knows and this book lays it out.

INTRODUCTION

All hell had broken out in the Ozark Foothills in the late summer of 1980. A Titan II Intercontinental Ballistic Missile (ICBM) had just exploded destroying its silo. The violent explosion had ripped the silo open and tossed the missile's 10 Megaton Nuclear Warhead several hundred yards into the drainage ditch alongside the site's gravel access road.

This aging fleet carried the United States' largest warhead known as a city cracker and consisted of 54 missiles that couldn't hit the broadside of a barn. Close only counts in horseshoes, hand grenades and nuclear weapons. Something was wrong with the guidance package.

The Space Shuttle Launch Complex SLC-6 (pronounced Slick Six) was designed and built on the California west coast at Vandenberg Air Force Base to launch space shuttles into a north-south polar orbit. The complex cost billions of dollars and was never used. It was supposedly shut down due to environmental concerns. Could it be that the real reason was that it was too dangerous and "forbidden" to launch manned space vehicles across the poles?

What do the Greenland Icecap, the Mojave Desert, and the Bermuda Triangle have in common? They contain material of near constant density, such as ice, volcanic tuff, and seawater respectively. Constant density of large volumes of mass is a prerequisite for harnessing gravity waves and torsional waves.

If the age of the Earth were represented by a twelve hour clock, humankind has inhabited it for only nineteen seconds. Or has it? There have been billions of years on this Earth that would have, could have, and must have sustained ancient races of beings with equal or superior intelligence to the human race. This book delves into these lost civilizations and how humankind has accidentally rediscovered them and is now tapping into huge libraries of knowledge, harnessing vast amounts of energy, and is now on the threshold of interstellar travel.

What do all of the following events have in common?

- The 1945 atomic bomb detonations
- Admiral Bird's flight to the North Pole in 1947
- The Roswell Incident in 1947
- A Titan II ICBM Blowing up in its silo in 1980
- Hurricane Andrew in 1992
- DNA
- Crop Circles
- ESP, Remote Viewing, and Kirlian Photography
- The Bermuda Triangle
- The Coral Castle

You'll be surprised to find out!

CHAPTER 1

The Big Bang

Standing on an aluminum grated platform 150 feet atop a Titan II ICBM silo, a technician is tightening a fixture with a nine pound socket wrench. As he struggles to get a good grip, it slips out of his hand and falls between the work platform and the missile. Just like Newton's apple, it accelerates downward, tumbling as it falls. It makes a metallic clanging noise when it hits the missile's thrust mount, and then ricochets up into the bottom of the first stage fuel tank making a sickening thud. This was then followed by a voice shouting the two most uttered words heard at all accidents and catastrophes. "Oh, shit!" echoed off the silo walls.

A few hours later and a thousand miles away, the sound of footsteps flying up the narrow wooden stairs roused newly commissioned Second Lieutenant David Sheridan out of his bed. His father was racing upstairs to wake him up and tell him a missile silo had blown up. It was one of his missile silos, or at least, soon to be his, in a manner of speaking. Sheridan had just been commissioned from the Air Force Officer Training School, known as OTS, in San Antonio, Texas. He was home on leave in northwest Ohio prior to heading to his first assignment. Sheridan was assigned as a missile engineer with the 308th Strategic Missile Wing just north of Little Rock, Arkansas.

Dave threw on his pants and raced downstairs. CBS news was reporting that a huge explosion had just shaken north central Arkansas and that towns were being evacuated and the entire area was being cordoned off. It wasn't known yet if there was an actual nuclear detonation. It was Friday, September 19, 1980.

The Titan II carried the largest warhead in the US inventory. An Office of Technology Assessment study had estimated that a 10 megaton air burst on Leningrad would result in 2.4 million fatalities and 1.1 million injuries.

As more and more information trickled in, it was reported that an Air Force technician doing routine maintenance in the silo had dropped a wrench which rolled off a work platform and fell to the bottom of the silo. The socket bounced off the thrust mount and struck the missile, causing a leak from a pressurized fuel tank. The missile complex and surrounding area was evacuated. Eight and a half hours later, hypergolic fuel vapors within the silo ignited and exploded with enough force to blow the 740 ton silo door several hundred yards. The incident was classified as a Broken Arrow and would trigger events and procedures for the Strategic Air Command to locate, secure, and recover the ten megaton nuclear warhead that was found six hundred feet away in a drainage ditch. The explosion killed an Air Force specialist and injured twenty-one other USAF personnel.

When Second Lieutenant Sheridan arrived at Little Rock AFB the following week, all hell was breaking out. Talk about your baptism with fire. Sheridan was escorted from the base personnel office by his new sponsor and supervisor, Major Larry Norris. Norris explained how things were very hectic and that it may take a couple of weeks for things to die down and get back to normal. Little did they know, normalcy never would come back to Little Rock AFB. On his way to his new office, Norris brought Sheridan into the Missile Maintenance facility. Laid out on the concrete floor were several shards of twisted metal. Also, what looked like two sets of astronaut suits were laying in a far corner. They were shredded and blood stained as if someone had blasted them a dozen times with a shot gun. One helmet was cracked in a half dozen places. Norris explained that these were the RFHCO or Rocket Fuel Handlers Clothing Outfits worn by two airmen that had volunteered to take explosive fuel vapor buildup readings in the silo just before it exploded. They had just registered and reported explosive level readings pegging the needle and were exiting the silo entrance portal when the blast occurred. One airman was relatively sheltered behind the silo portal door. The other was peppered with shrapnel, concrete, and gravel. He lived only a short while.

Lieutenant Sheridan moved into his new office. He was introduced to Bill Green, a civilian engineer, who had been on the base for nearly twenty years. He also met Chief Mitchell. One piece of advice he remembered from OTS was that when you have an opportunity to work closely with a chief master sergeant, latch on to him and then soak up all the experience and knowledge you can. Between Bill and the Chief, there was nearly fifty years of missile experience to glean.

Bill had arranged for a site visit the next week to an operational missile site. Before that, the days were spent in safety training and security training. This also meant Sheridan had to come up to speed quickly and become intimately familiar with the Titan II systems and their silos. He spent the next week pouring over the weapon system drawings, operations manuals, and schematics.

On the surface, the Titan II launch facilities covered an area of approximately 600 x 600 feet or about eight acres. All of the launch facilities were underground. The silo was built of heavily reinforced concrete, and was 147 feet deep and 55 feet in diameter. They were designed to be "hot launched" from within the silo. To deflect and channel the exhaust gases, each silo was fitted with a flame deflector at the base and two exhaust ducts that ran up the length of the silo, venting to the surface. Inside the silo there were nine levels of equipment rooms and missile access spaces. The 740 ton steel and concrete silo door could be opened in 17 to 20 seconds.

The silo was connected to the missile control center by a 250 foot long access tunnel. Between the silo and the launch control center was the blast lock, a single level, heavily reinforced concrete structure containing three rooms. To enter the launch facility the missile crews descended through a 35 foot deep access portal that opened into the blast lock area. Each end of the blast lock was covered by a pair of large steel blast doors, each weighing 6,000 pounds. They were designed to protect the launch center from either a surface nuclear blast, or the explosion of the missile within the silo. The doors were designed to withstand an overpressure of 1000 psi; while being so perfectly balanced on their hinges, a single person could manually open them.

The launch control center was a dome-shaped, reinforced concrete structure 37 feet in diameter containing three levels. The three floors within the launch center were suspended from the ceiling by massive springs to minimize blast shock. The control center provided space for all of the launch control and communications equipment, as well as a mess and sleeping quarters for the four-person combat crew.

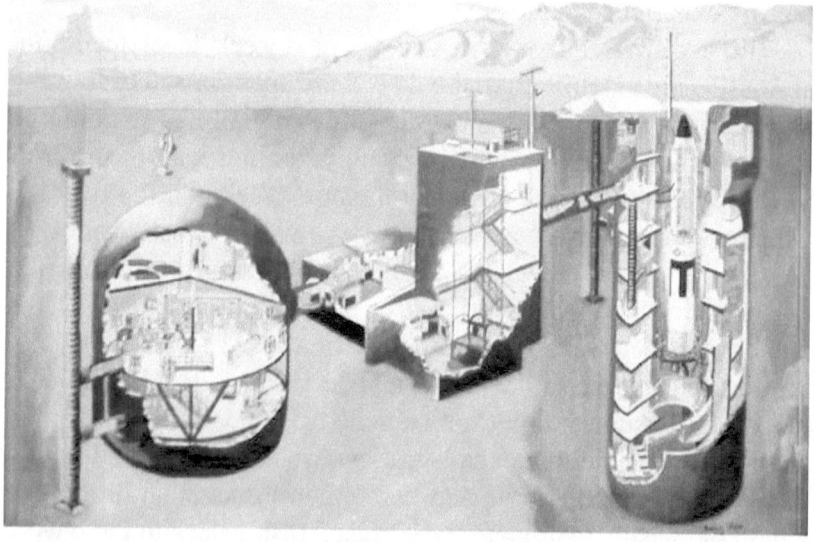

The TITAN II ICBM measured 110 feet in length and 10 feet in diameter, utilized in excess of 200,000 pounds of two part hypergolic propellant, igniting on contact, and produced 530,000 pounds of thrust. The TITAN II had a target range of 5,500 miles.

It is a two stage liquid fueled booster, designed to provide a small to medium weight class capability and able to lift approximately 4,200 pounds into a polar low-Earth circular orbit.

There were 54 Titan IIs placed on alert despite the fielding of more than 1,000 of the much easier to operate solid fueled LGM-30 Minuteman. This was because the huge 10 megaton warheads of these few Titan IIs represented almost 30 percent of the overall ICBM megatonage of the USAF's Strategic Air Command (SAC).

The Titan II was a very reliable missile; it was therefore used by NASA in the Gemini manned spaceflight program. Initially, the USAF made very limited use of the Titan II as a space launch vehicle under the strategic launch vehicle (SLV-4) designator.

Sheridan's first official task as a newly commissioned officer was to support the accident investigation and assist in disaster recovery. This included methods to monitor groundwater contamination and assist in fuel decontamination of the destroyed silo.

Bill made arrangements to get a base chopper to ferry them out to Silo 4-7 early that morning. When they arrived at the helicopter operations center, both went through the safety and preflight brief and then walked out onto the ramp. The sun was just coming up and it was hoped that the fog would burn off before they got airborne and out to the site. This was his first chopper flight and he couldn't wait. The crew chief helped him strap in. The seat belt and shoulder straps had a weird quick-release system. After he was snugged up, the crew chief just smiled, gave a com check on the intercom headset, and then pointed to where the barf bags were. The unwritten rule was if you chuck it up, you cleaned it up. It didn't matter if you were a buck sergeant or a four star general.

After the preflight and all the "remove before flight" ribbons were removed, the flight crew hopped in. This was going to be a training flight. There was another butter bar in the right seat of the chopper. The turbines were started, radios set, flight instruments set, and then rotors engaged. The rpm spun up and the chopper began to shake violently.

Several rivets, screws, nuts, and bolts were dancing around the floor. The crew chief grinned and calmly pulled out a whisk broom to sweep them into a coffee can. "More of these where those came from, Lieutenant."

Just then the pilot pulled on the collective stick and the chopper rose about ten feet off the ramp. The chopper hovered for a while and then taxied off the ramp onto the runway. As the pilot pushed in the cyclic stick, the good ol' Huey nosed downward. It looked like the ramp was going to smack them all in the face. Instead, the chopper hung nose down as it accelerated down the runway gaining altitude on its outbound trek.

By this time, the fog was burning off and the sun was rising as a big beautiful orange ball on the horizon. The chopper turned north and climbed over a ridge line. Complex 374-7, as it was known, was about sixty miles northwest of the base near a little town called Damascus. The chopper flight was exhilarating.

Up until this time Dave had only flown a total of four times. Once when he was thirteen after spending the summer with a friend in Massachusetts and he flew home in a 727. His father took him up in a Cessna when he was fourteen. His last flight was his flight from Columbus, Ohio to Texas and back after Officer Training School (OTS). He soaked up the experience.

As an engineer he couldn't keep his eyes off the instruments. The crew enjoyed flying with a novice. They did not intentionally try to get him to puke his guts out. Nobody likes the smell of barf. But they did like to show off their piloting skills. The pilot dropped the chopper down to about a hundred feet off the deck.

He told the crew, "We're now crossing the Fort Chafe Army Base, federal land. No need to worry about scaring the cows and chickens here. We're going to do some low level VFR work here." In other words, they were going to fly around using visual flight rules to check out the float streams.

They followed a stream and Dave overheard the pilot tell his copilot, "That's where I'm putting my float boat in this weekend to catch beaucoup mega bass." The chopper continued to follow the stream and then climbed sharply and turned back to the north.

The pilot said, "Enough fun and games, don't know if we're going to be able to get you guys in out there. The fog is still fairly thick at 4-7. We might have to shoot some instrument approaches to hone our skills. I'm going over the lake to do some instrument work."

They spent the next half hour practicing instrument turns. You couldn't tell up from down. They were flying in and out of a fog bank over the lake. Every time they'd turn into the fog bank it was like flying through a milk bottle. Dave was experiencing vertigo, but he held his own. He kept his stomach contents down.

"Okay, we're going to continue out bound to 4-7. The sun is starting to thin this stuff out," the pilot said. The chopper turned to the north, flew along a highway for several minutes and then started to circle the site. The fog had burned off enough for them to look down and see a gaping hole in the ground about 150 feet wide. Chunks of concrete and debris were scattered everywhere. The pilot lined the chopper up for the helipad and made a slow approach.

He said, "Okay, Mike, this one is all yours. You have the aircraft."

The young copilot replied, "Roger, sir, I have the aircraft. Pre-landing checklist is complete."

The crew chief spoke up, "Tail clear left and right."

The chopper hovered ten feet off the pad. The power and pitch were adjusted and the Huey made a nice bounce on the pad. The pilot chided the young lieutenant. "You rushed that one a little bit. We'll have to work on that." After the chopper shut down, Bill and Dave climbed out and they walked up to the entry control point a hundred yards up the road.

It didn't take long for things to make an impression on his first visit at the destroyed missile complex. After passing through the entry control point and walking up the site access road, they noticed a half dozen vehicles strewn about. These were remnants of the maintenance crew vehicles after the explosion. Most had their windows blown out. One pickup had both doors blown off. There were twenty to thirty people on the complex that day. Anything below ground was still strictly off limits. There was no radiation hazard. However, the hydrazine and nitrogen tetroxide fuels were highly toxic and corrosive. There was concern that there might be residual fumes that migrated to the launch control center.

"Unbelievable." Dave said. "It is hard to believe everyone within a half mile of the complex was not killed."

Another thing he noticed was that the security fencing surrounding the complex was bent, twisted, and full of holes in several locations.

"What's that over there?" he asked.

"It's one of the flame deflectors." Bill replied. "Those massive steel structures divert the launch exhaust outward away from

the missile as it rises out of the silo. They are made of two inch thick high carbon steel."

The mangled pile of plate steel was about 20 x 40 feet and 10 feet high. It was torn to pieces like a cardboard box, lying in the middle of a bean field several hundred yards away.

Basically the entire silo headworks above level three were peeled back and blasted out of the ground. It reminded him of a shotgun barrel that got plugged and then shredded after pulling the trigger. There were massive pieces of equipment, chunks of concrete, rebar, wiring, and steel everywhere. Part of the headworks included several ten foot thick I-beams that crisscrossed much like a tic-tac-toe pattern. These structural members were lying in a pile of concrete several hundred yards to the other side of the complex. They couldn't even see the massive silo closure door. It was blasted over a sixty foot tall pine tree at the back of the complex and landed in a field.

One of Lieutenant Sheridan's assigned tasks was to calculate the explosive force in kilotonage that resulted in blowing a 740 ton door nearly 750 feet. That was nearly a ton per foot. He got the calculator out and crunched the following numbers:

- The energy in one pound of TNT is about 2,300 BTUs.
- The Titan burns hydrazine as a fuel and has 12,178 BTUs per pound which is nearly six times as energetic as TNT.
- The Titan II carried 104,000 pounds of hydrazine.
- Thus the explosive power in kilotonage of TNT:

$$104,000 \text{ lb} \times 12,178 \text{ BTU/lb}$$

$$= 1,266,512,000 \text{ BTU} \div 2,300 \text{ BTU/lb}$$

$$= 550,675 \text{ lb of TNT.}$$

He thought out loud, "Holy shit! That's one hell of a big bang! This was equivalent to a small tactical nuke going off." It came out to over a quarter of a kiloton in explosive force and this didn't even include the energy in the oxidizer. The Hiroshima atomic bomb was only fifteen kilotons. This was put in the accident investigation report. He was on the job less than two weeks and he was already published.

The young lieutenant walked up to a slab of concrete hanging over the edge of the silo crater. He peered over the edge.

Just then someone yelled, "Get off that, you dumb shit!" A big burley Master Sergeant rushed over yelling more obscenities as he ran. Dave was taken back a little. They didn't teach you at OTS what to do when a 240 pound, 6 foot NCO calls you a dumb shit and starts running at you.

Just then, Bill raised his hand and yelled back, "Calm down, Mitch. He's with me."

Mitch stopped dead in his tracks. He immediately apologized, "Sorry, sir. I didn't recognize you. However, I must respectfully ask you to step back from the edge. This whole area is in danger of falling into the hole. We've got enough problems out here without fishing out a butter bar. No one is allowed near the crater without being tethered off."

Lieutenant Sheridan gave a professional response, "Thanks

for the warning. By the way, I am not a butter bar. I worked hard for these gold bars."

Mitch responded, "You're right, Lieutenant, my mistake."

He reached out his hand and said, "Look, I don't want to get off on the wrong foot here, especially since it would've resulted in a 150 foot drop." Mitch grabbed it, shook it firmly and smiled.

Bill spoke up, "I hear you're having some problems with the pumping out here. What's going on?"

The silo bottom had been filling up with groundwater and rain water the last couple of weeks. There was about thirty feet of water in the hole. They were dumping five gallon buckets of HTC, a pool treating chemical, to neutralize the fuel in the silo. They had lowered a pump down the hole and were attempting to pump it into tanker trucks topside.

Mitch responded to Bill, "We went through three pumps already. We burned out two of them. I've sent two guys into town to bring back a couple of bigger pumps. They should be back in a few minutes. We haven't pumped a drop all morning."

Bill looked at all the hoses running from the hole to the tanker truck. Just then there was a commotion at the gate. A staff car had pulled up. It was the Wing Commander, Colonel Haase.

When he walked over, everyone stood erect and gave him a crisp SAC salute. Bill reached over to shake his hand. "Good morning, sir."

"Morning, Bill. Who's your partner in crime?"

Lieutenant Sheridan immediately spoke up. "Good morning, sir, I'm Dave Sheridan, your new missile engineer."

The colonel responded, "Welcome to the 308th, I heard we had a new butter bar in the Wing. Sorry, I haven't had a chance to meet with you since you in-processed. Things have been kind of hectic. Speaking of hectic, SAC HQ and the state EPA are riding my ass. They want to know if we're contaminating the groundwater up here. They're worried that the chickens will no longer lay eggs and the cows' tits will dry up. I heard there is some problem with the water treatment and pumping. What's going on?"

The brand new lieutenant had his first encounter with an O-6 and was about to show his brilliance. He responded, "Well, sir, from what I can see with these submersible pumps, is that they burned out because they were not the right type to begin with. It is not that they were underpowered. Unlike on *Star Trek*, more power is not always the best answer."

Haase looked surprised. Bill just smiled.

Sheridan continued, "What they need here are positive displacement pumps. They are trying to suck water up over 150 feet plus the height of the tanker truck. It's a physical impossibility to suck water more than about thirty-two feet."

Haase chuckled, "You mean you gotta blow, not suck. I always heard blow was a figure of speech."

Dave laughed along with the others. At least, the colonel had a sense of humor. He went on to explain that three, fifteen horse power submersible positive displacement pumps would do the job. "As a matter of fact, you might want to pump up the water and then mix the HTC in the tanker. Then just let some of the water fall back down a hose to the bottom of the silo to insure good mixing and to get into the cracks and voids down there."

Haase swung around and ordered Sergeant Mitchell to make it so.

They were mixing and pumping water by late that afternoon. Colonel Haase had some positive information to pass on to the generals in Omaha and the state EPA. Dave had come through with flying colors on his first engineering challenge and he impressed the boss.

CHAPTER 2

The Broadside of a Barn

Dave walked into the office Monday morning and was immediately whisked off to the conference room by Chief Master Sergeant Bowls. There was a commotion for sure. Colonel Haase and Bill Green were in a heated discussion over something. Normally you don't see a full bird, especially the Wing King, and a GS-14, going toe to toe. But Bill was standing his ground and not backing down. Lieutenant Sheridan started to catch on to the gist of the conversation.

The colonel asked, "Bill, what do you mean when you say that we couldn't hit the broadside of a barn? Do you mean that all fifty-four birds are pointing in the wrong direction? You're crazy!"

"No, sir, but it is very simple," Bill responded coolly. "Every silo that was aligned for targeting, and was calibrated when the standby generator was running, now has a built-in error. It is simple thermodynamics. Let me explain. The exhaust gas from the generators runs directly under the collimator room on level two of the silo. The huge chunk of concrete and steel that the collimator sits on collects the heat from the exhaust. Then all that concrete and steel expands. Even if it is by only a quarter inch or so, this makes for a huge targeting error."

The colonel's lip curled up a bit. "Okay, hold it right there. This conversation is over. This conference room is not cleared for discussions this sensitive."

Haase picked up the phone and punched in the CCC, the Combat Control Center. "I'm bringing my engineering staff over in ten minutes, make the SCIF room available." This was the Secure Communications & Intelligence Facility.

Haase, Bill, Sheridan, and both Chiefs walked out of the HQ Building and down the road to the CCC. The colonel coded in and signed in the rest under his escort. He pointed to the SCIF room. Everyone crammed themselves in around the conference table and sat down.

"Okay, Bill, how'd you figure this out?" Haase asked. "If you're right, then thirty percent of our nuclear capability is sitting out there pointing at who knows what!"

Bill stated that he figured it out when they were doing work on a blast valve overhaul project at complex 374-5. The silo exhaust air shaft has a valve that protects it from an outside blast wave. Any explosion topside would simply push the blast valve shut and the overpressure would then be routed through and around the delay piping to dampen the shock. As might be expected, the tolerances on the actuators and seals associated with this critical valve are very tight. When putting things back together after chrome plating the components, nothing seemed to fit. The dimensions were triple checked. However, nothing lined up. It had to be a misalignment of the silo structure itself.

Bill explained that when surveying equipment was brought out to the Site, they needed to establish a baseline or reference to measure the blast valve housing alignment. The steel plate on the collimator shaft was a known benchmark. After all, it was used for targeting the ICBM. Its exact location on Earth was known down to a gnat's ass.

During the process of using a theodolite to shoot their measurements from the collimator room, the Launch Control Center radioed Bill and notified him that they were about to fire up the standby generator. The generator is run for eight hours a week to ensure its operational capability. The standby generator is a critical piece of launch equipment. Bill acknowledged the transmission from the LCC. The generator kicked on and then the clicking sounds were heard a few minutes later as the motor control center relays and switching gear transferred site power from commercial over to standby.

Bill explained that when he went back to taking his measurements after about three hours it was getting a little warm in the collimator room. This was expected and understood. After all, they were sitting over the exhaust pipe and water jacket of the generator. However, what wasn't expected was that when he took a theodolite reading from his surveying equipment it completely missed its mark. It was a full half inch off. The implications immediately sunk in. The bench mark was not a fixed stable platform! This could lead to alignment and targeting errors when performing targeting sets!

Haase absorbed all of this. He knew Bill was right. He calmly stated, "All right Bill, you've convinced me. Now we are going to punch up SAC HQ and you're going to explain it all over to the battle staff."

Haase punched up SAC HQ on the STU-II. The STU-II is a special telephone instrument that can be switched to a secure mode for discussion of classified information. The abbreviation STU-II stands for Secure Telephone Unit-2nd generation.

If a person needs to discuss classified information, you can use the STU-II in non-secure mode to place a call to another party who also has a STU-II. After the connection is made, you ask the party receiving the call to "go secure." You and the other party then put your crypto-ignition keys (CIKs) into the phone terminal, turn them on and press the SECURE button. It may take about fifteen seconds for the secure connection to be established. He then punched up the speaker phone.

After Bill and Haase explained the situation to the battle staff, both sides of the conversation went quiet for a minute. Haase had to ask if there was anyone on the other end. After a few seconds the word came back.

The topic was closed for discussion and any mention of it would be a breach of national security. Besides, planned upgrades in the guidance package would fix the problem.

Lieutenant Sheridan spent the next couple of years modifying the launch complexes and upgrading the guidance package for the Titan II ICBMs.

As it turned out, one of the best kept secrets of the cold war was that the Russians and the US could not hit the broad side of a barn with their land based ICBMs. Several of the assumptions and constants taken into consideration in the targeting algorithm were in error.

The fact that most of our ICBM force would not have hit the broadside of a barn during the cold war might startle some. However, accuracy is a relevant term when it comes to nukes. When you're talking about a ten megaton nuclear war head (the largest in the US inventory at the time) being close means taking out an entire city such as Moscow or only half the city.

The ol' SAC adage of "Nuke them until they glow and then strafe them at night" had some ring of truth to it.

The funny thing about targeting errors is that the same thing happened as artillery became more powerful and ranges increased to over twenty miles. The simplistic parabolic trajectory calculations no longer applied. The projectiles were actually following a suborbital path. This path was elliptical and must take into account the curvature of the Earth.

By World War II, there was a demand for more accurate calculations to improve accuracy. Rooms full of humans were employed in computing artillery trajectories, and the result was unacceptable error. A variety of computing research projects were undertaken at Princeton University, Harvard University, and the University of Pennsylvania. These resulted in room-size computers such as the Mark-I through Mark-IV, and the ENIAC. All of which used vacuum tubes. The vacuum tube machines were erroneous. Tubes were always burning out or their response drifted frequently. This consumed a huge amount of power and generated a large amount of heat. And, they were slow. Less than 10,000 integer multiplications per second compared with the gigahertz or billions per second common today. They were also difficult to program, but provided a useful test bed for basic computer concepts.

It seemed that we have now come full circle. ICBM targeting could also no longer be counted on to depend on the simplistic targeting algorithm of the day. The Titan II missile system was designed to destroy enemy strategic targets in a minimum amount of time. To do so, the warhead must be placed on a target with a high degree of accuracy and from a distance of over 5,500 miles. This degree of accuracy is comparable to hitting a golf ball into the cup 150 yards away or making a hole in one from a par three. It is obvious that many variables must be considered in attaining this degree of accuracy. The powered portion of flight lasts less than one sixth of the total flight time or about five minutes. Control of the flight path was not possible after powered flight ends. The missile goes into a ballistic free fall for the remainder of the flight.

Several parameters must be met before the end of powered flight to permit the warhead to arm itself and free-fall to the target. All missile systems exist solely for this purpose. The targeting of a Titan II ICBM involved an algorithm containing only 13 parameters. These include obvious variables such as launch site and target coordinates, velocity, altitude, and even barometric pressure. However, there are other not so apparent variables that enter the equation.

Polar motion produces variations in several parameters employed in targeting computations which are traditionally treated as constants. These include the Earth's angular velocity vector, launch site gravity magnitude and astronomic coordinates, and target and launch site inertial velocities. The resulting targeting error is assessed for each of these quantities. The dominant error is shown to be the Inertial Measurement Unit (IMU) azimuth alignment error. This results in a large cross-range error caused by a shift in the Earth's poles.

Why is this important? Because all of the test launches of our ICBM fleet were launched from Vandenberg AFB on the California coast and launched westward towards the Johnson Island Atoll or Kwajaline Atoll about 5,550 miles out into the Pacific Ocean. This westward launch did not adequately simulate an actual launch over the pole to the north. Going over the pole represented a whole slew of challenges and problems not fully understood or anticipated.

The IMU azimuth alignment relied upon celestial navigation. The azimuth was determined using an optical collimator that consisted of basically a periscope using a mirror and prism system that was piped down through the silo and into the reentry vehicle (RV), the polite and politically correct term for nuclear warhead.

This optical system established the missiles exact coordinates on Earth in reference to the pole using the North Star as a bench mark. This was done based upon the position of the North Star timed with the aid of an atomic clock. A small measurement error on the launch end represented a huge error on the target end of the trajectory. Gravitational "anomalies" were also encountered when flying over the poles as was experienced with spacecraft placed in polar orbits.

Every object in the universe attracts every other object in the universe with a force (F) directed along the centers of the two objects proportional to the product of their masses (M1 and M2) and inversely proportional to the square of the distance between the two objects (R). This is the basis of the famous Newtonian formula below:

$$F = G \, (M_1 \times M_2)/R^2$$

where G (Gravitational constant) = $6.67300 \times 10^{-11} \, m^3 \, kg^{-1} \, s^{-2}$

Don't confuse this "big G" with "little g". Big G is considered a universal constant or the same number throughout the known universe. Little g is the known as the acceleration due to gravity. On Earth, it is normally about 9.82 meters per second squared. That means that when an object is dropped it falls at a rate of 9.82 meters per second for the first second. After the next second it falls at 17.64 meters per second. After the third second it is falling at 26.44 meters per second and so on and on as it picks up speed. It is also conceded that little g is not a true constant but varies from the pole to the equator and due to the pear shape of the Earth. It can also be affected by the relative mass and density of materials such as mineral deposits, mountain ranges, ice packs, and ocean depths. It has to do with the amount of mass beneath your feet.

These deviations in little g have been fairly well understood and even mapped by geologists, oil companies, and the Colorado School of Mines. Even with all the targeting deviations, precessions and errors known, it was nearly impossible to validate that the algorithm was correct when you had to launch a missile toward the North Pole to prove it. The Russians and Chinese would take a dim view of this. Anything remotely approaching the pole would be considered a threat.

Thus, the only other alternative was to map out the gravitational anomalies and account for them in the targeting algorithm. This gave birth to a multibillion dollar black program called Delta G in deference to the changing gravitational constant.

Newly promoted First Lieutenant Sheridan was now about to embark on another career broadening experience. He was summoned to Headquarters at North American Aerospace Defense Command (HQ NORAD) at Cheyenne Mountain near Colorado Springs. One of NORAD's primary functions was to track space-borne objects in orbit around the Earth. This included all satellites, and space junk down to the size of a tennis ball. As a matter of fact, one of their smallest objects tracked was a glove that floated loose from a spacewalk operation out of a Gemini capsule. NORAD uses a combination of radar and optical sensors to track and catalog over 9,000 space objects.

Another mission includes a Laser Clearinghouse (LCH) for laser operations and Collision Avoidance (COLA) for NASA; both functions are intended to protect on-orbit assets. COLA and LCH use the computer projections to propagate objects over the laser emitter or launch site to determine if there is a possibility of collision.

Sheridan was escorted into Cheyenne Mountain by Captain Dennis Murphy. The entry procedures were similar to those for the Titan sites. Once inside the giant drive-thru blast doors, they hopped into an electric golf cart that whisked them the 300 yards into the cavernous operational control center. This place looked like a launch control center on steroids. Again, everything was shock mounted and situated on huge isolation platforms. Murphy led Sheridan into one of the modules and then down a hallway into a conference room. Sheridan had to smile at the cherry wood paneling, table, and furniture. For a place built to last beyond doomsday, no expense was spared on the details and little things in life.

General Ron Giffen entered the room along with a staff of a half dozen technicians and asked, "Sheridan, do you really know why you are here?" The question took him back a little. He responded sharply, "Sir, I was told to attend a briefing on orbital tracking, space operations, and targeting algorithms."

Giffen replied coldly, "Sheridan, this operation is classified TS and just to be clear that you know the ramifications, I'm sending you to the North Pole afterwards to implement the operational plan," added the General. Dave didn't see that one coming as his jaw dropped.

Giffen continued, "You're now a world class subject matter expert on ICBM targeting and are intimately aware of the fact that launching an ICBM over the pole makes it about as accurate as my tax return. The only saving grace with the Titan is that it carries one hell of a punch. That ten megaton warhead means you only have to be close. However, we have other problems."

SLC-6 Complex at Vandenberg AFB

The General paused for a moment for dramatic effect, "ICBMs aren't the only thing we launch over the poles. The Space Shuttle is due to be launched out of Vandenberg from SLC-6 in a year or so. We're going to put it in a polar orbit to augment our reconnaissance satellites that are currently in a polar orbit."

General Giffen stood up and walked over to the wall display, "Now with that said, I want to show you something very interesting." He had one of the technicians call up a program showing a graphical representation of the Earth and several thousand objects apparently in orbit. "Sergeant, delete all objects not in polar orbit at or below eighty degrees north latitude." The screen now showed only a few dozen objects.

"Lieutenant, these objects represent the satellites that we and the Russians have in polar orbit. Sergeant Keen, filter out the space junk now." Only a handful of satellites were visible on the display. "Lieutenant, there is nothing particularly fascinating about this plot. However, if you plot the orbit by looking down directly over the pole you will notice some interesting dynamics taking place. These satellites were designed to stay in orbit for seven years. There is enough maneuvering fuel on board to reposition and provide for station keeping. Now, Sergeant, show a plot of the orbits for the next five years filtering out known deviations, perturbations, precession and known errors without station keeping."

Lieutenant Sheridan couldn't believe his eyes. The plot looked like a kid's Spirograph with lines spiraling off in every direction. "Okay, Sheridan, you've seen it. There is not enough steering fuel on board to keep these birds in a polar orbit for four years let alone seven. Clearly there are some forces acting on these satellites that are unseen and unaccounted for in our orbital calculations. They are not random errors. A statistical analysis proves there is a very perceptible left hand twist to these polar orbits. Depending upon altitude, each one of these satellites takes up to a one second degree of left hook on each orbit. At ninety minutes per orbit, this adds up to quite a deviation over a month or two. We can't afford to keep sending up more hundred million dollar satellites every few years. Thank God, the Russians are even worse off than us."

"Your job is going to be to figure out what the hell is going on. We're sending you to the Greenland icecap to find out. Congratulations, Captain Sheridan," as General Giffen handed Dave his new silver bars.

CHAPTER 3
Greenland

The C-141 Starlifter cargo plane had been in the air for about three hours heading north out of McGuire AFB, New Jersey to Sondrestrom Air Base on the west coast of Greenland. The accommodations weren't too bad. For the grueling five hour flight, actual passenger seats were clamped onto the aluminum cargo deck in lieu of the cargo net seats. Surprisingly, there were a dozen or so passengers on this flight along with several cargo pallets on their way to the Arctic. As Captain Sheridan grabbed for a cup of coffee, he accidentally dropped it. The hot liquid literally froze to the metal floor before the crew chief could come back with some paper towels to clean it up. The pilot had announced that the outside air temperature was a balmy minus sixty-four degrees.

When he got up to use the six hundred dollar toilet seat, he took the opportunity to look out one of the door windows. He had never been this far north before. Looking above, there was a dark indigo sky without a cloud in sight. Down below, the colors and geography were magnificent and striking. The ocean was majestic blue, the icebergs and ice flows were blinding white, and the black rock cliffs along the fjords gave a foreboding, yet, tranquil appearance.

A couple of hours later, the pilot began his approach up the ninety mile long fjord into Sondrestrom. Glaciers fanned out into the ocean and adjacent fjords for as far as the eye could see. Water in the ice crevasses was a beautiful blue, like someone had poured Aqua Velva aftershave onto the ice.

Dave had studied up on Sondrestrom prior to his departure. What he found was fascinating. Beginning in September of 1941,

Sondrestrom Air Base was built under the guidance of the famed Arctic explorer and aviator, Bert Balchen. During World War II, Sondrestrom was known as Bluie West 8 or BW-8, and was an alternate base for the ferrying of aircraft to England. It soon became one of the most important stopover sites for flying missions between the US and Europe, due to the fine flying conditions for which Sondrestrom became known.

The base was laid out on a sandbar near the beginning of the fjord. The fjord was about a mile wide at this point and was surrounded by thousand foot cliffs and mountains with a five hundred foot tall glacier entering the fjord a couple of miles upstream. The massive Greenland icecap, twice the size of Texas, was only twenty miles to the east. Greenland is a Danish Territory. The 50,000 residents, mostly Inuits, were in the process of voting for home rule and independence from Denmark.

It took a great deal of piloting skill to land at Sonde, as it was affectionately called. You had to be specially trained and signed off to make the risky approach and landing. There had been quite a few nasty accidents over the years. As a matter of fact, one of them involved a C-141 in the late summer of 1976. The first third of the runway here has an upslope. During landings, the rest of the runway seems to disappear over the horizon. This optical illusion may have caused the pilot to think he either overshot the runway or that the runway was very short. As a result, after touchdown the pilot evidently decided to go around for another try. During the liftoff the plane over-rotated, developed a nose-high attitude and then stalled. It crashed on the runway, killing seven crew members, and sixteen passengers. The navigator and three passengers survived.

Rumor has it, that the base chef was one of the survivors. He has now been on base for the past nine years, because he absolutely refuses to get on another aircraft.

The Starlifter made a smooth landing on the 12,000 foot runway exactly on schedule at 1100 hours on a balmy spring day in 1985.

An Air Force bus met the passengers at the plane and dropped them off at base operations. Dave was met there by the Base

commander, Lieutenant Colonel Dan Snyder. "Welcome to Sondrestrom, Captain. I know this flight is an ass kicker. Let's get
you over to billeting. Your bags will be delivered there shortly."
Snyder drove him over to the Visiting Officers Quarters (VOQ)
and walked him up to the desk. "Henry, take care of this young
man. Give him a wakeup call for 1400 hours and then run him
over to my office."

Snyder was right. The flight was grueling. He'd been up since
0400 to get ready for the 0600 flight that morning. He took the
key from the desk clerk, thanked Snyder and stumbled off to his
room. He was surprised at how modern and nice the room was.
He had envisioned something between an igloo and Quonset hut.
Instead, this reminded him of any Ramada Inn in the States. He
took his boots off, flopped on the bed and crashed.

Three hours later, the phone rang. Henry was on the line with
his wakeup call and told him that his bags were outside his door.
He guessed that they didn't have to worry about someone running
off with your luggage up here. Their getaway route would only be
six miles long at the most. That was the longest road in Greenland
that ran down to the port. Amazing, the amount of trivia he had
already tucked away.

Henry told the Captain that transportation would be waiting
in half an hour. He used the time to get cleaned up, put on a fresh
uniform, and walk down to the lobby. He was met there by Master
Sergeant Andy Caudill. "Good afternoon, Captain. I'm here to
drive you to your 1400 meeting. We'll be stopping by the Danish
Hotel on the other side of the base to pick up Dr. Paul Rapp and
Dr. Ralph Timken. These gentlemen are doing the ice core drilling
out at the DYE-3 site."

He hopped into the staff car and got the guided tour of the base
on their way around the runway to the Danish side of the base. He
was surprised by the number of buildings, and warehouses. He
was even more surprised to see cabins and bungalows scattered on
the sides of the hills. Sergeant Caudill explained that many Danes
flew in from Copenhagen to spend the summers here. Also, several Inuits that worked at the base lived here, too.

The Danish Hotel was even more impressive than the VOQ.

They walked into the lobby and met Dr. Rapp and Dr. Timken waiting for them. "Hello Captain Sheridan, nice to finally meet you. I've heard a lot about you," Dr. Rapp said as he shook his hand. This surprised him. He didn't know he had a reputation, let alone one that preceded him. "Thanks…I hope," he quipped.

The sergeant interrupted politely and pointed out they were five minutes late for their 1400 meeting. They hopped in the staff car and drove back around to the Air Force side of the base. Along the way, he noticed a huge shaggy looking buffalo critter a hundred yards off the end of the runway. Dave asked, "Is that a musk ox?" The sergeant replied, "Yes, sir. It sure is. Those things are too stupid to know that they are supposed to be extinct. They are all over the place. Have to watch driving at night. And believe me; the nights can be really long up here."

The car pulled up to the Base Headquarters building. All four men walked up to the front door. Every facility had a cable running between them strung between bollards every fifty feet or so. The sergeant smiled and said, "We use those to find our way home when the wind kicks up and puts us in a whiteout; nice to have around after a beer or two over at the Caribou Club."

The sergeant led them into Colonel Snyder's office. "Good afternoon, gentlemen. Have a seat." Dave sat down at the end of a huge black leather couch. "Captain, I know you haven't had much time to get acquainted with our two distinguished professors here. So I'd like to take this opportunity to bring you up to speed." Dave relaxed a bit and listened intently.

"Quite frankly, General Giffen at NORAD called me VFR direct and wants me to provide you all with any support, facilities, and resources you need to accomplish your mission here. This includes C-130 support to the icecap. I only know the basics of what you're doing out there: some kind of ice-core drilling for gravitational mapping up here, and something about improving targeting for ICBMs and orbital station keeping for our spy satellites. I don't need to know the details. I'll just follow my orders to support you anyway I can." Colonel Snyder called in the sergeant, "Andy, bring us a pot of coffee and have the club run over some sandwiches."

Colonel Snyder continued, "Captain, we have an office set up for you. You will be acting as Quality Assurance Engineer up here watching over the contractors running the DYE sites here in Greenland. Also, the transition from Tactical Air Command to Space Command is going to take some time up here. We've got quite a few projects underway to support the Space Shuttle polar orbit operations when they start launching off of SLC-6 at Vandenberg. This cover will give you access to all the facilities and communications capabilities up here. Before you ask, this room has been cleared for TS discussions, no Russian bugs in here. We also have a secure conference room here for your use. Dr. Rapp and Dr. Timken have their lab and facilities located at DYE-3. Their cover, as I understand, is ice-core drilling for researching weather patterns and airborne pollutions. The ice out there is over a hundred thousand years old and over two miles thick. That should keep them busy for a while."

Dr. Timken acknowledged this, but also made an interesting point. "Thank you, you are correct Colonel Snyder. Hopefully, we are going to kill about four birds with the same stone out here. We have funding and grants from several different organizations, so we will be doing other science as well as our gravitational experiments. As a matter of fact, gravitational experiments are not new. There is nothing super-secret about what we are investigating out here. We will be trying to delve into the universal gravitational constant. Scientists have attempted to do this all over the world. The trick is you need vast areas of constant density materials to conduct the experiments, such as salt mines. We've elected to come up here to the icecap because ice has predictable qualities and near constant density for over the twenty-five square miles that we require."

Colonel Snyder interrupted, "Excuse me Dr. Timken, I'm a simple soldier that has a degree in Military History. What's so special about this constant you are trying to figure out? I took enough science and physics to make me knowledgeable but dangerous. From what I understand g is not a constant. It varies with where you are on Earth. Isn't it something like 9.8 meters per second^2? It's only about a sixth of this value on the Moon, so how can it be considered a constant?"

Rapp answered, "Forgive me, Colonel, but you are confusing the acceleration due to gravity known as little g with the Universal Gravitational constant big G."

Snyder laughed and said, "That's nothing new, my wife's always telling me I can never find the correct G spot." Everyone had to chuckle at this one.

"What we are doing up here is trying to prove that the big G is not a constant throughout the known universe. I'd like to take a few minutes to refresh your Physics 101, if I may?" Timken continued.

Snyder leaned back in his chair and threw his feet up on his desk. "Go right ahead. Continue with your explanation. It's not like I have a tee time to make or anything. We've got all day... which up here can be six months long." Dave had the sickening feeling that this fact would be stressed time after time.

Timken laughed and assured everyone that they would not be there anywhere near that long. He continued on with his history lesson. "A few flashes of inspiration and genius occur about every half century that fundamentally change the human race. One of these was the falling apple that inspired Sir Isaac Newton to formulate his findings on gravity."

He stood up and walked over to the dry erase board. "Colonel, may I use this to humor my academic nature?" Snyder replied, "Sure, I'm left brained and you'll need to draw me a picture anyway."

"Thank you, sir," Timken continued, "as you all know, Newton once saw an apple falling from a tree and had an inspirational thought. He observed that as the apple fell, it accelerated since its velocity changed from zero as it was hanging on the tree and then sped up as it moved toward the ground. Thus, Newton concluded that there must be a force that acted on the apple to cause this acceleration. He called this force, gravity, and the resulting acceleration, the acceleration due to gravity. This is the little g as we discussed earlier. He then wondered what would happen if the apple tree was twice as high. Here he again expected the apple to be accelerated toward the ground and pick up even more speed.

Thus, he concluded that the force gravity would reach to the top of the tallest apple tree." Timken paused for a minute and grabbed a cup of coffee that had been poured for him.

He continued enthusiastically, "I realize this might not sound like one of those eureka moments, but you must understand, it's what Newton did with this knowledge that counts. His brilliant conclusion was that if the force of gravity reached to the top of the highest tree, should it not reach even further; in fact, might it not reach all the way to the Moon! Then, the orbit of the Moon about the Earth could be a consequence of the gravitational force, because the acceleration due to gravity could change the velocity of the Moon in just such a way that it followed an orbit around the Earth."

Timken drew a picture of the Earth-Moon system on the board and exclaimed, "Eureka!" and continued with his presentation.

"Newton figured out that every object in the universe attracts every other object in the universe with a force directed along the centers of the two objects that is proportional to the product of their masses and is inversely proportional to the square of the distance between the two objects."

With this said, he labeled the Moon, M1 and the Earth, M2, then drew a line between them and labeled it r.

Timken continued, "Thus, one of the most famous and universally accepted formulas was born." He again picked up the marker and wrote down the famous Newtonian Equation.

$$F = G (M_1 \times M_2)/R^2$$

By pointing to big G, he concluded his lecture stating, "Where big G equals the Universal Gravitational Constant." He continued to write out the value for G on the board.

$$6.67300 \times 10^{-11} \ m^3 \ kg^{-1} \ s^{-2}.$$

Timken put the marker down and pointed to the formula, "This strange looking number followed by these weird series of units is termed a "universal constant" because it is thought to be the same at all places and all times, and, thus, universally characterizes the intrinsic strength of the gravitational force."

Everyone just stared at the board for a minute or two. Dr.

Timken sat back down.

Colonel Snyder spoke up, "Wow, how'd you remember the value for big G. I can't even remember my own Social Security number half the damn time."

Dr. Timken continued his lecture by pointing out that, "Just like the value for Pi is a known constant that is used in countless formulas and calculations. And just like Einstein's famous and inspirational equation $E=MC^2$ equating mass and the speed of light, to energy; Newton's Gravitational Formula is the glue that holds the heavens together."

Dr. Rapp spoke up this time, "However, there is a caveat. Notice that big G only has three significant places past the decimal point. For a very universal constant it is one of the least known numbers in terms of accuracy. In contrast, Pi is a known constant out past a million decimal places. The natural log e is another magic number and constant in science and mathematics. It is also known out to millions of decimal places. I can recall 22 decimal places for the natural log e. It is 2.718281828459045235."

Everyone looked at the doctor like he was the mystical Karnack the Great. He calmly said, "Okay, I do that at the faculty Christmas parties to impress the chicks. All that I have to do is memorize the equivalent of three telephone numbers and string them together."

Dr. Timken now proceeded to wrap up the lecture. "We're not here to improve the accuracy of big G. We're here to prove that the constant is not constant. We're going to blow Newtonian physics out of the water. As a matter of fact, this has implications in both relativistic and quantum physics as well."

Colonel Snyder jumped in, "Whoa, slow down a bit. You're getting in over my head now. What are you talking about?"

Sheridan spoke up now. It was time to put his $50,000 engineering degree out on the table. "From what I understand, Colonel, if the constant is not a constant, then there is a delta possible. This difference, or delta as it is known mathematically, allows for some interesting recalculations. If you acknowledge that G is not constant, then you can throw things like negative numbers in for mass and time into Einstein's relativity equations and quantum physics equations. It then becomes possible to exceed the speed of light which would no longer be constant. Theoretically, time travel would even be possible both forward and backward."

Colonel Snyder looked at Dave and said, "Holy shit, Captain. I thought you were up here because there was some targeting glitch with our ICBMs and our satellites keep taking a left hook worse than my tee shot. Now you're talking about H.G. Wells' time machine crap. Hell, even I can figure out that the constant is accurate to within plus or minus a few hundredth of a percent. That's not enough to account for antimatter and time warps."

Before Dave could recover from the frontal assault, both professors came to his defense. Dr. Rapp simply held up his hands and said, "Eureka! You've got it Colonel, the Captain is essentially correct. You'd be surprised what the supercomputers show is possible over galactic distances and eons with this small inconsistency. This is going to revolutionize science and physics. Humanity is at the dawn of an earth-shattering revelation that the Universal Gravitational Constant is not a constant and thus not universal. The implications are just now being understood! Welcome to the threshold of the brave new world."

"Okay, Professors, you've definitely piqued my interest. Now please tell me how drilling a few holes into the world's largest ice cube is going to prove your case?"

Dr. Rapp spoke up, "Well, I'm glad you have an open mind and haven't thrown us out on our asses in the snow. It's damn cold out there. What we plan to do out at DYE-3 is drill five holes about four miles apart. These holes will be about eight inches in diameter and two kilometers deep. We'll then drop a LaCoste & Romberg borehole gravity meter down the holes and measure the gravity about every eight hundred feet or so."

Colonel Snyder asked. "What the heck is a gravity meter?"

Dr. Rapp explained patiently, "A gravity meter consists of a weight on the end of a horizontal beam supported by a zero-length spring. A zero-length spring is defined as one in which the tension is proportional to the actual length of the spring, that is, if all external forces were removed the spring would collapse to zero length. The gravity meter can detect very small changes in gravity by measuring the restoring force necessary to bring the horizontal beam to a reference position. It is important to note that the instrument does not measure the total force of gravity, only changes in gravity."

Dave asked, "What's the status of the drilling at DYE-3?" Dr. Timken answered, "We have two drills delivered at the site and have started drilling with one. We have enough pipe to drill about halfway down. This is our biggest logistics tail. We need about 350 lengths of 20 foot long pipe. Also, once we reach bedrock under the icecap we are going to take some core samples with a diamond core drill bit. Nobody really knows what's down there."

Colonel Snyder picked up a folder off his desk, "I have the manifest here for the two support flights out to the DYE-3 site in the morning. I see a bunch of pipe, some instrumentation, core hole lubricant,…..that sounds kinky,….and other instruments and equipment on the two planes. Captain, you'll be on Raven One that leaves at 0730. Professors, you'll leave about an hour later on Raven Two."

Dr. Timken concluded the meeting by saying, "Thank you for your help and interest in this project. Dr. Rapp and I need to go over to the Logistic warehouse to make sure everything is prepared for the morning's flight."

Snyder stood up and shook their hands. Dave gave the colonel a crisp salute and shook his hand as well. Snyder punched the intercom, "Sergeant, please run these gentlemen over to the Raytheon Warehouse and run our good Captain back over to the VOQ. Before you go Captain, take this back with you." Snyder handed him a three ring binder, "That's a little home work for you to get familiar with where you are going in the morning."

After returning to his room and changing into his sweats, he laid across the bed. He opened up the orientation notebook and began reading about the DYE sites.

There were four DYE sites located in southern Greenland close to the Arctic Circle. DYE-1 was located on the west coast on a two thousand foot peak overlooking the Baffin Sea. DYE-4 was on the east coast on another mountain peak on the Island of Kulusuk, an extinct volcano.

The USAF also had two radar and communications stations out on the icecap. DYE-2 was built approximately one hundred miles east of Sondrestrom AB and ninety miles south of the Arctic Circle at an altitude of 7,600 feet. DYE-3 was located approximately one hundred miles east of DYE-2 and slightly south at a higher elevation of 8,600 feet.

The locations for the icecap sites were found to receive from three to four feet of snow fall each year. Since the winds were constantly blowing, at times over one hundred mph, this snow accumulation constantly formed large drifts. To overcome this potential problem, it was decided that DYE-2 and DYE-3 should be elevated approximately twenty feet above the surface of the icecap.

Eight huge I-beam columns, along with two 350 ton hydraulic jacks per column were used to lift the site above the snow. These jacks were designed to level the building whenever it became necessary due to different rates of settlement between the beams. The "big eyes" were forty feet long by four feet wide by five feet high and weighed fifteen tons each.

The icecap sites were built like offshore oil platforms, similar to the Texas Towers. They were 125 feet tall with five stories of support equipment, storage, and crew accommodations. The radome was fifty feet tall. The sites encompassed 45,000 square feet and weighed over five million pounds each.

Each site was manned by a twelve to eighteen man crew. Dave thought to himself, "This is the real Ice Station Zebra. Just like Dreamland at Area 51, it did exist." He read on with fascination.

Each site was built by flying in the components one piece at a time on specially equipped C-130 Hercules cargo planes. Thousands of flights were required to haul all the pieces to the top of the icecap. Over 127,000 tons of steel and equipment were landed on the icecap.

Dave closed the book and pondered a thought of how many billions must have been spent up here. "Wow, your tax dollars at work." He flipped off the light and tucked in for the night. He felt like a kid waiting for Christmas morning.

CHAPTER 4
The Ice Station DYE-3

The next morning Dave had breakfast at the Air Base dining hall with Brad Johnson, the Chief Engineer for the contractor running the DYE sites. He drove them over to Base Operations hangar. It was a balmy 28°F this morning. On the ramp were two C-130 Hercules cargo planes. These four engine turboprops were the workhorses of the Air Force. These planes belonged to the 109th ANG Squadron based in Schenectady, New York. They were proudly known as the Raven Squadron and nicknamed the Firebirds. These Hercules were part of a select few that were outfitted specifically for operations on the ice. They  were fitted with several million dollars worth of retractable Teflon coated skis that allowed them to operate on both paved runways and the icecap. The nose ski was ten feet long by six feet wide, while the main skis were twenty feet long by six feet wide. Each ski weighed approximately a ton.

The 109th is the only military unit in the world that flies ski-equipped C-130s. These cargo planes can carry 30,000 pounds for over 500 miles at 275 mph.

The Greenland icecap is a foreboding place. It is a dome of ice twice the area of Texas. The ice is about 11,000 feet thick at the center of the world's largest island. It is completely ringed with mountains with hundreds of fjords and glaciers making their way through them out to the Atlantic Ocean on the east coast and Baffin Bay on the west coast. The weight of the ice actually suppresses the bedrock to below sea level.

Dave took time to read an article posted on the bulletin board concerning the icecap. He found the facts and figures fascinating:

- The Greenland icecap contains one eighth of the total global ice mass. The total ice mass on Earth is 125 million cubic miles; Antarctica has 112 million cubic miles; Greenland 11.5 million cubic miles.

- The average height of the Greenland icecap is 7,000 feet above sea level with 65 percent of the area above 6500 feet. That is why Greenland deserves the name of most extreme highland in the world.

- Lowest recorded temperature: -94° F (1953 Station Northice). Mean annual temperature: -22° F: So the Greenland icecap is without any doubt the coldest place in the northern hemisphere, even colder than the North Pole.

- Because the snow surface reflects most of the sunlight, the temperature is lowest near the snow and increases in upper air levels. This is an exceptional situation because usually temperature decreases in higher air levels. The dome structure of the icecap causes cold air to flow constantly to lower areas at the edges. So, crossing the icecap, you will always experience head wind until the top of the icecap and then backwind.

- Above the seas around Greenland, the air is less cold and thus creates a substantial difference in temperature and air pressure between the coast and the inland. This can cause terrible storms.

- At present the maximum thickness of the icecap is 10,500 to 11,000 feet. If the entire icecap should melt (which is extremely unlikely), the sea surface worldwide would rise 20 to 25 feet!

The planes were being prepared and loaded with the supplies and ice drilling equipment. Timken and Rapp were working with the crew chiefs to get them loaded properly. He was met at Base Ops by Major Rick Boop. Dave gave Major Boop a crisp salute. Boop returned it and welcomed him to the Ravens' Nest.

Boop grinned a big smile and said with a southern drawl, "Good morning, I'm the mission commander for your flight out to DYE-3 this morning. Kid, you're in for the ride of your life. People would fork over a year's pay to do what you are about to do. Not many people have been to where you're about to go. DYE-3 does exist. Unlike Dreamland it can be found on any air chart. Its coordinates are 65 degrees, 10 minutes, 57 seconds north latitude by 43 degrees, 49 minutes, 10 seconds, west longitude. Its code name is Sob Story. Don't know why. To this day, the history behind this name is lost. Might have been some random string of names put together by some computer in the basement of the Pentagon. Anyway, it is 250 miles inland at an elevation of nearly 9,000 feet above sea level."

Boop continued with the mission brief and gave Dave a Flight Safety briefing. He familiarized him with aircraft safety features, systems, and what to do in the event of an emergency or crash landing. Since Dave was scheduled for his arctic survival training in a few weeks, he took the discussion very seriously. The temperature at DYE-3 was 26 degrees below zero. This was relatively warm. It could get down to 50 below. It gets cold enough to turn jet fuel into slush. As a matter of fact aircraft engines are never turned off on the icecap. Chances are you'd never get it restarted.

After climbing aboard the C-130 he was led up a short flight of stairs into the flight deck where he buckled into the jump seat behind the pilot. The crew buckled in and ran their pre-departure checklist. Clearance to taxi was given and the huge transport rolled out onto the taxiway. The jagged fjord cliffs dove into the waters of the fjord. Surprisingly, the fjord wasn't the deep calm blue envisioned from a Norwegian postcard. It was brown and flowing turbulently and full of silt. It was about a mile wide at Sonde Stromfjord. Melt water from the icecap and glacier a few miles up the fjord was making its way the ninety miles back out to Baffin Bay.

The C-130 taxied onto the runway. It was given a hold while a Greenland Air Helicopter taxied across the other end of the runway to the Scandinavian Air Service (SAS) terminal. Take-off clearance was granted and the huge cargo plane's four turbo props spun up to full speed. The variable pitch propellers were tilted forward and started biting into the cold arctic air. The plane accelerated down the strange, saddle humped runway towards the west. As it climbed up and out of the fjord it made a steep bank for a full U-turn back to the east. The view from a C-130 cockpit is panoramic. The full view of Sonde filled the windows. There was actually some green in Greenland. The end of the fjord was now in view were the glacier sloped down from the icecap. A huge ripple was seen were the ice was calving off the glacier face as the plane soared over the edge and out over the icecap. The icecap at the coast is only a few hundred feet thick. It gradually ramps upward to over two miles thick a few hundred miles inland.

DYE-3 is about 250 miles to the east slightly below the Arctic Circle. Amazingly, navigation in this state of the art Air Force beast was on the crude side. Although it used an Inertial Navigation system to get them near the site, approaches and landings were visual. No navigation aids existed at the DYE sites. To give them an edge in times of low visibility, Major Boop was going to practice shooting a total radar approach. He explained the procedure to Dave, "DYE-3 is literally the only metal structure within hundreds of miles. Once we get closer, it will ping very nicely on the plane's Navigation Radar (NAVRAD). We will also use a radar altimeter to find our way to the station."

Major Boop continued, "This radar has extremely high resolution. As we get closer to the site at about four miles out we will be able to distinguish even the metal flag poles spaced every seventy-five feet apart along both sides of the skiway."

As the plane soared over the glaciers, Boop clicked the microphone. "We're coming up over the pressure ridges. The crevasses you see are up to a thousand feet deep. They'd swallow this plane whole if we lost power now. The glacier would grind us up and spit us out in about a thousand years. By the way, are they giving you hazardous duty pay, Dave?"

To this Dave laughed, "Hell, no. They even argued about giving me a flight suit and parka back in Colorado."

Boop said, "You've got my sympathy, my friend. But they did have you prepare a will and power of attorney, right?"

Dave asked nervously, "You know something I don't?"

"No, I just have the bureaucracy figured out," Boop replied dryly.

The mighty C-130 droned on for the next two hours. Dave was mesmerized by the white desert-like scene below him. They were flying at 18,000 feet and Dave could still see huge drifts of snow and some shadows from a few clouds. The clouds were getting a little thicker the further they flew.

Major Boop hit the intercom, "Carl, these clouds are getting thicker. They are at about 13,000 feet. There is little danger of icing. They are relatively dry stratus. However, this isn't going to be a visual approach." The copilot responded "Roger that. I'll set us up for a radar-assisted approach. Just then a radio call came in, "Raven One, Raven One.....Sob Story, do you copy?" The copilot responded, "Roger, Sob Story. Raven One's with you,....four fiver miles west,.....inbound,.....descending through 16,000." DYE-3 responded, "Roger, Raven One, I have you on the scope. Be advised winds are three four zero at one zero. Ceiling is about 2,000, visibility is 3 miles. Marginal VFR. Cleared to land at pilot's discretion." Rick handled this call. He was pilot in command, "Roger, Sob Story, Raven One is making a straight in approach using NAVRAD assist." DYE-3 replied back, "Roger, Raven One, the flag poles are deployed. Will advise of winds and visibility." Boop responded, "Roger, winds no factor. Will call you on the ground."

With that, the plane was set up for a landing. The NAVRAD scope clearly showed the site now on the thirty mile band. The plane descended into the stratus layer. Boop turned to Dave and said, "This is why we get the big bucks and get to wear these nice flight suits." The windscreen turned milky white and he had flashbacks to his first chopper flight back at Little Rock. But he kept his cool. The copilot started calling off the pre-landing checklist. The flaps were lowered, the throttle adjusted, and the nose tilted downward. The NAVRAD scope was now pinging the DYE site clearly. They were six miles out and 2,500 feet above ground level (AGL). There was still no visibility. The poles along the skiway started to light up on the scope at five miles out. Dave was amazed. The scope truly did look like follow the dots with a V-shaped taper towards the top. At three miles and 1,500 feet AGL the plane broke through the stratus. What he saw in front of him was a magnificent black mega structure sitting on eight massive columns with what looked like the world's biggest golf ball sitting on top.

The plane slid in for a landing smoother than snot on a glass doorknob.

Boop turned to Dave and said, "Welcome to Hoth on Earth." Dave smiled and nodded. He got the joke. This was a clear reference to the ice planet in *The Empire Strikes Back* movie.

The plane taxied back to the ice apron adjacent to the massive complex. Boop hit the intercom again, "Everyone, it is twenty five below zero outside. Bundle up. The wind chill factor will be fifty below in the prop wash."

Sergeant Dylan Sheppard lowered the ramp. Dave was surprised to see a tracked vehicle pushing a large sled up to the aircraft for off loading the drilling pipe and equipment. Carl opened the aft side crew door and lowered the stairs. Dave pulled his parka hood up over his head and put on his fur lined gloves. He didn't bother to take his fur-lined, sealskin boots, or mukluks, as they were called up here, out of his crew bag. After all he was only going to walk a hundred feet to the complex. Major Boop climbed down the ladder followed by Dave.

Sheridan felt the prop wash blast against his body. It was a challenge to stay up right. They walked over to the stairway and were met by the Site Commander, Vince Beach. They shook hands but it was very difficult to carry on a conversation with the props running. Vince led the way up the two flights of stairs and into the site. Dave's eyeglasses fogged up immediately with a thick layer of ice as he hit the warm air of the entrance way. He pulled off his glasses to see. Vince welcomed him and Major Boop to DYE-3 and had them sign in on the site log. Vince then led them through a series of hallways into the dining room for a cup of coffee. He introduced him to the site's chef, Olga. She shook his hand and then gasped, "Captain, do you know that your ears are bleeding?" He reached up to feel a smear of warm blood on his ear lobes. However, it wasn't his ears that were bleeding. It was his temples. Apparently when he stared into the prop wash, his metal frame glasses froze to his skin. When he removed the glasses because they fogged up, he also unknowingly removed several layers of skin. He thought to himself, what a way to make a grand entrance by bloodying up the kitchen.

Dave soon found out the coffee in Greenland really gives you a jolt. It is a little thicker than back in the States. After Olga helped put on a couple of bandages, he downed his second cup and devoured a phenomenal real Danish pastry. Then Vince gave him a tour of the complex.

"Most of the chefs up here in the Arctic are the best of the best. They come out of the Merchant Marine. The military had learned a long time ago that in order to keep the moral high and the troops happy they didn't skimp on the meals. The typical daily caloric input up here in the Arctic is over 5,000 a day and it's not just all sugar. It's full of good protein with plenty of meat and potatoes. Keep in mind those extra calories might keep you alive for a few more hours if you go down on the icecap. Too bad you're really screwed if you go down in the water."

"We have enough food on site to last us sixty days. Water is no problem. I'll show you our drag line and snow harvesting operation in a little bit." He showed him the huge freezers and warehouse pantry. "The first floor consists of warehouse space, receiving, and our power plant with six huge, 12 cylinder White Superior diesel generators." Vince remarked, "We need three running at one time to supply site power. We have two in standby mode and one down for overhaul at all times. It takes the Ravens six weeks of round the clock flying to supply our diesel fuel requirements for the year. They make about two hundred flights out here from Sonde in a six week period and off load over a half million gallons."

They next climbed a flight of stairs to the lateral tropospheric communications room. Vince explained that radio waves are bounced off the troposphere to adjacent sites. This allows for over the horizon radio communications versus line of sight VHF. It is also very difficult to jam. Half of this floor was a gymnasium with a weight room. "We have to have some place to work off all that pastry." In the back corner was a varnished plywood wall with a door that said "BAR." "We also have to have a place to drown our sorrows."

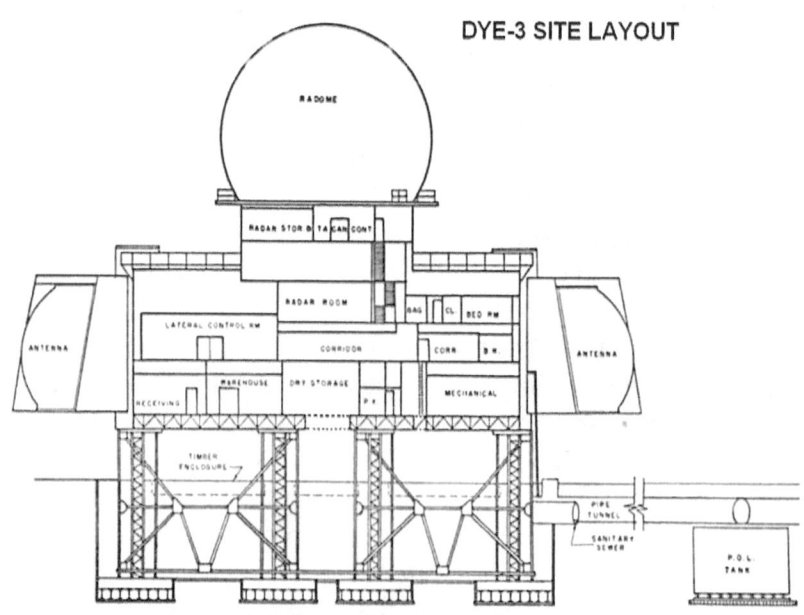

DYE-3 SITE LAYOUT

Next, Vince showed Dave the third floor living quarters. There were a dozen or so rooms arranged on the outside perimeter of this floor. The walls were a good three feet thick and were highly insulated. Each room had a window, more for fire escape than for view. This floor also housed the radar console room in the center of the complex. Vince explained the radar system to him, "We use the FPS-30. With the FPS-30, you could throw an orange into the air thirty miles out and we would see it." Dave asked what the range was. Vince answered, "The actual range is classified, but it is over 250 miles. We have overlap with each of our adjacent sites." Vince punched four digits on a cipher lock and opened the door to the radar room. "This is the heart and soul of our complex. This is our console room, ops center, and communications center. It is manned 24/7. If you need to take a leak there is always someone on standby to cover for you." The room wasn't all that large. It had two scopes side by side, a low altitude scope and a high altitude scope. "There are sixteen permanent party members on-site. We have twenty one with you and the drilling crew. We operate with three RadTechs, two ComTechs, a chief mechanic and two apprentices, an electrician, a laborer, a janitor, a chef, and two dozer operators that constantly plow snow away from the site and keep our skiway smooth for aircraft operations. Then there is myself and a LogTech."

Vince introduced Dave to Jim Ewing. "Jim has been on the line for nearly six years without getting burned out. They all make good money up here and really have no place to spend it. Unlike many of the guys stationed up here, Jim doesn't have an ex-wife down south to worry about. He just keeps banking it away." Jim shook his hand and pointed his thumb at Vince. "Talk about your money bags. The reason we have a twenty million dollars worth of com gear on this site is so Vince can talk to his broker every day."

Just then the radio speaker crackled to life, "Sob Story, Sob Story...this is Raven Two over." Jim keyed his hand set and replied, "Raven Two, Sob Story is with you." "Roger, Sob Story... We are at 15,000 and descending...Please give us a weather and radar check." "Roger, Raven Two, I have you one two zero miles, bearing two eight zero. Weather is as follows, outside air temp (OAT) at minus two fiver degrees Fahrenheit, winds three six zero at ten, visibility three miles, ceiling two thousand and overcast with marginal VFR. Be advised Raven One is on the Apron taxiing out. ETD fifteen minutes."

Raven Two acknowledged the information. Vince said, "Raven two is the load of drilling gear along with Dr. Rapp and Dr. Timken. We have a half an hour to finish up your tour before I have to head back outside to greet them and supervise the offloading."

Vince took Dave up another twisting flight of stairs. He could feel the altitude getting to him now. He was huffing and puffing.

"It'll take you a couple of days to get acclimated to the altitude. Remember, DYE-3 is nearly two miles above sea level."

They exited the stair shaft and were on the third floor. Here there were several rooms dedicated to the station chief, and any VIP visitors. "Here is your room, Captain." Vince opened the door and Dave was pleasantly surprised to see a large room with a queen size bed, dressers, couch, chair, coffee table, and TV, all the comforts of home. "I'll have Sven bring up your bags in a little bit. We can't go up into the Radome with the antenna hot and spinning. It would fry your gonads in a fraction of a second. My room is at the end of the hall. Dr. Rapp and Dr. Timken have the other two rooms. We'll go down to my office real quick and I'll give you a visitors' safety briefing on what to do in case of fire, medical emergencies, communications procedures, and all that good stuff."

The PA system echoed off the halls, "Raven One off the ice and out bound to Sonde. Raven Two inbound…ETA ten minutes." With this much going on at the site, Vince had air traffic calls put on the PA to keep everyone informed what was happening.

After the visitors' brief, Vince said, "I've got to bundle up and head back outside. You can wait in the dining room or you're welcome to join me. Your choice." Dave was no fool. "Until I get acclimated and my temples stop bleeding, I think I'll wait inside. I'd like to wait in the console room if that's okay with you. Besides my mukluks are in my luggage out there somewhere." Jim said, "That's fine. Just announce yourself to Jim on the portal phone outside the door. You're cleared for access to all areas of the site. But just a word of wisdom, never let that arctic survival gear bag out of your control. Never know when you will need it."

The PA system came to life once more, "Attention on-site, attention on-site…Raven Two, Raven Two on the ice. Taxiing to the drill site." Jim told him it would take about forty minutes to offload the piping and drilling equipment. He showed him every knob, switch, and dial in the console room. He even showed him how he was tracking a couple of commercial flights out of Europe doing the great circle route over Greenland on their way to Detroit and Toronto. Dave's cover story was to be the Air Force Contracting

Officers Technical Representative, COTR for the Space Command modifications. He was the on-site inspector. Sort of like the IG. No wonder everyone was treating him like royalty here and he was getting the VIP room.

Jim asked him about the Space Command site upgrades that he would be overseeing to support the Space Shuttle polar orbit launches out of Vandenberg AFB in California. Dave smiled, "Well, if I tell you, I'd have to shoot you." Jim smiled and said, "Well, I'll bet you my gun is bigger than your gun. We have two old M-1 carbine rifles in the cabinet over there. I don't think they've ever been fired in over twenty years. Do bullets have a shelf life?" Dave laughed, "Don't know. What do you suppose they have them up here for? Hold off being overrun by the Russians, put down a mutiny, take out a few polar bears, and protect the site from space aliens?" Jim replied, "Might be some element of truth in all the above." Dave gave him a disbelieving look, "You mean they're here to protect you from little green men?" Jim laughed, "Hell, no, I'm talking about the polar bears. We do get them every once in a while up here. Even though we're over a hundred miles from the east coast, they do come out here. And when they get here, they are very hungry, and mean as hell. I'll continue with your site safety training. Anyone working outdoors is issued a bear cracker. And, no, it isn't something to eat. It is a quarter stick of dynamite. You light it like a flare and then toss it at a bear to scare it away. However, they don't work very well. All that happens is that a bunch of other bears hear the noise and figure out that there must be food this way."

Just then the handheld radio came to life, "Jim, this is Vince. Our good professors request the presence of our VIP. I've had his arctic gear delivered to his room. Could you run him down and have him suited up? I'll have Jorgen waiting for him with a snowcat at the bottom of the stairs." Jim replied, "Roger, Captain Sheridan is in the console room with me. He copies."

Jim gave Dave some pointers on how to bundle up and cover exposed skin. He then went to his room and opened the arctic survival gear duffle bag and put on long johns, fatigues, iron pants, two pair of thermal socks, a parka, and a pair of deerskin gloves.

He pulled on his mukluks which were genuine seal skin. Nothing was ever found that could substitute for a good pair of mukluks. He then put on his ski mask, glasses and goggles.

Dave stopped by the console room on his way out. Jim gave him a status check to make sure he was properly suited up for a trek on the icecap. The extra pounds he was wearing were taking a toll as he exited the complex and climbed down the stairs and headed towards the snowcat. Jorgen saw him descend and opened the door for him as he climbed up into the cab. In a thick Danish accent, Jorgen welcomed him to DYE-3 and told him to sit back and enjoy the ride over to the ice drilling camp. They could barely see the tail of a C-130 off on the horizon. "Why are they so far out?" Jorgen replied, "For a couple of reasons. Their gravimetric instrumentation is very sensitive. They need to get clear of the DYE site vibrations and structural steel. They are also located in a radar beam side lobe gap. They aren't constantly bombarded every sixty seconds with umpteen thousand watts of radar energy. The camp is about five miles out. They are far enough away to be clear of the site and close enough for logistics support and emergencies. We will be there in about ten minutes. Captain, help yourself to some hot coffee from the thermos there. It is always good to warm up the gut if you can before you venture out onto the ice."

"Sounds like good advice." He poured himself a cup of thick Danish coffee and sipped it down. He was beginning to wonder if the Air Force had a caffeine addiction program. He could see he was going to have to learn to like this stuff.

About halfway there, they could see that the C-130 was beginning to taxi towards them.

"They must be finished offloading the drilling supplies. They will taxi the five miles back to the DYE-3 site and use the skiway to take off. It is too bumpy out here for them to get enough air speed to attempt to lift off." It was kind of strange to pass a C-130 coming at you, but Dave and Jorgen waved to the pilot as he passed off to the left on his way back to the skiway.

As the snowcat neared the drilling camp, they could see a few tents set up and a few large cargo containers strung together. Off to one end was a drilling derrick. Another snowcat was pulling a huge sled full of piping and crates towards the derrick. Jorgen pulled the snowcat up to the cargo container and got on the hand-held. The handheld was a small radio which had a thirty mile range that was line of sight limited. "Vince, this is Jorgen. We are outside now."

"Roger, we'll be out in a minute." Vince and Rapp exited the cargo container and opened the back door of the snowcat and climbed in. The snowcat had bench seating along both walls and had a couple of cable drums turned on their sides to use as desks and tables.

Rapp's beard was already frosted over when he climbed in. "Welcome to the Apple Orchard, Captain." Dave thought the code name for this camp was kind of funny. "Why is this place called the Apple Orchard?" Rapp smiled and said, "In deference to Sir Isaac Newton and his falling apple that revolutionized the world of physics. We are about to change the world here, too."

Rapp pulled a PVC tube from the wall of the snowcat and pulled out a set of drawings. He rolled them out on the table. "This is one of six camps located up here. We are spread out in a pentagon pattern of about four miles apart with the sixth located in the center. We are drilling eight inch diameter holes through the ice down to within five hundred feet of the bedrock nearly two kilometers below us. We are looking for several things. First, any signs of torsional waves. Second, any signs of gravitational waves. These are much harder to detect due to their long wavelengths, and then, lastly, for any variances in the Universal Gravitational Constant, alias the big G, that we explained to you in Sonde."

Vince told Jorgen to head for the drilling rig. The snowcat lurched forward. When they reached the rig, Vince and Rapp leapt out the back as Dave crawled out of the cab and was surprised at how warm it felt outside. The sun was bright and there was no wind. The snow was crisp and powdery dry under his feet. He followed Rapp and Vince into the canvas covered derrick. Inside was a tripod frame about fifty feet tall with chain hoists and rigging. Several pieces of pipe were stacked vertically along one side of the frame. Timken and another man were bending over the generator on the backside of the rig. Dave couldn't quite make out the discussion, but it was pretty intense and sounded like a few Russian expletives were thrown in for good measure.

"Dostal, dostal. Dis a pizdet. Da balvin." Just then Timken turned and saw Dave, Vince, and Rapp. He threw up his hands in disgust and exited the tent. "What's wrong with him?" Dave asked. Rapp replied, "He is pissed off at Boris here, because he let the fuel run out in the generator while he was off loading the C-130. They can't get it restarted. The battery is nearly drained." Dave looked over at the generator. He wasn't a mechanical engineer, but he grew up in northwest Ohio and knew how to jump start a clunker to get her started on a winter morning. He asked if the snowcat had a set of jumper cables. He was surprised to hear from all the men standing around him, "What are they?" He thought to himself, "You've got to be kidding. All these PhDs oozing with brain power and they didn't know how to jump start an engine." They were actually contemplating having a new battery flown in from Sonde.

"Okay, gentlemen, this is what we're going to do. This is a standard twelve volt marine battery. Have Jorgen open up the hood or whatever you call it on the snowcat." He found an extension cord plugged into one of the flood lights. Just like his dad had taught him, he always carried a pocket knife on him. This time he had to dig through three layers as he had left it in his fatigue pants pocket under his iron pants. He cut off the ends and then peeled back the insulation a couple of inches, exposing the copper wire. Jorgen had lifted the cab over the diesel engine. Luckily Dave spotted a couple of C-clamps in the top tray of a tool box. He grabbed them and walked out to the snowcat. He clamped a wire to the positive terminal and then walked back into the derrick shelter. He clamped the other end of the cable to the positive terminal of the generator battery. He walked back outside and clamped the other wire to the negative terminal on the snowcat. He then walked back in and looped the leftover cable around the generator frame for a ground. Just then Timken re-entered the tent. "Are you sure you know what you are doing, Captain? This is some delicate machinery." Dave was a little annoyed at this point, "Delicate my ass, this is a standard 60 kilowatt, 240 volt, three phase Cummins generator set. This ain't rocket science. I should know. Okay, crank her over. She should start up." Boris turned the lever and sure enough the generator cranked over and sputtered to life. He let it idle a minute or so and then threw another switch. Presto!! The lights came on. He figured he'd earned his pay with this little piece of technical knowhow. Obviously, this crowd had never had to jump start a '65 Mercury in a dark parking lot at ten below before. Piece of cake.

CHAPTER 5
Ancient Blue Ice Cubes

With his new found status as a mechanical genius, Rapp and Timken were duly impressed. They opened up a little more to their newfound friend. The drilling continued for a couple of weeks and all was going well. Ice cores were taken every five hundred feet and sent back to Denmark for analysis. Scientists in Europe were studying climate change, looking for pollutants, volcanic eruptions, and carbon dioxide content all going back almost 100,000 years.

One day Rapp and Timken entered the site bar. Vince and Dave watched as they uncovered a contraband bottle of Russian vodka and poured the contents into several glasses. Rapp announced, "Now for the piece de resistance." He pulled out a large metal thermos and grabbed a set of tongs from inside his jacket. He opened the thermos and then grabbed a chunk of blue ice and dropped it into the glass of vodka. The ice immediately snapped, crackled, and popped. "What you see here gentlemen is an exothermic reaction from a compressed nitrogen oxygen mixture reacting with an ambient ethanol concoction."

Timken held out a martini glass and said, "Or, in other words, please join us in a salute with some vodka and Greenlandic ice cubes that have been compressed from being buried under two miles of ice for over a hundred thousand years. We have just completed our core drilling." Dave grabbed a glass and was amazed to watch the blue ice cubes pop like a Fizzie when he was a kid. The air bubbles trapped in the ice were under great pressure and had not seen the light of day for a hundred millennium. They all raised their fizzing glasses as Timken made a toast. "To unraveling the secrets of the universe, may we have the intelligence to understand them, the wisdom to guard them, and the humanity to use them wisely." To this everyone replied back with a hearty Danish, "Skol!!"

"We are on schedule. The holes are drilled to the proper depth and the alignment is well within tolerance. We will lower the gravity meters in the morning and start our experiments on Wednesday."

"What exactly will you be looking for?" Dave asked. "I've seen your instrumentation shack and understand the concept. But how sensitive are these meters and how do you know when you are successful in finding gravity waves?"

In a not too exaggerated Russian accent, Timken replied, "We have our ways, my good Captain. Besides we are really looking for the torsional waves. It appears that the Earth's magnetic field pulls torsional waves into both the North and South Poles. Torsional waves align themselves perpendicular to the magnetic field. However, torsional waves are coupled to gravity waves. Unlike gravity, electrical fields and magnetic fields are coupled 90 degrees apart. Gravitational waves are coupled at a little over 68.75 degrees to torsional waves, half the golden angle. This famous angle is found all throughout nature and the universe."

Timken took another sip of vodka and continued, "There are many other strange manifestations of spin-torsion interactions also at the subatomic level we call nuclear spin waves or nuclear wave resonance which are the basis of the fifth force of nature or unified field."

"We now know that gyroscopes and gyroscopic forces can generate and are also affected by torsional waves. Experiments with gyroscopes have found slight but measurable variations of the gyroscope's weight depending on the angular velocity and the direction of rotation. Even more bizarre, fall-time of freely falling spinning gyroscopes also varies depending on the angular velocity and the direction of rotation, resulting in microgravity. This effect is even more noticeable at the poles to a small degree with the rotation of the planet Earth. In effect, gravity here is polarized through the frame-dragging effect of large rotating masses coupling angular momentum, inertia, and T-waves."

As the evening wore on, a couple more bottles of contra-band vodka and a bottle of Norwegian Aquavit (Viking Fire-water) made their rounds. Half the complex was in the site bar making toasts to everything from Ronald Reagan and the Space Shuttle, to boobs and babes. Dave was reassured that the regs he was sent out here to enforce, did not say anything about passing around free liquor. The regs only mentioned it was not permissible to sell anything but beer at the site bar, with the funds generated to be used to purchase recreational equipment. Since he was a SAC-trained killer, he had to go by the letter of the law and he deemed no regulations were being violated.

Rapp and Timken were feeling no pain and started opening up even more and more to Dave. He was not feeling any pain either. However, he held back some and had the feeling that the good doctors were not telling him the whole story of what they were up to. They were sending out way too much crypto radio traffic to be supporting an above board scientific experiment. Now was a good time to pump them for some answers.

In a slightly slurred Russian accent, Timken blurted, "You know, Captain, this whole thing started about eighty years ago in Siberia."

"What 'thing' would that be, Dr. Timken?"

"This whole thing with torsional waves and antimatter, of course. Have you not ever heard of the Tunguska event?"

"Wasn't that supposedly a huge meteorite or comet that struck somewhere in your home country at the turn of the century?"

"I assure you, Captain, it was certainly not a comet or mete-orite, and there is nothing "supposedly" about this event. It really happened. Back in the summer of 1908, the explosion, as you call it, leveled over 800 square miles of forest and knocked down over 60 million trees. This is more than five times the size of the Mount Saint Helen's eruption. It occurred in a vastly remote and relatively unpopulated part of western Siberia about five hundred miles northwest of Lake Baikal. There were witnesses and even a few casualties."

"What do you think it was, if it wasn't a meteorite or comet? From what I remember reading, whatever it was did not leave an impact crater, implying it was a massive air burst."

"Well, Captain, being that we are comrades now, and in the spirit of glasnost, not to mention the spirits of vodka and Aquavit, I am about to let you in on a little secret. The Tunguska event was in fact an extraterrestrial event. It was a six kilogram ball of antimatter traveling at nearly 100,000 miles per second or half the speed of light. That ball hit the Earth at a relatively shallow angle of about 30 degrees at about seven in the morning of June 30, 1908. As a matter of fact, it passed a little less than five hundred miles directly under this very spot as it grazed the outer core and then exited the Earth in the North Atlantic about a thousand miles off the coast of Nova Scotia. It created a huge steam geyser on its way out as witnessed by several ships at seven in the evening, their time, a half a world apart. The torsional energy left in the wake of this antimatter bullet is still spinning in the core of the Earth. In effect, the molten core and magnetic field are still reacting to this torsional wave. That is where the gravity anomalies are coming from and what is causing the left hand twist on all of the satellites in orbit. You see, Captain, Space Command has a desire to find an explanation for the orbital shifts. All we have is a theory. These experiments will validate our mathematical models."

"I appreciate your candor in discussing this topic with me, Dr. Timken. But I do have a question. Why wouldn't this antimatter be annihilated instantaneously when it interacted with the Earth's atmosphere, let alone be able to pass through thousands of mile of dense rock and magma and stay intact? Also, I assume that there is enough matter in the form of space dust and solar wind material to interact with the antimatter long before it even reached the Earth."

"You are a very bright young man, Captain. The antimatter was protected by being wrapped within the wake of a torsional shockwave. No matter could penetrate this plasma flux.

The explosive damage done by the Tunguska event was purely kinetic. That's not meant to imply that other damage or effects were not felt. The wake left behind is still present after eighty years not to mention other strange after effects."

"What other strange effects do you mean?"

"Sorry, Comrade, I'm not that inebriated."

"I'm sorry, but I find it kind of strange that just off the east coast of the U.S. in 1908, you have the equivalent of a 20 megaton nuke going off with very little notice. I assume the slug had the same effect coming out as it did going in. Wouldn't there have been tidal waves, shockwaves, blinding flashes of light? There had to be hundreds of ships out to sea."

"Captain, I am very fond of the American saying, how do you say, you know what happens when you assume? It makes an ass out of you and me.   When the antimatter slug passed out of the Earth it was traveling from higher to lower density material reducing the torsional energy, with the seawater being mostly constant density material. The torsional wave sliced through it like butter with very little kinetic energy transfer. I would assume that the surface geyser phenomena reported by several ships at the time would have been quite impressive. These ships were hundreds of miles away; however, they reported seeing a mile wide steam cloud rocket miles into the sky."

"Now look who is assuming."

"Very well, Captain, it is getting late. We have much work to do in the morning. Could I get someone to help me get my colleague up to his room?" Dr. Rapp was slumped over in his chair under the dart board at the end of the bar. He was oblivious to the incoming darts passing only a couple of feet over his head.

The alarm clock rang at 0630 hours. Dave thought that the alarm clock was amongst the worst inventions in the world. They fell somewhere on his list between nerve gas and disco. After all, it wasn't natural to send an audio shock through your nervous system to wake you out of a perfectly good REM sleep. This was especially true after kicking back a few shots of vodka.

It would be much better to wake up naturally by a stream of warm sunshine on your face. Oh yeah, right. He was above the Arctic Circle. The sun had been up already, for a good couple of months now. Luckily, there wasn't much to a vodka hangover. After a quick shower and shave, he suited up in his cotton fatigues and headed down for breakfast. He was going to have to request a flight suit from Colorado Springs. With this much static electricity floating around the complex the last thing you wanted to wear was all cotton. However, he wasn't officially on flying status, even though he probably logged more flying time than half the F-16 pilots he knew. The zipper-suited sun gods were quite protective of their flight suit status and took a dim view of desk jockeys wearing their holy garb.

He was surprised to see Rapp and Timken finishing their breakfasts. They looked no worse for wear. Olga was behind the grill ready to custom make any omelet imaginable. Dave thought he'd throw her a challenge. "How about a western style omelet?" She gave him a wink and said, "Sure thing, Tex." She was definitely in a flirty mood this morning. He was beginning to wonder what he did in the bar last night that he couldn't remember.

After pouring himself a cup of thick black coffee, he sat down at the table with Vince, Rapp, and Timken.

Vince greeted him, "Good morning, Captain. We were just going over today's schedule. My crew is lowering the instruments out of the supply warehouse and down to the snowcats now." Rapp said, "We should have all five gravity meters down-hole by this evening and start calibration in the morning. Hopefully, we'll get our first readings by tomorrow afternoon."

Dave took a sip of coffee and commented, "You're not wasting any time are you?"

"We plan on taking advantage of the good weather. They are forecasting some gusty winds on Friday. If you will excuse us, Captain, we are going to move out with the equipment."

Vince spoke up, "We'll give you a couple hours to get the equipment unpacked, wired up, and then we'll be out there to bug you." Dave said, "I assure you I'll stay out from under foot. I know you are on a tight schedule." To this Rapp replied, "You are more than welcome anytime in the Apple Orchard. You saved the day with your brilliant power transfer solution."

"Oh, you mean the jump start I gave you guys. It pays to grow up in the Midwest. I've got to catch up on some paperwork this morning and tend to some of my own equipment installations. We have a K-band satellite antenna to install to support shuttle operations."

The professors excused themselves as Olga walked over to the table with Dave's omelet and a freshly made peach Danish pastry. In a cute Danish accent Olga mentioned, "The pastry is from my grandmother's recipe book. The omelet I learned from watching Graham Kerr on TV. I hope you enjoy them both. Is there anything else I can do for you?"

"No, I am fine. Thank you, Olga. I really appreciate the hospitality." Olga smiled and strode off into the kitchen.

Vince said, "I think she kind of likes you, Captain. I told her to take good care of you."

Dave smiled and said, "Thanks. But being the only female within three hundred miles she can afford to flirt with any guy she wants. I assure you I intend to keep things very professional out here. I don't need any more complications than I have."

To this Vince said, "I'm sure her intentions are honorable. She is a great cook. I'll talk to her if you wish."

Dave replied, "No, don't do that. No need to embarrass her. Now, let's run up to the communications room. I've got to check on some measurements and verify rack space availability for some of the K-band equipment to be fitted. I need to meet with your Com technicians, too. They will be instrumental in installing the equipment. I've also got to figure out how to install the antenna. I noticed you have a satellite TV reception antenna installed outside. That's not on any of the as-built drawings."

Vince responded, "Yeah. We bought that with our bar proceeds. Got it pointed pretty low to the horizon to pick up on a European satellite TV station."

Dave answered, "Well, if your guys can rig that system up

to watch the European boob tube, I'm sure a simple K-band set up will be no problem. We just have to tie it in with the tropo-feed back to the States."

Vince asked, "Why in the world do you need to use this site as a shuttle telemetry and downlink station? Why not use Thule or Sonde?"

Dave replied, "Oh, to be sure that they are being fitted up, too. All the DEW (distant early warning) line sites are being equipped with the K-band capability. The military logic is this. When the shuttles come arching up over the poles in the lowest part of their orbit, they can flash down link their communications, data, telemetry, or any intel to the DEW line sites. This data stream can then be sent directly on to Colorado Springs via the DEW lines existing troposcatter radio, saving a precious ten or fifteen minutes before they are in range of any other communications sites further south. Also, the aurora borealis plays havoc with polar orbit communications. This is also a vital backup to our satellite to satellite communications relay system, which is also not very dependable. It is important to note that the Russians and Chinese are not thrilled with us over flying every square inch of their territories, too. We are sure that they have some 'passive' jamming capability. I prefer to discuss the classified portion of this topic out in the snowcat."

After taking his measurements and confirming the dimensions on the communications rack, Dave next verified the power supply leads and terminal strip configuration. Space on the rack had already been identified for the K-band receiver and transmitter. A troposcatter interface was being designed and built at Hanscom Air Force Base in Massachusetts. His job was to confirm that the rack positions and power leads were available to support the new communications gear. He would also be responsible for its installation north of the Arctic Circle. Plus, a totally brand new system was going to be built and installed. It would have a rack of its own and needed to be located in a secure location onsite. The most secure location was the console room and Radome. This new system was known as the Shuttle Lunar Laser Reflectometer Data Relay.

In the event of magnetic storms, electromagnetic pulse detonation, or enemy jamming, the shuttle had another innovative
communications capability. They had the capability to use a
laser beam reflected off a quartz reflector left on the Moon's
surface to communicate.

The icecap is a perfect place for a lunar observatory. A
study using ten years of imagery measured very good sky conditions on the icecap; 60 to 68 percent of the observations had
clear skies or scattered clouds and only 12 to 18 percent were
overcast. The clouds over the icecap are also likely to be thinner than those on the coast as the cold air inland is not capable
of holding as much moisture as that at lower altitudes.

Even though a whiteout condition occurred on the icecap at
times it seldom reached up and over the Radome 80 feet above
the surface. Thus a laser optics receiver was to be placed atop
the Radome and synchronized to track the Moon's trek across
the sky.

CHAPTER 6
Fire in the Sky and Lake on the Ice

There was a knock on the VIP room door at 0030 hours in the morning. One of the radar techs woke Sheridan telling him that there was an ELT, (emergency locator transponder) radio beacon going off, and one of the ice drilling rigs had reported seeing a glow over the northern horizon. He threw on his fatigues and boots and headed down the stairs toward the radar console room. The door was open when he got there. Vince Beach was studying the radar display and the ELT beacon was audible on the speaker set.

All aircraft are equipped with an ELT transponder. This beacon is activated when a switch built into the unit is activated by high G-forces, such as in a crash. It is analogous to an air bag going off and the car notifying OnStar of the deployment via cell phone. However, this is a radio beacon that uses a universal frequency of 1030 to 1090 MHz. In the event of a crash the radio beacon can be used as a directional finder to locate the crash site.

The funny thing about this ELT activation was that nothing was on the radar screen prior to its activation. No distress signal was given. The beacon was coming from the north in the direction of the glow over the horizon.

Vince got on the tropo-phone hotline and notified the Space Command HQ in Cheyenne Mountain of a suspected crash. NORAD confirmed that there was no military or civilian aircraft in the region prior to the ELT. Then encrypted message traffic came in over the KW-7 instructing them to cease discussing the incident over the tropo-phone. They were to use the encrypted keyboard. The reason given was that it could be a Soviet aircraft that was testing the radar coverage area and it was flying below the radar. It may have actually crashed.

The ice drilling rig operator was now on the radio telling us that the glow on the horizon was moving slowly to the east. This sure didn't look like a crash site. Captain Sheridan and Vince put on their parkas, iron pants, goggles, and gloves and headed outside onto the catwalk near the snow harvester dredge. They looked to the north and sure enough could see the glow. It was more than a glow though. It was a fuzzy inverted V-shaped object, glowing yellow, and then green. It looked to be just over the horizon. Whatever it was, it wasn't burning and it was huge. Distances and size are deceiving on the icecap.

Space Command HQ authorized a Search and Rescue operation to be organized and sent out. Vince got on the PA system and hit the crash alarm. Everyone was up in an instant and met in the gymnasium. Blankets were gathered. Four men headed down stairs to the maintenance shed to fire up the site's three snowcats. The tracked vehicles with a crew box were sort of like mating a minivan with a bulldozer. They held up to a dozen personnel each and were onsite in the event of a catastrophic event on the station. They were life boats so to speak. Each one had its own survival gear and first aid equipment stored on board.

Vince picked another half dozen men and had them report to the shed. He then had Jorgen man the infirmary. The snowcats were loaded up within a few minutes. The diesel engines were preheated and fired up quickly.

The glow was still moving slowly to the east as the three snowcats with the four men each lurched out onto the icecap. They made pretty good time. They would easily do about twenty-five mph. However, the snow rifts and drifts made it a slow go. Dan Wilson was in the lead snowcat. He was a little apprehensive. It sure did not look like a plane crash or fire on the horizon. The closer he got the higher the glow seemed to get until they reached a point where they could clearly see it hovering over the horizon and still apparently moving to the east. The only thing that kept everyone calm was the fact that an ELT was still going off. Only airplanes have ELTs, right? The snowcats were now out for about forty-five minutes. They were about fifteen miles out and could barely make out the DYE-3 site behind them. They were still quite a ways from the glow. It still looked like it was on the horizon, but higher now. It was still fuzzy and shaped like an inverted V. Sort of like the *Star Trek* symbol. Talk about irony. Dan was feeling less guilty now for insisting they bring one of the only two weapons from the site, the old M-1 carbine. Nobody had ever even loaded the magazine in one of these things let alone fired it. However, Dan was now taking a crash course in ballistics. He gave up trying to figure out the stripper clip and manually placed one round in the chamber. Luckily he didn't shoot a hole through the wind shield or blow his foot off, but he felt a little more secure and confident.

The snowcats were now out more than an hour and were twenty miles from the site. The glow was now moving faster to the east and was several degrees above the horizon now.

Vince flipped a toggle on the console communication panel and the radio speaker cracked to life. DYE-4 had contacted him to let him know they now had an ELT pinging. They could not see any glow however. DYE-4 was on an island mountain top near the Inuit village of Kulusuk on the east coast of Greenland about 150 miles from DYE-3. This confirmed it was not an equipment malfunction at DYE-3.

DYE-4 had notified Keflavik, Iceland of the ELT. Two F-15s were put on notice and short alert status. They could be airborne in a couple of minutes and make the seven hundred mile trip to DYE-3 in under an hour with use of afterburner. A midair refueling would be needed for the trip back. HQ SAC at Offutt AFB controlled the Air Force's tanker fleet and were now involved with putting together a rendezvous with a KC-135 over the North Atlantic.

Dan had now been heading northeast of DYE-3 for over an hour. The site wasn't visible now. Compasses are pretty much useless in the Arctic. They're too close to the Pole to be reliable. One comfort was that the radar had picked them up using what is known as a side lobe. Using the same technique the Ravens use on setting up for a landing, the side lobe radar was now pinging on the only solid metal objects on the icecap. It couldn't distinguish three separate vehicles but did register them as a group. They were twenty-two miles out with a relative bearing of 40 degrees true.

Vince was now watching the anemometer and barometric gauge. What he saw was unsettling. The wind gauge was starting to pick up and gust to twenty knots. The barometer was dropping. It didn't take much wind up here to kick up the snow and produce a white out condition.

Vince told Dave to get suited up because they were heading outside on the catwalk around the Radome. From the catwalk, they could see the swirls of snow writhe up and over the snow-drifts. The odd thing was that there was not a cloud in the sky. The stars were out. The night was perfectly clear. Only the green-ish yellow glow shined on the horizon. Whatever it was, it was really picking up speed now. It was now lifting up off the horizon with clear air visible beneath it.

Vince made a command decision to tell Dan to stop any for-ward motion. A few minutes after this the ELT suddenly went dead. DYE-4 reported theirs went dead, too. At about the same time, the glow suddenly reversed course, heading west at a rapid rate of speed. The glow got brighter, too. It got more yellow. Then it stopped dead in its tracks about where it was first spotted. It rose higher on the horizon, started spinning, and then flashed out of sight in an instant: no noise, nothing on the radar, and no trace. Swoosh, it spun and shot straight up. It was gone in an instant. They just looked at each other in disbelief.

The wind was now picking up to twenty-five knots and the snow was kicking up. The catwalk was a good forty feet above the surface. The blowing snow was only about fifteen feet off the deck. Dan had now reported that he saw the object spiral straight up and vanish in an instant. He was also worried about getting back to the site. They had plenty of fuel, but it was getting danger-ous. They were more than twenty miles from the site blinded by the snow and he knew white outs could last days up here.

The funny thing about the M-1 carbine now was that it was now as useless as a bull with ten tits, since Dan couldn't see more than ten feet in front of him now. It was time to figure out how to keep all three vehicles together and make a 180 degree turn back to DYE-3. Dan had them lined up side by side. The flashing yellow caution lights gave off another eerie glow that significantly increased the pucker factor among the team. They could make better time flying in formation and have less white-knuckled steering with not having to worry about climbing up and over each other in a single file.

Dan made a slow turn to the right. Both the other snowcats were now running parallel ten feet apart and could barely see each other. The wind was whipping the snow horizontally. Dan called back for a heading check. The side lobe radar was losing them in the surface effect of the wind driven snow. Dan asked for the wind direction, thinking he could use the blowing snow as a reference for a relative bearing back to the site. However, the snow was swirling too much to get an accurate bearing. He went with his instincts and pressed ahead dead reckoning.

They were now out for nearly two hours doing about ten mph. The wind was now gusting to over thirty mph. Vince and Dave went back out onto the catwalk. The blowing snow was visible below them. It was still only a wind event. The stars were clearly visible above them. The temperature had dropped to ten below with a wind chill factor now of sixty below. Vince had an idea. Each snowcat was equipped with a flare gun with six shells each. He asked Dan to stop, open the roof hatch and fire a flare straight up. They should be visible if they were not too far out. According to the directions on the flare gun the flares would reach an altitude of 120 meters and burn for 8.5 seconds. They were about fifteen miles out now. Vince and Dave were fifteen meters above the surface and could theoretically cancel out the curvature of the Earth. The flares should be visible and it would be a simple task of walking the snowcats back to the Site visually.

Vince had every light on the station turned on, including every flashlight that could be rounded up and had them pointed in Dan's general direction.

Dan opened the roof hatch and was immediately hit with a blast of cold air. His goggles froze over immediately. He was prepared for this and took a cloth he had pre-sprayed with windshield wiper fluid and swiped it over his goggles. Looking into the whiteout was like staring through a milk bottle. He lifted the flare pistol straight over his head and fired.

Both Vince and Dave saw the red flair instantly as it shot up on the northeast horizon. With his handheld brick radio, Vince gave Dan a relative bearing of forty degrees from his compass. It was impossible to estimate the distance. Dan looked at his compass and read the opposite direction of 220 degrees. He knew the magnetic declination was huge this far north and that they would have to trade relative bearings back and forth with each other after flare shots to make it back.

This process worked very well for the next hour and a half, after only five more flares were used. Finally, Dan saw one of the metal flag poles along the ice-runway. He followed them back toward the site and simply made a left turn up the taxiway and into the shelter of the maintenance shed. There, they broke out a bottle of scotch and thawed out.

Nobody could really believe what had just happened. Vince and Dave went to the console room. Vince banged out a simple request to NORAD on the Crypto keypad:

"Object vanished. Please advise."

Dave was very much surprised when there was an almost immediate simple response. He figured the bureaucracy would delay any answer.

"Log event. Recover search crew."

Neither Vince nor Sheridan knew how to interpret this. Evidently there was someone at NORAD that was taking the initiative. They would have had a "Please Standby" message if not.

"So, this is how it's going to be. They've pretty much told us to ignore it in a polite way and not bother them anymore. Nice to know they are concerned about the crew," Vince said.

Vince complied and wrote the event up in the daily site log. He even put it on the contacts and radar track sheet. He wrote it up with an interesting "spin."

- 0030Z060685
  ELT Activation

- 0045Z060685
  Visual sighting of glow on northern horizon
- 0050Z060685
  Contact NORAD HQ
- 0055Z060685
  Contact Iceland
- 0105Z060685
  Dispatch Search & Rescue
- 0130Z060685
  Visual track west to east over north horizon
- 0200Z060685
  Whiteout conditions – low level
- 0300Z060685
  Object spins and climbs out to the northwest at warp speed
- 0430Z060685
  S&R Crew Return to Site

Dave was a little more detailed in his daily report. He wrote three pages on the "event" and sent it in with his weekly activity report. Since he was not told to keep quiet and no *Men in Black* showed up, he simply sent the report in through normal channels.

The next morning all hell had broken loose at NORAD. Dave was not reprimanded. He was not chastised. He was simply summoned back to HQ Space Command at Cheyenne Mountain for a meeting with the commander. "Oh, shit," he thought. "I've screwed the pooch. But hell, what were they going to do to me, send me to Alaska?"

The next morning a Raven showed up. It off loaded 3,300 gallons of diesel fuel, as well as food, and a heavier anchor chain to be used to smooth the ice runway.

He learned his lesson and did not stare into the prop wash as he boarded the C-130. The crew chief escorted him to the flight deck where he shook hands with the flight crew and strapped in. He put his headset on and did a com-check and was glad to see it was Major Rick Boop who was commanding this flight. He told Dave that they had about ten more minutes before departure. They were going to haul out a D-7 dozer back to Sonde for extensive overhaul.

Flying the C-130 on the Greenland Icecap requires special skills, techniques, and guts. The high altitudes at which the DYE sites are located reduces engine performance by as much as thirty-five percent. Lift also is reduced. Ski landings are similar to normal landings. However, takeoffs on skis are another matter. Skill is required to keep the aircraft lined up on the runway. Because of the friction of the skis on the snow, the runs are longer, especially on warmer days when the surface is softer.

The crew chief checked and armed the eight Jet Assisted Take Off (JATO) bottles attached on the aft end of the fuselage. Under heavy load and certain snow conditions, JATO bottles were often used to literally blast the aircraft off the ice. On this flight, the dozer weighed over 20,000 pounds.

Major Boop taxied the Hercules out onto the skiway. He said that there was another C-130 inbound with another load of diesel. It was circling the site waiting for them to depart. Boop radioed the console room notifying him that he was departing VFR direct to Sonde low level. This meant that they did not have to burn much fuel to climb with the heavy load.

"Raven Two, Sob Story. Roger, VFR direct to Sonde, two thousand feet AGL." This meant they would follow the icecap at two thousand feet above the surface until they got back.

The C-130 prop pitch was tilted forward and the sound of the four big T-56 turboprops biting into the cold arctic air was reassuring. The C-130 accelerated and bounced down the skiway.

Over the headset, the copilot was calling off the critical airspeeds as the plane accelerated. "V one...V two...Rotate...Victor, Victor, Victor." Just then a switch was flipped and Dave was thrown back in the jump seat. They were pulling some heavy Gs now. The nose pitched up, and the noise was deafening as the rockets lifted the huge aircraft off the ice at a thirty degree angle. In seconds, the Raven was five hundred feet off the ice. The JATOs cut out and the nose tipped over. Wow, what an adrenalin rush and a real buzz in your shorts.

The Raven went from zero to two hundred in about twelve seconds. That was about equivalent to a rail dragster. As the nose settled on the horizon, Dave looked out. The sky was clear and the snow below just about blinded him. The Raven banked to the left and circled back towards the site. They were coming in at 289 knots and 500 feet. The Site Radome was growing larger by the second as they roared over the top.

Just then over the radio, "Raven Two...Sob Story." The copilot acknowledged the call. "Raven Two, Raven One is ten miles west inbound VFR direct. Suggest you proceed on current course until he clears IP (inner perimeter)."

"Roger, Wilco, Sob Story, Raven One." They cleared the area to the north to give him plenty of room. There was plenty of space up here; might as well make use of it.

The C-130 climbed to two thousand feet above the ice and started a turn to the west after they heard Raven Two was safely on the deck. Just then a flash of light caught the flight crew off guard. There was a reflection of the sun off the ice. Where was that coming from? Just to the north a few miles was a pool of aqua green water several miles in diameter. This was impossible even in June in Greenland and at an altitude over a mile and a half above sea level.

Dave asked over the com set, "What the hell is that?" Major Boop responded, "I don't know, we're going to go check it out." He told Boop about the strange event that had taken place the week earlier. It was clear that this was no plane crash. Whatever left this perfect circle in the middle of the icecap used a hell of lot of energy to melt that much ice. There were signs it was a whole lot bigger to begin with but the edges were refreezing towards the center. Somebody is making the equivalent of crop circles in the ice.

The Raven headed for the center of the lake. As it crossed the southern edge the plane suddenly dipped down and to the right. The stall warning horn went off. The airspeed indicator dropped to 170 knots even though there was no apparent deceleration. The turn coordinator showed a full slip to the left even though they were turning opposite. The artificial horizon was rolling in its cage useless. Even though a magnetic compass was useless this far north it was spinning madly.

Boop's quick reflexes and muscle memory kicked in. He did a text book stall recovery. He lowered the nose, applied power, and kicked the opposite rudder to the turn. The hardest thing for a pilot to do in a stall is to counter intuitively push the nose down. Many stalls result when the pilot sucks the yoke back into his chest trying to milk altitude for airspeed. This is usually a fatal mistake.

The plane recovered with a few hundred feet to spare. There was not time for an "Oh, shit." It all happened too fast. As they cleared the opposite side of the lake the instruments settled down and returned to normal.

Boop got on the radio back to Sob Story. He wanted to warn Raven Two to stay clear of this area. He'd explain it once they got back to base.

Boop got on the intercom, "Okay, crew, we just had what they call a departure from normal flight conditions in clear weather and calm air. We're running the stall recovery check list now. You guys all take notes on what you felt, heard, and observed. There will be a debriefing at Sonde."

The plane climbed up to a comfortable altitude and headed back to Sonde. Boop wanted a few thousand feet under his butt just in case something else happened.

The flight recorder was on as well as the voice recorder. The crew was in no mood to ask a bunch of stupid questions no one knew the answers to. Since it was likely the recorders were going to be removed and scrutinized everything was by the book, professional, and no chit chat. This did make for a quiet flight. However, Boop did pass a note back to Dave.

The note simply said. "Need to talk back at Sonde. Not the first time! Caribou Club at 1700 hours."

Dave felt like a third grader passing notes. He nodded to Boop that he understood. There were certain things that the crews did not want said with the voice recorder running. Saying you saw a UFO, and, oh, by the way, it about made me crash was not one of them.

Raven One droned on. Sonde was now an hour to the west. All instruments were in the green. Flying over the icecap was like flying inside a milk bottle sometimes. There was no sense of altitude or speed, due to the lack of landmarks.

The closer the plane got to the west coast some of the mountain peaks started to pop up over the horizon. The plane started its descent. It cleared the glacier and followed the fjord down to the runway. The pre-landing checklist was performed and audible per the book. No one said anything other than what was necessary or mission essential.

After the plane touched down and taxied over to the operations ramp. Dave and the crew went into Operations. They were met by the Ops chief, Maintenance chief, and the Base Commander Colonel Snyder.

"You understand, gentlemen, this is an official investigation. Anytime you have a deviation from controlled flight in a C-130 or any other aircraft, the Air Force wants to know about it. Everything you say now is for the official record. We are going to interview you individually first, and then as a group."

Major Boop followed the three officers to the crew lounge. An NCO was there with a tape recorder and steno pad. Boop knew he was in for a grilling. You don't just drop a C-130 fifteen hundred feet out of the sky. It just isn't done unless the plane is improperly trimmed, loaded incorrectly, hits rough air, flies too slowly, etcetera. In other words, he was being set up for the "oh shit factor," or technically known as pilot error.

After it was over, Major Boop gathered his three man crew and walked with them over to the Caribou Club. The Caribou Club was a combination NCO and Officers' Club. Dave was already waiting. He had ordered a beer and turned around to see the four crew members walk through the door and make their way to the lounge in the back room. He followed them back. The lounge was known as The Suicide Lounge. Urban legend has it that this was where several people went to drink about their sorrows and depression before jumping into the deep fast moving, freezing waters of the fjord, never to be seen again.

Boop pulled out a felt tip pen. He went up to a corner in the room surrounded by his crew and scribbled something on the wall. Afterwards, they cleared the corner, and all went over to a table. Dave's curiosity got the better of him. He strode over to see what words of wisdom Boop had scribbled on the wall. It simply read, "Into the thin air and beyond. 06/05/85 RPB Maj USAF." Under his signature was a strange spiral symbol.

Boop motioned for Dave to come on over to the table. He said, "I'd buy you one, but I see you're already sucking one down. This place does suck at times. They're over at Base Ops right now going over our debriefing to see how bad we screwed the pooch. They can't make any determination up here and the chicken shits will defer any decision to New York. We haven't been grounded. Raven One is still operational, no damage. Only thing missing is the voice data recorder. Not much on it, but it is out of the plane now along with the flight data recorder. Nothing in the regs that says we can't fly that bird to support a mission critical flight. As a matter of fact, I've got an idea up my sleeve. We're going back out there. You with us, Dave?"

Dave didn't have to think twice. "You, betcha. I wouldn't miss it for the world. What's your plan?"

Boop laid out the plan, "This type of thing has happened in the past. Planes up here sometimes encounter what we call thin air. It is much different than your basic turbulence or vortex. You're flying along and all of a sudden you just lose lift. Our little event this morning got my attention. However, I kind of anticipated it to be honest with you. When we began to stall, I noticed a drop in airspeed and a drop in turbine pressure. The vertical speed indicator didn't even budge. The altimeter reading also had a lag in it. This all added up to one thing. The air we flew through had just become instantaneously much thinner. It was like we were flying in a vacuum. We had hit thin air."

Boop continued, "What we're going to do is simple. We're going back out there. However, we need a good reason to launch the bird. A medical emergency or some other reason is what we need to get back out there ASAP. Dave, can you contact DYE-3 and push the envelope a little for us? See if they'd be willing to give us the Bat Signal or something. Maybe they need a critical part or something. On second thought, a medical emergency would raise too many red flags. Maybe if their tropo antenna went down for a few hours. That happens all the time up there. Their equipment is antiquated and spare parts are flown in all the time, right?" Dave responded, "Yes. I'll figure something out. When do you want to get airborne?" Boop replied, "Give us an hour to refuel. Put the call in straight over to Ops. We'll be there ready to go." Dave said, "Okay, but I'm going along for the ride." Boop smiled and said, "Wouldn't have it any other way."

Dave then asked Boop what he meant when he said this has happened before. Was he talking about aircraft stalling or the presence of UFOs? Boop grinned again and simply said, "Both. Let me show you something. See these walls in this lounge. Look at all the graffiti, signatures, and words of wisdom. People have been leaving their mark up here on these walls for over forty years. It is a tradition. This is part of the base history and legacy. It would be a crime to paint over these walls. I'll give you a hint. There are thousands of signatures and words on this wall. See if you can find any with the spiral symbol next to their name. I'm part of a group of flyers that have encountered the thin air phenomena. Others have as well." Boop got up. He only had to walk a couple of feet. "Check out this one." It read, "Balls to the wall with thinning hair – DJC – 11/17/65. There was a sketch of

Kilroy looking over a wall with a single spiral curl of hair on his head. Boop explained. "See how the last three letters of hair are underlined. I don't think that is coincidental. There are at least a couple dozen sayings and initials with reference to thin air. They all put the spiral symbol in somewhere to signify a spin or other "sightings." Let me show you one of the more famous."

Boop walked behind the bar and pointed to a prominent framed spot on the wall over the cash register. "This is a shrine, so to speak, for Colonel Bernt Balchen. He had once been chief pilot for Admiral Byrd in the Antarctic. He built this base and was its first commander. Let me read the inscription.

'Today goes fast and tomorrow is almost here. Maybe I have helped a little in the change. So I go on to the next adventure, looking to the future but always thinking back to the past. Remembering my teammates and the lonely places I have seen that no man ever saw before.' This also is inscribed on his tombstone at Arlington."

Boop turned the frame over, "Speaking of Admiral Byrd, does this sound familiar to you?" On the back of the frame was taped a piece of paper.

0830 Hours: Turbulence encountered again, increase altitude to 2900 feet, smooth flight conditions again.

0910 Hours: Vast Ice and snow below, note coloration of yellowish nature, and disperse in a linear pattern. Altering course for a better examination of this color pattern below, note reddish or purple color also. Circled this area two full turns and return to assigned compass heading. Position check made again to base camp, and relay information concerning colorations in the ice and snow below.

0912 Hours: Both Magnetic and Gyro compasses beginning to gyrate and wobble, we are unable to hold our heading by instrumentation. Take bearing with Sun compass, yet all seems well. The controls are seemingly slow to respond and have sluggish quality, but there is no indication of Icing!

0915 Hours: In the distance is what appears to be mountains.

0949 Hours: 29 minutes elapsed flight time from the first sighting of the mountains, it is no illusion. They are mountains and consisting of a small range that I have never seen before!

0955 Hours: Altitude change to 2,950 feet, encountering strong turbulence again.

1000 Hours: We are crossing over the small mountain range and still proceeding northward as best as can be ascertained. Beyond the mountain range is what appears to be a valley with a small river or stream running through the center portion. There should be no green valley below! Something is definitely wrong and abnormal here! We should be over Ice and Snow! To the portside are great forests growing on the mountain slopes. Our navigation Instruments are still spinning, the gyroscope is oscillating back and forth!

Dave asked, "Is that what Colonel Balchen was referring to in his epitaph? Strange events and places that no man has seen before."

Boop shrugged. "No one knows, but this is a copy of a page ripped out of Admiral Byrd's log book from a flight he made to the pole in February, 1947."

It took a few seconds for all this to click and sink in. "Damn, you're right, Major. This has happened before. We've seen the open water and hit the thin air. We've got to get back out there and figure this out."

Boop put his hand on Dave's shoulder, "Want to hear another strange coincidence? Colonel Balchen also flew German rocket components and scientists to Alamogordo, New Mexico after the war. It is also rumored that he was one of the pilots called upon to haul the Roswell aliens from New Mexico to Wright-Patterson." With that one, Dave took a big swig of his Carlsberg beer, swallowed, and then got up and left the bar.

Boop took a swig of beer himself and then asked an interesting question, "The Russians and us have been putting men in space for nearly three decades now. How come no one has put anyone into a polar orbit? Makes you wonder, doesn't it?"

Dave went over to his office and made a phone call. He dialed up DYE-3 on the tropo line. He dialed directly into Vince Beach's office. Vince picked up the phone, "DYE 3, Beach here." Dave responded, "Yeah, Vince, Dave Sheridan here. Just wanted to let you know we made it back to Sonde in one piece. We had an interesting flight though." Vince responded, "Yeah. We heard. We were monitoring your radio traffic in and out of Sonde. What did you see up there?" Dave was surprised at the breach in protocol. Vince was kind of blunt. He chose his next words carefully; he knew the tropo line was not the most secure voice communications in the world. "Not much Vince, just the ice spiraling up in my face. We hit some thin air." Vince caught on quick. "Glad to hear everything turned out fine. I've flown with Rick Boop for years. He's one hell of a pilot. Not many can kick a C-130 out of a half turn spin and recover in 1500 feet, especially when you've got a ten ton dozer strapped to your ass. Must have had the plane balanced perfectly." Dave replied, "Yeah, he's one cool customer."

He now fed Vince the bait and hoped he'd bite. "Just thought you'd like to know that Klystron tube you ordered is in the warehouse here. It came in on the last C-141. I know that you're down to the last one and it's kind of flaky. You must have a problem with your signal conditioner to keep burning out the tubes the way you are." Vince took the clue, "Yeah, funny you should mention it. Dan is in the radar equipment room doing a diagnostic now. If we lose this one, we'll be offline for half a day. I better put in a priority MICAP request to get that tube out here." A MICAP request meant mission capability is impaired if the equipment or material is not delivered ASAP. If the radar went down, there would be a hole 150 miles wide in the NORAD early warning system. Dave responded back, "Roger, MICAP for a Klystron spare."

"I'll start drawing up the paperwork here and contact base ops," Vince said. "Thanks Dave, for looking out for us. I owe you a beer."

Vince got on the intercom and told Dan to send a message to Sonde Logistics requesting a Klystron Tube MICAP. Dan keyed in the message and hit the send button on the krypto set. Dan called back, "Fire in the hole."

The message hit the logistics warehouse at Sonde just as Dave walked in. He wanted to be there when it came in to explain the importance of getting that tube out to the site. The Klystron tube was the heart of any radar system. It generated the pulse and radar wave.

The LogTech understood and placed a MICAP order. He punched in the stock number, got a warehouse location and sent a man out for it. "It says here it's only three pounds. You plan on walking it over to base ops, Captain?" Dave responded, "Sure, I'll sign for it." The LogTech printed out a hand receipt. He signed it, put the box under his arm, ran back out to the warm pickup truck, and raced over to Base Ops.

He entered the ops center and walked up to the counter. A burley Master Sergeant, stood up and asked, "What can I do for you, Captain?" Dave said, "We've got a MICAP situation out at DYE-3. The radar is about to drop offline, unless we get this Klystron tube out there." The sergeant was very cooperative. It was pounded into every good NCO; you've got to support the mission. "We've got Raven One that is fueled and we can have it airborne in less than an hour," he responded. "Thanks, Sergeant, I'll wait in the lounge." Dave poured himself a cup of coffee. He'd only had one beer this evening, but he wanted to piss that out of him. The sergeant got on the alert phone and hit the klaxon alarm button. He lived for this. It was like getting to pull the fire alarm in your high school. All over base little red lights started flashing, pagers went off, and phones rang. The alert crew was notified that they had a critical flight and were to report to base ops immediately.

A few minutes later Major Boop came through the door, followed by his copilot and navigator. He said, "What have you got for us, Sergeant?" The sergeant pointed to Sheridan and said, "You've got a MICAP priority run to DYE-3. Their radar is about to go offline." Dave spoke up. "How are you doing, Major? I need to get this Klystron out to DYE-3 ASAP."

Boop responded, "We can accommodate you, Captain. We are fueled and ready to go. My crew chief is just getting ready to off load the dozer. We've had the heaters on it since we landed. We can't get her off until we get the lowboy trailer truck fired up. It won't start. I'll tell you what, Sergeant, get on the radio with the crew chief and tell him to leave it on the plane. We'll off load it when we get back. Can't afford to let that radar go offline. Glenn, start up a mission plan. Carl, start a pre-flight. I'll be out in a few minutes." Both Captains went off in different directions to carry out their orders. Rick gave Dave a thumbs-up and said, "We can be airborne in a half hour."

Dave followed the navigator out onto the apron. After they ran up the cargo ramp, the clam shell doors were closed and ramp pulled shut. Dave made his way up to the flight deck and strapped into the jump seat. The ground crew was busy cranking up the AGE carts and blowing warm air into the engine air intakes. Captain Carl Davis, the copilot, secured himself and started the pre-flight. Master Sergeant Bob Svisco, the crew chief, made a quick walk around and then plugged in the headset to the plane's umbilical. He motioned to the copilot through the cockpit window to fire up the number one engine. The plane came to life and he did the same for the number two engine. Just then, Boop climbed up the flight deck ladder and strapped himself in. He said, "Okay, gentlemen, we've got another twelve hours of daylight. We're in the Arctic, remember. Carl, get departure clearance. As soon as Bob gets in, we're ready for taxi." Boop dialed up Ground Control on the radio, "Sonde Ground Control, Raven One with you with the numbers, ready for taxi instruction."

"Roger, Raven One. Taxi to runway two three via taxiway alpha and hold short." Rick acknowledged. Bob climbed on board, closed the cabin door, and hit the intercom, "Clear left and right, load secure, fire up three and four." Boop acknowledged the crew chief and engines three and four were started.

The copilot was busy talking with the control tower, writing information on the air charts, and setting radio and navigation frequencies. Captain Glenn Rylah, the navigator sitting behind

Dave, was busy crunching the numbers and computing takeoff roll. He punched in the destination coordinates into the Inertial Navigation System (INS) 68° 58' 45" N by 42° 59' 40" W. He then got on the intercom and said calmly, "Major, we're going to need every foot of this runway to get the beast in the air without the JATOs with the dozer on board." Rick responded coolly, "Roger that, Glenn." With that said, the plane began its taxi. Immediate takeoff clearance was granted with a VFR flight plan to DYE 3. The weather was clear, and the wind calm. Rick was hoping for at least a little head wind to shorten the takeoff distance. No such luck. Rick lined the C-130 nose gear up on the center line. He set the break, applied full throttle and then changed the propeller pitch. Once full power was achieved he released the breaks and the C-130 lurched down the runway.

The plane rotated with about 2,500 feet of runway left and sucked up the gear just after liftoff. The plane slowly climbed up and out of the fjord and turned back out over the icecap. Once they reached 5,000 feet Boop dialed in DYE-3 on the radio, "Sob Story, Sob Story, this is Raven One with you on one one niner point two niner." After a couple of seconds, Dave recognized Dan's voice on the other end, "Roger, Raven One, Sob Story control. We have you, please say altitude. Squawk one seven zero zero and ident." The copilot acknowledged and dialed in the radar transponder code 1700. "Raven One, Sob Story Control, understand you have MICAP equipment on board. Please be advised, we are now offline for diagnostics and repair." It was unusual for the controllers to acknowledge over an open mike that the radar was down. However, this was code for: "Hey, you guys, the radar is offline and we can't see you. Go fly wherever you want to." Plus, the fact that the voice data recorder and flight data recorders had been pulled meant that Raven One was now free as a bird.

Boop nodded to the copilot. He turned around to Dave, the navigator, and the crew chief. He turned the radio console off, and keyed the intercom mike. "Okay, I told you we have a plan. Here it is. We saw something up there near the lake. It showed up on our NAVRAD. It was the only metallic structure other than DYE-3 for a couple hundred miles. We're going to go find out what it is."

Boop continued to brief the crew on the plan, "Once we get up there we are going to circle the lake. We're not getting any closer than one mile from the edge. We're not going over the center of it like we did last time, not pressing our luck. We are going to search for the object with our NAVRAD. Once we get a bead on it, we'll make a low level pass if we haven't run into thin air. We'll land, taxi over to it and check her out. Any questions?" No one spoke up. Rick hit the master switch toggle for the radios. He had shut them off just out of precaution. It wouldn't be the first time someone had accidentally broadcast over the open air when they thought they were speaking on the intercom.

"We're going to follow the ice to the lake at about 2,000 feet AGL. The icecap gradually climbs up to about 9,000 feet where we are heading. That will put us at about 11,000 feet above sea level (ASL)."

As the plane droned on for the next hour a glint of aqua blue tint was showing up just on the horizon. Boop said, "Dial in the NAVRAD, wide beam, fifteen degree down angle." The navigator complied and the radar screen lit up. "Nothing on it", said Carl. "Roger that. Make a heading towards DYE-3", ordered Boop. The navigator spoke up, "DYE-3 should now be two o'clock at three zero miles." Rick turned the plane to the right and lined up the nose with DYE-3. Just then the radar pinged and lit up like a Christmas tree. Carl said, "Nothing wrong with NAVRAD. Suggest we make a turn to the north after passing ten miles abeam DYE-3 and retrace our steps from last time."

"Sounds like a good plan, Carl." Rick waited a few minutes and then cranked the C-130 over to the left. After he leveled off, there it was, clear as a bell. Something at eleven o'clock out, twenty miles on the NAVRAD screen. The lake was about three miles wide and perfectly circular in shape. It was deep. The bottom was not visible.

Rick slowed the plane down to two hundred knots and keyed the mike. "It looks like whatever it is, is off to the left side of the lake." Carl acknowledged, "Roger that, we're about ten miles out, showing 1,800 feet AGL, and two zero zero knots. Ease her over to the left. Now pinging one mile off the left side of the lake." Rick cranked in a shallow left turn and then leveled the wings. Then Glenn clicked in, "ETA three minutes."

"Roger that Glenn." Everyone's eyes peered straight ahead like laser beams. Carl broke the silence, "Something pinging this far out is surely visible. ETA one minute." The lake loomed large on the right side of the cockpit windows. Off to the left a black speck was a sharp contrast to the bright white ice. Boop called it, "Black object on the ice, twelve o'clock, 2 miles."

"Tallyho, object," Carl said. Dave still didn't see it. It was probably below his field of vision sitting in the jump seat.

Boop said, "Okay, gang, I'm going to descend to 1,000 feet AGL and set up a standard left turn orbit. Glenn, get your camera out." Glenn had brought a video camera. Rick set the turn, and trimmed up the plane. "Okay, I've got it in sight. Keep us away from the lake on the right side." Glenn unbuckled his harness and went back into the cargo bay. He was going to video through the cabin door window. It was easier than leaning across Dave and Rick.

Dave looked out over Rick's shoulder and could indeed see the black object now. What the heck was this thing? Not much detail from up here. But it was definitely solid. It looked about thirty feet in diameter. It wasn't your classic saucer shape as Dave had half expected. It looked more like a turtle from up here.

Rick asked, "Glenn, what's the outside air temp?"

"Just a second, Major." Rick had forgotten that he had gone to the back of the plane. Glenn came forward, climbed back into his seat and checked a dial on his engineer's panel. He didn't take the time to reconnect his mike, but instead tapped Rick on the shoulder and made signals with his fingers showing a one followed by a zero and then a thumbs-up. This was interpreted to mean ten degrees above zero. Fairly warm even by Greenland summer standards.

Rick keyed the intercom, "Okay, gang, we're going to set this thing up for a landing. Ice looks smooth, no crevasses and only small drifts. We will come in from the low side. Wind isn't a factor. Carl, run the checklist. Glenn, watch the airspeed closely.

I'm going to come in low and hot. No flaps. I want to be twenty knots over stall speed. I'm going to fly her onto the deck."

Rick turned the plane back to the west. He went out about ten10 miles and made a shallow turn back towards the object. "Carl, call off the air speed. Glenn, call off the altitude from the radar altimeter." Rick set up the plane in a shallow decent and throttled back slightly. He let the airspeed bleed off. Carl read off the airspeed, "190...180...Stall speed is 110 with this load and configuration...130." Rick eased the nose down a little. Glenn called out the altitude, "1000 AGL...800...500..." Carl continued, "Airspeed steady at one three zero." Rick responded, "Roger. Maintaining one three zero." Glenn called out the altitude, "400 feet AGL." Rick answered "Skis coming down now." The million dollar skis were about to take a beating. They only dropped a few inches below the wheels so no additional drag was encountered. At 130 knots, this was about like a NASCAR driver about to rub the wall on turn four just before he crossed the finish line. Rick was aware of the fact that the terrain was gradually sloping up to meet them. All he had to do was to maintain straight and level, as well as air speed, and the skis would eventually come in contact with the ice at a very shallow angle. There should be very little friction and stress on the skis. The operative word was "should." The pucker factor was very high now. However, Rick kept a loose one handed grip on the controls. Dave thought to himself, "Look, Mom, no hands." But Rick was more concerned with airspeed and kept his right hand tight on the throttles.

Glenn called out, "200 feet AGL, 100 feet, 50... 25...10." Just then Dave could feel the rear skis hit. The plane bounced a few feet and settled back down. The plane shook and then the nose dropped down. Rick pulled back slightly to keep pressure off the nose. He throttled back and let the plane slide to a stop. No need to reverse the prop pitch. He has plenty of room out here.

Once stopped, Rick said, "We should be about a half mile from the object. I'm going to taxi over to it." He was now sorry that he let the Raven come to a complete stop; getting it moving

again was like starting a freight train. He pushed the throttles forward and the plane began to move. As the plane neared the black object, they could see it was actually cobalt blue. Everyone's jaw dropped when they saw what it was. Or, at least, what it appeared to be. If Dave didn't know any better, he'd swear he was at the beach. Lying directly in front of the nose of the plane, one hundred yards away was the biggest nautilus shell that he had ever seen. It was huge. It was sitting upright. It was about thirty feet high and ten feet wide. How the hell did this thing get here? Better yet what was it?

Any hopes of flying it out were dashed. It wouldn't fit on the aircraft. The C-130 cargo bay was only about 9 feet high and 40 feet long. It would be like sticking a square peg in a round hole.

Major Boop keyed his mike, "Bob and Glenn, go suit up. Dave, get your iron pants on. Carl, stay put and watch the bird." The engines are never shut down while sitting on the icecap. All four were left running. They had plenty of fuel. They had another four hours worth and they were only an hour and a half out from Sonde.

Everyone suited up with their iron pants, parka, mukluks, gloves, and face masks. Bob opened the cargo bay doors and lowered the ramp. The group walked out the back and made a big sweeping walk back to the front of the plane, staying well clear of the spinning props. Carl could see the group out the cockpit window and gave a big thumbs-up.

Rick and Dave walked up to the shell and looked it over. Too late now, but Dave yelled in Ricks ear, "What if this thing is hot?" and made a gesture to cover his gonads. Rick shrugged it off and did what any typical Air Force pilot would do. He went up to the blue object and gave it a good kick. Dave said, "That's a hell of a welcome to Earth. How do you know you didn't give it a kick in the balls?" There were no markings, no moving parts, and no color other than the dark cobalt blue. Whatever it was, it was big, solid, and heavy. Rick sent Bob back for the tool chest. When he returned Rick grabbed a wrench and then gave the shell a hefty whack. It definitely sounded hollow and gave out a metallic ring. But he couldn't dent it or even leave a mark on it.

Rick said, "Okay, gang, we're here. It's here. We don't know what the hell it is. We're not doing much good out here. I'm freezing my ass off. Let's head back into the plane." Once on board, Bob buttoned up the cargo doors and then went up to the galley to pour everyone a cup of coffee.

Rick asked Dave, "What do you think that thing is?"

"I'm not sure, Major. I can't even tell if it's extraterrestrial."

Rick smiled and said "Bullshit, this thing wasn't made here. It's almost impossible to stall a C-130 at over 150 knots over stall speed. Whatever is out there wanted to get our attention. Well, they've got it. We're going to drag this thing back to DYE-3. It's only twenty miles. We've got a dozer. Does anybody know how to operate this thing?" Bob spoke up, "Yeah, I used to operate one similar to this on my folk's farm. I can run it. Not sure we can rustle up enough chain and cable to rig up a tow line though." Rick said, "Okay, you open the doors, fire that thing up and we'll see what we can come up with."

It was Dave's turn to make his engineering talents known. "We don't have to tow. We can push. Just use the blade to knock that thing over on its side and we can push it to DYE-3. Just when Dave thought everyone would bow to his brilliance, Bob busted his chops. "That's a great idea, Captain. Too bad we don't have enough diesel fuel in the D-7 dozer to get it off the plane, let alone push this thing twenty miles to DYE-3."

"Damn," Dave said, "How about towing it with the plane? We've got enough cable in the flight controls to scavenge if we need to." It was Glenn's chance to throw in his two cents. "Okay, we can use the web seating. We have about twenty feet of cable, plus the cargo netting. I think we can rig a harness to wrap around this thing. How much you figure this thing weighs?" Dave put his Physics 101 class to use. "Well, we can try pushing it with the dozer. If it moves we know it's less than 20,000 pounds." Rick spoke up. "Okay, sounds like a plan. We're burning valuable JP-4 now. Let's get it in motion. Bob, fire up the dozer. Go see if you can tilt that thing over. Then see if you can push it behind the plane so we can rig it for towing. While you're doing that, we'll strip the web seating, and lash up some chains to make a harness."

The cargo doors opened again and Bob fired up the dozer. This was definitely against tech orders. But how often do you get to tow a UFO? Bob got the dozer moving and drove it down the ramp. He moved around to the front of the plane. The fuel gauge was bouncing on empty. Rick and Dave watched as he nudged the blade up to the shell and gave it a push. The shell moved a foot or two but did not fall over. Bob raised the blade as high as it would go and then gave it another shove. This time it teetered as he gunned the throttle. It fell over like a drunken sailor.

Dave, Rick and Glenn grabbed all the webbing, cargo netting, and chains that they could get their hands on. Bob got behind the shell and began pushing it. It did move. Now that it was on its side there was less contact with the ice and it slid much easier. The dozer wasn't getting very good traction though.

However, it did move and Bob was doing fairly well pushing the shell around to the back of the plane. He got it lined up about twenty feet behind the plane. Just then the diesel sputtered a few times and then the engine quit. It was out of fuel. He leapt off the dozer and went to help the other guys with the harness and rigging. He then climbed back up the dozer and walked out on the blade to the top of the shell. Glenn tossed him a corner of the cargo net. He placed it over the top. Four other cargo nets were attached around the sides. The web seating was taken out and attached to the corners. Bob said the thing weighed about 15,000 pounds and that the webbing should hold. The webbing and netting was tied off and it was secured to pallet hooks. Everyone boarded the aircraft. Bob went over to the ramp control lever and swung the ramp up off the ice. Everything looked secure and was ready to rock and roll, or in this case, slip and slide. Rick grinned in satisfaction, "Guess we're leaving the D-7 dozer for the shell. Hope we got the better trade."

CHAPTER 7

A Snail's Pace

Rick stood next to Bob and plugged in a headset. "Bob, I'm staying back here with you." He pointed to Dave and motioned for him to go forward with Glenn up into the cockpit. Carl would need some help taxiing the C-130 the twenty-five miles over to DYE-3. Carl had no doubt they could get this "object" to DYE-3. The longest taxi on record was when a Raven had to taxi from halfway between DYE-2 to DYE-3 because of an emergency landing due to hydraulics failure. That was a taxi on the ice of over seventy-five miles. That took over four hours. Rick figured it would take two hours at the most to taxi to DYE-3.

Dave didn't bother to strap in. What was the use? They were on the ground, right? He sat in the pilot seat where there was a better view. He sat there worrying to himself. What was all the secrecy about? Why did Rick feel he had to drag this thing over to DYE-3? Why not call up Sonde and have them send out another Raven? Why not tell Sonde what you found? Dave mulled this and a hundred other questions around in his head. This was surreal.

Rick had explained his logic back at Sonde. First of all, he wasn't sure what the reaction would be if they found anything up here. He may be ordered back to Sonde and brought up on charges. After the disinterest that he experienced in the debriefing, along with the attempt to brand him as a poor pilot by claiming he was hot dogging, stalling a twenty million dollar aircraft and endangering his crew, he no longer trusted the chain of command. It was time to show some balls. Besides, the DYE-3 crew had twelve men on it. All of them knew some-thing was going on out here and had at least seen something strange last week. The DYE-3 crew were contract employees. They supported the military, but were not beholden to it. If you pulled this thing up to their front door, it would be hard to brush it under the rug, or bury it under fifty feet of snow. Rick wasn't necessarily looking to blow the lid off this thing. If that were the case, he would have loaded the plane up with a bunch of Danes from Sonde, the hotel manager and his staff, or half the Caribou Club patrons. However, his purpose was strictly to gain some leverage and to have a bargaining chip. This was the chance of a lifetime. He had heard the rumors. He had watched as pilots came and went. The thin air crowd got scoffed, ballyhooed, and even ridiculed. This wasn't going to happen to him.

Dave on the other hand was a little worried. He had defi-nitely seen what this thing could do. He had made an official report. Nothing had come of it, yet. But after talking with Rick at the Club, it didn't take long to convince him to go along for the ride. Carl, Glenn, and Bob trusted their commander implic-itly and were in the same boat as him. A crew lives and dies for each other.

He convinced himself that it definitely made sense to drag the thing over to DYE-3. There was not much that could be done out here anyway. DYE-3 could provide the personnel and equipment to maybe help figure this thing out. It would eventu-ally become the base of operations anyway. They might as well drag this thing the twenty-five miles over to where they've got warm food, warm beds, a shower, plenty of power, equipment, tools, and all that good stuff. Besides, this thing can take the punishment. And by the way, how else would you move this thing anyway? A chopper could never get up here and lift it. It is better to sometimes beg forgiveness rather than ask for permis-sion. This was one of those times. "Good grief, is this what hap-pens to your thought process after dating a JAG officer for the past three years?" He shrugged it off. He knew she never lost an argument, and would only concede a point from time to time.

Rick gave the order to throttle up and head towards DYE-3. Carl acknowledged and reached over to grab the throttle levers. "Glenn, you need to keep a good eye on the oil pressure and temp gauges. We're going to be putting a lot of stress on these engines. I'm sure we're going to need full military power to sustain our forward motion dragging all that weight behind us. I'm also concerned with sucking up chunks of ice. I'd hate to FOD out an engine up here." Turbines were notoriously susceptible to foreign object damage. Their intakes acted like a vacuum cleaner and would ingest just about anything they could. A chunk of ice could rip the guts out of a turbine. However, the nice thing about a turboprop was that the propeller tended to deflect ice, rocks, and pebbles. The C-130's engines were very high above the ground which helped, too.

Carl pushed the blade pitch levers all the way forward. The constant speed propellers bit into the arctic air and the plane slowly moved forward. Carl was worried about the tension on the harness, "Major, you need to stay clear of those tie down straps. If they break loose, they'll cut you in half."

Rick responded, "Thanks for the advice, but we're very well aware of that. Everything is secure back here." Carl responded, "Roger that. Do you want me to contact DYE-3 on the handheld radio? I think we're in range." Rick replied, "Negative, we'll wait until we're in sight of the complex."

Now Dave understood why Rick wanted him out of the way. He had enough things to worry about back there. The huge transport plowed through the two foot high drifts with ease. They were doing about 10 to 15 mph. They had been moving for forty-five minutes. This was turning out to be easier than everyone thought until the nose gear plowed suddenly and plunged into some soft snow. The plane stopped like it hit a brick wall. Even going this slow, Dave was slammed against the console. Rick and Bob lost their footing on the ramp. "Shit, Carl, what was that?" Rick asked.

Just then he looked back at the shell. It was continuing its forward motion, all 15,000 pounds of it. It slid into the back of the plane with a sickening crunch. "Damn," Rick exclaimed, "we just got rear ended by an extraterrestrial. Close encounters of the fourth kind." Rick was trying to put everyone at ease. It didn't do much damage to the plane. Carl asked, "You both okay back there?" Rick replied, "Yeah, we're okay. Put a nasty dent in our ramp though. Not going to be able to pressurize this bird. We'll have to keep the ramp down on the way back to Sonde. We'll have to stay low and slow." Glenn piped in, "Not much lower and slower than we can get right now. By the way, we're not at fault. We were rear ended, right? Besides I think that bump pushed us out of that rut." Glenn was right. The extra push did pop them out of the hole. Carl applied power and they continued on their way. Rick clicked in, "Okay, Carl, take it a bit slower, no pun intended, but we're going to have to keep her down to a snail's pace."

The Hercules started moving again. It wasn't long until they were back up to a comfortable eight or 10 mph. The plane actually picked up a rhythmic bounce bounding over the drifts much like a speed boat slapping its way across the swells. The weather was perfect. The sun was high on the horizon. There wasn't a cloud in the sky. The snow even had enough moisture in it to give the skis a good ride.

They had been pulling the shell for over two hours now. The harness was holding up fine. They were about six or seven miles out from the site at this time. They were now seeing the Radome peak up over the horizon. Rick got on the intercom, "If we can see them, they can see us. Better contact them on the handheld. Use the local frequency, not the emergency frequency 125.5. No need to stir a panic on the site."

Carl replied, "Roger sir, will do." Carl grabbed the handheld. He'd been rehearsing in his mind what he was going to tell the site. You can't just casually call up a NORAD radar and communications site and say that you were about to pull up to their door step, towing a flying saucer. "Sob Story, Sob Story …..Raven One, over." He repeated the call two more times. Finally he got a response. "Raven One. This is Sob Story. We have you visually five miles out. Contacting you via handheld. Copy?" Vince Beach was no dope. He did not want this conservation transmitted to the outside world either.

"Sob Story, roger. ETA thirty minutes. We are towing a rather large and strange looking object we found discarded on the ice approximately twenty-five miles northwest of your location. We're bringing it in for handling and inspection. It appears safe and inert, over." Vince grinned from ear to ear. He turned to the console operator, "Dan, they found something. I knew it. Go round up the crew. Meet in the gym in five minutes and have everyone suited up. Get the dozers and snowcats started and out of the shed."

The news spread quickly. Everyone was quickly dressed and in the gym in a few minutes. Vince walked in. "Gentlemen and lady, I've got Raven One on the handheld. They are towing in an object they found on the ice near where we saw the light a few days ago."

Everyone yipped and hollered. High fives were slapped around as if this were an NBA game. Everyone knew the implications. They did not need Vince to spell it out, after years of sightings and rumors. After careers were dashed and after subtle threats were made, this crew finally had proof. Vince threw up his arms. The crew quieted down. "We are about to make history here today. We have proof of an extraterrestrial visit. From what the aircraft crew has told me, they are pulling a snail shaped metallic object that weighs about 15,000 pounds. Don't worry, no little green men inside or in sight."

One of the Danish crew members shouted, "That's good, but is it hot? It ain't gonna fry our gonads is it?" Olga spoke up, "To hell with your balls, it ain't going to make my tits fall off will it?" This broke the tension as everyone laughed. Vince didn't really know the answer to this one but told them, "No sign of radiation." Technically he was correct. After all, radiation was colorless, odorless, and tasteless. They didn't have a Geiger counter on-site, so they were taking their chances.

"Listen up guys. This is what we need to do. The damn thing is huge. We're going to tuck it in under the site. After we've got it secured, we'll get on the horn with a Mayday from Raven One. We'll have the other three Raven planes and crews out here looking for them along with every other aircraft within range. The idea is to get as many people involved in this as possible. No sweeping this under the rug."

Just then the handheld crackled to life, "Sob Story, this is Raven One. We're at the skiway. Request assistance to drag this thing up the ice apron."

Vince responded. "Roger, my guys are on their way out now. You heard the man. Get to it."

CHAPTER 8

Things Can Boomerang on You

Just as the harness was being removed from the shell, Dan got on the radio, "Vince, get up here ASAP. Better bring the pilot with you. Hurry up. Got a hit on the scope. Unscheduled inbound from the north. Whatever it is it's huge." Vince, Dave, and Rick hit the ice running. Climbing the three flights of stairs at nine thousand feet above sea level winded them all even though they were all in excellent shape.

The console room door was open. Major Boop and Vince rushed up to the scope. What they saw blew them away. "What the hell is that?" Vince asked. Dan replied, "Not sure. But it's at maximum range and moving this way at seventy knots." Boop responded, "Shit, they're on to us. They're sending in a chopper. A plane wouldn't fly that slowly."

Dan responded, "I don't think you understand, Major. I've set the scope to the two hundred mile range; this blip is showing a return that is over a mile wide." All four of them were quiet for a few seconds. Dave had a flash back to when he was eight years old watching a Godzilla movie on a Friday night with his brothers and sister. Everyone knew Mommazilla would always come back looking for her kid and she was usually very pissed off.

"Are you sure?" Vince asked. "Dead sure, Vince." Rick quipped, "Poor choice of words, Dan." Vince glared. Dan looked back at the scope and said, "At this rate, whatever this thing is, it will be here in a little less than three hours."

"What's the altitude?" Boop asked. Dan switched the setting on the console and again shook his head in disbelief.

"This thing is at 20,000 feet," Dan said, "and it's definitely not a chopper. It couldn't fly that slowly at that altitude. The air is too thin."

Dave asked Boop a few very calm and calculated questions. "What do you want to do, Major? Should we fly out of here now? Or should we go check this thing out?"

Boop replied calmly. "No, we don't have the fuel to fly half that distance. We can't get out of here. Face it Captain, no place to run and hide up here. This is going to boil down to a waiting game."

Vince then threw in his two cents, "As site commander, it's my responsibility to look out after my crew and site. This is getting out of hand fast. We don't know what we're dealing with here. I'm notifying NORAD right now. Dan, dial up Cheyenne Mountain." Dan picked up the hotline. There was nothing but static on the line. "Shit, guys, we're up a creek. The tropo is down."

"Damn it to hell," Vince said. "Okay, I'll try to radio over to DYE-2. He picked up the headset and keyed the mike, "Sob Story, Sob Story calling Sea Bass…Sob Story, Sob Story calling Sea Bass." Vince flipped the frequency selector over to the emergency frequency and tried again. Still with no response from either DYE-2 or DYE-4. "Is that thing jamming us?" Boop asked. "Looks like it, Major." Vince replied in frustration.

Dave offered another option, "Set off the ELT in the plane. That should get someone's attention."

Vince replied, "Not sure of the range up here. They might be able to pick it up out to DYE-4. They received the same ELT that we picked up last week. What do you think, Major?"

Boop paused for a moment and then asked, "How long do you figure we have before anyone realizes we're offline?"

Vince replied, "Good point, Major. We have to do a com check every two hours with the adjacent DYE sites. We're due for one in forty minutes. They'll start wondering when we missed that window. But they won't send anything up this way from Sonde for hours. By that time whatever this thing is will be on top of us."

Boop had to make a command decision, "Okay, you're sure this thing is for real. It ain't a radar glitch?"

"It's a real bogie, Major. I checked both primary and secondary scopes. However, if they're jamming our UHF radios and tropo, why not jam the radar?" Dan asked.

"Simple," Dave said, "They want us to know they are coming."

"That makes about as much sense as anything, I guess," Vince replied.

Vince asked Dan if there was any commercial traffic overhead. This was the great circle route from Europe to Chicago and planes flew over Greenland all the time. "The last track was a DC-10 out of Copenhagen for Chicago about an hour ago. He's long gone. We usually have a daily track of something coming out of Brussels for Chicago. It might show up in an hour or so."

Vince added, "The radios are out, but it's a clear day today. We've got plenty of flares. We can flag somebody down." Boop replied emphatically, "That plane will be 25,000 feet over our heads. He'd never see a flare pop. However, we could get their attention with a fire. We've got plenty of diesel fuel up here. There's plenty of trash, pallets, and plastic to burn to make dark smoke. That should show up on the icecap from 35,000 feet."

Dave then busted all their chops by pointing out the obvious, "Excuse me, but what are they going to do if they do see the smoke? We're talking about a passenger jet. He's not going to come buzzing down here for a look see. He'll try to get a hold of us and the radios will be out. He'll simply report that fact along with the smoke and fly along his merry way. It's impossible for him to land and pick us up. He can't save the day by rolling in on the bogie for a strafing run and drop napalm like John Wayne. Bottom line is, what's the point?"

Boop and Vince agreed and acknowledged that panic mode was creeping in. "We can't run. We can't hide. We can't even yell for help. How about we play dead? Assuming that thing has radar and can see us, let's hop in the Raven, take off to the north and let them ping us good. It'll look like we're heading for DYE-4. They don't know our fuel situation. We can then circle back low level and come up from the south and let the DYE site mask our approach. One of two things will happen. They'll either turn to the east to follow us or they'll continue on their current track. Everyone is speculating that this thing is here because of what we dragged up to your front door. Maybe they'll take it and leave."

Right in the middle of all this beautiful logic, Glenn burst into the room. "Major, we've got a problem with the aircraft. Number two and four are starting to overheat. We're down to less than an hour's worth of fuel at this rate."

Boop pounded the console and responded in the pilots' universal language, "Shit. Okay, get the bird moving; taxi her back to the south side of the complex. Maybe they haven't pinged us yet. When they do, maybe they'll lose it in the ground clutter. Stay close to the complex. Once you are on the south side, get the nose pointed directly to the complex and tuck her in as tight as you can. Maybe we can hide her both visually and from their search radar until they are on top of us." Dan spoke up, "No sign of them pinging us yet."

"Dan, did you tell anyone else on this site we got a radar target?" Vince asked. "No, after I checked the secondary scope in the equipment room, I got a hold of you right away." Vince turned to Boop and asked, "How about your crew, Major? Think they've told anyone?" Boop replied, "No, they've been too busy worrying about the aircraft. No time for small talk." Vince responded, "Okay, let's keep it that way. No use letting panic spread throughout the site. I'll be having enough trouble keeping from crapping my own pants. Let's all take a step back and figure this thing out."

Dave had an idea and tossed it out for discussion, "We have only enough fuel on board for us to fly halfway to DYE-2 or DYE-4. How about we load up the snowcats then fly out to the maximum range and then take the tracked vehicles the final distance. They have a range of seventy-five miles or so, more if we strap diesel fuel drums to the roof."

Major Boop again pounded his fist on the console and this time without the profanity. "Dave, you may have hit on a possible way out. Diesel fuel is the answer. We can burn diesel in the C-130. They have no aviation fuel stored here, too volatile to have around. Fumes don't evaporate up here. However, we can burn diesel fuel in an emergency. I'd classify this as an emergency. The engines won't operate at peak efficiency, but it just might get us airborne. We can stay low and slow and just hop the drifts. I think DYE-4 is our best bet. It's all downhill to the east." Vince's face lit up, "Yes. We can pump the diesel into your wing tanks."

Boop scrambled to grab the handheld, "Change of plans, Carl, we're not going to hide our head in the snow like some arctic ostrich. We're going to be sensible and make a strategic retreat." Carl came back on the radio, "Does that mean you figured out how to get us the hell out of here, Major?"

"No, our good Captain up here figured it out. We're about to fill her up with diesel, good buddy." Carl understood, "I'll pull her up to the pump." Boop replied, "Negative, continue around to the south side, no time to jerry rig the pumps and plumbing from the bunkers. We'll drop a hose to you from the generator room. There's a few thousand gallons in the day tank stored there." Carl responded, "Roger, I'll nose her in as close as I can."

The C-130 made a big sweeping turn around the south side of the huge complex. Vince, Dave and Rick ran off toward the generator room. The site had six huge twelve cylinder White Superior diesel generators. The generators burned a tremendous amount of diesel and there was a huge emergency storage tank at the back of the generator room for day use. Boop figured they'd need about a hundred feet of hose to make it to the plane. The most likely source would be fire hose. Boop ran to the fire hose cabinet. There was only about fifty feet in this one. Dave ran up to the next level and pulled another fifty foot section. He dragged the heavy hose down the stairwell. He nearly tripped over Olga coming up the stairs. "What's going on?" she asked. "We've got to refuel a C-130. Come help me." She gave him a quizzical look but grabbed up some of the hose and followed him into the Generator Room.

Vince grabbed the Generator Room technician by the shoulder and startled him. It was noisy in the room and he was wearing ear protection so he didn't hear him coming up behind him. He pulled him inside his small office and started to explain the situation to him. A minute later the technician was pillaging through some storage bins and smiled as he held up a short piece of pipe. He ran over and grabbed the end of the fire hose and spun it on the threads. He grabbed the other fire hose and attached the two pieces together. Vince grabbed a wrench and broke out a window behind the storage bins. He snaked one end of the hose down to Glenn waiting below. The other end was being plumbed onto the day tank.

Vince got on the handheld, "Carl, don't contaminate the fuel in the wing tanks with this diesel. Keep it separate. Put it in the empty under wing tanks. We may need the good juice once we're out over the east coast. I'd prefer to burn the good stuff over the mountains." Carl acknowledged.

Glenn had gotten under the wing and was now in position to run the hose into the pylon tanks. Vince turned the valve on the day tank and diesel began to flow.

Boop grabbed Vince and yelled into his left ear, "Get your people together. We're going to pull out of here ASAP." Vince ran into the office and got on the PA system. He hit the fire alarm. This would get everyone moving. He turned the klaxon off and told everyone to meet again in the gym.

They all rushed out of the generator room and made their way into the gymnasium. Most everyone was there already. Vince wasted no time telling them about the radar target heading their way and their plan for evacuating the complex. He didn't tell the crew that the target was a mile wide.

It took the crew about fifteen minutes to gather survival gear, and get suited up. Boop agreed to load one of the snowcats on board, just in case. He didn't want to deal with the weight and balance problems of loading all three.

The fuel was flowing smoothly into the plane. But at this rate it would take about forty-five minutes to drain the day tank. Dan got on the PA. He was still in the console room. "Target bearing 360 relative, range 120 miles, speed seventy knots, altitude, 10,000. ETA ninety minutes. Tropo and UHF radio still out." Vince appreciated the update and was glad Dan didn't announce on the PA that this was one big MF and to run for your lives. Chalk one beer up for Dan if they ever got out of this.

Dave grabbed Jorgen, the drilling technician, and ran down to the shell with his video camera. The radar energy was affecting the video but he wanted to get some proof they really had this thing. He got video from every angle imaginable. He even had the presence of mind to try and scrape a sample of the material off for positive proof and analysis. He thought to himself, "Damn, this shit was bullet proof. Nothing's going to make a dent or a scratch." Then he had another brain storm. The drill bits for the bedrock core sample experiment were diamond impregnated. He could use one of the ice augers to try and cut a piece of the shell out. He had Jorgen drag one of the augers over to the shell. He attached the cutting head to the auger pole and started the motor. He dragged the auger onto the lip of the shell and engaged the drive gear. He hit the feed lever and they both watched as the cutter head started scratching into the shell's outer surface. Dave thought, "Holy shit, I think this is going to work."

Just then Boop ran over. "Captain, we're done pouring fuel in the bird. What the hell are you doing? Let's get out of here. That thing is fifty miles out."

"Major, we're making some progress here. I think I can cut a piece of the shell out."

Boop responded curtly, "You've got fifteen minutes, Captain."

Boop ran off towards the plane. He could see men clambering down the access stairs and heading over towards the plane following him. The crew chief was directing one of the crew members up the ramp with a snowcat. Dave figured it would take a few minutes to secure the plane, crew, and machinery. He gave the thumbs-up to Jorgen and continued on with the drilling. The bit was doing its work. It was biting into the shell. The shell was about a quarter inch thick. The hollow drill bit was about four inches in diameter, designed to take rock core samples. Whatever they were drilling through was tougher than any rock Jorgen had ever encountered.

Both men looked up in time to see the ramp of the C-130 being sucked up off the ice and clam shell doors shutting. A couple of minutes later the engine propellers changed pitch to full reverse. The big C-130 was backing away from the complex. The C-130 had the capability to back up under its own power and was doing a good job of it now. Just then he heard the rpm of the auger speed up as the auger punched through the shell. A metallic clanking noise was heard as a four inch metallic disk fell out of the drill bit and onto the lip of the shell. Dave grabbed it and they both spun around and raced towards the moving C-130. The plane had backed off from the site about one hundred yards. Running in snow at nearly two miles above sea level was a very hard thing to do. The side door was open and Dave crawled in followed by Jorgen. Several crew members helped pulled them inside.

Glenn was standing in the flight deck doorway. "For crying out loud, Dave, the Major was serious about leaving your asses out here." Dave just smiled and held up the disk shaped piece of metal like some kid who'd caught a home run ball. He made his way to the cockpit to show off his trophy. Boop turned around and said, "Way to go kid. Now strap in. The chief has been busy, too. He's only had time to hook up four of the JATO bottles. This might give us a running start. Probably won't get us airborne but it'll save a few hundred gallons of valuable fuel by getting us air-speed for liftoff."

Just then the plane made a hard turn to the left and taxied to the end of the skiway. It made a 180 degree turn into the wind. Boop applied full throttle and pitch. Carl called off the V speeds and once rotated, Rick hit the JATO switch. There was not as big of a kick in the ass as with the six bottles from the last time, but it still got your attention. The crew in back did not have ear protection and were deafened by the noise. The plane leveled off at a couple hundred feet and accelerated.

Boop clicked his mike, "Okay, we're going to level off at two hundred feet and hug the ice, no sharp turns. How are the engines, Glenn?" The copilot replied, "We're burning JP-4 now. Ready to switch over to diesel on your command. We should see some rpm drop. Better be prepared for the power loss." Boop acknowledged, "Roger, change tanks now." Glenn turned a switch on the engineer's panel and watched as the fuel flow meter started to click off. "Major, watch for the power drop in both inboards in about ten seconds."

"Roger that, Glenn."

The expected power drop happened on cue. The rpm surged and then dropped. "How are the engine temps?" The copilot responded with a cool tone, "Actually the temps have gone down. Must be the air flow around the cowlings. All in the green. We are twenty knots over stall speed." "Roger that. Maintain heading one one zero and an altitude of two hundred feet. If we lose an engine or start torching one, we're going to have to put her down fast."

Something caught Rick and Dave's peripheral vision at about the same time off to the north. An orange streak was racing at them from the left. It was coming from a huge flying wing shaped like a boomerang about thirty miles to the north. Rick knew immediately what was heading their way from his days over the Hanoi trail. Somebody was firing a missile at them. "Shit, missile inbound, nine o'clock, ten miles. We're too low and slow to take evasive action." If Boop had turned the plane sharply, chances were he'd lose airspeed, dip the wing into the ice and cartwheel into a fireball. No choice, but to keep her straight and level. Boop also noticed that the missile was overtaking them. It was a good sign that there was some relative motion to the orange ball of fire. This was not the proverbial golden BB or object that just keeps getting bigger and bigger as it comes straight at you and smacks you between the eyes. Rick knew it was going to miss well in front of them.

But "miss well" was a relative term. The missile struck the ice about a quarter of a mile in front of them. A huge plume of ice and snow shot up in the air. The plane flew straight into it. The windscreen was cracked by several large chunks of ice. The prop blades spun several large chunks completely through the fuselage with a loud bang. Luckily, no one had been sitting near the red line bulkhead. The plane had been pelted with a thousand snow-balls doing over 200 miles an hour.

"That damn thing just shot a warning shot across our bow." Just then another orange streak raced in on them. The same thing happened only a little closer. Carl calmly reported, "Flameout in number two, rpm drop in one. We have no choice, sir. We've got to put her down."

Boop feathered the props on the dead engines. Just then the fire warning lit up on number one followed immediately by number two. "Hit the HALON, Carl. Left engines only." Carl flipped up the switch guard and then toggled the fire extinguisher on the number one and two engines. Both port side engines were dead now. The plane was losing airspeed fast. Boop put the plane in a shallow nose down attitude to maintain airspeed. He had the right rudder peddle pushed halfway through the floor board to compensate for the adverse yaw. He told the crew chief to prepare the passengers for a crash landing. He was stating the obvious. Bob was way ahead of him. However, Bob had been too busy arming the JATO bottles. He didn't have time to secure the snow-cat. If the plane crash landed, the 10,000 pound vehicle would smash through the flight deck like a Mack truck through a Pinto. There was about one minute of flight time left. He threw the pallet straps over the vehicle. Luckily one of the DYE site crew members knew what to do with it on the other side and clipped the hook into the floor anchor and started cranking it down. A second strap sailed over the vehicle and another crew member secured it as well.

Boop had his hands full with the control yoke. They were down to fifty feet. The stall warning horn was going off. Carl was on the radio calling, "Mayday. Mayday. Mayday. Raven One going down two zero miles east of DYE-3." Boop lowered the nose more and yanked back on the yoke just a few feet off the deck. The front ski bit into a drift. The nose gear was now bouncing back into the air. The main gear skis hit the ice and the plane ground to a quick halt. Bob was thrown forward along with the other two crew members into a mangled heap of bodies and cracked bones up against the front bulk head. Luckily, the snowcat held in place.

"Carl, Glenn, get back there and see if everyone is okay. Dave, grab the fire extinguisher, exit the plane and hit the left inboard." Dave opened the flight deck door and sprayed the contents of the fire extinguisher into the intake. There was no visible fire just a lot of smoke and steam hissing as ice was tossed onto the engine cowlings. Glenn came back up to the flight deck. "Bob and a couple of guys are busted up pretty bad; a few broken ribs, arms and legs, nothing compound and not much bleeding. Not sure about internal injuries. All three are conscious, but in a shitload of pain. Props on one and two are gone, with a massive hole in the left side of the aircraft. Could have been much worse."

Boop didn't have to hit the ELT. It went off automatically. He just hoped DYE-4 could hear the Mayday and pick up the ELT. He doubted it. They were below the mountain crest on the east coast. They were too low for the Mayday. The radio was strictly line of sight.

Just when everything seemed hopeless the radio crackled to life. "Raven One, Raven One......request you change frequency to 121.9." Boop keyed the radio, "Who is this? We're down on the ice, crash landed, two zero miles east of DYE-3, several injuries." A reply came back calmly and with a bit of a Canadian accent, "Roger Raven One, change frequency now to 121.9." Boop changed frequency, "Now, who the hell is this? We need help up here ASAP."

The other end of the transmission responded. "We know. We forced you down." Dave and Rick looked at each other. Rick

was pissed now. "Who the hell do you think you are? You just fired on an unarmed United States Air Force aircraft." The response was unexpected, "We know Major Boop. This is the *Delta G Airship Nautilus*, now twenty miles off your left wing. Please stand down and prepare to be boarded. I assure you we mean you no harm. If we'd wanted you dead, our aim would have been more exact."

Major Boop grabbed the handheld radio, unbuckled and raced to the back of the plane. The rest of the cockpit crew followed suit.

Looking out a door portal window, Dave saw the boomerang

shaped airship looming over the horizon about five miles out. The radar signature did not do it justice. It was a mile wide, but it was also a quarter mile thick in its center. Details were now visible. It was closing in on the helpless crew. The temperature was plunging inside the cargo bay. Major Boop had thrown blankets over the injured men to keep them warm.

Just then the handheld crackled to life, "Major, this is Admiral Scott Dukes, commander of the *DGA Nautilus*. What is the status of your injured crewmen?"

Major Boop put the handheld to his lips and pressed the key, "We have three men down, broken ribs, legs and arms, in severe pain, treating them for shock."

"Roger that, Major. I am sending a medical team to your location. ETA is fifteen minutes."

Major Boop was still pissed, but still looked out after his crew and passengers. "You damn near killed us all and now you're coming over to patch my crew up? I suppose you're going to fix my broken airplane and then send us on our merry way, too."

The voice on the handheld simply said. "It's much more complicated than what you think, Major. We did not intend to hurt anyone. I'll talk to you once you're aboard my ship. Follow my crew's instructions to the letter, Major. Is that clear? This will be our last communication. Out."

Dave was still standing in the doorway peering out through the porthole. The small portal window was starting to ice over. He pulled a credit card out of his wallet and began scraping the window. The object was now directly overhead. There was absolutely no sound whatsoever. The shadow of the airship was covering several acres of ice. A few minutes later a pair of snowmobiles showed up outside the doorway. The men dressed in white arctic camouflage opened the door. There were four men. The first thing out of their mouths was, "Where's your injured mates?" in a thick Australian accent. They were carrying a medical kit.

Dave led them back to the crew compartment. Major Boop stood up and faced the visitors. "These men are in shock and they are in severe pain. Do you have any morphine?"

The bearded one carrying a satchel knelt down and flashed

a pen light into the eyes of one of the injured men. "I have pain killers. First I want to see what I'm dealing with here." He turned to the other three men that came in with him and said, "Signal the *Nautilus* that we cannot move these men, and prepare to rig the plane for an extraction lift. We'll deal with them once on board."

He then turned to Major Boop, "I am Dr. Logan Chase. I can administer morphine to only two of your crew. This crewman here is semiconscious with a severe head wound. I dare not take the chance with him. We have facilities aboard to conduct scans for a skull fracture."

Dave went back to look out the window. Several large straps were being lowered from the airship and slung under the wing roots. Dave turned to Rick, "These crazy bastards are about to lift us up off the ice." To that Rick replied, "Beam us up, Scotty."

Vince Beach came up to the doctor and asked if his crewmen would be all right. Dr. Chase said the injuries looked superficial. However, he could not rule out internal injuries.

Just then, with no warning, the entire plane lifted up into the air. It tilted a little nose down and swung like a pendulum a few times before settling down. Just like an elevator ride, the plane and crew were lifted upwards what seemed like several hundred feet. Nobody moved. Dave watched as the snowmobiles shrunk out of sight and then stared in amazement as the plane passed beyond the metal decking and vast void of what appeared to be a storage bay of some sort. He watched as a massive set of doors closed underneath the plane. The plane was gently lowered with a slight clanking noise as it was placed on the deck.

The crew door was again opened. Eight armed men with M-16s formed a V-shaped wedge outside the door. At the point was a tall muscular balding gentleman in white fatigues. He had eagles on his collar.

He strode up to the door, "Major Boop, permission to come aboard." This surprised Boop. "Do I have a choice?" Admiral Scott Dukes replied calmly, "Actually, Major, I'm following protocol. Believe it or not, you actually outnumber me and my crew. I intend to ensure you do not outgun us as well. Frankly, Major, you're actions are unpredictable as evident with your barnstorming stunt that we all just witnessed."

Boop gave him a salute and asked, "Admiral, am I under arrest? What are your orders?" Dukes responded with a professional salute, "Major, my orders do not concern you directly other than I've been told to treat your injured and escort you and the crew back to Thule." This little slip implied that they had come from Thule AB near the northern tip of Greenland. Boop let it slide for now.

"I've been told by Major General Charles Ahrens to treat you, your crew, and your passengers with all military courtesy. Yourself, your aircraft crew, and the young Captain Sheridan here, are to come with me to the conference room. Your injured will be moved to the infirmary where they will be treated. The rest of the crew will remain here in the cargo bay of the *Nautilus*. My crew is going to purge your aircraft of fuel and seal the aircraft. Follow me." Boop asked, "What about Mr. Beach, the DYE site commander?" Admiral Dukes replied, "My orders are not specific to him. I'll give him the option of coming along or staying here with his crew." Vince elected to stay with his crew.

The military cadre exited the aircraft and followed Admiral Dukes. The *Nautilus* crew was busy wrapping plastic wrap around the leaking aircraft engines and sealing them with some sort of fast setting foam. Dave looked overhead and was amazed to see a gigantic gantry crane straddling the C-130. There were three of them traversing each bay that covered several dozen acres. It reminded Dave of being inside the Pontiac Silverdome stadium in Michigan only much bigger. There were no structural members visible overhead. The ceiling had an inflated look and was slightly arched. There were a series of tubing and cables crisscrossing the width of the ship.

Admiral Dukes turned around and told the crew to hurry along. He had a briefing prepared for them and would answer their questions in due time.

They passed through a bulkhead door and secured it behind them. Two electric carts were waiting on the other side. Dave thought, "Damn, I wonder if this place has a golf course."

He followed the cadre into a large briefing room and was

startled to hear a loud, "Room, ten-hut." Eight men and a woman were now standing at attention. Admiral Dukes responded, "At ease, ladies and gentlemen and please take a seat. Before we get started, I have to mention a few things. I've been instructed to welcome you to the Delta G White Airborne Recovery and Analysis Laboratory."

Dave immediately perked his ears and asked, "Excuse me, Admiral, are you a part of the Delta G Program Office?" This was starting to make a bit of sense now.

Boop turned to Sheridan and asked, "What the hell is Delta G? Pardon the French, Admiral."

"To answer your question, Captain; yes, we are a part of Delta G. Let me explain, Major. Our good Captain here has spent the last six months up here conducting gravitational anomaly measurements with Drs. Timken and Rapp. Apparently your work and results have gotten the attention of some of our friends who live about fifty light years away from here."

Boop cut in, "You mean what we found out there is definitely a UFO?" Dukes turned and looked him in the eye. "On the contrary Major, it has been identified, and by the way, it does not fly, or at least how we would define it."

Boop got a little defensive, "Admiral, with all due respect, please quit playing word games with us. We've had a hectic day. Finding and dragging an alien craft across the icecap and then being blown out of the sky, kind of makes one edgy."

"Fair enough, Major. What you have found, or were allowed to find, was what we call a torsional wave generator or TWG. Since 1947, we and various governments around the world, have found and recovered nearly a dozen of these devices. The airship you are sitting in was built to recover the devices from all over the world. We've picked up devices like the small ones you dragged over to DYE-3, up to colossal ones weighing over 200,000 pounds. We've plucked them out of the jungles of Brazil, the sands of the Sahara, the farms of the Midwest, the bottom of the ocean, and, yes, even the ice of the Arctic. This craft carries a half billion cubic feet of helium. It can lift and haul a half million pounds of cargo halfway around the world with a crew of only eighteen."

The admiral continued, "You are all now members of the Delta G Team, like it or not. We are not here to threaten you, arrest you, or do surgery on your brain to make you forget this incident. As a matter of fact, the team is growing. We need qualified men and woman to figure these things out. Above all else, we also need the time to figure these things out. We are counting on a couple of things; patriotic duty may or may not apply. That's because we now have an international effort underway to cooperatively figure these things out. World war among super powers is highly unlikely at this point in our history. It's the nut cases and terrorist groups that we all have a vested interest in cleaning up.

"We could bribe you. However, there is always someone out there to offer more bucks. Hell, every member of my crew knows these extraterrestrial things exist." Dukes considers, "What keeps them together as a crew? Why doesn't my lowest ranking enlisted technician run off and write a book, blow the lid off of this whole thing? It boils down to this: curiosity, being on the cutting edge, building a legacy for their grandkids. There is a lot of power in being able to someday tell your grandkids that you were the first ones to visit another star."

Dave's mind was racing a mile a minute, but he could only think of one stupid question to throw out on the table, "A half billion cubic feet. Where do you get all that helium?"

Admiral Dukes had to laugh at this, "I can see I'm moving too fast for you to absorb all of this. I've just told you that aliens exist fifty light years from here. We're cracking their technology and they've invited us to a neighborhood block party. However, I can't tell you how we get our helium. That is a closely guarded military secret."

CHAPTER 9
The Shell Game

A female voice came over the PA system, "Bridge to crew, we are now hovering over the DYE-3 site." Admiral Dukes picked up a phone and punched a button. "Prepare for shell extraction and inform me when it is aboard." Dukes turned to his guests, "It will take them about a half hour or so to rig and lift the shell. During that time, we have much to mull over and discuss. Major, I am authorized to offer you and your crew the chance to join the Delta G White Group. Your expertise is desperately needed. Before you say anything, I am also to remind Captain Sheridan, that he is already a member of the Delta G Team. His area of expertise has just been expanded."

Major Boop folded his hands across his chest and leaned into the table, "Admiral, speaking for myself, sign me up. That is, as long as I don't have to leave my wife, kids, and/or home back in New York."

Admiral Dukes reassured the crew, "We're not going to kidnap you. As far as your family, friends and coworkers are concerned, you are on an extended temporary duty (TDY) to Thule. Naturally, the DYE site crew will have to return to the site within the next hour or two. They will be bribed in a way. They will be offered lucrative jobs here in Greenland and/or back in Europe. They will then be taken care of for the rest of their lives. Unless they start making waves, then their support structure gets cut off at the knees. It's amazing what peer pressure and the good old psychologist Maslow's hierarchy of needs do for the space program."

The admiral's phone rang. He picked it up to his ear. "Thank you, Dr. Chase, that is indeed good news." He hung up and turned to his guests, "The three injured men are all alert and show no signs of internal injuries. However, your crew chief does have a mild concussion. We will have them all at Thule in about three hours. Captain Rylah, please go with my exec back to the cargo bay. Convey the good news to Mr. Beach; tell him I will be there shortly. Also prepare him and his crew with the news that we are going to leave them at DYE-3. I will give them the marketing pitch in an hour or so. I will brief Major Boop who will be free to back brief you later."

Glenn simply stood up, saluted the admiral and said, "Yes, sir." Glenn and the exec left the room. The admiral turned to Rick, "I'm very impressed, you have a very professional crew. Captain Rylah did not defer to you, nor did he hesitate. He followed my orders without question." Rick smiled and said, "I have the best crew in the world, Admiral. They know the score."

"Well gentlemen, let me at least feed you and then show you around my pride and joy. I love showing her off. If you can wait a few minutes, sandwiches and coffee are on the way. In the meantime, I have a presentation I would like you to see. Lieutenant, please proceed."

"Good afternoon, gentlemen, I'm Lieutenant Carolyn Perkins. I am the flight engineer aboard the *DGA Nautilus*. This briefing is classified Top Secret, NATO. You are guests on a one of a kind, lighter than air, semi rigid airship. Even with its enormous size, it costs less than an aircraft carrier to build and maintain."

Admiral Dukes interrupted, "Don't look so surprised, gentlemen. After all, the CIA paid Howard Hughes over two hundred million dollars to build his ship the *Glomar Explorer*. It was used to lift a sunken Russian nuclear submarine from the bottom of the Pacific. It was built in 1968 under the cover story that she was a deep sea mining vessel, used to recover manganese nodules from the ocean floor. Also, at the same time, Hughes built a huge mining barge known as HMB-1. It was a submersible barge used to carry the claw needed for the recovery effort; it was also used to hide the recovered submarine. So you see, gentlemen, there is precedent for these clandestine recovery systems. Please carry on, Lieutenant."

The lieutenant continued with the presentation, "This vessel serves as both a recovery ship and airborne laboratory for studying, analyzing, and experimenting with TWGs. It is propelled by ion drive propulsion. The leading and trailing edge of our airframe is ionized positively and negatively changing the air density in front of us and behind us, thus generating thrust, or horizontal lift. We have one TWG on board that provides the ionized atmosphere for propulsion."

Again the admiral interrupted, "Gentlemen, we have only begun to understand what these shells mean, what they can do, and how they were put together. We have been in sporadic contact with their makers. However, it isn't as simple as reading a set of blueprints or asking for a copy of the directions. The beings that made these obviously are highly advanced. Right now, communicating with them is like us trying to talk to a bunch of dolphins. We know that each other exist. We are in awe of each other. We trust each other. However, we really haven't figured out how to talk to each other very well. Our frames of reference and the environments that we live in are totally different. We are no threat to them and they are no threat to us.

"The beings that leave these shells have been visiting the Earth for at least a million years or more. This is based on finding these shells in ancient sea beds, talc deposits, arctic ice, and lava tubes. We tried Carbon 14 dating them, but they are not organic. Any radiation shot into the shell becomes absorbed and doesn't return back.

"As a matter of fact, you asked how we get all of our helium. Since you are on board, I'll concede that it is no longer a military secret. The truth is the shell makes it for us. We found this out by accident. We were trying to cut a shell with a hydrogen torch. The flame went out and hydrogen gas seeped into the shell. A few minutes later everyone in the room was talking with a higher pitched voice like Mickey Mouse. As Asimov once said, the most exciting phrase to hear in science, the one that heralds the most discoveries, is not 'Eureka!', but 'That's funny.' What came out of the shell was helium, a funny thing indeed."

Dave was astonished, "Do you mean, Admiral, that these shells are some kind of cold fusion device? Do hydrogen atoms go in and get fused into forming the next element up in the periodic chart which is helium? What happens to all the energy that's released?"

The admiral perked up and looked excited to be talking to somebody that could actually understand the implications, "That's a great question, Captain. Nobody knows for sure, but there are a shitload of PhDs trying to figure this one out. Another thing, this isn't your normal everyday helium. It is actually an isotope called helium-3. Funny about this stuff, there is only about ten kilograms of it occurring naturally on the planet Earth. However, the Moon has a shitload of it entrapped in its geology. The Moon has no magnetic field. The prevailing theory is that the sun sheds this type of helium off in its solar wind. The Earth's magnetic field deflects it around the Earth. We haven't figured out if there is a tie in with torsional waves or not.

The prevailing notion is that the shells keep curving in on themselves in a perfect logarithmic spiral. The curve goes so far as to break down into a point source. Thus, an actual Zero Point Energy (ZPE) Source exists in the heart of these things. When you pump hydrogen gas in, the only thing that does come back out is helium-3 gas, no heat, no light, no radiation, just helium-3 gas. We can't X-ray the damn thing and can only get so deep with probes."

Major Boop asked, "Admiral, do you mean these aliens leave these things lying around just for us to find to generate helium gas?" He responded politely, "No Major, it's just one of many byproducts. After all, we know they generate torsional waves, a type of gravity wave. I'm sure your meters in the bore holes went off scale last week when our guests showed up. Didn't they, Captain Sheridan?"

Sheridan grinned and replied, "You are correct, sir." The admiral continued, "Well gentlemen, as long as we are on the subject of gravity and helium let me enlighten you further. You know that pocket of thin air you hit with your aircraft that caused your stall? It was a pocket of helium gas. There is another shell at the bottom of that lake that is drawing off the hydrogen from the water and converting it to helium-3. We haven't figured out how to get our hands on that one yet."

Major Boop responded, "I'll be damned. The rumors are true. Pilots have been hitting pockets of thin air for years up here. With this much gas floating around up here, why haven't there been any explosions?" Admiral Dukes looked genuinely hurt with that comment, "Major Boop, what was your field of study in college?" Boop responded defensively, "Business Administration. Why do you ask sir? Did I ask a stupid question?" He laughed and said, "I'll let that one slide, but you have a common misconception. Helium is an inert gas, it is not explosive. That's why we use it now in our airships. The Hindenburg used explosive hydrogen which was also lighter than air, but with catastrophic results. There are very few places in the world were helium is found. Amarillo, Texas is one and Canada another. It is a valuable strategic commodity."

Admiral Dukes said, "I apologize, Lieutenant, for interrupting and leaving you standing there. Please continue."

Perkins replied, "That is quite all right, Admiral. I expected this to be a two way discussion and cross feed of information. It makes it more dynamic and interesting that way." Dave thought to himself, "Wow, gorgeous, smart, and diplomatic. I've been on the ice way too long. She makes those fatigues look damn good. Down boy, I'm on the cutting edge of technology and science here, but still a red blooded male and horny as hell."

The lieutenant continued, "We have three shells on board. One generated helium for us, but it is also being studied as a microwave energy generation device. We cannot generate the torsional waves with these shells. We only know they exist when our visitors show up and leave us one. Speculation is that they are leaving these shells for us to figure them out and follow them to the stars."

Just then Major Boop cut in, "Forgive my business analysis approach on this one, but how do you know the aliens are leaving us valuable technology to reverse engineer and experiment with? They may simply be leaving their trash. Or, are they just discarding excess weight like throwing out a beer can?"

Perkins responded, "Good point, sir. We do that all the time with space boosters, space junk, shuttle external tanks, and all that stuff we left on the Moon. So, I can see your point. However, we had advance notice or warning of where to find this shell."

The major asked, "I thought we couldn't talk or communicate with these people. How'd they give us a heads up? Are they running on some kind of schedule?"

The lieutenant replied, "Very good Major, your business sense is paying dividends now. They are operating on a schedule. They've even published it for us. Admiral, may I proceed with this topic of discussion?"

The admiral replied, "Lieutenant, go right ahead, but not too much off the table." She told the sergeant flipping slides for her to start at slide twenty. "I'll skip over the airship diagrams. Besides, I assume we'll be giving our guests a guided tour soon anyway."

Up on the overhead screen was a spiral shaped diagram. It was very intricate, beautiful, and strangely enough recognizable. The navigator, Captain Carl Davis had been quiet most of the time. Yet, he spoke up, "That gentlemen, is a crop circle. I've seen them before. I've flown over them in my Cessna over Kansas."

Lieutenant Perkins replied, "You are exactly correct. This particular one is located in Manitoba, Canada. Our scientists have figured out that our alien friends think logarithmically. We humans think more digitally on ten based numerical systems. We also think linearly or serially." She took a deep breath, smirked, and then followed up with a zinger, "Unless of course, you are a woman that is capable of parallel processing. But even this multitasking capability is still linear thinking." She glanced at Sheridan giving him the gotcha stare.

Admiral Dukes broke up the flirtatious teasing. "Now, now, Lieutenant, please do not harass our guests. We all love you for your mind." The lieutenant smiled and continued, "Very well, sir. Sergeant, please flip through the following twelve charts, ten second pauses for each." The sergeant complied. Photo after photo of crop circles crossed the screen.

"Do you notice any common denominator among these photos?" Glenn spoke up, "Well, excluding the obvious, that they are circular, they also contain spirals. Plus what you might not know, the crop is barley wheat." Perkins replied, "Very good, Captain. You are correct. It is barley wheat, but from the same seed batch. As a matter of fact, the seeds were irradiated."

Dave had to ask, "How do you know that?

Admiral Dukes replied, "We have access to the brightest and best. One of them is the world's best bioinformatics engineer." He punched a button on his cell phone, "Dr. Anne Ahrens, please report to the main briefing room. Lieutenant, we'll defer the biology of the crop circle discussion for our good doctor."

"Each of the crop circles you just saw was digitized, scaled and overlain in order of appearance into a composite diagram. The early ones had simple circles, arcs and lines. This was the Greys' attempt to think linearly like us and attempt at two dimensional communications. When we didn't figure it out at first, they gave up, and then went back to their three dimensional logarithmic way of thinking. This involved spiral patterns, fractals, and intricate curves. Their linear equivalence to distance or time is related to the proportion of crops that are pressed down versus left alone. Also, you'll notice, the layout of these patterns always has a dominant orientation, that of 137.5 degrees towards the southeast. This is known in mathematics as the golden angle. It is also what defines a logarithmic spiral." The lieutenant walked back to the podium and grabbed a pointer.

"This portion of the briefing gets a little technical, detailed and hard to follow. I know you are not all rocket scientists here, but please bear with me as I delve into some advanced geometry, orbital mechanics and cartography or mapmaking. Gentlemen, time to turn on your parallel processors. Sorry Captain, I couldn't resist." She took the pointer and swirled it around the composite diagram. "Notice all the light and dark areas on the composite diagram. This diagram represents areas of depressed wheat when you overlay all seventeen crop circles, one on top of each other. The resulting pattern in itself is very intricate and beautiful for that matter. Yet there is something familiar to it as well.

"Now I'm going to discuss a little bit of cartography. As you know, there are several ways to draw a map representing the globe," continued Perkins. "It is nearly impossible to accurately represent the spherical surface of the Earth on a flat piece of paper. How do you display the globe in a usable, scalable format? We use maps. Maps are a 2-D representation of a 3-D reality. Imagine peeling an orange and pressing the orange peel flat on a table. The peel would crack and split as it was flattened. It would then be transformed from a sphere to a flat plane. The same is true for the surface of the Earth and that's why we use map projections.

"The term map projection can be thought of as a projector. If we place a light bulb inside a transparent globe and project the image onto a wall, we'd see a map projection. However, instead of projecting a light, cartographers use mathematical formulas to create the projections.

"Depending on the kind and accuracy of any map, the cartographer will attempt to eliminate distortion in one or several aspects of the map. You must understand that not all aspects can be represented accurately. So, the mapmaker must choose which distortions are less important than the others and must consider four aspects as shown here." The next slide popped up and showed the following bullets:

- Conformality: the shapes of places are accurate.
- Distance: measured distances are accurate.
- Area/Equivalence: the areas represented on the map are proportional to their area on the Earth.
- Direction: angles of direction are portrayed accurately.

Lieutenant Perkins spun around quickly and grasped her pointer. It reminded Dave of a nun trying to catch a third grader with a spit wad. "Now, if you do a reverse projection of this crop circle composite diagram onto a three dimensional sphere using the equal area equivalence method you get some very interesting and complicated curves and patterns.

"As this name implies, the equal area projection conserves area. Shapes are not preserved, but shape distortion is not too bad in the near hemisphere. When we do this, the entire half sphere can be plotted, but in reality shape distortion beyond ninety degrees, shown here in red, becomes severe. Beyond about 130 degrees it is so extreme as to be unusable. To be exact, anything beyond 137.5 degrees becomes not viewable. It is the event horizon in this case. Again, we see the appearance and limits of the golden angle. Meridians and parallels become complex curves such as ellipses, parabolas, and spirals. Another interesting property of this type of map projection is that it is used in computers as a choice for statistical comparison of spatial data. The Greys think spatially."

Dave spoke up, "I think I am having one of those Eureka moments. I've seen this pattern before. I saw it at a briefing given to me by Space Command inside Cheyenne Mountain. That pattern is the same one shown for the tracking of our satellites in polar orbit."

Lieutenant Perkins looked dutifully impressed, "If you are correct Captain Sheridan, then you may have hit on the Rosetta stone for interpreting the meaning of these patterns."

Dave said, "I'm sure of it. These are the nodal patterns or a plot of our Keyhole imaging satellites as seen from the North Pole. It even includes the left hand twists that the satellites experience."

It was the admiral's turn to speak up. "Captain, I think you are correct. The significance of this is that we will now be able to predict the arrival of our visitors. One of our Keyholes was directly over the DYE-3 occurrence when the object generated a torsional wave and disappeared. I think we now have their flight schedule by matching the composite pattern nodes with the Keyhole satellite orbital nodes. Lieutenant, overlay the Keyhole orbits with the event horizon orientated at 68° 45' towards the poles. Then match that up with the known locations from the Bruce Cathie Energy Grid. Captain Sheridan, you just earned your pay for the year. Damn, you're good."

It took a few minutes to get the slides together, but the results were worth it. Admiral Dukes immediately got on the phone to Cheyenne Mountain to have them start plotting out a time schedule for new locations and map out the shells currently on the planet.

CHAPTER 10
Non-Linear Thinking

Admiral Dukes got up and walked up to the podium, "Whatever it was that melted the area north of DYE-3 made a perfect bowl shape depression in the ice. The bowl is three miles wide and over a mile deep. As a matter of fact, it has a perfect parabolic contour. We assume that there is another shell or object at the bottom of the lake that is generating all of the helium gas. We looked for it for two days. We even took sonar readings and even lowered a submersible with no luck. Another amazing thing is, even though the outside air temperature up here is -6° F, the water does not freeze. We now conclude that the helium gas was trapped in some sort of molecular matrix in the ice and then released. Also, the residual torsional energy also keeps the ice from crystallizing so it can't freeze.

"As a matter of fact gentlemen, it was pure dumb luck that you stumbled upon the lake at all. This airship just happened to be back at Thule Air Base loading the submersible when you flew by and first encountered the helium plume and then returned a few hours later. We had our Keyhole satellite watching the area very carefully. The Keyhole did get some very detailed photographs of that lake. What's more impressive is the radar imagery that they got. We also got some very interesting and entertaining photos of your snail dragging activities on the ice.

"Our earlier discussions of map projections gave us the idea to review the radar imagery. The Cray supercomputer has been crunching the numbers for the last half hour. It turns out that there is a definite pattern etched on the bowl shaped ice walls of the lake. These patterns match exactly the Keyhole orbital node traces that

Captain Sheridan hit upon along with even more detail. We have to constantly keep reminding ourselves that the Greys do not think linearly. When they do try to communicate with us, it is not one idea that they are trying to get across. There are always meanings within meanings and they are always expressing multiple ideas and thoughts.

"For example, even though we had to overlap each of the crop circles to come up with a composite, each one of those crop circles had an individual purpose and meaning as well. We think we are on the verge of figuring out what a few of them mean. The key is the golden spiral and helix."

Just then another beautiful woman with long brown hair in a tight jump suit entered the room. She spoke with a subtle Long Island accent, "Excuse me Admiral Dukes, for interrupting. I was running a simulation on the Cray and could not break away."

Admiral Dukes smiled and responded, "Not a problem Dr. Ahrens. I'd like to introduce you to our newest members of the Delta G North Team."

Captain Sheridan's eyes were fixated. He thought to himself, "to hell with the lieutenant with the baggy BDUs. Now, here is a real woman."

Admiral Dukes followed military protocol and introduced each new team member in order of rank and specialty. When he got to Sheridan, he had to throw in a couple of attaboys and qualifiers. "Now, we come here to our good Captain David Sheridan. He is the bright young officer that your father keeps bringing up that is singlehandedly putting the pieces of this puzzle of ours together. We've been compartmentalized for too long. General Ahrens is making Captain Sheridan the Delta G Integration Officer. Congratulations, Captain. Unfortunately there is no pay raise or increase in rank that goes along with the responsibility."

Dr. Ahrens strode over to Sheridan. She reached out her hand. He didn't know quite what to do, but caught on quickly. He grasped her hand and shook it politely. Dr. Ahrens responded, "I'm impressed. My father does have a keen eye for talent and brilliance."

Admiral Dukes responded, "I'll second that. Now don't let

that go to your head. You're still only an O-3 and face many challenges, resistance, and hurdles ahead."

Dave responded, "Well, to tell you the truth, I'm not quite sure what to make of all this. And what the hell does an integrator do anyway?" Dukes laughed and replied, "Well, at least you're honest."

CHAPTER 11
Sacred Geometry

Dr. Anne Aurora Ahrens was anything but boring. "I appreciated your presentation on the crop circles, Lieutenant. I understand that you were just about to discuss the Golden Spiral. Now, what I'm going to tell you is really going to blow your minds." Dave thought to himself she couldn't possibly top the fact that flying saucers existed, that they were responsible for the crop circles, and were attempting to communicate with us. But he was wrong.

Dr. Ahrens continued with her presentation, "If you don't already know, I am what is known as a bioinformatics engineer, one of only a handful in the entire world. What if I were to tell you the secrets to the universe and be able to answer yes to the question, is there a God?" Everyone in the room just stared. She was definitely on her way to topping this morning's conversation on space ships and aliens. Dr. Ahrens grabbed the dry erase marker and walked over to the white board. She drew a single point on the board. She labeled it God. She then drew a spiral outward and then labeled several layers as conscience, knowledge of self, and then, knowledge of God.

"Ladies and gentlemen, this is not a sermon or a philosophy lecture. I assure you what I'm about to discuss is purely science. The secrets of the universe involve spirals and to put it simplistically, torsional energy emanating from a Zero Point Energy source. This is so simplistic because it links matter, energy, light, and biological forces together. This energy is 'all present' at all times and results in matter being self-aware of its physical state."

Dave had to speak up. "This is all an elegant discussion, but if you don't mind me asking, what do spirals and torsional waves have to do with biology?" Anne gave a smile to him and simply said, "Let me expand on this secret to the universe. All life is based on the spiral, or specifically, a special type of harmonic logarithmic spiral, based off what Fibonacci, a famous mathematician discovered.

"He is known for the Fibonacci sequence. It is 0, 1, 1, 2, 3, 5, 8, 13, 21, 34, 55, and so on. It begins with the first two numbers 0 and 1, and each new term from there is the sum of the previous two. The limit ratio between the terms is 1.618034..., an irrational number variously called the golden ratio or the divine proportion or the term Phi. Not to be confused with the Greek letter π (Pi), or 3.14, which is another famous number in mathematics used to find the area of a circle.

"Golden Spirals appear everywhere in nature: from the leaf arrangement in plants, to the pattern of the florets of a flower, the shape of a pinecone, or the scales of a pineapple. The Fibonacci numbers are, therefore, applicable to the growth of every living thing, including a single cell, a grain of wheat, a hive of bees, and even all humans.

"The most notable and far reaching examples include the double spiral helictical pattern of the DNA molecule. I don't have to tell you, ladies and gentlemen, that this molecule is the program for all life. But I'll bet you didn't know it is based on the golden section. It measures about 34 angstroms long by 21 angstroms wide

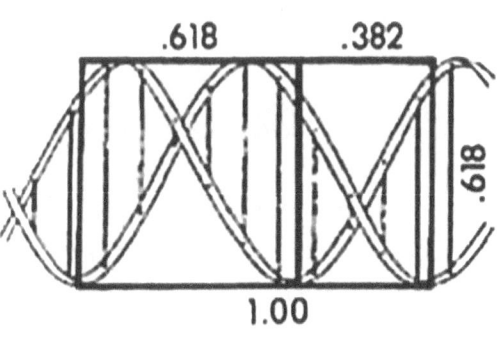

for each full cycle of its double helix spiral. Before you waste a stupid question by asking what an angstrom is, all you need to realize is that 34 divided by 21 is 1.6190476 which closely approximates the value of Phi 1.6180339. As I've said, the number that keeps cropping up in nature."

Anne flashed a few slides up on the screen to drive her point home. "A cross-sectional view from the top of the DNA double helix forms a ten-sided decagon. Here is a decagon. It is in essence two overlapping pentagons, with one rotated thirty-six degrees from the other. Thus, each spiral of the double helix traces out the shape of pentagon.

" You will notice the ratio of the diagonal of a pentagon to its side is Phi to 1. So, no matter which way you look at it, even in its smallest molecule, DNA and life are constructed using phi and the golden proportion! We've found that torsional energy resonates with the DNA strand and can change its makeup and, thus, accelerate or alter evolution.

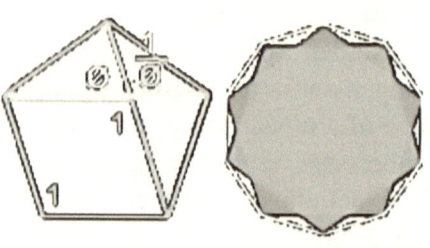

"The Equiangular or Logarithmic Spiral was discovered by Descartes. Its properties of self-reproduction were recognized by Jacob Bernoulli, a sixteenth century Swiss mathematician, who requested that the curve be engraved upon his tomb with the phrase '*Eadem Mutata Resurgo*' meaning 'I shall arise the same, though changed.' He was somewhat of a poet, too. Was he referring to reincarnation and evolution? His most notable poem is:

Even as the finite encloses an infinite series
And in the unlimited limits appear,
So the soul of immensity dwells in minutia
And in the narrowest limits no limit in here
What joy to discern the minute in infinity!
The vast to perceive in the small, what divinity!

This man was a half a millennium before his time. His epithet is now our motto," Anne commented.

Dave couldn't resist a wisecrack. "Wasn't '*Eadem Mutata Resurgo*' what had to be said to the Giant Robot to keep it from

vaporizing Washington, D.C. in *The Day the Earth Stood Still*?"
Anne didn't miss a beat, "No that was 'Klaatu, Barada, Nikto.'
However, I'm impressed that you could remember our motto."

He gave her a sly wink, "Sorry, I must confess. I didn't. It's
written on the front of the podium you are standing behind."

"So it is, Captain. You are very observant. But I'm still
impressed"

Major Boop looked at Sheridan and then Anne and said, "Not
half as impressed as I am. How do you remember all of this stuff,
especially that poem you just recited?"

"Simple, I have a photographic memory."

Admiral Dukes broke up the banter and busted Anne's bubble,
"Not to mention the teleprompter on the other side of that podium.
Now back to our discussion, please."

"Sorry Admiral. With the advent of X-ray photography, we
have discovered that the physical structure of elements is gov-
erned by a patterned array of intervals surrounding a central node.
The general assumption that the nature of matter is fundamentally
composed of particles is rapidly giving way to the concept that
the underlying patterns of the material world are geometric spiral
wave forms."

Anne gave this concept a few seconds to sink in and then continued, "The irony here is that by choosing to examine and explain
the world using geometry, many ancient cultures were closer to
the positions now adopted by modern science, and vice versa. The
Egyptians, the Greeks, and even the Swiss got it right. Geometry
is sacred and holds the secrets to the universe.

"You've just witnessed that crop circles are all based on the
golden spiral. At least the real ones are. We speculate that spiral torsional energy waves coupled with microwaves were used
to form the crop circles. We also suspect the same forces were
responsible for melting the ice lake that we are currently hovering
near."

Just then Admiral Dukes interrupted, "Excuse me everyone,
but we are no longer hovering near the lake. We have successfully
lowered the DYE-3 crew down to the surface. My exec will be
staying with them for a while. We are on a course up north to our

staging area near Thule. Our top speed is classified; however, we are seven hundred miles out and will be there in approximately three hours." He smiled and then said, "We are in a hurry to get your injured crew members to a hospital. You do the math."

Major Boop turned to Admiral Dukes, "How is Sergeant Sheppard doing?" Dukes reassured him that he was now conscious yet confused. "Your navigator is still with him." Boop looked relieved and asked to see him. Dukes responded, "The best thing for him now is to rest."

Boop conceded this, then asked, "Why didn't we feel any acceleration or hear any noise?" The admiral replied, "You wouldn't expect a ship such as this to suddenly pull G's, would you, Major? The *DGA Nautilus* weighs in at over five million pounds. She's hard to get moving, but like a battleship, once moving not much is going to stop her. Excuse the interruption, Doctor, please continue."

Anne Ahrens strode over to the white board, erased it and then picked up the marker. "That is quite all right, sir. It gave me a minute to collect my thoughts. Forgive the math lesson, but what you are about to hear is very important." She took another deep breath and reengaged her train of thought, "The shape of the nautilus shell you helped us recover is a type of spiral based upon the golden ratio. Two quantities are said to be in the golden ratio if their whole, that is, the sum of the two parts, is to the larger part as the larger part is to the smaller part. I know that was a mouthful, but written mathematically it looks like this." She wrote the formula on the board.

$$\frac{a+b}{a} = \frac{a}{b}$$

"Where *a* is the larger part and *b* is the smaller part.

This ratio is denoted φ(Phi) and is an irrational number." She continued with her mathematical wizardry on the white board and wrote the following equation.

$$\varphi = \frac{1}{2}(1 + \sqrt{5}) \approx 1.618033989$$

"This is the same number I mentioned earlier when I mentioned the DNA molecule. This golden ratio is also known by many other names such as: the golden mean, golden number, golden proportion, divine proportion, extreme and mean ratio, or, with emphasis on the division of the whole into parts, as golden section, golden cut, or sectio divina." Anne took a deep breath and let out a sigh. "Wow! Say that ten times real fast."

Admiral Dukes seemed to enjoy watching the group scratch their heads, pull on their chins, and grapple with all that has been laid before them. It was time for him to give Anne a break. He followed up on the discussion, "Sacred mathematics, as it is known, has been around for thousands of years. Builders and artists have used shapes proportioned according to the golden ratio because they are aesthetically pleasing to the eye. As a matter of fact, the term Phi is derived from Phidias, the architect who designed the Greek Parthenon. The golden ratio suggests a natural balance between symmetry and asymmetry. The ancient Pythagoreans also believed that reality is numerical and that the golden ratio expressed an underlying truth about existence."

Anne regained her stride and continued, "Thank you, Admiral. I can take it from here. In case you are wondering what the heck a bioinformatics engineer does, let me enlighten you before we give you a tour of the ship." With this comment everyone stopped squirming in their seats. As fascinating as this discussion was, Major Boop and Dave were quite anxious to see the ship.

After taking a sip of water, Anne continued with the discussion. "I can see all of you are anxious to tour this fantastic vessel, so I'll leave you with just one additional thought. It has been discovered recently that spiral energy is an unmistakable part of the human physiology. The human senses include the five known: hearing, touch, taste, vision and smell. And we all suspect there is potentially a sixth, the extrasensory one. These senses not only have a spiral physiology, but they also have response curves that are logarithmic and have a Fibonacci structure. For example, human cellular action membrane voltage potentials, which are important for muscles and nervous systems, have voltages equal to the log of the ratio of the ion concentration outside the cell to that of inside the cell." Anne could tell she had just blown this one over everyone's heads. "Let me put it in simpler terms. The brain and nervous system are made from the same type of cellular building blocks and look similar microscopically. So the response curve of the central nervous system is probably also logarithmic like the brain. As a matter of fact, we now think that the pineal gland in the center of the brain might be the centroid for this physiology. In conclusion, torsional waves touch the very fabric of space, time, and perhaps are even the true life force in the universe. Please keep this in mind when exposed to the Delta G Program."

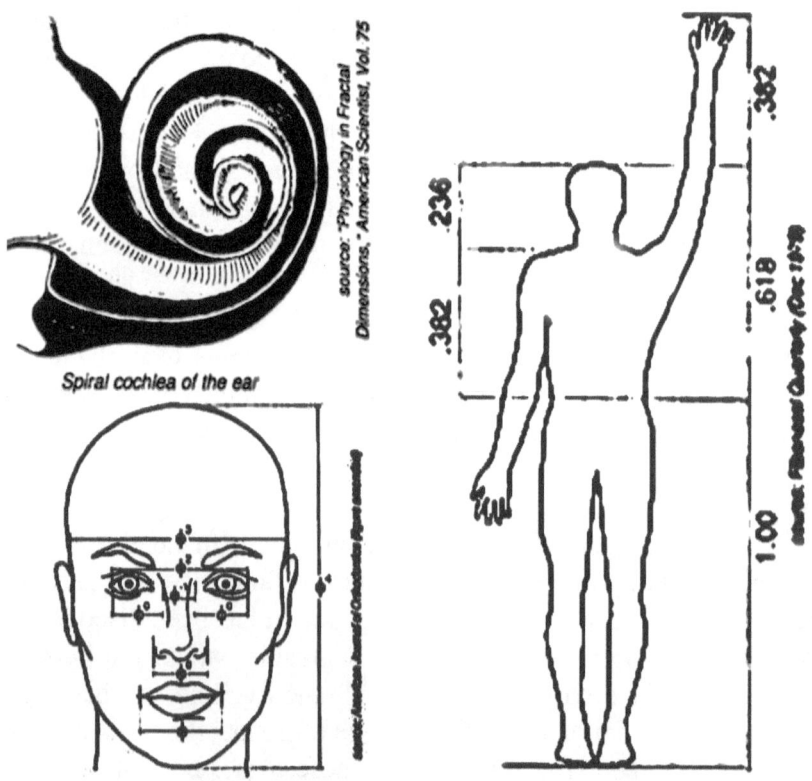

Examples of the Golden Ratio and
Logarithmic Spiral in the Human Body.

CHAPTER 12
Admiral's Tour

Admiral Dukes' pride in his vessel was apparent. He took the group of Air Force officers on the guided tour he promised. Major Boop, Dave, as well as Captains Davis and Rylah were awestruck, but kept a calm and professional demeanor about them. He brought them back into the high-bay to take a look at the C-130 under the adjacent hoist to the shell. Boop asked why his plane was being wrapped in white plastic. "That's a fair question Major. Your plane is full of hydrocarbons. These shells are like giant chemistry sets. Certain molecules react with the shells and give us some peculiar reactions. I explained what happened when a hydrogen cutting torch gas reacted and gave us helium-3. We are taking no chances. The shell was hermetically sealed on the surface before being hoisted up. We are wrapping your Hercules and inerting your fuel tanks with nitrogen. This is also a precaution against fire and explosion. There is no fire department up here."

Dave couldn't help noticing the diamond metal deck used for flooring and the hefty epoxy carbon graphite structural members lining the high-bay. "They told me at the Nevada Test Site that when we were doing the cold-launch eject tests for the MX missile that our launch tube was the largest epoxy-graphite structure in the world. Obviously, they were wrong."

Dukes laughed and replied, "Don't feel bad, Captain. With this vessel, size does matter. We have plenty of lifting capability. Our main structural concern is with the high winds we get up here. And since this ship covers over two hundred acres in area, the structural loads constantly shift and change in intensity."

Boop asked, "Why is this ship so huge? You could obviously

lift the shells with something a lot less grandiose."

"Well Major, it's not so much the volume we need as it is the space and distance. We have several of these shells on board. They seem to act more efficiently if they are not in close proximity with each other. We call this the shell breathing room factor. Two of our shells are located at the ends of the vessel and provide plasma for our ion propulsion. We have another two located forward and aft that make our helium-3, and now we have this one in the center bay.

"You will soon see that this ship is a flying laboratory. We are experimenting with MASERS, particle accelerators, cold fusion magnetic containment systems, radars, ESP, neutron detection, gravity wave detection, magnetic field flux detection, even radio astronomy, and of course, DNA and biological experiments with the shells. You need a lot of real estate to accomplish these tasks."

It was about time for Boop to start asking some obvious questions, "Excuse me for asking, Admiral, but with all of this at your disposal you said our expertise is desperately needed. Why do you need my crew, my plane, and me? What kind of expertise were you talking about?"

The admiral pondered the question, "Well, let me put it this way. We've spent billions on this vessel. We have most of its operations and even the maintenance of her automated. Even the experiments on board are mostly automated. The ship darn near flies itself. We have a small crew on board and to tell you the truth a fairly small support staff and crew up near Thule. What we lack is some dependable transportation and hauling capability. But as you can well imagine, we can't just fly this thing anywhere in the world. That's why we need a plane and a crew."

Major Boop looked a little suspicious, "You have all the resources of DoD at your disposal. Why pick this crew and this plane? Besides, it's a little busted up at the moment."

The admiral said, "Okay, I'll be blunt. You were in the right place at the right time. Not to mention, you have one of the few ski equipped large transport planes in the world. That makes you very valuable to this program. Don't worry about putting her back in shape. We'll get that done in no time. However, as far as the rest of the Air Force is concerned, Raven One crashed and was destroyed on the icecap."

Boop replied coolly, "I assume the crash had a happy ending and all the crew survived." Dukes looked puzzled and truly hurt, "Of course, Major. Just the plane met an untimely end. The crew was rescued by the DYE-3 crew. DYE-3 will report this fact back to Sonde. DYE-3 will then report a white out condition for the next few days. Communications to and from DYE-3 will be routed through this ship, and as far as the rest of the world is concerned, you and your crew are resting comfortably at the DYE-3 site sucking down Carlsberg beers and watching porno flicks waiting for the weather to lift.

In the meantime, we are going to get your plane to Thule. We have an extensive maintenance complex there. I can assure you our team there can get, or make, the parts and pieces to patch up Raven One. We will then prep and train you and your crew on your new mission." Again, Boop asked, "What might that be?"

Dukes replied, "We think that we've come up with a way to detect these shells located all over the world, and even on the Moon for that matter."

Dave spoke up this time. "How do you go about detecting these things? By sniffing for helium-3, by triangulating torsional waves using satellites, or have the aliens left us a detailed map? I assume they are not easily located, since none are on display at the Ripley's Museum in Vegas. I wouldn't think the node projection chart and timeline that we just discovered are accurate enough for you to go around and dig up the planet."

Dukes replied, "Well, none of those obvious methods you mentioned worked. Trust me, we looked and we tried. The crop circles only help to locate where they are going to be in the future, not where they've been. The helium-3 dissipates after a few weeks and becomes undetectable. Also, we haven't figured out how to detect torsional waves from a distance of more than a few miles on Earth due to interference with magnetic and gravitational fields. Now, what we've come up with involves MASERS. Remember when I said these shells eat radar energy. You can't use ground penetrating radar to look for them. They are nonferrous, so you can't detect them magnetically. However, they do reflect MASER energy. We are going to turn Raven One into an Airborne MASER search platform."

This time Captain Carl Davis asked, "What the hell is MASER energy?"

Dukes pointed to Dave and said, "Do you want to tackle that one, Captain Sheridan?" Dave felt like he was back in third grade again, being asked an English question and could only offer a shrug of the shoulders and shake his head no. Luckily, Dukes was a little more understanding than the third grade nun that would tug on his ear lobe every time he shrugged his shoulders with a negative reply.

"Anne, would you tell our new crew members a little something about our MASER experiments?"

Anne replied, "I'd love to. MASER stands for **M**icrowave **A**mplification by **S**timulated **E**mission of **R**adiation. This uses the same principle as a laser only using the microwave frequency of the spectrum instead of light. MASERs have been around for several years. As a matter of fact, an atomic hydrogen MASER Oscillator was launched in 1976 to prove Einstein's time dilation theory on objects in orbit versus earthbound. He was right.

"Also, since the MASER oscillator had a frequency stability of approximately one part in ten to the sixteenth power for over a day it easily verified Einstein's predicted Gravitational Red Shift principle with a precision of seventy parts per million. He was proven right again, thus was born the MASER clock.

"We then wondered what would happen if we pointed a MASER beam down the gullet of one of the shells. Nothing ventured, nothing gained, right? So we built a half-mile long high power MASER and put it here in the *DGA Nautilus*.

"Trust me when I say we followed proper safety protocols. We flew the *Nautilus* to the most remote places on the planet Earth to test our MASER on a shell. God forbid, if we would start a chain reaction and incinerate the planet. We were about to twist the dragons tail and needed a huge buffer zone. For your information, here's a nifty piece of trivia. The North Pole is not the most isolated place on the planet Earth. The North Pole is less than five hundred miles from the Canadian Air Base at the village of Alert on the tip of Ellesmere Island in Canada, and is less than a thousand miles from Spitsbergen, Norway, where you can land on an asphalt runway and pick up a rental car at the airport. And no, before you ask, it's not even at the South Pole. If you take into account all the outposts that are only a few hundred miles apart down there, such as McMurdo on the Ross Ice Shelf, which is only 750 miles from the South Pole."

Carl, the navigator, spoke up. At least, he had some knowledge of world geography and a feel for relative distances. "I'd put the most remote place on earth somewhere in the southern mid-Atlantic."

It was Anne's turn to repay with a sexy wink and say, "You win a cigar, Captain. Our primary test location was an Island known as Tristan. It's about seventeen hundred miles west of Cape Town, about halfway between South America and Africa. What we found there with our MASER is quite interesting.

"The MASER Energy was not absorbed, but reflected back out of the shell. It didn't matter what microwave frequency we shot down the gullet, it reflected back at 38.2 degrees out of phase. This was a complete shock. It was assumed that MASER signals maintain a constant frequency of interplanetary distances. We also became interested with MASERS when we suspected that this was how our alien friends were creating the crop circles. We began an experiment with *Nautilus* as a platform to see if we could create crop circles, too. It worked amazingly well. We never achieved anything as remotely intricate as our friends can; however, we were able to lay down some wheat. We had our roll in the hay so to speak. However, we had even better results on soybean fields.

"Another interesting fact about masers is that unlike lasers, they occur naturally in the universe. Radio telescopes have detected them. As a matter of fact, the 22 GHz water MASER line is the brightest spectral line in the radio universe. It is found in shocked star forming regions, dense circumstellar gas shells around evolved stars as well as circumnuclear disks around black holes of galactic centers.

"Again, like torsional waves and DNA, MASER energy is

associated with the building blocks of life. Water molecules are violently produced during the birth process of a star as a result of the powerful shockwaves generated from the star formation process. The birth of massive stars generates strong stellar winds with velocities up to several thousand mph. These winds interact and react with shockwaves surrounding the star cloud material. By looking for shockwaves with velocities exceeding 10,000 mph in the vicinity of high density magnetized material, MASERS can be located with the H_2O MASER spectral reading."

Admiral Dukes went over to a wall phone and punched in three numbers. "Are things in order for our guests up there? Very good. We will be up shortly. Gentlemen, we'll defer our discussion of MASERS and ZPE for a few minutes while we move upstairs to our MASER lab."

CHAPTER 13
Charlie Sierra

Admiral Dukes ushered everyone into a large square room in the back center of the high-bay. He put his palm on a biometric reader and immediately a klaxon alarm sounded along with a rotating blue light. The klaxon quit after a few seconds and was followed by a firm mechanical voice, "Stand clear of the entrance and perimeter walls. Stand within the bounded area." This was repeated three times as the entire room started to move upwards. The elevator was huge, about fifty foot square. It reminded Dave of a carrier flight deck elevator, no walls just a moving platform. Dave watched as the elevator cleared the high-bay ceiling and he could peer into a cavern of duct works, conduits, piping, ladders and catwalks. It kept moving up about another hundred feet and then stopped. In front of the cadre was a long arched hallway about a hundred yards long. Again, there were several electric golf carts waiting for them.

Admiral Dukes said, "I assume you all are checked out in the operational characteristics of your standard issue electric golf cart? However, these are a far cry from standard issue. They are robotically controlled, voice activated, and follow a preset grid pattern located in the deck plate. One must remember this ship is over a mile wide, and covers several hundred acres with its five decks. We don't have turbo shafts. If it makes you feel better, these are hydrogen fuel cell operated vehicles." With everyone seated comfortably in a cart, Dukes uttered a simple command, "Cart four, five and six, destination Zebra Papa Echo, main lab."

The carts accelerated down the corridor and made a smooth turn to the left at the end of the hall. They were now in a large corridor that curved slightly backwards. Dave could tell it ran the width of the ship and followed the contour of the ships leading edge. Even though the hallways were huge, he still had a slight pang of claustrophobia. He had a burning question, well, actually two. First one, "Admiral, do you have any windows on this ship?" The answer surprised him, "No, Captain, we do not. Remember, we travel in a stealth mode. The entire exterior skin of this ship is dedicated to that task as well as ion drive propulsion. Windows and glass are a security threat as well as totally unnecessary. As we will show you in time, our sensors are quite capable of letting us know what is in our surroundings." The second question was now a little more urgent, "Excuse me, Admiral, but you couldn't perhaps stop by a roadside rest? The coffee is beginning to takes its toll on my kidneys." Major Boop spoke up, "Good call, Captain. I was just thinking the same thing."

"No problem, gentlemen," the admiral said, "just keep in mind there are only two dozen of us on this ship. The latrines are few and far between other than our private quarters. I'm glad you asked to stop now. The comfort station is only a few hundred feet ahead. The admiral amended his original order, "Carts four, fix, and six. Stop at Charlie Sierra four." The admiral half kidded, "You'd better know your phonetic alphabet and the layout of the ship or you'll have to cross your legs for quite some time before we get another pee break." The carts stopped at an alcove that had several leather couches. There was a water and fruit drink bottle dispenser along with a coffee machine. Funny, it did remind him of a road side rest. The bathrooms were huge. Instead of tile, everything was a white fiberglass, except the fixtures which were stainless steel.

After Dave exited the latrine, he asked Dukes a perplexing question, "I notice that in your smaller rooms, offices, and enclosed spaces you have standard fluorescent lighting. However, the large open cavernous space is lighted in a translucent, almost natural glow. If you have no windows, were does that light come from?"

Dukes replied proudly, "Again, very perceptive of you. It is quite a design and operational challenge to light and environmentally control this much volume. We have again borrowed or reverse engineered some unique technology. We call it nano-technology. The ship has millions of Micro Iridescent Suspended Transponders, or what we call MIST particles. These particles are micro-bubbles of silicides infused with helium about the size of a BB. Each MIST has a transponder that emits its exact location on this ship to within a hundredth of an inch. The MIST can be excited and activated by microwave energy to provide light and/or heat. They are neutrally buoyant and can be grouped, rounded up, and even sent to any place they are needed. They have a built in logic program on a microchip the size of a grain of sand that allows for learned commands, limited artificial intelligence, and built in fail-safe systems. They are tied directly into our ships mainframe, can be used for surveillance, and even patching holes if need be. My computer people tell me the technology is fairly simple. The breakthrough came when we could miniaturize it using some innovative electron beam nano-additive manufacturing processes that we learned from the Greys." Dave and the others took a collective breath at the mention of alien technology in use before them.

After the comfort break the group climbed back in the carts and again proceeded down to the end of the gently curving passageway. An area of about an acre opened up with what appeared to be offices and labs. On the other side of a thick Plexiglas wall, a huge nautilus shell, sitting in the center of a smaller bay, was surrounded by scaffolding and cat walks. There were bundles of conduit running over the top with a few small cables running into the gullet.

Just then, from behind them, walked two bearded men in blue lab coats. They were several hundred feet off, but Dave felt he could recognize the stride. He thought, "I'll be damned. It's Professors Rapp and Timken."

Dr. Timken held out his hand to shake Major Boop's, "Good to see you again gentlemen, as well as you, too, my dear," as he bowed towards Anne.

Major Boop put his hands on his hips and shook his head from side to side, "Well, I'll be damned. Nothing surprises me anymore."

Dr. Rapp responded, "Now, now, my good Major. You must not forsake the unexpected, or the unexplained. I assure you that nature is full of surprises yet to be discovered."

Boop replied, "Good point, Doctor, I'll keep that in mind."

Dave asked, "I gather you both are a part of the Delta G Program, and not just passing through?"

Admiral Dukes laughed, "I assure you, no one just passes through my ship."

Dr. Timken broke in, "Captain, we have been part of Delta G for several years now."

Dave asked, "The ice drilling and gravitational experiments were all a ruse or cover? If so, what else was really going on?"

"No, what we were doing on the icecap at DYE-3 was very vital to the Delta G Program. Before I get into the details, let me show you our laboratory. We are quite proud of it."

Drs. Rapp and Timken walked through an arched doorway and into the shell chamber beyond. "Welcome to the Dragon's Lair. What you see here is TWG #3 or torsional wave generator number three. You may already know that we have four permanent shells on the ship, not including the fifth one you dragged to the DYE site and that we have sealed up in our cargo bay.

What we are doing with TWG #3 is investigating if the shells are actually Zero Point Energy sources. We know they can fuse elements together. We know that for some reason they react strangely with other gases than just hydrogen. For instance, they react violently with ozone. Ozone or tri-oxygen (O_3) is a tri-atomic molecule, consisting of three oxygen atoms. It is an allotrope of oxygen that is much less stable than the diatomic O_2. That is why you do not see very much in the way of electronics, motors, or circuitry anywhere near the shells. As a matter of fact, the room we are now in has a constant positive air flow outward."

Captain Rylah asked, "What about all those cables hanging over the shell?" Rapp replied, "Very good powers of observation, Captain. Those cables are coaxial microwave guides and also Lucite fiber optic cables."

Admiral Dukes handed everyone a pair of glasses and ear plugs. "Believe it or not, we have a lot of stray laser light at times in here. Also, when the shell decides to pop a helium cloud, it does make a bang. We'll need these."

Captain Davis asked, "Okay, I'll bite. What the heck is Zebra Papa Echo?"

Dr. Rapp turned to him and in a theatrical flair held his arms outreached and palms up. "Zebra Papa Echo represents an almost infinite energy source formed from the very vacuum of space."

Davis looked a little baffled, "That sounds a lot like an oxymoron. Like everything from nothing. Sort of like how my wife operates with my salary and the credit cards."

Rapp smiled and said, "You are exactly right. The concept of Zero Point Energy has been around since Einstein's famous $E=MC^2$. Let me explain. In the early seventeenth century, the concept of a vacuum was thought to mean simply removing all matter from an existing space, such as pumping out all of the gasses from a vacuum chamber. This concept was then modified in the late nineteenth century, when it was realized that thermal radiation still existed in the vacuum. Thus, the space was not void. So, someone had the bright idea to simply cool the vacuum chamber down to absolute zero (-459° F or 0° Kelvin). This sounded logical at the time.

"However, wouldn't you know it? Those experiments also showed that the now super cold vacuum chamber was occupied by other types of nonthermal radiation. This was called zero point radiation. It was later verified when scientists had the technology to cool helium down to within micro degrees of absolute zero. A funny thing about helium is that it becomes a liquid at 4.2 degrees above absolute zero. Then at only a little over two degrees above absolute zero things get really weird, the helium suddenly becomes a superfluid. It is the only element that has this property. And only ZPE (Zero Point Energy) can account for the source of energy that keeps helium from freezing. This is even more so with the rare form of helium-3 isotope."

Dr. Rapp continued, "Another interesting property of helium is that normal liquid helium is a very bad conductor of heat, but the superfluid helium is a perfect heat conductor or superconductor. To put this in perspective, it would be like someone putting a match to a mile long steel rod and you suddenly feel the heat at the other end because of the zero resistance. Another strange thing is that at these temperatures, helium atoms are indistinguishable from one another. They act as one big quantum entity, kind of like one huge helium super molecule. Or as our beautiful bioinformatics engineer, Dr. Ahrens, is fond of saying, the super molecule is all knowing and almost conscious of all of its constituent parts.

"Unfortunately, studying the transition phase shift of trillions of atoms to one huge molecule is not very easy. The problem is that Earth's gravity creates minute pressure variations in the samples so that one part remains normal liquid helium while the rest is superfluid helium. We are experimenting in a zero G space laboratory now and…"

Admiral Dukes cut off the good professor in mid-sentence. "Excuse me Doctor, but our discussions are limited to this vessel and any experiments directly related to it. Our guests are not cleared for other Delta G Programs." Dr. Rapp put his hands in his lab coat pockets and apologized.

Dukes requested Rapp to continue with his explanation of the ZPE lab. "One other fascinating thing about ZPE is that it involves larger heavy particles of matter with high atomic numbers. If there is matter out there or should I say in here (pointing to the shell) that has an atomic number greater than 137 or higher, it will cause a constant virtual particle flux of the ZPE vacuum because of intense electrical field gradients when the binding energy equals or exceeds the rest mass of its orbiting electrons."

Everyone sort of looked at Rapp as if he had grown a third eye or something. Dave made a swooshing sound as he passed his hand over his head. "I think you blew that curve ball right past us, Doctor. We are not PhDs and have very little understanding of particle physics."

"My apologies, Anne and gentlemen, let me try again. If super heavy atoms are created with an atomic mass of greater than 137, the binding energy will then exceed twice the rest mass of the electron. A pair production, resulting in matter and antimatter along with photons and gravitons, will appear out of the vacuum. The electron is then driven into the nucleus and spontaneous positrons or anti-electrons are produced. Do you know what this means?"

Major Boop spoke up this time, "From my limited Star Trekian experience, anytime you mix matter with antimatter nasty things happen. Planets blow up. People in red shirts die, and space gets warped and ripped."

Dr. Timken actually grinned at this one. "Not far off, Major, but the simple truth is that this reaction results in a true source of unlimited free energy. It becomes paradoxically a vacuum that cannot be emptied. It means matter can travel faster than the speed of light. As a matter of fact, the electrons generated from the reaction have a rest mass energy of $E=2MC^2$ or twice the normal energy levels. The amount of energy contained in one cubic meter of empty space is mind boggling. It has been estimated to be from 10^{36} to 10^{70} Joules."

Captain Davis made a crash and burn sound effect, "Can you put that in layman's terms?"

"Surely, my good Captain, that means that there is enough energy in the volume of one cup of coffee to boil away the Earth's oceans."

All Davis could say was, "Wow, now that's one hell of a cup of coffee."

Dave was a little more analytical, "You have found a stable long-lived element with an atomic number of 137?" Rapp said, "You are looking at it down this thing's gullet. And actually, it has an atomic number of 182. We call it Grey Matter 182 or GM 182 for short. Even though it is extremely dense, it lies in what is known as a stability island well beyond the range of human made capability. The current element chart only goes as high as 118. There are a few theoretical elements such as unbihexium that is speculated to be stable also. It has an atomic number of 126. We have also been experimenting with ununpentium 115. It has some interesting gravitational properties. As it turns out, several of these upper heavy elements actually have enough mass within their nucleus to effect or perturbate the weak nuclear forces. This has huge potential for…" Admiral Dukes cut him off abruptly, "That will be all Dr. Rapp. We don't want to overload our guests with too much information."

Dave smiled and caught the fact that Rapp was about to expose them to some very, very classified information. Sheridan diplomatically changed the subject, "I hope with all this particle physics going on around here we are not getting fried to a crackly crunch." Anne smiled and said, "No need to break out your lead lined jockey shorts. Your gonads will be just fine. The proper protection and shielding is in place. As we stated earlier, that is another reason for the scale of this ship. Obviously for weight purposes, we are selective in our placement of shielding and thus rely on distances. Otherwise, we would in fact need to be literally flying around in a huge proverbial lead balloon."

CHAPTER 14
Ride in a Lead Balloon

The bridge of the *DGA Nautilus* was phenomenal. Dave was expecting it to look something like a cross between the bridge of the *Queen Mary*, the *Starship Enterprise*, and the SAC underground Command Post. He wasn't too far off. However, the bridge was literally a flying bridge. It was located at the very top center of the ship forward of the high-bay. It had two intersecting flyways, with a gondola suspended in the center about one hundred feet in diameter. It was surrounded with computer screens, work stations, and in the very center was command center with the admiral's chair. Dave walked around it and could make out Greenland on a heads-up display console. He could see a blue circle glowing over the center of the icecap tracing a path north towards Thule. From up here, he could peer down through every deck. He could see both wing tips a half mile on either side, the ion drives, the lab modules and the entire high bay with Raven One straddled by one of the three gantry cranes. The scale took your breath away.

Admiral Dukes climbed into a large reclining leather swivel chair at the front of the gondola. He swiveled it around to face his guests. "Welcome to my world. From here I can fly this vessel to any point on the planet. I'm linked to every satellite in orbit. Because of the one mile width of this ship, I am provided with 3-D stereoscopic projections of the outside world. I can zoom in at any place on Earth down to a six inch resolution. The sheer size of this ship also makes for some interesting stabilization problems. The weather is a constant battle. Air pressure and winds can be quite different from one end of the ship to the other. The ship relies on precise positioning using laser range positioning and laser ring gyros for navigation and stabilization. So you see, we put every piece of equipment on this ship to work."

Major Boop's jaw dropped when he looked over the admiral's console. He knew enough about glass cockpit displays to read the particulars. "It looks like we are cruising at 100,000 feet at two hundred knots according to your console, Captain."

"Very perceptive of you, Major. It is very easy to get the ship to this altitude. After all, lighter-than-air ships have been flying over 100,000 feet for over twenty-five years. In 1961, the current official altitude record was set. A Commander Ross and Lieutenant Prather of the US Navy rose to nearly 114,000 feet. The name of their balloon was Strato-Lab Five. Unfortunately, Prather drowned and died after his flight. His pressure suit filled with water when he landed in the ocean after his record breaking flight.

"Altitude is not a problem. Propulsion, on the other hand, took some rather simplistic ingenuity. I mentioned the ion drive. The whole exterior skin of the ship is a huge collection of blocks of photovoltaic cells, triodes, and optical capacitors. With millions of these cells we can propel the ship, hide the ship, and also even provide power for the ship. At over two square miles, the top surface of our ship is a huge platform to convert sunlight to electricity. We then store the electricity in the capacitors. We then fire the capacitors at a high enough frequency and pattern to ionize the air around them. The heated air becomes a plasma, thus, reducing its density. The result creates either the vertical or horizontal lift that we need to navigate and propel the ship. What could be simpler?"

Dave asked, "How did you keep the construction of this vessel and the others secret for so long."

Dukes got up out of his chair and leaned over the guard rail, "Captain, it is actually easier than you might think. The ship was built in modules, not unlike the DYE sites. I understand those weigh over five million pounds apiece. That's less than this ship weighs. All the laboratory equipment can be explained away as particle physics experimental packages, of which they in fact are. The cover behind the millions of Electro-Optical Capacitors as we call them, was created as an advertising and eye candy project for the Vegas strip to replace neon. As far as the eight suppliers are concerned they are now lighting up Glitter Gulch on Freemont Street. Little do they know that with only a minor tweak and some focusing parameters, cold plasma can be generated from their diode displays. When we combine this technological breakthrough with Cray multiprocessing giga-flop supercomputer power, we are able to reverse or retro-project colors and scenery from any point on the ship to the opposite diode on the other side of the ship. This gives the illusion that you can see right through the ship and provides us with the active electro-optical camouflage that keeps us invisible to the naked eye. The ionized diodes also absorb radar waves giving us virtual radar invisibility and stealth capability. And of course as we discussed earlier, we make our own helium. We store it in one hundred twenty bladders or what we call helium casks to create the ships buoyancy.

"By the way Anne and gentlemen, speaking of Vegas, we will be putting in at Vegas on the first of October, or at least a hundred miles north of there anyway. Captain, if you have not already suspected it that is where this beast was put together. But before we put in for some long overdue modifications, we'll be conducting more MASER, RV and DNA experiments. Now that we know where to look and can pinpoint, we may even get a chance to extract a shell or two on the way down south. Captain, I'll talk to General Ahrens, but it looks like you will be our guest for a couple of months."

Dukes picked up what looked like a TV remote and pointed it at the head-up display. He clicked a couple of buttons and a series of red laser dots covered the earth. "What you see here, team, are the locations of all the shells that we have recovered." There were over two dozen. It surprised Dave that there were some even in the ocean and even more surprising near some large metropolitan areas. "These represented some very interesting and challenging logistical problems with their recovery." He pointed to the globe again and then hit the remote. The scene changed to a bunch of flashing white spots or about fifty shells located all around the globe. "These are the shells we've located but have not recovered yet." Anne took a laser pointer and swirled it about the globe. "If you gentlemen will notice, there is a pattern to these locations." She was right, of the eighty or so lights they all fell between about sixty degrees north and south latitude. There was a perceptible staggered triangular grid to the pattern as well. However, there were some apparent holes, too.

Dukes then hit another button and a series of about twenty-five green pinpoints lit up the void areas. "We think that other shells can be found here near these locations. These fill in closely the Planetary Energy Grid system that Bruce Cathie postulated back in the fifties. This is why we need your plane, Major. To go out and find them."

Just then Lieutenant Perkins interrupted, "Excuse me, Admiral, our ETA to Thule West is twenty minutes."

"Very good, Lieutenant, start the descent, and initiate landing procedures." In a Navy response, the Air Force lieutenant responded, "Aye, aye, sir."

Major Boop and Captain Rylah looked at each other with a perplexed smile, Rylah asked, "Where is Thule West? We've flown into Thule dozens of times. There is not much west of Thule other than the Baffin Sea and ice flows."

Admiral Dukes replied, "You are wrong, Captain. Have you ever wondered what that strange island is five miles off the west coast? It is Mount Dundas. It is a geological wonder. That is our base of operations. That ancient mountain fits our needs perfectly. We took over the Inuit Village of Dundas a few years ago. That hasn't made the Air Force too popular with the Inuits or with Greenpeace for that matter. Actually, a B-52 bomber crashed just off the southern shore of Mount Dundas in 1968. It was carrying four hydrogen bombs. Two did crack open releasing low levels of radiation. The radiation is no longer a threat. However, the nuclear triggers and detonators were never recovered from the wreckage. Thus the area was cordoned off and a village of eighty-seven Inuits relocated. The ten square mile plateau on top of the mountain serves as our landing pad. We also have facilities there should we need supplies or conduct repairs. Major modifications are still done in Nevada."

Major Boop asked, "How do you keep the persons stationed at Thule from knowing this ship is sitting on an island only five miles off their coast? You must be visible from the approach path to the runway."

Dukes replied deviously, "We might be visible, but that doesn't mean we have to be recognizable. To aircraft landing at Thule we blend in with the ice and snow on top of the plateau. With the ships flat underbelly and relatively low profile we blend right in. We look like part of the geology. Actually very few people from Thule Air Base know we exist on the island, just the base commander, the ATC controller, and about a dozen other people. As far as they are concerned, we are a huge flying missile defense shield and have been in place to support the president's Star Wars program. They haven't got a clue about our extraterrestrial mission."

Dave couldn't help but to ask, "Speaking of missile defense, you popped a couple of missiles yourself at us a few hours ago. So I assume you have defensive armament on this ship somewhere."

"That is correct, Captain. We are for the most part a very large, very efficient, and might I say, very effective research vessel. However, we are a military vessel and do pack a punch if need be. As you saw we are equipped with anti-aircraft missiles. We also have four GAU-8 30 millimeter Gatling guns." Looking over to Major Boop and Captain Rylah whispering, Dukes replied, "No, Major, we do not use our sophisticated lasers and MASERS to blow things out of the sky."

Just then Lieutenant Perkins broke in, "Admiral, we have started our final approach." Dukes walked over to his command chair, sat down, and then said, "Excuse me for a few minutes; I will be busy during the docking procedures. Sergeant Jerry Svisco will escort you back to the conference room. You can watch the arrival on closed circuit TV from there. You will be more comfortable and frankly out from under foot there. I will be down in half an hour or so."

Sergeant Svisco, directed the group to the same three electric carts and gave the voice command, "Charlie, one, two and three. Proceed directly to the conference room." The cadre was whisked down the long corridors to the elevator. They drove onto the platform and were lowered to the hangar deck. They then raced across the high-bays and up the short hallway to the conference room. Suspended from the ceiling were two huge TV monitors. On one was a forward looking video feed. On the second there appeared to be an instrument display of heading, speed, and altitude with a split screen showing the outline of the ship with a strange glowing pattern surrounding it.

Captain Rylah read the display, "Looks like we are coming in from the northwest. We are only five hundred feet off the water. Mount Dundas is masking us from Thule Air Base. The airspeed indicator was showing forty-five knots. The DME or Distance Measurement Equipment was showing twelve miles. Major Boop looked over the instrument screen as well, "This ship weighs ump-teen million pounds. It will be like trying to stop an aircraft carrier."

Just then there was a perceptible change in pitch in a humming noise and a perceptible deceleration. Sergeant Svisco said, "We haven't figured out the Greys' inertial canceling mechanism yet. We are reversing the ion drive to the leading edge. If the computers are right, we'll come to a complete stop about a mile off shore. The top of the *Nautilus* will be even with the major portion of the island. We'll do a popup maneuver and then let Mother Nature's prevailing winds drift us over our mooring pad. We'll use the ion drive then for station keeping while we hover about twenty feet off the surface."

Major Boop asked, "What happens if you ever have total engine failure. What prevents this beast from drifting where ever the winds take it?"

Sergeant Svisco replied, "The ion drive is very simple and very dependable. It has been in operation for over two years since our last major O&M cycle. In the event of a propulsion emergency we ascend to 100,000 feet and let the ship drift until propulsion is restored."

Dave asked, "What if propulsion is never restored? That is a long parachute drop to the hard pan."

Svisco gave a nervous laugh. "We do have escape pods in case of fire or in case of a catastrophic event. We can egress safely. But I assure you that will never be necessary."

"Excuse my skepticism, Sergeant, but didn't Captain Smith make a similar claim on April 14, 1912." Dave was referring to the Titanic sinking.

Major Boop replied, "I believe you are correct, Captain, and I believe he was surrounded by icebergs at that time, too."

Dave responded, "I'm a firm believer in Murphy's law. If something can happen, it will."

Boop said, "I thought that was Finagle's law. If anything can go wrong, it will." The sergeant smiled and said, "Excuse me, sirs, but I think you are both incorrect. We enlisted refer to this as the Shit Happens rule! Any bad shit that seems to want to happen will happen no matter what the fuck you do about it and you'll get blamed for it!" With this the room exploded in laughter. Boop rubbed his eyes clear and said, "Leave it to the wisdom of the enlisted troops to put things in perspective."

The *Nautilus* was registering full stop. Sergeant Svisco explained the color coded symbols on the TV monitor illustrating the Ion Propulsion System status on the various surfaces. Red meant negative pressure and blue was positive pressure. Various shades in between gave the relative propulsive strength. The diagram was showing a distinctive negative pressure on the side of the windward surfaces. Just then there was a perception of lift as the *Nautilus* rose above the cliffs of the island. The colors shifted and the ship drifted in over the center of the island. Again, full stop was signaled and registered on the video screen. Just then, Admiral Dukes made the docking complete announcement via an intercom. He added, "I will be down in ten minutes. A helicopter has been dispatched from Thule, ETA five minutes. It will carry your injured men to the Thule Base hospital. The doctor says they should recover just fine. However, there is a C-141 Starlifter on the ramp should we need to medivac them to the states. They can be in Boston in a few hours."

As promised, Admiral Dukes walked through the conference room doors ten minutes later. "The injured will be brought here in a couple of minutes. The chopper pilots are one of the few Delta G personnel cleared on the base. They serve as our logistics arm. They are bringing my maintenance crew with them. They will determine if we can repair Raven One here at Thule or if we will bring her with us to Nevada."

CHAPTER 15
Plan B

The injured men were placed in a portable ICU and lowered from the high-bay to the surface below. It was secured to a sled behind a snowcat and pulled to the helipad about a quarter of a mile away. "Your crew members are in the best of care, Major Boop," Dukes said in a reassuring tone, "They will be just fine. I would like to know if you would like for Sergeant Shepard to continue as your load master when he recovers."

Boop didn't hesitate, "Of course, Admiral. He is indispensable to this crew."

"Very well, when he recovers I will have him brought back on board. We will be here for approximately five days and will put that time to good use. My maintenance crew is looking over your damaged aircraft. Let's see what they have to say. Captain Sheridan, while we are examining the aircraft I would like for you to go with Dr. Ahrens and get acquainted with our computers as well as her laboratory. Also Anne, show him our crew quarters area. I'll have Sergeant Svisco prepare the major and him a room. We'll put the rest of the crew together down here in a portable hab shelter until we can construct more rooms. Cripes, I have a hundred acre ship and only quarters for two dozen people"

A tall lanky Chief Master Sergeant Donald Eldon met the admiral halfway across the bay. "Good afternoon, sir, I'm afraid Raven One is not reparable."

Major Boop interjected, "That was a pretty quick assessment, Chief. Can't we just slap a couple of new engines on her and patch up the hole in the fuselage? I've seen some pretty beat up and shot up Hercs make a grand recovery back in 'Nam."

"No disrespect intended, Major, but she ain't shot up. Patching holes is not the problem. Even replacing the engines wouldn't be much of a problem. It took me a grand total of thirty seconds to see that the wing root is cracked. Must have been a hard landing. With a cracked root, it is just like a horse with a broken leg. I'd hate to put a bullet through her head. But the damage is beyond repair."

Admiral Dukes strode on over to the plane anyway. "I see what you mean, Chief. However, this is most distressing. We had high hopes and expectation for this unique bird."

The chief called over one of his technicians, "What do you think, Smitty? Can we cannibalize the skis and retracting mechanism? Admiral, that is the only thing unique about this bird. They're worth a few million and we all know that they aren't tooled up to make them anymore."

Sergeant Jamey Wilson crawled up into the landing gear bay and beat on a couple of struts for good measure. He shimmied back out and said, "Sure thing, Chief, they aren't too beat up. The skies are in great shape. A couple of the hydraulic actuators are bent. But those can be replaced easily. We should be able to pull these off and put them on a new bird."

Admiral Dukes smiled, "Very good, Chief. Plan B, Major. It looks like you get a brand new airplane, but we'll reuse your skis. While modifications to your new plane and the *Nautilus* are underway, we are going to prep and train you and your crew on how to use the MASER equipment and sophisticated sensors to find the shells that are missing from the grid."

Major Boop grinned and slapped his copilot Davis on the back. "Damn, I knew all that flying up and down the Ho Chi Man trail looking for trucks to shoot up would pay off some day." Boop had piloted a C-130 gun ship in Vietnam and earned his distinguished flying cross locating and destroying over 120 vehicles on the trail.

"Any questions, Major? Captain Davis?"

Boop replied, "Just two. Do our families get to come to Vegas during the training? And how do you explain away our reassignment, especially after I broke one of the squadron's precious airplanes?"

"Oh, Major, I assure you the accident investigation board will not find you at fault. As a matter of fact, you and your crew will be commended for your bravery, quick thinking, and miraculous crash landing. Too bad your aircraft was burned up in the resulting fire. We'll just drop off Raven One about six miles off the end of the skiway, minus your skis of course and give her a proper Viking funeral. Of course the DYE-3 crew will also be commended for putting together the search and rescue team to bring you safely back to the site.

As for your families, I hope they enjoy their time in Vegas. They will accept the fact that their loved one flies off into the mysterious desert north of Las Vegas. They'll know better than to ask you questions you can never answer."

CHAPTER 16
Calm Air

Anne escorted Dave to the crew quarters area of the ship. It was located forward of the high-bay. It looked like a five star hotel lobby complete with plants (although they were silk), art work, and photographs on the walls. The art and photos were impressive. However, he was more impressed with the architecture.

"Anne, this ship is a work of art. It is indeed a masterpiece. It is beautiful, yet functional. Just like her namesake from the Jules Vern novel, *Twenty Thousand Leagues Under the Sea*. Only now, we are a hundred thousand feet above Thule."

Anne replied, "You are a hopeless romantic, Captain Sheridan. You don't look like the poetic or philosophical type."

"Well, I'd have been a lot more poetic, if I could have converted leagues to feet. That conversion factor wasn't taught to us, engineers."

In her imitated southern accent, she replied, "Au contraire, my good Captain, engineers are very good philosophers and artists. For example, one only has to look at Michelangelo. I'm going to let you in on a little secret; his genius is physically the first piece of artwork now on its way to another star system. It was not coincidental that his sketch of *The Vitruvian Man* was selected to represent the human race on the plaque bolted to the Voyager space craft. This sketch was done with the holy proportion or golden ratio in minds. Don't tell anyone, though. The PC police and feminists wouldn't like the fact that we left half the human race behind. Funny, isn't it? We're pretty sure they are asexual. The concept of male and female would be totally foreign to them. Also, another tidbit of info was that we don't think they really have stereos to play the solid gold record we attached either. It is the spiral pattern of the information on its grooves that we hope they get and interpret someday."

Dave continued the flirtatious banter, "So I guess now that I know the big secret, the little ones are up for grabs."

"No, Captain, there is a good reason they call it Dreamland. Dream on, fella!"

Now that he'd been put in his place, he changed the subject back to the architecture and asked Anne about the walls, "The walls on this ship are super thin, no more than an inch thick. However, they seem to have very good sound insulation."

Anne replied, "Everything boils down to increase the volume, but decrease the weight where and when possible. The walls are made up of an epoxy-graphite fiberglass panel sandwiched between an insulation material known as Aerogel. The Aerogel has phenomenal insulation characteristics. As a matter of fact, silica-aerogels are the least dense human made material on earth, only three times denser than air. It is nicknamed solid smoke. Not only are the wall panels lightweight, they also act as fire barriers. You could literally lay a crayon on top of one of these panels and hit the underside with a blow torch for fifteen minutes and the crayon would not melt. The stuff is very expensive and very dangerous to manufacture involving spinning silica in vats of complex, volatile and toxic solvents, and formaldehydes."

Dave stated, "That's one nasty batch of cotton candy."

She smiled and said, "True, but the walls also help in my area of experimentation. They help in the detection of Cherenkov radiation which is a result of particles going superluminal or breaking the speed of light. The acoustic absorption comes in handy in my remote viewing experiments."

Dave wished he could talk to his dad about this. They used to get into some philosophical discussions when he was in college about Einstein and traveling faster than light. Dave contended that a spaceship traveling faster than the speed of light couldn't use its headlights. The beam would peel back, not unlike the shockwave of a sonic boom. It would be like a supersonic jet trying to honk its horn. You'd never hear it coming. In the case of the spaceship, you would never see it coming and get to your destination before you left. On the other hand, his dad took the relativistic approach and claimed that the speed of light was relative to the moving platform.

Dave continued through the lobby, past the recreation room, the gymnasium that included a lap pool, and into the galley.

"Let me buy you a cup of coffee, Captain."

"Sure, I'd like that. I'm a cheap date, but please call me Dave, Dr. Ahrens."

"Okay, if we're going to be informal, then call me Anne. But let's keep it formal around the crew and the admiral."

"Fair enough. It's just that I feel like I'm in some sort of resort now. I'm letting my guard down now and am very relaxed."

Anne turned and said, "That is no accident Dave, the crew area is designed to do that. Every detail of this ship was meticulously planned and thought out to combine comfort with function. Given that the crew is made up of an international group from different cultures, different skills, and beliefs, who have to work together as a well-disciplined team, the artwork, architecture and details bring the comforts of home when we are away for months at a time in this windowless environment. Unlike a submarine, we have plenty of room and we maximize its use for human habitation. So, if you really want to be relaxed, let me lead you to my web."

He wasn't quite sure what to make of that comment. He enjoyed the mutual flirtation, but wasn't sure if he was just propositioned. He had to come up with a response, but not be too forward. "My, what a sticky web we weave. You're not like one of those black widow spiders, are you?"

"You don't know the half of it, Dave. I'm not going to screw you, then kill you; if that's what you are afraid of. I was talking about showing you my RV lab, not my room, dummy."

Dave continued the flirtation, "You realize you are talking to a SAC trained killer, don't you?"

Anne poured him a cup of coffee and then zapped him with a zinger, "I suppose we can proceed with our date, just as long as you don't come across as a lady killer." She handed him his cup.

He laughed and said, "Sure, I'd like to see your web. But to a SAC trained killer, RV means re-entry vehicle, or a politically correct term for nuclear warhead. I assume you are talking about remote viewing. I've heard the term a few times but am not sure what that involves."

Anne replied, "Well, let me enlighten you."

Dave laughed and said, "You've already done that, several times today."

"Well, seeing is believing. I am about to give you some hands on training." Dave was a gentleman and let that innuendo pass by without jumping on it.

He followed Anne up a flight of stairs, as he was thinking, "Damn, that jumpsuit had to be tailored." Every curve was accentuated just right as she bounded up the stairs.

They walked down a long hall for about a hundred yards where she put her hand on another biometric reader and as the door slid back, they entered her web. The lab was huge, three stories high. A Plexiglas covered catwalk traversed across the lab at mid-level. There were a half dozen modular units suspended from geodesic domes on both sides of the walkway. They were connected to a literal web of cables, and conduits patched into instrument racks and computer monitors below the catwalks. In the back of the lab were a series of cylindrical padded columns about ten feet in diameter. The base of the columns looked like they were surrounded by some sort of bench seating. The columns were cut away on one third of their circumference to expose a hollow core packed with servers and memory cards. Dave then read a name plate on one of the towers and then recognized them as Cray supercomputers.

Anne pointed at the Cray towers and said, "These are my babies. There is enough computing power to model the gravitational interaction of a million body system in near real time. These chambers are sensory deprivation chambers. They are completely suspended and isolated from vibration, motion, noise, heat, and light. Here is where our date gets interesting, Dave."

"How's that, Anne?"

Anne responded with a wink, "I'm going to play doctor now and ask you to get naked and climb into my bed chamber."

Dave leaned up against a wall spread eagle and said, "I donate my naked body to the service of science and humankind. Take me to your chamber."

Anne said, "Okay, but first the enlightenment portion and then an explanation of the experiment."

Dave said, "I get it. This is where you want to cuddle and talk first. I guess you can call this lecture mental foreplay. Why do I get the feeling that my mind is the only thing going to get screwed with today?"

Anne said, "Yes, but what I'm about to do is going to blow your mind." Again Dave was an officer and gentleman, by Act of Congress no less, and let that innuendo pass, too.

Anne said, "Have a seat, I want to explain the RV technique to you. Remote viewing is a type of ESP. However, you don't have to be a psychic to be able to learn and use it. You can tap into incredible mental powers that you don't even know you have. This isn't magic. It is pure science and a way of tapping into the universal mind, transcending time and space, and bringing the unconscious into the conscious."

Dave said with a nervous laugh, "You sound like Rod Serling and this is the Twilight Zone."

Anne put her hand on his knee and gave it a pat. "I assure you, no Hollywood script writer has even come close to what you are about to experience." She squeezed his knee and said, "Does that peak your interest?"

He replied, "You've got my juices flowing."

Anne smiled and said, "Down boy, keep the testosterone and hormones in check. I'll take care of the adrenaline later when I stimulate your pineal gland."

Dave let the first innuendo slide but couldn't let this one pass. "Are you getting kinky on me, Doctor?"

Anne gave a wink and replied, "In a way I am. The pineal is a kinked spiral-shaped gland in the center of your brain. It is called the third eye chakra in yoga. It was believed by some to be a dormant organ like your appendix. However, we now know it to be a T-wave receptor that can be awakened to enable telepathic communication and astral travel or remote viewing."

Anne continued with the pre-brief, "Remote viewing is a psychic ability to perceive places, persons and actions that are not within the range of the senses. A remote viewer, can perceive a target in the past or future that is located in the next room, across the country, around the world or, theoretically, across the universe. With remote viewing, time and space are meaningless. Because it uses specific techniques, remote viewing can be learned by virtually anyone."

Dave pouted and said, "And just when I was feeling special, you had to bust my bubble."

Anne said, "Au contraire, you are very special. You are new to the program and thus, your mind has not been cluttered with a lot of what ifs and speculation. You are a ripe, neutral subject. Sort of a RV virgin, I guess you would say."

He smiled and said, "Should I wear a white gown and be sacrificed to the RV gods?"

Anne said, "If you don't stop, I'll sacrifice you to the RV gods all right. I'll have you dropped in front of a speeding Winnebago from 100,000 feet."

Anne continued, "Remote viewing is not an out-of-body experience. You will not astrally project to the target, although some remote viewers occasionally report a feeling of bilocating to the site of the target. You will not be medicated. You will be fully awake and alert. You will not be digging deep into your mind. You will relax and let the deeper parts of your mind bubble up."

Dave grinned and said, "Damn, I knew I shouldn't have eaten those beans."

Anne let that one slide, "We are experimenting to try and figure out how remote viewing works. One theory is that remote viewers are able to tap into the Universal Mind which is a kind of comprehensive storehouse of information about everything, where time and space are meaningless. The remote viewer can enter a hyperconscious state in which he or she can tune in to specific targets within the universal consciousness of which all people and all things are a part. It is sort of like the superfluid state of helium that Dr. Timken explained. Truly mind over matter."

"It sounds like I'll have a religious experience or vision."

Anne replied, "I guess that is one way of looking at it. You will be in a virtual reality."

Dave switched to serious mode, "What do you want me to do? What is the protocol and what am I going to be looking for?"

Anne swiveled in her chair, "I'll show you." She turned on a computer terminal and began banging away at a keypad. A 3-D cutaway animation of the chamber was shown. It showed a human figure spread eagle naked lying on his back. Anne walked him through the process and protocol for entering the chamber and hooking up the feedback circuitry.

"We use these chambers for many things. We tried to RV the location of the shells. However, we've had no success. We think since the shells represent Zero-Point Energy sources, they are already in effect everywhere and, thus, nowhere.

"We also use the chambers to RV where the shells come from. We've had some interesting results here that I cannot discuss with you now. You'll see what you see and record what you see.

"We also want to see if we can use these chambers to com-municate with the Greys. Again we've had limited success in this area. Much, much data has been acquired. It's just very difficult to interpret. We haven't yet found the Rosetta stone.

"What we are going to do now is this. You're going to get undressed, lie on your back in a shallow pool of saline solution adjusted to your body temperature. Your ears will be plugged so you can't even hear your own heartbeat. The salinity of the water will allow you to float with your face above water so you can breathe comfortably. The pool is only eight inches deep so you can't sink and drown. You will wear these special goggles that will project a virtual reality 3-D projection of soothing scenery. This does two things. It relaxes you and it keeps you from freak-ing out from extreme claustrophobia. After about fifteen minutes, when you are relaxed, the goggles will fade to a black board of sorts. You can use it to draw your thoughts by using the retina of your eye to trace objects and what you view. I'll have you hooked up to an EEG so we can overlap brain wave patterns to what is viewed. You will not talk. However, you can quit any time by verbal command. I'll be monitoring you visually via closed cir-cuit TV."

Dave grinned and said, "From the neck up, I assume?"

"You don't come across as the shy type, Dave. But yes, I'll respect your modesty and privacy. You are naked because we want total sensory neutralization, nothing clinging or touching your skin. The EEG leads and goggles are the only exception. Besides some of the remote viewing experiences can be quite, what's a good word, erotic, I guess. Therefore, we don't want any constraining clothing, do we?"

Dave emerged from a changing room in nothing, but a towel. Anne sat him down and connected the electrical leads to his bare skin and scalp. She opened the door to the RV chamber and helped him in. She closed the door, instructed him to lay the towel on a shelf beside the door, and then lay down in the pool.

Before Dave stepped into the pool, he asked, "I'm not going to get myself fried, am I? I've always been taught that a Jacuzzi and electrical wiring do not mix." Anne smiled cutely and said, "I ain't fried no one's brains yet. Don't worry they are very low voltage leads. Please enter the pool and sit down, but don't lean back yet."

When he did step into the pool, he barely felt the water as it was perfectly matched to his body temperature. He sat down as instructed. Anne said, "Now grab the virtual reality goggles suspended in front of you and put them on like a swimmers mask." Again, he complied.

Anne continued, "Now I want you to put the earpiece in each ear. After you have the earpieces in simply lean back and allow your body to relax and float on your back."

He leaned back and was amazed how buoyant he became with his face, chest, manhood, and knees floating slightly above the water. It was very relaxing.

Anne now spoke into her mike and said, "I'm going to turn on the mask. You should see some relaxing images in a minute or two. I'm cranking in some random white noise now, so this will be our last communication until you ask to quit or I terminate the procedure. Remember, use your retina to sketch what you see on the screen in front of you. The software will track your eye and record the sketch. There is an alphanumeric keypad on the bottom of the screen. Blink three times on a letter or number to write text. Are you set, comfortable, and ready to go?

Dave replied, "I'm ready. Anything in particular you want me to target?" Anne replied, "See if you can find where these shells come from, coordinates, directions, and how we can communicate with the Greys."

He relaxed and enjoyed the moment. After a few minutes of a serene beach scene with gentle waves lapping at his feet, he soon began sketching with the retina motion recorder. There were no clear images. No visions of alien beings, flying saucers, or unimaginable technology. He sketched what came into his head which were two strange beings with an x behind them. Dave was no artist, but these figures were bizarre and had a childish look, like stick figures. It included spirals, a Moon-Earth diagram and some strange time line.

Dave soon heard Anne's sweet voice. "I'm shutting down the procedure. I think we have what we need."

He asked, "You mean you can make heads or tails out of all that gibberish?"

Anne replied, "Sure, with the help of fifty million dollars in Cray supercomputing power and a few hundred dollars per hour psychologists. These drawings are treated more like Rorschach sketches than Polaroids. You will be interviewed by the shrinks soon to see what you think they represent."

Anne said, "Let's get you out of there, showered off, and then I'll buy you lunch."

Dave couldn't resist, "First time I've gotten naked before a date."

While Dave was immersed in Anne's experimentation, Raven One was dropped off fifty miles west of DYE-3 and torched, minus its skis, of course. The crew was saved by the DYE-3 rescue team, who had become the heroes of the day. The accident investigation board ruled the crash was due to fatigue failure of the number one prop and that the crew was lucky to be alive except for some extraordinary flying skills. The plane was a total write-off and no one even tried to reach it to salvage anything since the drifts were too large and dangerous to land another C-130 there.

CHAPTER 17
Cruise of a Lifetime

As expected, General Ahrens approved Dave's temporary duty assignment spending the next three months as part of the crew of the DGA Nautilus. As far as the rest of the world was concerned, he was busy bouncing around the Arctic at various sites preparing for the shuttle launches. All communications to him would be routed through the ship.

On the fourth of July in 1985, the DGA Nautilus departed Thule West. This cruise, as it was called, would take several months and take advantage of the time to conduct some MASER, gravimetric and electromagnetic experiments. And, of course, there were two shells plotted along the way for extraction.

Dave took the opportunity to absorb everything he could. He learned many of the ship's systems and helped with several of the MASER, DNA, and RV experiments. Anne and he had grown very close during those months, but kept it on a friendship basis. Fraternization or having a relationship with fellow crew members was frowned upon, not that it did not happen.

The DGA Nautilus was making good time as it cruised at a 100,000 feet over the extreme northwest corner of Baffin Island near the Arctic Bay. It had flown through a hole in the North Warning radar net that Cheyenne Mountain had made for them. Dave was busy in the MASER lab helping Dr. Rapp pull some fiber optic cable out of the Greenland shell.

"My good Captain, I'm going to put a beam splitter on the end of the cable to get it in the shell as far as possible. I want the MASER to be split into two beams 67.5 degrees apart. If we can cram it in as far as she can go, we can get away from some of these edge effects that distort the reflection back. We are going to aim the MASER reflection back over to the beryllium-coated mirror in the corner over there and then shoot it through the roof hatch over here to these lunar coordinates."

Dave looked over the lunar photo Rapp had handed him. At the bottom it was titled, Reiner Gamma, centered at the -59.11° longitude, +7.41° latitude. The photograph was of a lunar crater that showed some strange swirls of dust around it.

Dave said, "This is an interesting crater. I thought all eject-ed matter on the Moon fanned out in a straight line pattern. The Moon has no atmosphere or magnetic field to affect ballistic tra-jectories. This has an interesting swirl pattern."

Rapp replied, "You are absolutely correct. It is one of three craters on the Moon with these features. The other two are on the far side of the Moon. We are 99.9 percent sure there is a shell there. The swirl pattern is a telltale sign that there was a torsional wave generated there. Sort of like lunar crop circles."

"Damn it." Dave yelled, "I knew I should have signed up for that lunar landscaping course back in college."

Rapp said, "Never know when those liberal arts classes pay off. I got an A- in Medieval Plumbing 101 and it has paid divi-dends." Dave wasn't sure if Rapp knew he was joking or if he was pulling his leg now.

"Now, Captain, you have a chance to get your name put in the history books. Well, at least some obscure technical manual anyway. We're sitting over a special place on Earth where the magnetic flux is stable and predictable. It is fairly quiet on the radio frequency spectrum, too. Also, we are low enough on the horizon to see the Moon clearly without too much atmospheric interference for the MASER.

"We are going to bounce this MASER beam down the gullet of this shell. It is going to split, demodulate, then reflect back, and become correctly tuned to the shell frequency. We'll aim it at those coordinates and if there is a shell up there, we should see a detectable blue flash or shift in the reflection back. Simple Dop-pler physics. To put it in plain terms, we're building a big-assed MASER beam shell detector. The only thing is that we can't point this MASER towards the ground. To overcome the magnetic field effects, that much power would fry everyone's gonads for a square mile. So, what better target than one that is a quarter of a million miles away on the Moon?

"This experiment will help us build the portable detector for the C-130. We can shrink the size of the MASER once determining the proper tuning frequency. This will allow us to lighten things up with relatively low power to detect the return. Right now it is kind of like us lighting up the whole woods with a million candle power search light looking for the reflection off a coyote's eyes. If we knew the reflective properties of a coyote's eyes, we could use a low power infrared camera to detect them. Does that make sense?"

Dave replied, "Simple as one plus one equals two." Rapp replied sarcastically, "I hope not. I can prove with a certainty that one plus one equals zero."

Rapp walked over to the chalkboard and wrote down the following proof:

$$Proof\ that\ 1+1=0$$
$$Where\ a = 1 and\ b = 1$$
$$then\ a = b\ and\ a^2 = b^2$$
$$and\ also\ a^2-b^2 = 0$$
$$a^2-b^2=(a-b)(a+b)$$
$$(a-b)(a+b) = 0$$

Then dividing both sides of the equation by (a-b) leads to the following:

$$(a-b)(a+b)/(a-b) = 0/(a-b)$$
$$1(a+b) = 0$$
$$(a+b) = 0$$
$$1+1 = 0$$

Dave said, "I see what you mean, clear as mud. I can't fault your mathematics or logic, but clearly there is a trick." Rapp replied slyly, "No trick, Captain. The algebra is foolproof. I'll let you sleep on this one. Go get a good night's rest." Dave walked out of the lab murmuring under his breath, "Damn, more homework."

While tossing and turning in bed, he had a lot on his mind. As he drifted off, he suddenly awakened and sat straight up. He had another Eureka moment and jotted a note to himself on the night stand. It simply read, "The trick is that division by zero is not allowed in mathematics. It results in infinity, something from nothing, the whole basis of ZPE." He'd redeem himself with Rapp in the morning.

The next week was hectic preparing for the MASER Moon Shot, as it was known. The more technical term was MASER Experiment to Detect and Analyze Lunar Shells, or MEDALS. This was a multibillion dollar test that had a lot of visibility in the Delta G Program. As much as they hated to deal with the bureaucracy, even NASA was involved. Several classified payloads aboard the orbiting space shuttle were, in fact, space borne gravimetric and T-wave detection satellites.

The Nautilus was in position. The roof doors were cranked back. From the pressurized control cab, Dave could look up through the roof and see a huge beautiful full Moon.

Virtually every lab on the ship had a stake in this test.

Anne and three of her colleagues were lying in the chambers awaiting the countdown. They had their RV protocols set on three different targets. First, did the MASER hit anything, if so, exactly where on the lunar surface? Second, what would be the effects of the MASER return on the Greenland shell? Third, once the residual T-wave was lit up by the MASER, trace the path back to the original source.

The ZPE lab was going to measure the energy output of a reflected MASER beam once it passed through a T-wave to test their theory that more energy would be produced than expended. They also had a ZPE chamber on the shuttle, which will prove the energy spike will occur simultaneously with the MASER release, not the 2.5 second delay to the moon and back. Thus, proving that ZPE and T-waves were instantaneous across the vast distances of space.

The DNA lab also had samples in lunar orbit to detect effects on genetics from a T-wave interaction.

Rapp was on the Delta G SATCOM frequency running through

the last few minutes of the countdown. "T-minus one minute and all is GO. All systems and monitoring stations are reporting green lights. MASER is powering up. Sequencing is on auto fire.

"T-minus 10 seconds, all is GO. MASER cooling holding steady. Slight He3 leak, within tolerances. Still GO. Five.... four....three.....two.....one......MASER fired."

Dave was kind of disappointed. There was no blinding flash of light. There were no phaser or photon torpedo sounds. There was no sound at all. As a matter of fact, Dave had to watch the monitors to see if the power had peaked and the capacitors drained. By this time, the MASER had hit the lunar surface and reflected back. But MASER energy is not in the visible light spectrum. The computer and sensors would have to do the detecting and number crunching now. It would take weeks before anything substantive was determined.

After the MASER shot, the Nautilus simply closed its roof doors and moved onto its next mission and location. It was a six hour flight and a thousand miles to the southeast. The suspected shell was located on the eastern shore of Hudson Bay near the coordinates 56° 12' 17" N by 74° 29' 27" W in the center of Lac a L' Eau Clair, a lake created by meteor impact. The lake showed abnormally high concentration of He and He3. From satellite views, the lake appeared much clearer and warmer than the other lakes in the vicinity. Plus, it fell almost exactly on the global projection map.

They hoped that the shell could be easily found and extracted with relative ease. The lake was only twenty feet deep at this location just off an island in its center and easily diveable. Three of the crew members were former Special Ops Navy Seals and were getting suited up. This part of Quebec, Canada is covered

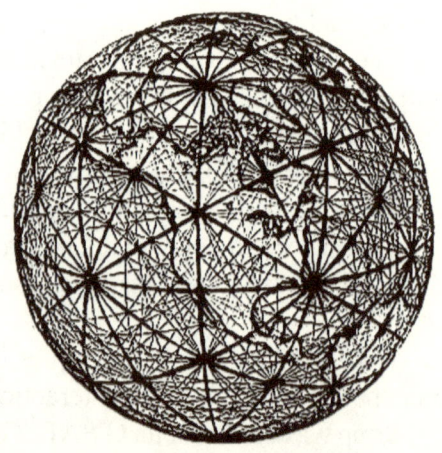

with thousands of small lakes less than a mile in length. The only problem would be if they ran across a hunting party or a mining survey team. However, a check of hunting permits and flight plans showed the area to be clear of anyone within a hundred miles. The ship descended to less than a thousand feet over the lake. There was so much helium in the air that the ship was having a hard time maintaining a constant altitude. It was similar to the thin air phenomena in Greenland. So the Nautilus backed off a mile and sent the extraction crew down the cablevator. The dive team would have to hike the mile over to the lake. They were told to wear their breathing gear within two hundred yards of the lake.

As it turns out, this was a fairly easy extraction. The dive team located the shell sitting on its side towards the northwest end of the lake. Speculation was that this part of Canada was under the edge of the retreating glaciers of the last ice age only 7,000 years ago. The shell simply dropped out of the ice and into the crater as it retreated. The site was carefully documented and samples from under the shell were excavated for carbon dating. This shell did have some dents and dings indicating that it had fallen out of the ice face.

The team lowered the extraction cage and lifted it into the ship with very little effort. It was discussed whether they should extract it in a tank of water to preserve the helium-3 generation process. But from previous experience, the process was known to be self-initiating and sustaining when exposed to water. It could be pulled and dried with no adverse effect. The whole process was done in less than a day.

However, the analysis on the shell took months. This was where Dave earned his keep. He was actually a pretty bright engineer, constantly thinking outside the box. He had the idea to try the shell in different types of water: deuterium, distilled water, mineral waters. The results were the same. The shell didn't differentiate on the type of water. All it was interested in was fusing the hydrogen atoms into helium-3 in a cold fusion process. The helium came out, but the energy did not. Also, he discovered that no matter what temperature the water was placed in the shell, the gas bubbled out at a constant 34° F.

Several samples of the shell were taken from the exterior and ran through various spectral analyzers, chemical tests, and electron microscopy analysis. What was weird was that the ages of the shells appeared to be nearly constant. Even though they were inorganic objects and could not be carbon dated, the chemical consistency between shells was exact. The Greenland shell was supposedly on Earth for only a few days, while the one they just recovered was on Earth at least 7,000 years. A shell found buried in a lava tube on Easter Island was there for at least 100,000 years. They all had exactly the same chemical consistency including trace amounts. The shells consisted of 55 percent cobalt, 34 percent nickel, 5 percent carbon, 3 percent tungsten, 2 percent beryllium, 1 percent iron, 1 percent yttrium, a Fibonacci sequence in its own right.

It had been suspected that under the right conditions carbon could become magnetized through photon beam bombardment. This led to the discovery that the carbon was actually ferromagnetic carbon fibers that were hollow, tube shaped and aligned towards the center of the shell. This was proof that it could be done. Again the weird thing about the magnetism was that all shells had exactly the same Gaussian field strength.

During his stay on the Nautilus, the ship would station itself above the Hudson Bay. It would rendezvous from time to time with a ship or submarine for supplies, personnel, and or laboratory equipment. Captain Dukes told him that the Hudson Bay location was strategic for logistical reasons. It was less than fifteen hundred miles from the center of population in the US yet had very little air traffic. It was the perfect place to operate. As a matter of fact, Delta G was thinking of moving the Nautilus Base operations from Thule West to an island in the northern part of the bay. Most of the work on the icecap was now completed. The next phase involved extraction within the grid zone further south. The Hudson Bay site would also be more accessible to the lunar MASER window.

The shells were consistent in materials; however, they had some totally different functions dependent upon their size. The smaller shells appeared to deal more with forces such as electrical, nuclear, torsional, and gravimetric, while the midrange shells were matter conversion shells. The large shells were mostly affecting biological, thought and temporal aspects.

In another flash of brilliance, Dave plotted the sizes of the known shells with their location and estimated arrival time based upon geological surroundings. After the last extraction, he even had the Cray plot potential drop points based upon glacial movement from the last three ice ages. Some interesting locations were plotted, including one in his home state of Ohio.

Finally, after about four months, the Nautilus returned back to Thule West. It was due for some routine maintenance. Dave caught a C-141 back down to Sondrestrom to await his orders back to the US.

After a week at Sondrestrom, the call from the Delta G Program Office finally arrived. Orders were on their way. Pack your bags, turn in your mukluks and parka, and grab the next available C-141 south to civilization. Your duty assignment will be at the Nevada Test Site.

One custom that is undertaken prior to departure from any military installation is the hail and farewell. Dave's was held at the Suicide Lounge in Sonde, so called because of the six months of dreary, depressing, sunless winter months that everyone endured up there. The place was built to drown your sorrows and expose your soul. Everyone that departed Sondrestrom wrote their name on the bar room wall along with a paragraph or two of wisdom and wit. The lounge made for some interesting reading. There had to be at least a PhD involved for someone to come in and document and analyze the decades of thoughts on arctic philosophy. The wall hadn't been painted over since 1944. Now that he was going to leave his mark above the Arctic Circle (not counting several streaks of yellow snow from time to time) he had to think of something witty and apropos. He took the felt tip pin and simply wrote, "Gravity is a figment of your imagination. Or, does this place just suck? DJS 11-18-85." This kind of summed up his experience. He put an extra tight curl on the question mark. He had wondered if the date had any significance.

This writing ritual was performed early in the festivities because after that another ritual took place. The bartender mixed a concoction called a Thule Blue Nose. The actual mixture of this particular cocktail is a closely guarded secret passed down from bartender to bartender over the past sixty years. Rumor has it that it contained fourteen shots of various kinds of liquor. The top layer was bluish flaming slush. The idea was to blow out the flame, tilt it back and chug it down. The last layer would always stick to your nose, thus Thule Blue Nose.

Sitting on top of the world's largest ice cube for over a year builds some very tight friendships. He only wished Anne was here to enjoy the moment. His only solace was that he knew that they would see each other in Nevada.

After the Blue Nose, your friends literally pick you up and pour you into the cargo plane. The loadmaster straps you in and you are whisked away. All of a sudden you wake up in the Visiting Officers Quarters at McGuire AFB in New Jersey about eight hours later.

Dave had only been sick drunk two times in his life: once after his sister's wedding reception and the other after a keg party in college. Each time he said never again.

The next morning, he caught a commercial flight back to Ohio to visit his family before heading off to Las Vegas. He had over a month's leave saved up from his remote tour. Dave and his family were very close. He couldn't wait until the day when he could actually sit down with his dad and tell him all the strange and neat things he did in the Air Force. His dad thought he was nuts, at first, to spend four years of college getting his engineering degree and then pass up several job offers only to join the Air Force. But he didn't want to settle down with some nine-to-five job. He wanted to see the world. He wanted to work with the cutting edge technology, aircraft, and missiles. There were not too many opportunities to do this in northwest Ohio. His dad eventually came around.

It was Thanksgiving, 1985. As he pulled up to the little green house on Charles Street, he took a few minutes to reflect on his childhood He was one of six siblings, the oldest of five boys.

His older sister had to put up with a lot, and with only one bathroom. His parents were married very young. They had six kids before they turned thirty. His dad worked every day of his life at various machine shops and factories in town for the last forty-five years. They lived paycheck to paycheck for years. Dave's mother is very loving, caring and giving. So is his father, patient and wise, too. His dad retired a few years back as a time study engineer. He was a self-made and self-taught man and very proud of his kids. He gave them all a lesson in self worth and gave them the work ethic and integrity that they all shared. When Dave's parents moved into the neighborhood thirty-eight years ago with five kids, and one on the way, the elderly neighbors surrounding them were a little nervous and probably thought, "Oh no!" All the racket from tricycles, bicycles, cap guns, fireworks and BB guns, along with the constant hammering and shouting from the tree house must have driven them absolutely nuts; not to mention the occasional broken windows from baseballs and snowball fights. These neighbors eventually grew to accept them (or at least tolerate them). Over the years more families moved in with other kids. Dave's mom was a big kid herself. The neighborhood kids ended up growing up in her yard and living room. She wasn't afraid of a messy house. The yard never had any grass growing in it. But the kids had fun, were safe, and all the parents knew where they were. They were also very kind and caring with the elderly neighbors in the neighborhood. They looked in on them, ran errands, and the kids shoveled the walks and raked the leaves. It was a good synergism.

Dave had a very relaxing month and Christmas at home. He was a new uncle and had gotten the chance to meet his new niece. He even got in some rabbit hunting with his old high school buddies and baby brother, Scott, before he had to catch a plane out to Vegas.

CHAPTER 18
NTS

It was the third of January, 1986. The Boeing 737s at the Janis Air Terminal, McCarran International Airport in Las Vegas looked normal enough. They did, however, lack any lettering or type of identification marks on their sterile red and white fuselage.

Fresh from his leave back in Ohio, Captain Dave Sheridan presented his written orders to the guard at the security desk. His orders told him to report in civilian casual attire, jeans and tab shirt. An escort led him into the security office where he was fingerprinted, photographed, and then given several security documents to sign. He was then briefed on the dos and don'ts of his next adventure. The briefing was ominous. The nondisclosure document he signed was four pages of lawyerese that boiled down to one thing; you will go to jail for a long, long time if you disclose any classified information.

After his badge was printed, he was escorted back out into the lounge area and waited with the hundreds of other passengers for their weekly flight to Dreamland. Dreamland was only eighty miles north of Las Vegas as the crow flies. However, it was three tall and rugged mountain ranges away.

The hundred or so passengers looked like any other group at any other passenger terminal. You had professional looking men and women as well as the beefier, hardened, callused types. The only things missing were the crying babies and pain-in-the-ass teenagers.

As he climbed the stairway to the 737, he noticed that there was no handheld luggage. There were not even any overhead bins on the plane. You were only allowed one carryon which was thoroughly searched. The window shades were all down. However, the seating was business class all the way, plenty of leg room. The flight was only thirty-five minutes, so no drinks or peanuts were served. Reading material was provided in the seat pockets.

He never did like to fly blind and always liked looking out the window to keep his bearings. He didn't like the thought of flying inside an aluminum beer can without visual reference. Dave flashed back to his first chopper ride ten years ago out to the missile field when he got his first taste of vertigo. The plane's engines started up and it rolled down the taxiway and onto the runway. There were no cute stewardesses to flirt with while telling you how to buckle your seat belt. They kind of figured if you were smart enough to board this plane then you surely know by now how to buckle a seat belt. They weren't too concerned with lawyer-speak on how to even evacuate the damn thing in an emergency. Who were you going to sue? The plane, after all, did not exist.

Once the engines started they were given priority clearance for takeoff. There was not a lot of time for chitchat from the cockpit. As a matter of fact, there was no announcement at all over the PA. The plane accelerated quickly down the bumpy runway. It rotated, sucked up its gear quickly, climbed out, and banked sharply to the right. The guy in the driver's seat was obviously a frustrated fighter jock wannabe. They were actually pulling some Gs.

The flight was uneventful, although a little bumpy. It was the mountain waves pushing turbulence up and over the 14,000 foot Mount Charleston to the west. There wasn't much small talk on the plane. The magazines that were provided included: *Time*, *Newsweek*, as well as the nerdy ones such as *Scientific American*, and *Popular Mechanics*. There were no rules against talking to anyone on the plane. Dave figured it was just etiquette not to bug each other.

About a half hour into the flight, the 737 made a steep descending turn to the left. Dave's stomach was still a few miles back. The gear came down and locked. The actuators for the flaps made their familiar whirring sound as he felt the plane slow down and nose pitch up a little. The plane bounced a little on landing. Dave was sure the pilot would owe the crew a round of drinks for that one. As the plane rolled out, no thrust reversers were used; they must have had plenty of runway. The plane veered off to the left on a high speed exit and taxiway. It continued to taxi for a minute or two, then it stopped and the engines were shut down. After a few more minutes the plane was towed forward a couple hundred yards and came to another full stop.

A couple of minutes later the cabin door opened. Everyone on the plane got up and headed to the front of the plane. Dave was a little hesitant. He had not been told what to do, where to go, or who to meet after the plane landed. He was simply told he would be processed at the other end. When he stepped through the cabin door, he was surprised to see that the plane was parked completely inside a huge hangar. Everyone was walking towards what appeared to be an entry control point. At the bottom of the stairs, he was met by a woman that simply said. "Good Morning, Captain, I'm here to escort you to the briefing room." He was a little surprised, but didn't ask the obvious question of how he was picked out of a crowd of over a hundred passengers. He figured either she was good at memorizing his photo or they had another system for picking out the newbies. She continued, "All you military types look alike to me, it's the color of your badge." He looked at the badge hung around his neck and sure enough there was a bright orange border around it with the letters *Escort Required*, so much for his ego. Well, he wasn't going to let her get away with the military slam and he replied, "It's nice to see the Government has a first rate escort service here, after all, this is Nevada." Paybacks are hell. She looked at him coldly and simply replied, "Touché, Captain, please follow me."

The woman accompanied him through the entry control point and signed him in. She then led him through a double set of doors and into a hallway on the backside of the hangar. She did a sashay as she strode down the hall. Dave had been out on the ice too long and appreciated the curves on this specimen. She stopped at another set of doors and punched in a four digit code on a cipher lock and opened the door. She said, "Pick a seat. I'll be back in an hour to escort you to your new digs." The room had a huge

U-shaped conference table with about twenty chairs. The outside wall was surrounded with chairs as well. There were a couple dozen people present. No one was sitting at the table. Someone came in a few seconds later and said, "Don't be shy, ladies and gentlemen, come on up around the table." This caused a shuffle. Dave dove for a seat at the end and settled in. The individual dropped a folder in front of each person. They were sealed with a red ribbon. The folder had a strange emblem that showed a spiral with a lightning bolt. The Latin words, *Eadem Mutata Resugo,* were on the lower part of the shield.

At the top and bottom in big red letters were the words: TOP SECRET. The individual again said in a stern voice, "Do not touch these folders until directed." Everyone put their hands in their laps instinctively like sixth graders getting ready for a math test.

Dave looked at his watch. It was 0850 hours. He figured the briefing he was about to hear was scheduled for nine. He thought to himself, ten minutes to kill. There was a coffee pot and some doughnuts along the back wall. Well, about time to show some initiative. He walked back, grabbed a mug and a danish, and proceeded back to the table with his caffeine fix. Besides, he had always heeded his grandfather's advice for a soldier to eat when you can, sleep when you can, crap when you can, and screw when you can. Well, batting .250 this early in the morning wasn't too awful bad he thought.

A few more people got up and poured themselves a cup. Then some repartee and handshaking started. He noticed that the room was split evenly, half guys, half women. Everyone was dressed casual, no ties. The women all had slacks or jeans on, obviously following their incognito orders. There was a mix of looks and age groups. Some were plain Janes, and some looked on the nerdy side. Most of the guys were older and had pot bellies. Dave was the youngest guy in the room. All the gals were staring at him as if he was the main dish.

Just then the door opened and a major entered the room. He said, "Ladies and gentlemen, please be seated. We will be starting in a few minutes." Everyone reclaimed their chairs and kept their hands off the table.

The room was called to attention as Lieutenant General Larry Powell entered the room. "As you were. Good morning everyone, please have a seat. Dr. Timken, please proceed."

Dr. Timken was your stereotypical tall lanky professor. He spoke with a slight Eastern European accent. For someone who had a PhD in quantum physics, he was having trouble turning on the laser pointer and getting the overhead projector to fire up. Dave did notice that at least his shoes were tied and his socks matched. He wasn't a complete nerd.

The screen in the front of the room lit up. The screen read:

TOP SECRET-CODE NAME-DELTA G

DELTA G TORSIONAL WAVE GENERATION PROGRAM

NOFORN

AUTHORIZATION-EO 12333 IN EFFECT

"Ladies and gentlemen, you all have been chosen by name to be here. Welcome to Dreamland. There are three groups of people in this room. The first think they have an idea why they are here. The second have no clue why they are here. The third think they know what we do here. All of you are here because in the course of your career, so far, you've run across or have been exposed to situations that have brought you in contact with advanced technology, advanced theory and concepts, or anomalies in known physics. You all have a piece of the puzzle. However, several pieces are still missing. Your job is not only to find them, but also to make them, if necessary. You are all either in the military, or government scientists and engineers. You've only had a few minutes to get acquainted. However, I assure you that you will all get to know each other very well."

Timken proceeded to give the group some background on the Delta G Program, "As you are all well aware, the Trinity Site in Southern New Mexico is where the first atomic bomb was tested at 5:29:45 a.m. on July 16, 1945. This was a small nineteen kiloton explosion. This event was about to change the world in more ways than one. Nobody really knew what would happen when you set off an atom bomb. There was even speculation from some scientists that it could crack the crust all the way down to the mantle releasing a torrent of lava. Some argued it could ignite all the oxygen in the atmosphere and scorch the entire planet. Little did they know at that time, that a more subtle event took place that would change life on Earth forever. Not only did this event lead to a quick end to the war in the Pacific, but also ushered the world into the atomic age and literally rang the extraterrestrial doorbell."

This statement got everyone's attention. The room was very quiet as Timken let his statement sink in.

He continued with his briefing, "The instantaneous release of energy associated with a nuclear blast is found in only one other place in the universe, in the core of a star. Using an atom bomb to detonate a fusion bomb or H-bomb reproduces what happens inside the sun on a much smaller scale."

The presentation on the wall showed a video clip of series of nuclear detonations: air burst, ground bursts, and even underwater bursts.

Timken continued on, "What did you see in all of these detonations that were common?" This was a rhetorical question and he didn't expect a response. Captain Sheridan spoke up, "All of these explosions released enormous amounts of heat and pressure that densified the surrounding air, water, and soil. In a single millisecond hundreds of square miles of earth, billions of cubic feet of air, and billions of gallons of water were compressed and densified."

Timken looked a little surprised and so did General Powell.

He replied, "Very good, Captain, but to what end do we capitalize on that phenomena?"

Without expecting or even giving time for a reply, Timken

said, "The rapid densification of billions of tons of matter creates a lens effect that warps space and time. A gravitational wave is generated. More specifically, torsional waves are generated."

Timken passed around a strange green chunk of glass. "In case you're wondering, this is a piece of trininite. This is the glassy substance found at ground zero. It is slightly radioactive, so don't drop it in your lap." Everyone started passing it around like a hot potato. When Dave got a hold of it, he definitely felt it had some heft to it. This was no ordinary chunk of glass.

The next slide had an aerial shot of the Trinity Site with the following caption: *"The following excerpt is from Time Magazine, September 17, 1945: 'Seen from the air, the crater itself seems (looks like) a lake of green Jade shaped like a splashy star, and set in a sere disc of burnt vegetation half a mile wide. From close up the lake is a glistening encrustation of blue-green glass 2,400 feet in diameter, formed when the molten soil solidified in air.' Chemical tests have confirmed that it is nearly pure melted silica with traces of Olivine, Feldspar, and other minerals which comprise the desert sand."*

Timken asked another rhetorical question, "What are torsional fields?" This time no one spoke up. Dr. Timken continued with an egotistical tone, "These fields come in at least three types: E-fields, S-fields, and G-fields."

General Powell interjected, "So much for the cold war, ladies and gentlemen, we've been working with the Russians and Chinese for decades trying to figure this out. We are getting close. Sorry for interrupting, Doctor, please continue."

"Thank you, General. Before he passed away a few years ago, another renowned Russian astrophysicist, Dr. Nikolai A. Kozyrev, also proved beyond any doubt that torsional energy fields had to exist. As a result he became one of the most controversial figures in the history of the Russian scientific community. The implications of his work, and of all those who followed him, were almost entirely concealed by the Soviet Union. We are finally gaining access to Russia's best kept secrets. Two generations of remarkable research by thousands of PhD level specialists have emerged from Kozyrev's seed findings, which completely change our understanding of the Universe.

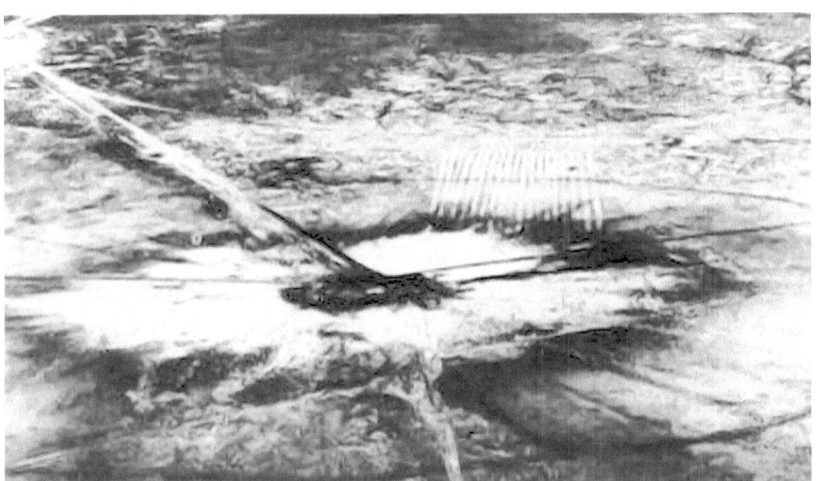

"The E, S and G stand for Electric, Spin and Gravity fields. The torsional field and its variations are types of energy fields. They are not like the standard and fairly understood Electric, Magnetic, and Gravity fields where the generators of these fields can be shielded against electromagnetic effects. The torsional fields still manifest themselves through such shielding due to their longitudinal nature. However, for some unexplained reason thin sheets of aluminum can block T-wave propagation. There might actually be something to those nuts wearing aluminum foil over their heads to block out the voices.

"Torsional fields can be generated, detected, switched on and off for communication purposes, and are a distinct type of energy field, not yet well understood and included in today's classical physics. T-waves can be generated by melting or solidifying some materials or as we just discussed rapid re-densification of large amounts of constant density material. They effect quartz crystals, effect some electronic components, and have been noted to even effect gravity.

"Speaking of quartz, did you know most quartz crystals are only between 100 to 125 million years old? They, too, have a mystical and magical history to them. All quartz crystals have a precise regular hexagonal internal arrangement of atoms, referred to as the crystal spiral. This spiral revolves either left or right, but we aren't sure why.

"The Tunguska event in Siberia in 1908 was in fact an anti-matter projectile that passed through the Earth and exited in four pieces on the opposite side of the planet in the North Atlantic and central Greenland. This was the basis of our gravity wave detection experiments at DYE-3. Not only did we prove that the universal gravitational constant was not constant, we also detected the wake left over from the eighty year old event. There is to this day a two mile wide exit crater in Greenland. We've detected trace amounts of beryllium in the crater. This is still a mystery to us. The T-wave passes about five hundred miles directly below DYE-3. The wave pattern is bent slightly to the left as it passes the polar axis by about five degrees. The resulting T-wave flux then effects gravity at a 68.5 degree couple. If you do the vector algebra, this explains the shifts in polar orbits.

"Torsional waves can travel at superluminal velocities as high as ten to the ninth power times the speed of light. That's one billion times the speed of light. That's nearly instantaneous." Timken paused to let this statement sink in, "The age of the known universe is approximately fifteen billion years old. This means that torsional waves can propagate anywhere in the universe within fifteen years. We have found that torsional fields can interact with laser beams by changing their frequency. On our agenda later this morning, famed bioinformatics engineer, Dr. Anne Aurora Ahrens will be discussing how T-waves affect biological processes."

This last statement is really what got Dave's attention. He thought to himself, "Hot damn, Anne is going to be here." He wondered if he'd get the nerve to ask her out. But before he could let his imagination get carried away and fade off into day dream and fantasy, Timken brought him back to reality.

"It appears Anatoly Akimov has happened upon the holy grail of physics. That being that torsional fields coupled with the standard electric, magnetic, and gravity fields provide means for a unified field theory. My colleague Dr. Akimov's view on the nature of matter, antimatter, and vacuum has changed the understanding of the universe. His mathematics are simple, elegant and yet intuitive. The notion of ether filling the void between the stars has been around for centuries. However, modern man discounted this concept when he assumed the void between the stars was a vacuum, void of all matter and gasses. It was even assumed that nature abhorred a vacuum and would try to fill it at any means. Dr. Akimov postulated that the vacuum is actually a physical medium that can arise out of polarization states and spin characteristics of sub-nuclear particles. When a vacuum is given charge polarization, the vacuum is manifested as an electromagnetic field. When given matter polarization, it is manifested as a gravitational field. And when given spin polarization, the vacuum manifests as a spin or torsional field. Thus, all fundamental fields known to physics correspond to specific vacuum polarization states. Therefore, the above torsional field theory of the physical vacuum can claim that all objects, from quanta to galaxies, create vortices in the vacuum.

These vortices are also information carriers, linking physical events, space, and time instantaneously. It has been demonstrated that particles are informed of each other's presence and state via the famous Einstein-Poldalsky-Rosen Experiment (EPR) performed a decade ago in 1976. This experiment provided evidence of the quantum dependence of two particles that occur when the particles have the same source such as obtained from the simultaneous decay of two excited atomic states.

"The experiment involved a photon that is split into two equal but opposite photons, that is photons of the same frequency that travel in exactly opposite directions. They then travel across the experimental apparatus to two identical half-silvered mirrors or see-through mirrors set at a forty-five degree angle. Each photon passes through the mirror or reflected back and photon detectors determine which path each of the photons has taken. The photon pair has a 50/50 chance of either being reflected by the mirror or passing through the mirror. However, the interesting thing is that there was a statistical 75 percent correlation in whatever one particle did, the other did as well. So, in other words, if photon A is transmitted through the mirror, then photon B is almost certainly to be transmitted also, despite the fact that the distance between each of the half-silvered mirrors is greater than the distance light could possibly travel during the time frame of the experiment. This means the particles communicate their spin status, polarization, and quantum flux parameters at faster than light speed.

"In layman's terms, when two subatomic particles split from a single particle, they somehow instantaneously communicate, regardless of how far apart they get in space and time. We call this non-local communication.

"Each and every one of you today brings together a set of skills vital to this project. We have bios and contact information on all twenty of you in the classified folder on the desk in front of you. It is put in resume format. This program overlaps many specialties, agencies, and countries for that matter. The number of members of the Delta G Team is classified, but it is less than a thousand. That makes you very, very special people. Since surprises will come up in this program and you will need to consult with subject matter experts outside your area of expertise, you are free to contact each other via electronic mail. You each will have an account on the CERNET Secure Network through the European Laboratory for Particle Physics in Geneva and the MFENet here at Dreamland's Cray Supercomputer Center. More will be discussed this afternoon, when you tour the computer facilities. We will all meet here each quarter to provide a continuous collaborative forum from cross feed of information.

"Ladies and gentlemen, in the classic military briefing format, I told you what I was going to tell you. I told you. And now I'm going to tell you what I told you. Now that I have gotten your attention, I informed you of the existence of torsional fields. We've humans made them with nuke shots. We've aroused the curiosity of some alien friends. T-waves travel a billion times the speed of light, and are the solution to the unified field theory tying the universe together. All matter, organic and inorganic, is aware of, and conscious of all other matter in the universe. Matter, whether in wave packets or solid form, can communicate physical states across space and time virtually instantaneously. Thus, T-waves are part of our psyches and physiology.

"With this said, I would like to turn this part of your immersion briefing over to my good friend and colleague, Dr. Anne Ahrens. Dr. Ahrens has a B.S. in Biology from Molloy College, and a M.S. in Biochemistry from Adelphi University, both on Long Island,

New York. Her PhD thesis was written on Bioinformatics at John Hopkins University in Washington, D.C."

Dave didn't see Anne enter the room as she strode up from the darkened back. She was still wearing one of her sexy tailored blue jump suits that fit her curves perfectly. She had her hair pinned up and was wearing the set of Minimoto pearl earrings that Dave had gotten for her birthday in Greenland a few months ago. He thought, "She had to know I was here in Dreamland, in more ways than one for that matter."

CHAPTER 19
Curves of a Different Kind

Anne opened her portfolio at the podium and handed the airman that was flipping slides a stack of transparencies. "This briefing is classified Beyond Top Secret (BTS) and is not to be discussed outside this room. It is being presented to you because of Need to Know, or N2K. Virtually every aspect of the Delta G Program touches on the area that I will be presenting. Torsional fields are more than just physical phenomenon as Dr. Timken alluded to. They literally touch our hearts, our souls, and our consciousness.

"Our brains are actually vacuum-based torsional field transceivers. The neurons in our brains create and receive torsional waves. This presents a physical explanation not only of quantum non-locality, but also of telepathy, remote viewing and the other telesomatic effects, which we will discuss later. I assure you this is not black magic, Voodoo, anything spooky, paranormal or mystical. This does not shake my faith in God the Almighty. If you look at it this way, it is just His way of being everywhere at all times and all knowing.

"Torsional waves are both superluminal and enduring. Torsional fields interact with DNA molecular strands in peculiar ways. Metastable torsion phantoms generated by spin torsional interaction can persist even in the absence of the objects that generated them. Hence, torsional waves last for a very long time after the event that triggered them is removed. The existence of these phantoms has been confirmed in the experiments of Vladimir Poponin and his team at the Institute of Biochemical Physics of the Russian Academy of Sciences. This may be the basis for the Kirlian effect I'll explain later.

"An interesting characteristic of DNA is that it acts as if it was a superconductor and is also able to store light and information. One theory by Fosar and Bludorf is that the DNA itself acts as an intelligence network which enables hyper-communication via wormholes. They were not far off. The strange orbs of light reported being seen during crop circle formations are a result of the wheat's DNA interaction with torsional waves. Torsional wave effects on DNA are even being studied by our colleagues in Russia on an antimatter collision which occurred in Siberia in 1908. This was known as the Tunguska Event. The biological consequences of the Tunguska event are very interesting. In the epicenter there has been an accelerated growth of biomass that has endured for decades after the blast. Several biological mutations have also been recorded, not only within the epicenter itself, but also along the trajectory path of the fireball of light as it passed over Tunguska. Abnormalities in the Rh blood factor of the local Tungus people have been recorded. There is also evidence suggesting genetic variations in certain local ant species, as well as genetic abnormalities in the seeds and needle clusters of at least one of the indigenous pine tree species. Pinecones have a classic spiral pattern based upon the logarithmic spiral. As a side note, other studies have revealed over magnetized soils in several locations in and around the Tunguska Site. Furthermore, over magnetized boulders have been discovered in the north of the Boguchanski district, which is positioned along the supposed path of the Tunguska body. In some cases the intensity of the magnetization was recorded as anywhere between ten to one hundred times higher than normal levels."

Dave thought to himself, "Hot damn, so this was the 'other strange things' Dr. Timken was referring to in the bar at DYE-3 that night." Anne continued her presentation.

"An investigation of the fluctuation dynamics of DNA solutions by laser correlation spectroscopy has since repeated the experiment at the Heartmath Institute in California. A sample of a DNA molecule was placed into a temperature controlled chamber and subjected to a laser beam. They found that the electromagnetic field around the chamber exhibits a specific structure, more or less as expected. But what was found is that this structure persists long after the DNA itself has been removed from the laser irradiated chamber. The DNA's imprint in the field continues to be present when the DNA is no longer there. Poponin and his collaborators concluded that the experiment showed that a new field structure had been triggered from the physical vacuum. This field is extremely sensitive; it can be excited by a range of energies close to zero. The phantom effect is a manifestation, they claim, of an overlooked vacuum substructure known as Zero Point Energy. All life and consciousness, is a manifestation of the constant, but subtle, interaction of the wave packets classically known as matter with the underlying physically real zero point vacuum field.

"This phantom effect also manifests itself in a new field of study called Kirlian photography. It is a special kind of imaging that some believe may be able to photograph the energy field of a person, plant, or even an inanimate object. Kirlian photographs are made by passing a small short electrical current through a specimen while the subject is in direct contact with a photographic plate. The film clearly shows a fiery aura of light around the specimen or a type of a coronal discharge. Skeptics felt that this field is usually too subtle to be photographed. However, the additional electrical current interacts with the torsional field which then enhances the field, making it photographically visible.

"This is where Kirlian photographs get interesting. When you photograph a leaf, the developed print shows an aura of light around it. But what happens when a portion of the leaf is torn away and the entire leaf is photographed again? The missing portion will sometimes still appear! This is known as the phantom leaf phenomenon. It does prove that an energy body exists even after the physical body is destroyed; hence, the existence of some ghost images. This can also explain why most people can still feel a limb after an amputation. Skeptics say it is smoke and mirrors or trick photography. I'm here today telling you it is a real phenomenon.

"And now this is where Kirlian photography gets downright weird. If I first take a leaf and snap a Kirlian photo and then cut off its end and then take a second Kirlian photo, the first photo shows a missing portion of the field. This is before the cut! Does the leaf have some sort of premonition of the impending cut? Or is this a case of all particles or cells knowing the state of all other particles, at all times, past, present, and future?

"Ladies and gentlemen, this is part of why you are all gathered here. You are part of a team that is going to blend physics with philosophy and even, theology. For instance, consider this. If time is infinite, space is finite in volume, but there is a finite number and amount of physical matter and antimatter, then one thing is statistically certain. The arrangement of all this material in the configuration pattern that we call the present has happened before. In short, there is only a finite amount of combinations that all material can be arranged given infinite time. Particle awareness or consciousness works very well if these conditions exist. Since all particles are nearly instantaneously aware of the state and conditions of other particles, it knows what will happen in the future and what has happened in the past. This explains parapsychology, ESP, remote viewing, prophesies, déjà vu, mother's intuition, animal instinct and many other strange occurrences in nature.

"One other point I'd like to make about DNA, through our laser and MASER experiments we have found some very interesting things. We have found that the compounds making up DNA can survive the harshness of vacuum and open space. The 'A' portion of the code is made of adenine. Acetylene and hydrogen cyanide can be combined to react and make this compound, both relatively abundant in the universe. Even though there are only a few molecules of these chemicals in open space, over millions of years enough could have been combined to spark a DNA molecule. We have found that torsional waves stimulated by laser and MASER energy accelerate the reaction and formation process. Thus, DNA is linked to space, time, and the mind."

Anne flashed the final slide up on the screen. "What you see before you now is an X-ray Kirlian photo of a nautilus shell. Please take note the energy void at the opening and that no aura is internal to the shell. As a matter of fact, the opening acts as an event horizon beyond which Kirlian energy ceases to exist. Your job will be to find out why.

"At the conclusion of my briefing, I would like to leave you with this thought. Forty years ago, a group was formed around the alien craft that crashed near Roswell. This group was known as the Majestic twelve. They were charged with protecting and understanding the nature of our visitors. Their primary mission was to determine if they were a threat, secondary was to understand their technology, and finally was to attempt communications with them. The Delta G Team is an offshoot of this small group. The mission of this team, that you are now a member of, is to eventually prepare the world's population for the release of this earth shattering information so as to not cause mass panic and collapse of institutions and governments. By the second decade of the next century, the world will be sensitized to accept this information. This group's code name is therefore the Millennium Sentinel."

Everyone in the room suddenly realized their lives were changed forever. Indeed, the world was about to change. They had just been exposed to the secrets of the universe. And it was their job to figure out how to break the news.

CHAPTER 20
NTS II

As part of his Nevada Test Site (NTS) and Dreamland indoctrination, Captain Sheridan was issued a radiation dosimeter badge and given a brief history lesson and informational briefing on the huge Department of Energy (DOE) installation. The unclassified portion of the briefing was presented. This briefing was given to the VIPs and tourists, who visited the DOE complex. The briefer began by giving a history of the site.

"The NTS is a massive outdoor laboratory and national experimental center that cannot be duplicated. Larger than the state of Rhode Island, its 1,350 square miles or nearly a million acres makes this one of the largest secured areas in the United States. The NTS is located in Nye County in southern Nevada. The southernmost point of the NTS is about sixty-five miles northwest of Las Vegas. The site varies from 28 to 35 miles in width (east to west) and from 40 to 55 miles in length (north to south). The NTS is bordered on three sides by 4,120 square miles of land comprising the Nellis Air Force Base Bombing and Gunnery Range, another federally owned and restricted area. This restricted area provides a buffer zone to the north and east between the test area and land that is open to the public, and varies in width from 15 to 65 miles. A northwestern portion of the Nellis Air Force Range is occupied by the Tonopah Test Range, an area of 624 square miles which is operated for DOE by the Sandia Laboratories primarily for airdrop tests of ballistic shapes. The combination of the Tonopah Test Range, the Nellis Air Force Range, and the Nevada Test Site is one of the largest unpopulated land areas in the United States, comprising some 5,470 square miles or 5 million acres."

After the briefer, Lyle George, gave the geographic details, he then proceeded to present the early nuclear testing program. "The United States conducted 119 nuclear tests here from the start of testing in January 1951 through October 1958. Most of those nuclear tests were carried out in the atmosphere. Some tests were positioned for firing by airdrop, but metal towers were used for many Nevada tests at heights ranging from 100 to 700 feet above the ground surface. In 1957 and 1958, helium-filled balloons, tethered to precise heights and locations 340 to 1,500 feet above ground, provided a simpler, quicker and less expensive method for the testing of many experimental devices. The tests of the atmospheric era took place in Yucca and Frenchman Flats. Of the 119 nuclear tests that were conducted at the NTS during the atmospheric testing era (1951 to 1958) ninety-seven tests were conducted in the atmosphere, two were cratering tests, detonated at depths less than 100 feet (30 meters), and twenty were underground tests."

He continued on with an explanation of the underground testing conducted for the last twenty- five years. "In 1962, two small surface tests, one tower test and two cratering tests were part of the nuclear weapons testing program. Six nuclear cratering tests were conducted from 1962 through 1968 as part of the peaceful applications (Plowshare) program. The overwhelming majority of the seven hundred tests that took place at the NTS from 1961 through the late 1980s were conducted underground either in shafts or in tunnels that were designed for containment of the radioactive debris. Most underground tests were conducted under Yucca Flat, but a few underground and cratering tests took place under Buckboard, Pahute, and Rainier Mesas in the northern part of the Nevada Test Site."

George then went on to explain the nuclear testing conducted in tunnels that were constructed under the mesas. "Tests have been conducted in sixteen different tunnels in Rainier Mesa. The first test was conducted on August 10, 1957, when a zero-yield safety experiment named Saturn was detonated in C-Tunnel. The Defense Nuclear Agency evaluated the effects of nuclear weapon explosions, thermal radiation, blast, shock, X-rays and gamma rays on military hardware, such as communication equipment, rocket nosecones and satellites. The typical horizontal line of sight (HLOS) test was primarily for radiation effects research. Researchers attempted to minimize blast and shock effects from the experiments. A large tunnel complex mined under the mesa contained the HLOS pipe. The HLOS pipe is 1,500 to 1,800 feet long and tapers from up to 30 feet in diameter at the test chamber to several inches at the working point. Experiments were placed in the HLOS pipe test chambers. At zero time the nuclear device is fired, and radiation instantaneously flows down the pipe, creating the necessary radiation environment. To prevent bomb debris and blast from reaching and damaging the experiments, three mechanisms were used to close the pipe. The first is the Fast Acting Closure which is slammed shut by high explosives in about one millisecond; the other two closures follow within 30 and 300 milliseconds.

"Over thirty underground HLOS events were detonated, releasing volatile radioactive materials (particulate or gaseous), which resulted in detection off-site. The remainder of the tests that took place at the NTS between 1961 and the present were either completely contained underground or resulted in releases of radioactive materials that were only detected on-site. A total of 299 events resulted in releases of radioactive materials that were detected on-site only.

"The total number of nuclear weapons tests that were conducted at the Nevada Test Site up to date is nearly 900, one hundred which were atmospheric, and the other 800 underground." The briefer paused for a few seconds to let that number sink in. He reiterated, "To date, ladies and gentlemen, nearly a thousand nuclear shots have occurred over the last thirty-five years. That comes out to about twenty-five per year or over two per month. That is a hell of a lot of energy."

The briefer continued to explain some of the technical challenges with achieving this phenomenal test rate. He explained some drilling challenges that were encountered and overcome. "When drilling vertical shafts for underground tests, the biggest problem was the time that it took to drill into the desert floor. A

36 inch diameter hole, 1,000 feet deep, could take up to 60 days. The initial method was to drill in three successive passes, each one larger. Eventually the tri-stage gave way to the flat bottom bit, with 12 to 24 cutters chewing up the rock as the entire unit rotated, a process that could drill a 1,000 foot hole in 20 days. A normal hole is from 48 to 120 inches in diameter and from 600 to 2,500 feet deep.

"Tests in vertical drill holes are of two types: smaller-yield devices in relatively shallow holes in the Yucca Flat area and higher-yield devices in deeper holes on Pahute Mesa." He pointed to the map and continued his briefing. "Tests at the Yucca Flat and Pahute Mesa event sites have the same general requirements, but differ in the magnitude of the operations. Deeper-hole operations disturb a larger area, require more on-site equipment, and have a higher requirement for electrical power and utilities. The distance from the core of the infrastructure is also a factor; Pahute Mesa operations are 30 to 50 miles farther away than Yucca Flat."

Dave stared with the others at the aerial photos of Frenchman Flats. It was cratered like the Moon. George continued as he pointed to the map. "The craters you see here are not blast craters. They are called subsidence craters. After the device is detonated, the overburden soil or rock and playa are melted and fall into the resulting cavity. As the heat rises, it creates a chimney effect and overburden soil falls downward to fill the void. Eventually, the ground subsides; this process can take up to a few hours or a half a day depending upon depth.

There are a few actual craters from the Plowshare Program. A famous one is Sedan Crater. It has become sort of a tourist attraction here at the NTS." George finished the briefing with the DOE spin. "Remember, even with all these nuclear detonations, the NTS is a safe place to work. There are several areas that are still hot and off limits. Just keep in mind we nuked two Japanese cities fifty years ago and they are safe places to live and work today." Dave thought to himself, "That was comforting to know."

Dave spent the next week in Dreamland being indoctrinated in DOE operations, Nuclear Safety, and Explosives Safety. Then he got into the interesting stuff: the history of the Greys, their involvement in Dreamland, sparse contact, and attempts at communications with humans. He had learned most of this from his stay on the *Nautilus* and discussions with the crew. However, he went through the official motions with the Delta G Program Office and again signed his life away on a classified DD Form attached to the standard DD form 312 Classified Information Nondisclosure Agreement. From the wording, they were deadly serious about the penalties for release of Delta G BTS information.

CHAPTER 21
Area 25–Jackass Flats

The UH-1 Huey was waiting on the Area 51 ramp with its turbines spooling up as Dave followed Rob Hill, the DOE Air Force liaison, out of the hangar into the desert sun and climbed aboard. They strapped in, put on headsets and did a com check. By this time in his military career, he had logged several hundred hours in the reliable ol' Huey.

And as it turns out, he had even gone to Squadron Officer School in Alabama with the pilot whom he recognized. The Air Force Officer corps was indeed a small world. They both just grinned and nodded to each other.

Over the intercom he heard the crew run through the pre-takeoff checklist. The radio crackled in a sharp tone, "Beaver One, Dreamland Control." The pilot responded, "Dreamland Control, Beaver One is with you." "Roger, Beaver One, you are cleared VFR direct to NTS area two fiver. Stay at or below five hundred AGL." Dave grinned again, he knew this was a formal way for the control tower to say take off and oh, by the way, have fun getting there. This mission would be chalked up to a low level training sortie. The crew would also use this opportunity to search the hills, valleys, and peaks, for unauthorized visitors. All chopper flights into and out of Area 51 were low level to scare off unwanted eyes. Also, staying low to the ground also meant you were less of an obstacle for the fast movers hauling ass in and out of the bombing and gunnery range. Dave was about to get another ride of his life.

This was the first time he would have to get a good view of Dreamland from the air. As the chopper took off he could look over the vast hangar complexes and facilities. Several dozen large structures lined up on the west side of the ramp. The runway was huge. It was over 15,000 feet long and even then protruded out onto the dry Groom Lake bed for another mile or two. This was a huge complex. Obviously several hundred people worked here. It was amazing they kept this place under wraps for so long.

It was a cool 70 degrees out just before 10:00 AM. The crew left the doors open during takeoff. That made the ride exhilarating and gave a refreshing rush of desert air blowing through the cabin. The chopper made a 180 degree turn back over the complex and hugged the terrain up a canyon and through a narrow mountain pass. As it shot up and over the mountain the chopper dipped down sharply into the adjacent valley in a negative G dive. The chopper was now 200 feet off the deck doing about 120 knots. This was a rush. The same technique was used to cross the second mountain range. The pilot picked a ravine and followed it up the mountain. At the crest he nosed over again for a roller coaster ride that was definitely ten times better than any Disney E ticket ride. They followed another dry river bed down the opposite side of the mountain. The copilot hit the mike, "Check out the dust cloud at two o'clock....two miles." The pilot responded, "Roger that, Rob. Heading that way." The pilot kicked the right rudder pedal and nosed it further down the mountain. The pilot clicked in, "It's days like this that make it worth getting up in the morning." Below them now was one of the most beautiful sights that Dave had ever seen. A herd of wild Mustangs was tearing down the dry wash in full gallop. There had to be at least a dozen or so horses. They were magnificent. Only their manes glistened in the sun as the dust enveloped their torsos looking like flames over their bodies. "Rob, you better contact NTS Control. They may want to know about this herd. They're getting kind of close to the White Hill Spring Road."

As the chopper followed along the alluvial fan protruding down the mountain the pilot clicked in again. "Dave, you are about to see the Dark Side of the Moon. Look off to your left." He couldn't believe his eyes. For miles as far as he could see the valley was pockmarked with the subsidence craters briefed earlier. The pilot keyed the mike again, "Directly ahead is Sedan Crater. This one is actually on the National Historic Places List. It's the result of a shallow 100 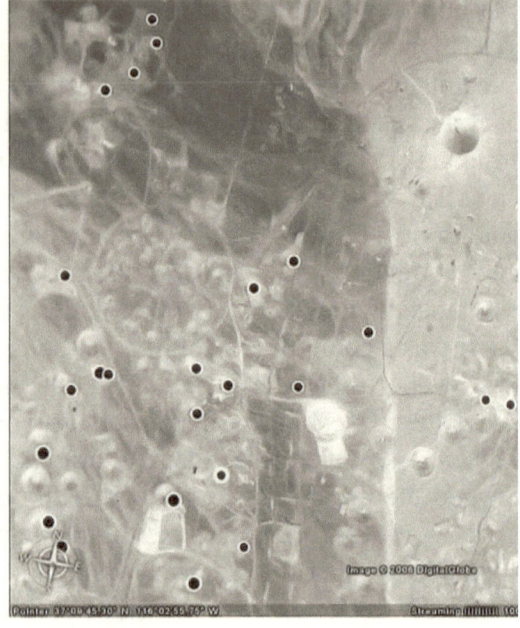 kiloton burst. The crater is over a quarter mile wide and thirty stories deep."

The chopper leveled off as it flew over the Frenchman Dry Lake. They still had about thirty five miles left to get to the southwest side of the Test Site. Area 25 was in an area known as Jackass Flats. It was home to the early Nuclear Rocket Engine Development program that President Kennedy started. This is the largest area on the NTS. It occupies some 225 square miles.

The pilot continued his tour guide duties by announcing the passing of the mesas on the left. "To the left about fifteen miles are Rainier and Buckboard Mesas. That's where the tunnel complexes are. We'll stay well south of there. Not wearing my lead-lined jockeys today, and my wife still wants a couple more kids.

"We're coming up on Calico Hills now." Again, the chopper twisted and turned up the dry river beds. The scenery passing below him was gorgeous.

The pilot clicked in again, "Rob, get clearance from Range Control to shoot the canyon. I feel the need for speed." "Roger, will do." The copilot switched frequencies on a radio and keyed the mike, "Nellis Range Control, Beaver One." An immediate response followed, "Beaver One, Nellis Range Control, go." "Roger, Control, we are VFR over Belted Springs. Request a low level clearance through Forty Mile Canyon southbound to RMAD area two fiver." "Roger, please standby." A minute or so later came the response, "Beaver One...Control." "Go control." "Proceed direct to Forty Mile Canyon, low level, maintain this frequency. Be advised of Red Flag activity in that area." The copilot responded, "Roger, will do."

Dave was in for another experience. Forty Mile Canyon was like a miniature Grand Canyon. It was about five miles wide at the start and narrowed down to a quarter mile in some places with sheer three thousand foot walls on each side.

The Huey accelerated and banked sharply on each turn of the canyon. They were pulling some G's again. Then, just when he was having fun, a streak of white smoke shot up and past the door, followed by a second and then a third. The mike clicked, "Shit, Chief, shut the doors." The chopper took evasive action and climbed up over a ridge line. It was now Dave's turn to key the mike, "What the hell was that? Who the hell is shooting at us? Get us the hell out of here!" The crew just began to laugh, "What the hell is so funny?" Dave asked. The pilot responded, "Relax ol' friend, no problem. I knew the spooks were going to be up here taking pot shots at anything that moved as part of the Red Flag war games. They're firing Smokey Sam's at us. They're just paper and Styrofoam Surface to Air (SAM) simulators. They'd bounce off us if they hit us. I forgot the doors were open. It would have been interesting had one come into the cabin. I thought this would give you a thrill. It also gives the spooks something to practice on for their Red Flag exercise."

Even Rob was checking his underwear now. He'd been on the range for twenty-five years and thought he'd seen it all. This was a new one on him, too.

This indeed had been some flight.

The chopper continued uneventfully down the canyon. As the canyon widened and leveled out, it turned southeast towards another complex of buildings in the center of a huge flat valley.

As the chopper slowed for approach in front of one of the buildings, the crew chief called tail clear as the chopper cleared the power lines and began its hover in preparation for landing on the helipad.

As the Huey's rotors wound down to a stop, Dave unharnessed himself and disconnected his headset. As the crew chief slid the door back he looked across the street from the helipad to a two story building. It had that 1960's look. It reminded him of his old high school. It looked out of place out in the middle of the Nevada desert. It even had landscaping, shrubbery, and grass. Rob spoke up, "Captain, welcome to Area 25, Jackass Flats. What you see across the street is the old nuclear rocket engine development administration building. Admiral Rickover, father of the nuclear Navy, had an office in there at one time. If you are wondering about the landscaping, we're actually on an oasis in the middle of this valley. There is a shitload of water below us. It's only 2,000 feet down. We've got a well just up the road.

"The facilities include a half dozen support buildings, the admin building, a machine shop, vehicle maintenance, supply warehouses, infirmary and communications facility. The large concrete structures on the slopes of Calico Hills over there are the Reactor Maintenance and Disassembly (RMAD) facility, rocket engine test stand, cryogenic facilities and then at the other end of the valley is the Nuclear Rocket Engine Test Facility. This whole area is interconnected by the Jackass Flats and Yucca Mountain Railway, a total of twelve miles of track and spurs."

There were a half dozen people standing in the shade of the entrance way of the admin building. Rob said, "Come on Captain, let's meet your new boss and staff." Dave followed Rob out of the chopper and walked the two hundred yards across the street.

He saluted his new boss, Lieutenant Colonel Jacob Williams. "Captain Dave Sheridan reporting as ordered, sir."

The tall O-5 responded, "Welcome to the Ballistic Missile

Office (BMO) Operating Location AA, Dave. Call me Jake. We're pretty informal out here amongst the heathens and the cactus." He shook his hand. "Let me introduce you to the staff. This lovely young lady is Catherine Lenihan, she is my Girl Friday. Actually, she runs the whole damn place. This is Chief Connor, he handles our logistics. This is Master Sergeant Nick Manda; he is the Safety NCO and explosives expert. You've met Rob, our field engineer. This is Lucas Cooper and Steve Tyler, our OEM reps, and this is our Crew Chief Brandon Riek. He's in charge of the two hundred man work crew out here. I know that's a lot of names and faces, but you'll get to know everyone real quick. We've all gotten pretty close over the last couple of years. Come on in and let's get out of the heat. Catherine, go over and invite the chopper crew in for lunch."

Everyone kind of stared out of the corner of their eye as Catherine bounced over across the road in her tight-fitting jeans and cowboy boots. She was drop dead gorgeous. She reminded Dave of Wrangler Jane on the TV show, *F Troop*. She definitely got the flight crew's attention as she leaned in the chopper door and invited them over. She sure had no problem convincing those guys to come over for a snack. And, you could tell she liked the flirting. She was outnumbered out here by about two hundred to one.

After lunch, Lieutenant Colonel Williams drove Dave out to the gravel access road leading up to the tunnel complex in the mountain ahead. He stopped the Suburban, got out, and told him to go for a walk with him. It was still a relatively brisk and cool desert morning in the high Mojave. Williams lit up a cigarette and pointed to the mountain five miles ahead of them. "Dave, welcome to Little Skull Mountain. Before we drive up there I need to go over a few things with you. I prefer to do my classified briefings out here in the open. I don't feel as paranoid out here. I'm not sure what they told you over the hill at Dreamland. Whatever it was, I'm sure it wasn't the entire story. This Delta G Program is so compartmentalized; it is based upon cover story upon cover story. It is as Winston Churchill once said, 'a riddle wrapped in a mystery inside an enigma.' He pretty much nailed this program. It's hard to tell what is a lie, what is a cover story, and what is real at times. You are now my deputy out here. We are going to have to trust each other and cover each other's backs. There are careers, hidden agendas, politics, and billions of dollars at play in this black world. You are a very lucky young officer. You have a great sponsor. General Ahrens thinks highly of you. That means a lot to me. Ahrens and I go way back to the Nuclear Rocket Engine Program."

Williams took another puff from his Marlboro and then bent over and picked up a rock. Underneath it was a scorpion. He stepped on it and ground it with his boot. He then chucked the rock into a yucca plant a few feet way. A kangaroo rat scurried off. Then there was the unmistakable buzz of a rattlesnake.

"Dave, this place is crawling with wildlife. Only thing is, most of it has fangs, stingers, or a nasty disposition. Frontier justice and survival of the fittest works well out here.

"Up the road a few miles are two tunnels dug into the side of this mountain. You can see the access portals about halfway up. We call them portals X and Y. What we are supposed to be doing out here is evaluate two different types of tunnel boring machines. We call 'em TBMs for short. Hell, the Air Force has an acronym for everything. We'll use them to drill in about a mile through the soft talc, build a work chamber and then turn the machines vertical. We'll then drill straight up through the hard basalt cap rock on top of the mountain and bingo you have a readymade missile silo ready to house our newest pride and joy, the MX or Peacekeeper ICBM.

"However, as you know, our primary mission involves the torsional wave business. We've been setting off nukes out here in the desert like they've got a shelf life. Make no mistake about it; they do a fine job of generating torsional waves. They definitely get our little green friends attention, actually they are grey. They do come buzzing around here every once in a while. I've never actually seen them. I've seen their craft, very, very impressive. But, I digress. Sorry, back to the tunnels.

"That little explosion a few years ago at the Titan Silo is one of the reasons we are out here. Small world isn't it? Somebody figured out that most of the nuclear detonation energy is wasted and is very inefficient. Something like 95 percent of the blast energy is wasted. The rapid densification of the strata is what counts. Everything else is a byproduct like the radiation, heat and overpressure. All that nasty stuff is from a nuke going off."

Williams took another drag on his cigarette and then asked, "Do you remember one of the first reports you put together as an Air Force officer?" Dave picked up another rock and tossed it toward the rattler. "Do you mean my work on the blast calculations that destroyed the silo?"

Williams leaned back on the fender and put his hands across his chest, "Man, Ahrens was right. You are sharp as a tack. Yes, exactly right. The one paragraph in your report that mentioned a half kiloton blast equivalent got somebody's attention. You'll be interested to know that the silo explosion set off a torsional wave." Williams grinned and stared, letting the implications sink in. He finished his cigarette and ground it out in the gravel.

Dave had to ask, "How the hell do we know it set off a torsional wave? It was a random accident. There was no gravimetric equipment in place to measure the event."

Williams responded, "Damn, you're good. Okay, here it is in a nutshell. Or should I say, a nautilus shell. Remember, every time we set off a torsional wave we get a response or a magnified echo that returns about five hundred days after the event. Sometimes these events are accompanied by our little friends. Other times they just ring our bell back. But almost five hundred days to the day a torsional event takes place. These torsional events are sometimes masked in a seismic event. Hell, out here a seismic event is as common as a Saturday night dance. So, we know about when they hit and we're prepared for them. Take a look at the seismic activity around the silo about sixteen weeks after the random event. There were a string of 4.0 quakes about twenty miles southeast of the complex. This falls well within the circle error probability for a return wave. These quakes had torsional waves embedded in them. Someday somebody is going to figure out the significance of the five hundred days. Hell, the planet Earth isn't anywhere near its orbital position around the Sun when we get the return. So it isn't line of sight, it's strictly time dependent.

"Also, you are correct. We didn't have any gravity detectors present there, but you got to know this stuff. Listen up; we've got a shitload of all kinds of sensors all over the world. Both the military and the universities are constantly measuring something with all these gizmos. All these measurements are then put into computer data banks. Then somehow and somewhere, over the telephone lines, all this data is gathered. It is compiled, analyzed, charted, graphed, "thunked on", and explained. In Dreamland they call it data mining.

"I was at a meeting a while back, over the hill there, when your name came up and they told me you were coming out here. In the meeting room, they had a ton of charts hung on the wall. They may have figured that as an Aggie I couldn't read their maps, or decipher their graphs, so they just left them up on the walls with their big red 'BTS Delta G' stamped and plastered all over the place. But, I'm from Texarkana, Texas; I've got a degree in Nuclear Engineering. I can recognize a map of Arkansas and recognize for sure what a magnetic Gaussian field survey looks like. On it were the Titan II missile fields. Next to that were maps of geological anticlines and magnetic anomalies in Arkansas. One map showed the area around Magnetic Cove, Arkansas, what a fascinating place. I've taken my wife and kids through there on a vacation to Hot Springs. One of only three places like it on Earth, there is one in the Alps, and the other is in the Urals in Russia.

"Since that meeting, I did some studying up. The place covers an oval shape area about five square miles. In it, there are over forty different mineral types and combinations. The place is a huge magnetic anomaly on the world map. Huge deposits of magnetic ore. Anyway, to make a long story short, I found out those anticlines run right under the silo that blew up. A University of Arkansas gravimetric study was underway at Magnetic Cove when she blew. The results are that the magnetic anticlines shifted and twisted thus detecting a torsional wave. Of course, this geologist didn't know the significance of his find, but the supercomputers did. So let that be a lesson. Big Brother is always watching, so is his whole damn family for that matter. But just between you and me, it looks like the Masons were right. This whole torsional wave thing might be the result of a bunch of very old rocks."

Williams then asked, "Back to the silo explosion. Do you know the significance of a conventional explosion setting off a torsional wave?" Dave returned the grin and said, "Yes. We can save our nukes for a rainy day, so invest in hydrazine." Williams laughed, "Glad to see you have a sense of humor, too. Well, we've come up with something a little safer than rocket fuel. What do you think of ammonium nitrate and fuel oil (ANFO)? We build ourselves a nice little shock tube in the side of a mountain, pack it with ANFO and set it off like a shotgun. The talc strata in the mountain, by the way, some very old rock, densifies, and bingo, we set off torsional waves."

Dave laughed and said, "Ingenious, why didn't anyone think of that before?"

Williams replied, "Well, funny you should ask. We did hit upon this concept a few years ago up in Rainier Mesa during one of our underground nuke shots. One of the tunnel shots in the Mesa contained a large diameter horizontal pipe. The pipe started out about thirty feet in diameter and tapered down to a few inches along its 18,000 foot length. This was called a horizontal line-of-sight (HLOS) test. Our scientists built humongous shutters or guillotines activated by explosives at strategic points along the pipe. The device or package was placed at the end of the pipe. Notice we don't call them nukes anymore. We're trying to be politically correct. They are called devices, packages, or experimental energy packets. Yeah, right. Anyway, the nuke was set off in a near perfect vacuum. The shutters were supposed to slam shut in a few milliseconds to protect the experiments and instruments from being damaged by the blast effects and debris. Well, to make a long story short, the explosive charges didn't detonate and slam close the shutters. A half billion dollar experiment was blasted across the valley to the opposite ridge. Pipe sections, rail, instrumentation, cabling, the whole tube was launched like a nuclear bullet. What wasn't vaporized is still glowing hot on that ridge line today. The blast also picked up the top of the mesa, shifted it over about twelve feet and set it down again. Another impressive show of force. Sorry, again I digress. Back to the torsional wave.

That pipe was not only blown out of the mountain it was twisted out of the mountain. The evidence of a huge torsional wave was that some of that debris came raining down on Frenchman Flats thirty miles away."

Dave said, "That's one hell of a blast, but artillery can do that."

Williams grinned from ear to ear and rubbed his chin. "You are correct about that. However, that shit landed five hundred days later!"

By this time, nothing surprised Dave. He took it all in calmly and professionally. He replied, "So, we have figured out how to make torsional waves and can now launch shrapnel to the stars."

Williams replied, "I guess so. The only problem now is that we can't keep using the nuclear shotgun approach. The environmentalists are all over our ass. And the truth is that blast did spray out a shitload of radiation. So that brings me back to our nifty tunnel complexes up here in Little Skull Mountain that I'm about to show you. We now know from the Titan Silo explosion that under the right conditions torsional waves can be generated. And we know from our little mishap in the tunnel shot that we can do it horizontally and actually launch stuff. Now we're going to marry the results of two 'ah shits', and come up with an 'ingenious approach' as you say."

Dave walked over closer to the rattler. It was coiled up and really pissed. "I've never seen a rattler out in the wild."

Williams responded, "They're everywhere out here. Be careful what you pick up. That rattler is a very deadly Green Mojave. We also get the little side winders in the office building all the time. They really get pissed in there because they can't get any traction on the linoleum floor. Next time we catch one, have Catherine take it home and make you a hat band."

"You know, Colonel, we are actually building on three 'ah shits'. The ANFO or Ammonium Nitrate and Fuel Oil explosives were accidentally discovered. Do you remember hearing about the Texas City ship explosion back in the late 40's? That ship was carrying a cargo of ammonium nitrate. It caught fire, diesel fuel entered the hold, and kaboom; the whole harbor went up in a blinding flash."

Williams responded, "Yes, I'm aware of it. I'm from Texas. It was the *SS Grandcamp* in 1947. They compared that blast to the nukes we dropped on Japan. It blew the ship's anchor over two miles away, caused a massive tidal wave and killed over six hundred people. You are right; this is the only program I've worked on that is built on one 'ah shit' after another."

Dave asked, "Do you think that Texas size blast or the Hiroshima and Nagasaki nukes set off a torsional wave?" Williams replied, "Good question, but I doubt it. Like I said, certain conditions must exist. It is not the blast per say that sets off the torsional wave; it is the sudden densification of near constant density material that sets one off. It's the Delta G remember. That's why we set off nukes over desert playa, volcanic tuft and now conventional high explosives in a talc stratum. These are all fine grained geologic deposits. I'd reckon that if you tried it in any other dirt, you'd muck up any wave generation because of various densities involved. Don't forget gravitational forces depend upon density of matter and objects. Not just the amount of mass."

Dave replied, "I understand this concept. That's why the Greys keep hitting the icecap. There must be a shitload of constant density ice up north."

He was enjoying his first banter with his new boss. He said, "Well, blasts happen all the time in nature. What about volcanoes and meteorites. Do you think Krakatoa set off a torsional wave?" Williams said, "If it did, nobody back then knew or cared. Again, a lot of stuff of different density was involved: magma, lava, rock, ash, and even trees and critters. Not to mention a shitload of seawater."

It was warming up as the desert sun beat down on the dusty gravel road. Dave put his sunglasses on and asked a deep philosophical question, "I wonder what constitutes 'a shitload'. It seems like this is an international standard of some kind; seems to be a pretty standard unit of measure."

Williams grinned and said, "Don't know how much a 'shitload' is but it's getting pretty deep around here. Getting pretty hot out here, too. Before I drive you up the mountain, I want you to take a look around. This is a very special place out here. It's rich in history, past, present and future. To the east over the Elk Range are the dry lakes where you saw all the craters from the nuke tests. To the north back behind the Calico range are the mesas where all the tunnel shots take place. To the west, beyond Forty Mile Canyon and Yucca Mountain, is the Tonapah Test range. There's something you need to know about that strange place. You can bet your ass the Delta G Project is very, very, very black. However, our buddies across the hill to the west at Tonapah are only very, very black. They are developing a stealth fighter plane over there. We are constantly sending funding and manpower over there to bail them out. Our cover story out here in Jackass Flats is to support the MX, or as the politicians call it, Peacekeeper ICBM basing concepts. Back behind the office building in the old RMAD facility will be the MX cold launch testing facilities, over to the west is our race track where we do MX mobile launcher road ability testing. Across the highway behind us is our shallow buried trench concept using the old hide and seek shell game for missile shelters. About a mile or so down the road is our half scale vertical silo works to do missile loading unloading simulations. So you see, my good Captain, we have a lot out here to do to keep us busy. There are a lot of places to literally bury millions of dollars in research and development funds to support our black programs. We work and play in the world's largest sand box. They give us expensive toys and we even get to blow them up for fun. Wow, I just love flying to work in the morning. You, my friend, are one lucky son of a bitch. Look around you. You are deputy commander of everything you can see for twenty- five miles. You are the chief engineer for everything you can't see for fifty miles and even a few miles under this mountain ahead. We are one of the biggest money launderers out here. We take clean money and turn it black. We're the Swiss bankers of Jackass Flats."

Williams climbed back in the Suburban followed by Dave, "Now I want to drive you up to the Little Skull Mountain Tunnel Portals. Keep an open mind. We're supposed to be pretty austere out here. Only a handful of us really know what the purpose is of these tunnels. Remember, our cover story is that we are having a competition between two contractors to see who can use tunnel boring machines to drill into the mountain and build readymade missile launch complexes and shelters. They don't know we are going to use them as shock tubes to generate torsional waves. As a matter of fact, our Russian friends have laid this whole experiment out. We get to spend all the money on the expensive toys for Christmas. Those cheap bastards get to play with the box they came in. But I've got to give them credit; the bastards are pretty creative at thinking outside that box. One of them has figured out the exact orientation for these two tunnels. They need to be exactly one mile apart. They need to be aligned with each other at a 69.5 degree angle. The shock tubes will be filled at their end with six million pounds of ANFO each and then detonated a few milliseconds apart. The resulting intersecting shockwaves will densify the talc rock under the mountain and set off a torsional wave. But this time, we're going to place a T-wave runner in the wave guide

and launch it into oblivion. Or we'll have another 'ah shit' and launch it over into Death Valley across the ridge to the south. Who knows what's going to happen. Let me show you our super-secret tunnel complex."

"Thank you, sir. But did you just call this mountain ahead, Little Skull?"

Williams replied, "That's its name, Dave. Why, does that give you the willies or something?"

Dave figured he could be, and should be, honest and open to his new boss.

"Sir, what if I told you I had a remote viewing experience that involved sketching skulls and crossbones. I think there is a connection here."

Williams smiled sheepishly, "What if I told you, I know."

Dave wasn't sure what confounded him most: the déjà vu feeling or the fact that Williams knew about it.

CHAPTER 22
Playing Nicely in the Sandbox

The Chevy Suburban continued its dusty climb up the barren slope of Little Skull Mountain. Williams grabbed the radio mike, "Better let them know were coming up. No need to surprise them, Mike X-ray, Mike X-ray, BMO One over." A few seconds later a crisp response came back. "BMO One, Mike X-ray, go." With a classical Texan accent Williams replied, "Roger, be advised we are ten minutes out, inbound. I have Captain Sheridan with me." The speakers crackled back, "Roger, BMO One, understand. Will advise ops chief." Williams grabbed for a bottle of water and chugged it down. "Better get a quart or so in you before we get out. Even though it's January in the high desert, it's going to get to over ninety this afternoon. It's also dry and dusty in the mountain."

Just then Williams pointed towards his right through Dave's passenger window. Dave looked out the window and was surprised to see two A-10 Wart Hog tank busters flying about a hundred feet off the deck heading straight at them. They roared over the top of the Suburban doing about 250 knots and then pulled hard G's straight up. The noise was deafening. Williams grinned and yelled out a Texan style, "Yippee! The boys want to play with us! They must have seen the dust cloud we're kicking up and are using us for a mock strafing run."

Dave turned to Williams and said, "The operative word here is mock, correct."

Williams replied, "Sure, those boys are given a lot of leeway out here. They know the range is not hot in this area. However, they take anything that is moving as a legitimate targeting opportunity. Good practice, ya never know when we're going to have to

blow the hell out of a column of tanks or some Arab convoy someday. Those guys can spit out 3,000 rounds per minute of 30mm
ammo the size of a coke bottle. A hell of a machine!"

Just then the A-10s set up for a second pass. This time they
both dove down from about a few thousand feet in a steep 45
degree dive. They again pulled up and peeled off behind Little
Skull, obviously practicing to use the terrain to mask their egress.

Williams stopped the Suburban and stepped out, "Excuse me
partner, but I got to go take care of a different kind of snake. I
hate to use them fiberglass shit houses up there. They stink to high
hell, plus the fact that they'll bake your brain while you're taking a
whiz. I prefer to water a cactus. Only have about a billion of 'em
out here." Dave thought what the heck, if his boss said it was okay
to water a cactus, why the hell not. Besides, he was again taking
his grandfather's advice of doing it where and when you can. He
stepped out of the Suburban and proceeded to write his name in the
sand. Just then from around the south side of Little Skull came the
two screaming A-10s doing a head-on pass. Both Dave and Williams kind of had their hands full as the planes rocked their wings
as the pair thundered over them at less than a hundred feet.

Dave let out his own "yeehaaaa" and said, "They're going to
have some interesting footage on their gun cameras."

Williams laughed out loud and said, "It ain't that big partner."
Dave grinned and said, "Sorry, sir, wasn't talking about yours."

After they finished their business they hopped back in the air
conditioned vehicle. Williams wiped the sweat from his forehead
and said, "Ya know, it wasn't the Winchester rifle that won the
west. Just look at us. It was definitely Freon." Dave smiled as he
adjusted the air conditioner blower to hit his face.

When they reached the tunnel portal site, Williams parked the
Suburban near the edge of the spoil pile. Dave had a bird's eye
view of Jackass Flats below him. He could see across the fifty
miles to Death Valley and then onward to the snowcapped peak
of Mount Whitney. Williams pointed out some interesting trivia,
"Dave, you're looking at both the highest point in the continental
United States and the lowest point. They are both in San Bernardi-
no County, California. This is one of the few places on the planet

you can stand and see both."

Dave followed Williams over to a pre-engineered metal building. He couldn't help but notice the large twenty foot diameter tube shaped object pointing to a carved out face on the side of the mountain.

Williams was met by the Boeing and Westinghouse Field Reps. They walked back to a large table with several rolls of drawings spread across it. Larry shook Dave's hand and said, "Welcome to the MX Deep Basing Test Bed Captain. We're here to get you acquainted with our horizontal tunnel boring machine (TBM) Project. Colonel, we've got most of the drainage diversion channels and culverts finished. That flash flood we had last week wiped out several power cables and the exhaust ductwork from water rolling off the top of the portal. It has all been repaired. We have all of the primary components for the Bechtel TBM and are waiting for some hydraulic motors and carbide cutting teeth for the Hanson TBM. We've got to put together the conveyor systems, but the portal faces have been squared off and we'll be ready for drilling in a week or ten days.

"Captain, we are going to spend the next several months drilling through this mountain. It will be sort of a race to see which machine can dig faster, cheaper, and more reliably. We'll go in about 2,000 feet, and then mine out a work chamber. We'll then point the whole kit and caboodle vertical and drill up through the basalt layers to make us one heck of a missile silo. The Russians couldn't possibly get to these babies."

Another old classic flashed through Dave's brain; "Good grief, I'm living the Jules Verne novel, *Journey to the Center of the Earth.*"

"We've got enough power up here to light up a small city. The TBMs are twenty-two feet in diameter and should have no problem drilling through the soft volcanic talc. We'll line the tunnel with a reinforcing rebar net and then spray it with a special type of concrete called shotcrete. We have plenty of ventilation."

The civil engineer within Dave kicked in full gear now. He asked, "How big of a work crew will you have?" Larry replied, "This is a union shop out here. Most people don't realize that the

Nevada Test Site is one of Nevada's largest employers. Each day thousands of workers migrate up here the ninety plus miles from Las Vegas, either by air as you're doing, by bus or van. We have over two hundred personnel working here in Area 25 alone. For this project we'll be using twenty miners, six iron workers, four carpenters, four mechanics, one oiler, three electricians, four heavy equipment operators, four laborers, two surveying crews and a photography crew. Of course, we, the aerospace prime contractors, will have our own support and technical crews out here as well."

Dave spent the next few weeks familiarizing himself with the operations, personnel and technical information on the various programs he was responsible for. He began to understand the intricate and creative financing that allowed for strange and wonderful things to be built and tested in this unique place.

Then, on the cool morning of January 28, 1986, Dave was driving on the backside of Little Skull when he got a radio call from Catherine, "BMO Two, BMO Two, BMO Control."

Dave replied, "Go, Control."

Catherine, in a choked up voice, finally got the words out, "Be advised on the BMO net, that the Space Shuttle Challenger has just exploded a minute or so after liftoff at the Cape. There were no survivors." It took a few seconds for this to sink in.

Dave replied professionally. He knew that dozens of people had overheard the conversation on the common BMO channel "Roger, understand. God bless them and their families. Request this channel be cleared and chatter kept to a minimum. Please inform BMO one via land line at the NTS Admin Office. I'm en route to the Admin Facility. BMO Two out."

Dave spent the next six months as the Air Force project engineer and deputy site commander responsible for preparing the Little Skull Mountain Deep Underground MX basing concept.

He understood very well his cover story this time was to demonstrate the feasibility of building readymade missile silos under the Mesa using the tunnel boring machines (TBMs). The idea was a good excuse to purchase TBMs for building the tunnels to launch the T-wave runner and not arouse too much suspicion. However, one thing that bothered Dave was the fact that several spare TBM components were acquired. These spare components added up to several full scale TBMs. Dave shrugged it off to "need-to-know". But now he had an interesting dilemma. How do you go about hiding the fact that you are really building the tunnels to be giant explosive shock tubes to set off torsional waves? Dave conducted dozens of classified meetings discussing this problem. It was hard to justify packing these tunnels with the millions of pounds of explosives and then set them off as some sort of nuclear shock simulations. After all, the shockwaves from a nuke were supposed to enter the complex from the outside, not the other way around.

One day while having lunch with Williams and his boss, General Powell, the subject of the newly proposed SICBM (Small Intercontinental Ballistic Missile) came up. The Scowcroft Commission recommended the development of a new, lightweight missile carrying only one reentry vehicle. President Reagan authorized full scale development of the Small ICBM in December 1986. They would be housed in mobile launchers based at widespread locations. When the shit hit the fan, the launchers would drive out onto the roadways and scatter across the country. It had been nicknamed the Midgetman.

In mid-bite of his hoagie, Dave had another one of his brilliant ideas. He set down his sandwich and brought up the idea as part of the discussion.

"Excuse me, General, but I think I have an idea for converting the underground silo complexes into our torsional wave generator without too much of a problem. I'm sure they are going to want to do shock and blast testing on the small ICBM mobile launchers. Why don't we propose that when we are done with the Deep Underground basing tests for the MX, we convert the tunnels into giant shock tubes to simulate nuclear weapons blast effects on the mobile launcher?"

Lieutenant Colonel Williams didn't skip a beat, "That is an excellent idea. That would explain the six million pounds of explosives we need to bring in here. We could say that we were setting up a full scale blast and shockwave test to simulate the over pressure effects on the launcher."

The general nodded his head in agreement. He got up and

looked out the window of William's office and stared off towards Little Skull Mountain a dozen miles away.

"I wonder if there is any way we can put our torsional wave runner inside the mobile launcher and use it as a transporter to the mountain. It sure would cut down on the security issues. I'm not sure how we would integrate the Midgetman Mobile Launcher with the T-wave runner. I'm not sure what the dampening effects or any interference the launcher would have on the T-wave. Maybe there is a way we could conceal it in the launcher, remove it in the tunnel, and then pull the launcher out and say we need to set off some calibration shots or something before the actual simulation test. By God, gentleman, I think we've saved the program. We can make this happen. I'm going back over to Dreamland to start the wheels in motion. Good thinking, Dave."

As Williams and Sheridan watched the general's Huey disappear over the mountains to the northeast, Williams patted Dave on the back and said, "Damn, Dave keep that brain of yours in high gear. I might retire as a full bird yet."

The TBMs were making progress through the mesa and chewing up the talc in record time. A few operational technical challenges always come up when you are literally and figuratively on the cutting edge of technology. It was assumed that the volcanic talc would be soft and thus an incorrect decision was made to use cheap carbide cutting teeth. However, the talc was abrasive and wore the teeth out quickly and slowed the operation. After replacing all one hundred cutters with titanium nitrite coated cutting teeth, the pace nearly doubled. This was a coating that the Russians developed to coat their turbine blades to prevent the sand in Afghanistan from wearing them out.

The race was on. In portal X, one contractor was busy using a TBM that was self-lining. Steel plates shaped as quarter panels were rock-bolted into the ceiling as the TBM progressed inward leaving a spiral shaped steel reinforced tunnel wall behind them. The Y-portal used a different approach. It still used a TBM cutting head, but then used a more conventional mining technology using wire mesh bolted to the walls and then sprayed with shotcrete. The idea was to see who could do it faster and cheaper. This testing method was tried and true in the Air Force R&D world in the same way fly-offs had been conducted in the past to select the best fighter planes from various competing design prototypes.

The challenge with this drill-off competition was to ensure that the tunnel walls were reinforced in such a way that a spiral torsional wave would propagate down the tunnel wall and amplify itself in the process. This had to be designed into the project without arousing suspicions from the workers or contractors for that matter.

The project was running twice as expensive and twice as long as projected. However, the stalling allowed the T-wave runner to be modified and fit into the small ICBM mobile launcher mockup.

After about seven months of work, the tunnels were nearing completion. The side drifts were dug at the end of the tunnels leading to huge excavated caverns. The TBMs were reoriented in the caverns into a vertical position to drill upwards through the basalt layers and the cap rock above. The TBMs used hydraulic rams to push them upwards as they rotated and chewed their way through rock on their way to the surface.

The vertical drilling phase was fairly easy. The only problem was that it was extremely difficult to get going once you stopped. This necessitated a twenty-four hour round the clock operation that lasted for a week. But both TBMs punched through the basalt cap rock within a couple days of each other. The concept worked. TBMs could be used to build deep underground missile launch complexes into the sides of mesas. Now was the time to switch gears and start converting the tunnels into the shock tubes.

It was an early Monday morning on a hot June 30, 1986. The parking lot was unusually full across from the Jackass Flats' command center as Dave drove in. There were a series of test readiness review meetings scheduled today.

Dave sat down next to Williams as Dr. Rapp was preparing for his classified portion to the Delta G contingent. He had accidentally dropped his overhead slides on the floor and was reshuffling them.

Williams got up and stood behind the podium. "Good morning ladies and gentlemen. Please secure the door and we will get started. This briefing is classified BTS and Delta G conditions are in effect. Dr. Rapp, please proceed with your briefing."

"Thank you, Colonel Williams. As you know, the full scale SICBM Mobile launcher mockup was flown into Desert Rock airstrip last week on a C-5 and then transported to the RMAD facility. The T-wave runner is located inside the launch tube. It is hermitically sealed in a helium filled chamber in the second stage dummy missile and placed in the launch tube to prevent oxidation."

Dr. Rapp flipped through the next set of slides until he came to the photo of the T-wave runner. He continued with his presentation.

"The T-wave runner is a very, very expensive single piece of forged beryllium. It was meticulously machined and chemically acid milled to shape it into this double helictical shaped sabot. It is approximately three feet in diameter and fifteen feet in length mimicking a double helix DNA strand. The one piece insures a near constant homogeneous density. The beryllium gives it near perfect reflectivity of torsional waves and photons. Once the T-wave is generated it will be amplified in the tunnel complex and then reflect perpendicular to the highly reflective beryllium vanes. As every child should know from our good old friend Sir Isaac Newton, for every action there is an opposite and equal reaction. Hence, the T-wave runner should literally catch the wave, hang ten so to speak, and be blasted into oblivion. As it passes thought the solar system at superluminal speeds, the gravitational wave detectors in orbit will triangulate and calculate its trajectory. As you are well aware, this first shot is just a slug. No instrumentation is on board to complicate things. The purpose of this shot is to see if we can launch and track a T-wave runner via the Lagrange point satellites by using conventional explosives. Any questions?" No one in the room spoke up.

It was Dave's turn at the podium, "I don't have any charts or photos. So, this is from the hip. As all of you know the tunnels are complete. We are stripping it of all lighting, air handling systems, and ancillary equipment. You will have a smooth-walled tunnel in a couple of days. As of now, only certified and trained personnel are allowed to enter the tunnels with self-contained breathing apparatus. There is no air change over in there now. This will make placement of the T-wave runner time consuming and difficult.

"When we drive the mobile launcher into the X-portal tunnel, we'll stop halfway in. We've left the rails in place behind the launcher. We will then open the launcher, extract the T-wave runner, place it on a rail skid, and then move it back into the side drift work chamber. Once secured in the side drift chamber, the launcher will be driven out of the tunnel. You do not need to know the details of why the launcher will be pulled. But suffice it to say that there will be some disagreement among scientists as to whether we will need to perform a calibration shot before the launcher is actually exposed to the first shot. We'll use this calibration shot to position the T-wave runner, and place the millions of pounds of ANFO at the end of the X-tunnel via the vertical shafts. We'll do the same in the Y tunnel minus the T-wave runner of course. Four million pounds of ammonium nitrate and twenty tanker trucks of diesel fuel is a huge logistical problem. We've been storing the ammonium nitrate in the old horizontal shelter tubing across the road. The diesel is stored in the old abandoned LOX tank farm at Calico Hills to the north. We will then pump the tunnels with nitrogen. This will be done for two reasons. First, it will prevent the T-wave runner from oxidizing. That's rusting, for you non-engineer types. Second, it will provide an inert atmosphere for the mixing and placement of the ANFO. We have only five days to do all of this. It is a tight round the clock schedule. This is going to be one heck of a Roman candle to celebrate Independence Day next week."

Lieutenant Colonel Williams got up next, "I don't have to stress the need for absolute secrecy concerning this test. It has been very challenging compartmentalizing all the layers of security required for this program. The two dozen members of the Delta G Team that are located in this room are only a handful of people that know about the T-wave runner. As far as the manufacturer is concerned it is a giant impeller built for a new experimental submarine. Ninety-nine point nine percent of the DOE Test Site community here thinks we are going to do blast and shock testing on the mobile launcher. Keep it that way. We will have a dummy load of instrumentation shunted into the control trailers. I cannot stress enough that this all boils down to timing. We are loading up both tunnels with ANFO and setting them both off within three milliseconds to initiate the needed densification and torque within the talc strata. Any questions for me?"

Just then a burly man from the front row raised his hand. "Sir, I have a question." Williams pointed to him and said, "Proceed Dr. Rapp."

"I was wondering how you explain the fact that it is necessary to blow both tunnels at nearly the same time. Don't people ask you this? Aren't you concerned with the shock testing demonstration only on the X-portal?"

Williams responded, "We considered that problem and after sitting under the tree of knowledge, sipping on Mogen David wine, we had a revelation. The second shot, or Y-portal shot, is the baseline event. It must be set off at the exact same time to represent the actual environmental conditions in the tunnel, such as outside barometric pressure, temperature, humidity. All these factors affect the resulting shockwave. So, we have one shot with the launcher in place and one shot with an empty tunnel to accurately map the shockwave with and without the test article in place. That sounds plausible doesn't it?"

Anne smiled and said, "You guys are amazing. How do you sleep at night keeping fact from fiction straight in your heads?"

Dave replied, "Truth of the matter is we sleep very well. But it is out of sheer exhaustion not contentment."

The rest of the morning was dedicated to technical considerations, such as instrumentation of the tunnel, explosive safety and countdown checklist procedures. It was imperative that everyone understood their tasks and responsibilities down to the second. The check list was 540 pages long and started the countdown at T-minus 48 hours. The launch team was camping out at the old infirmary that had been renovated to accommodate the two dozen Delta G members.

Anne's job in all of this was interesting. Her cover story was actually a classified program to investigate Remote Viewing. During the Carter administration, an RV program was developed concerning proposed deployment of the mobile MX missile system. In that scenario missiles were to be randomly shuffled from silo to silo in a silo field, a form of a high-tech shell game. In a computer simulation of a twenty silo field with randomly assigned (hidden) missile locations, Remote Viewers were able to show rather forcefully that the application of a sophisticated statistical averaging technique (sequential sampling) via RV targeting could in principle permit an adversary to defeat the system. As a result, much of the remote viewing activity was carried out under conditions where ground-truth reality was a prior known or could be determined, such as the description of U.S. facilities and technological developments, the timing of rocket test firings, underground nuclear tests and the location of individuals and mobile launchers. Thus, Anne got a huge budget to follow up and study the phenomena as part of the original CIA, DIA and DoD Sun Streak program.

With the test this week, she and her three colleagues were going to see how the T-wave energy enhanced their RV capability without any way to predict the outcome. They had several experiments lined up. Her team would be located in a specially equipped and instrumented trailer van located on top of Little Skull, a half mile behind the portal. Here they would be safe from the shockwave and over pressure. However, they would be directly over one of

the T-wave side lobes. The T-wave energy would be directed into the van and into a sensory booth much as was located on the *DGA Nautilus*. She would be looking for two things. Trying to RV the T-wave runner after its launch and trying to get a sense of what lies on the other end of the wave. Her deep cover story would be that the van was there to monitor environmental conditions and seismic activity.

Dave wished he had time to meet with Anne. He developed more than a crush on her in Greenland and hoped the feeling was mutual. However, things were nonstop and hectic getting ready for the shot.

He rode in the SICBM launcher vehicle from the RMAD facility up to the Little Skull turn off. There had been much consternation as to whether the launcher should be driven to the portal. Some felt it should be carried piggy back on tractor trailer flat beds. The schedule was too tight to risk the contraption breaking down.

The SICBM Program Manager made the call. He had faith and trust in his weapons system platform. The fifteen mile drive up the mountain to the X-portal would be part of its road ability testing. Dave switched with the assigned crew member into the right seat for its dusty leg up the gravel access road. The Mobile Launcher had no trouble at all on the flat paved road. There was a caravan of vehicles following the launcher.

Dr. Rapp was watching nervously as the launcher lurched up the mountain road. Even though it had no moving parts the T-wave runner cost as much as a B-1 bomber to design and build. New casting technology had to be developed to produce a beryllium component that huge.

As the Mobile Launcher turned and climbed the switchbacks, its 1200 HP Rolls Royce Perkins diesel engine put out the maximum torque to its eight tractor wheels through an electro-hydraulic transmission. The program manager had been right. This was a maximum effort road ability test. But it came through with flying colors.

At the top of the road at the X-portal, the mobile launcher was lined up with the tunnel. After several safety checks, the launcher inched its way into the tunnel. There were several feet of clearance all around. The biggest problem was with visibility. The diesels puffed out sooty exhaust and the vibrations kicked up a lot of dust. The crew stopped at the designated mark. They shut things down and then pulled on their Scott Air Packs and breathing masks and exited the vehicle. Other crew members had followed them in and started connecting instrumentation cables to the vehicle.

The next day, all hell was breaking out. The ruse was on. The Kirkland Weapons Effects lab was insisting the launcher be pulled from the tunnel. They had conflicting data from the Cray modeling software as to where the shockwave would stabilize prior to hitting the vehicle. They insisted on at least one full scale calibration shot to verify the computer model predictions. Two shots would be even better, done simultaneously in both tunnels. This would verify the model.

The SICBM Program Manager was highly pissed. But he had no choice. The Aeronautical Systems Center (ASC) commander had directed him to remove the test article and perform the calibration shots. The launcher was disconnected from the instrumentation umbilical and driven out of the tunnel and back to the RMAD facility. The ammonium nitrate was hauled up to the top of the vertical shaft in dump trucks. They literally poured it into a funnel and let gravity feed the beads into a five inch fire hose. The beads flowed fairly easily through the hose and they would be hosed into the back of the tunnel through a movable bulkhead. The bulkhead was twenty-two feet in diameter, concave, and made of frangible aluminum pie shaped wedges. Shaped HMX (high-velocity military explosive) charges were attached radially along the break points.

As the ammonium nitrate was placed behind the bulkhead it would move forward. A detonation cord had been coiled around the tunnel wall lining behind the bulkhead and under the steel walls of the tunnel. If the Kirkland explosives experts were correct in their calculations after the detonation the frangible wedges would separate and embed themselves in the talc walls and peel backwards much as a shotgun shell wadding. The resulting shockwave would blow past the aluminum wedges and propagate down the tunnel at hypersonic speed.

It took all day to pour the ammonium nitrate. Now came the dangerous and tricky part, saturating the ammonium nitrate with the diesel fuel. It too had been piped down from topside. It entered essentially a fire sprinkler system that sprayed the beads from overhead.

Once the proper saturation had been made, they only had four hours to blow the charge or the diesel would settle and drain to the floor of the tunnel. Everything was ready now. The clock was running and it was T-minus two hours and counting. The area had been cleared for ten miles out in front of the portals. The weather and winds were checked and perfect.

Lieutenant Colonel Williams ran the checklist, "Weather?" "GO." "Range Safety? "GO." "Instrumentation? "All boards are green, we're GO". "Explosives?" "We're a GO."

The dummy shunts had been removed from the fire control panel and replaced with live shunts. The mountain was now hot.

Williams continued with the countdown, "T-minus two minutes. Communications?"

"COM 1 and SATCOM Lima two checks green, we're GO."

"Activate sirens. Arm fire control panel. Insert keys. T-minus 90 seconds. Turn keys now."

The two man policy had been in effect, leftover from the good old SAC days. It took two keys located in separate trailers to be turned within two seconds of each other to activate the firing sequence.

"Confirmed armed and now on computer firing control."

Since timing was precise down to the millisecond, there was no way humans could initiate the firing of both tunnels within the three millisecond delay required. With less than ninety seconds before detonation high voltage capacitors were being charged. High speed cameras kicked in at T-minus one minute. For the next minute instrumentation channels started to record ambient conditions. When zero was finally reached the capacitors discharged routing a current through three redundant circuits to the firing control signal conditioners. The conditioners shaped the firing pulse to provide a distinct electrical charge to the detonation cord and with a half millisecond delay to the shaped charges.

Dave could feel the earth shake before he heard the loud explosion a few seconds later. The well insulated control bunker was six miles away, but the noise was surely the loudest thing that Dave had ever heard. Looking through the blast window towards the mountain, a huge fire ball shot out of the mountain several hundred yards. The shockwave could be seen dancing across the desert as cactus and yucca plants were blown outward. A smoke ring was visible several hundred feet in diameter as it slowly drifted upwards behind the massive tower of fire and smoke. Dr. Rapp had mentioned to Dave that one of the first tell-tale signs of a successful torsional wave being formed would be the smoke ring. Everyone in the control room was clapping now. It would now take a week or two to analyze the results. Hopefully, the orbiting satellites at the Lagrange points had recorded the T-wave passing.

Anne was laying naked in the saline bath and hooked to the EEG. She was relaxed and totally unaware of the outside world.

RVing is a form of virtual reality traveling that is brought under conscious control. She was wide awake and her senses were starving for input, including the sixth one.

Her colleagues were monitoring the instrumentation and the shot countdown. When their call sign was queried as to their status they replied, "This is USGS One, we are GO." The truck van had US Geologic Survey markings and logo stenciled on its exterior. Underneath was a huge pedestal that rested on the desert sand. It was supposed to be there to monitor the seismic event and map fault lines within Little Skull Mountain during the blast. The cover would be that this information was vital to the survey work being conducted for the high level nuclear waste repository being considered across the valley at Yucca Mountain.

In reality the pedestal was a shock damping system that would prevent any vibration or noise from reaching Anne in the chamber. They did not want to disturb her in her RV state.

When the blast took place the crew barely noticed any effects on top of and behind the portals. It shouldn't have been apparent to Anne floating in the saline. She was oblivious. Her mind was saturated with random thoughts and patterns. However, in one instant she could see or visualize herself as a spinning bullet accelerating down a gun barrel. As the bullet left the end of the gun, she could see the sun streak past her in the cobalt blue of space. She could see the beryllium billet spinning now. She had floated clear of it and was twisting and writhing along with it. The view behind showed the Sun-Earth-Moon system fading far below. Up above or in front, since there was no sense of direction, there was a burst of stars, a supernova spinning in on itself. The T-wave runner had exploded into a billion grains of dust when it hit the nova gas cloud. Anne was jolted awake when the door to the chamber quickly and unexpectedly opened. "Anne, are you okay? Speak to me." Anne's heart had actually gone into defib for a few seconds and the EEG went off scale. She came around and threw up into the bath. Her colleagues pulled her out wrapped her in a sheet and laid her on a cot.

She said, "Joe, hurry and get me a pencil and tablet. Joe, start the audio recording." She murmured something as they began recording her memories and she sketched her vision. It was imperative to get these thoughts now. The RV is like a dream, you can't remember them after a few minutes of waking up.

She drew the sun with a double helix with the T-wave runner inside with an arrow towards a spiral with a cross hair through the center. She

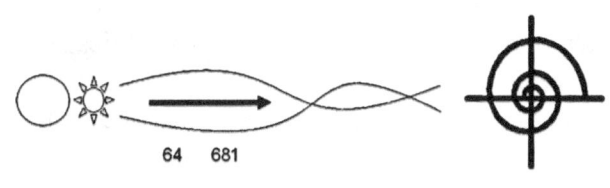

64   681

also wrote the numbers 64 and 681. She leaned to one side of the counter and threw up again.

"I'll be fine. I just need to lie down and rest for a while."

Dave spent the next six weeks involved with after action test reviews, writing reports, going to briefings and meetings to discuss when other meetings would be held. He was getting tired of the bureaucracy. General Powell had ordered a Program Management Review at Jackass Flats. This could be taken two ways, either the test was a huge success or it was a flop and everyone would be looking for jobs.

The room was called to attention as the general entered. "Please be seated. Now that you are figuratively on the edge of your seats, not just metaphorically, I'm going to cut to the chase. The TW test was about sixty percent successful. We successfully generated a near perfect wave in the tunnel. The T-wave runner exited the tunnel cleanly. However, we had some trouble with the tracking satellite at the Lagrange Point Two Site. We detected the TW but its wave length was so long we couldn't get a good fix on direction.

I have some good news and some bad news. The good news is we are still going to be generating torsional waves with conventional explosives. We knew we could do it. Now we proved the concept. The bad news is we are not going to be doing it here at the Nevada Test Site. Things have gotten too political. The tunnels require massive re-work to the steel and shotcrete liners. We broke a few windows in Lathrop Wells with this last blast. The brothel owner wasn't complaining, but the word got out to the press and now they are asking a million questions. We are now in a PR fight to explain why we are blowing up Little Skull Mountain and spewing who knows what out across highway 93. We have also detected a fault line running under Little Skull. The people involved with the Yucca Mountain project for the high level waste repository don't need the compounded hassle of explaining to the environmentalists that the place is seismically inactive when we just generated a 4.0."

General Powell picked up a pointer and indicated an aerial photograph projected on the screen. "So, gang, this is what we are going to do. We are going to move the operating location to an area east of Yuma, Arizona on the Luke Air Force Base gunnery range. We're moving the Small Mobile Launcher down there for more road ability and concealment tests. But we are not going to be drilling any horizontal tunnels. You'll have to wait until you arrive on station down there to get the details. This is part of the BTS compartmentalization process.

"Jake, you have three months to wrap up six years' worth of work and testing. You have the option to command the new location down there or I'll pull you into the NTS Air Force liaison office, or you can work with me here at Dreamland. You can pick your team. This is not a reflection on the outstanding work you all did here last month. We have to be rigidly flexible in this business. "Captain Sheridan, you will be the deputy commander of the Yuma operating location. You have one month to relocate down there.

"Before I leave I want to show you something." Powell flashed on the screen Anne's sketch from her remote viewing session. "If anyone can decipher the meaning of this, I'll give them a spot bonus and a promotion. I can't tell you where it came from, but you are all used to seeing strange symbols and playing with weird numerology."

CHAPTER 23
Yuma

Dave couldn't resist cranking up the rpm on his new Chevy Monte Carlo Super Sport as he barreled down Telegraph Pass on I-8 east of Yuma. The car took the desert curves nicely. Unfortunately, he had to back her off because he was looking for the Wellton exit to old US 80. Coming down the pass he could see the Mohawk Valley spread out before him. The irrigation from the Colorado River had made a farming paradise out of this Valley. It proved one thing; you could grow just about anything in the desert if you brought it enough water.

He overshot his next turnoff to South Avenue 25E and made a U-turn. The directions were somewhat confusing. Take S Ave 25E approximately one mile under the Interstate. Cross the railroad tracks and continue until you cross the Mohawk Canal where it turns into El Camino Del Diablo. Follow Camino Del Diablo approximately seventeen miles to the Entry Control Point (ECP).

Down this road located in a valley east of the Gila Mountains near Yuma, the Air Force Ballistic Missile Office had an operating location dedicated to nuclear shock and blast testing. It was here that Captain Sheridan brought his expertise to bear in developing vertical shock tubes for torsional wave generation. The shock tubes that were tunneled into the side of Little Skull were very successful, yet extremely expensive. Besides that, they were pointed in the wrong direction. It was discovered that the T-wave runner should be launched perpendicular to the Earth's magnetic field, not low over the horizon.

The cover for Sheridan's next assignment was to go to Yuma and build half scale missile silos and then detonate millions of pounds of explosives over the top of them to see how they shake, rattle and roll during the nuclear blast simulation. In reality, just like complex 374-7 near Damascus, Arkansas six years ago, the controlled explosions would be used to generate a torsional wave. The silos would be built in such a way to maximize and direct the torsional energy as the playa under them was densified in a millisecond.

He finally got his bearings just as he ran out of pavement. El Camino Del Diablo was once a 250 mile dusty road that led from the northwestern frontier of Mexico to the colonies of California. It began at Caborca in the Mexican state of Sonora. It hadn't changed much in over four hundred years. It still runs north northwest through a landscape of Socorro cactus, dry lakes, sand dunes, ancient lava flows and unbearable summer heat. It also passes through the Barry M. Goldwater Air Force Range where he was headed. This road is known as "The Road of the Devil."

Sheridan was a little hesitant to take his brand new sports car out on the gravel road for the next seventeen miles. He should have rented a car. After all, the best off road vehicle you can have is a rental car. It's too late now. He had a 0900 meeting and only a half hour to make it. He pulled on to the gravel and pressed on the accelerator. The road wasn't in too bad of shape. It seemed to point to no man's land which in fact it did. On the right were the Gila Mountains and to the left, an outcropping of volcanic rock and cinder cones. Somewhere in front of him was the Mexican Border.

The car got in a nice rhythm as it now glided over the wash boarding on the road. He was kicking up a dust cloud that must have been visible from orbit. His FM radio was fading in and out but thank God the A/C was throwing out the cold air. It was over a hundred degrees out. He rounded a curve and came upon a water truck spraying the road to keep the dust down. Dave thought to himself, "your tax dollars at work." He pushed on the final ten miles and came to a guard shack. A few hundred yards beyond was a modular building complex with an American flag blowing in the hot desert breeze.

Captain Sheridan showed the guard his military ID and was

waved in and told where to park. The guard announced his arrival. Not bad, he now had ten minutes to spare.

Dave was greeted by Lieutenant Colonel Kirk Johnson, the Commander of Ballistic Missile Office Operating Location – AF. "Nice to see you again, Dave. Welcome to BMO OL-AF. As you can see we are a little more Spartan down here than what you had up at NTS. We are a tenant on a Marine Corps range out of the Yuma Air Station, MCAS. They are a no frills bunch. Besides, we've got to leave this place as we found it when we're done here. We are actually adjacent to the Barry Goldwater Range a few miles to the east. That is an environmentally sensitive chunk of real estate. The crew should be trickling in a couple minutes for the 0900 staff meeting. Until then, let me show you your new office." They walked across the modular unit to the back corner. Dave said, "I'm impressed. A corner office with a view."

"If you think that's impressive, check out what's on your credenza." Dave checked out his new state of the art desk top computer, an Apple IIe. "Wow, a real engineer's computer." Lieutenant Colonel Johnson hit the power switch and said, "What we lack in facilities we make up for in creature comforts and top notch equipment. Someone, somewhere has a bank roll for this program. We'll have Debbie get you up to speed on this thing ASAP." The screen came to life complete with the BMO logo and log on block.

Just then, the outer door opened and in walked a gaggle of a half dozen persons. "Here comes the crew, just in time. You've got one minute to spare."

Dave sat down at the opposite end of the conference table from his boss, Lieutenant Colonel Johnson. Johnson started the meeting by introducing his newest member of the team. "I'd like to introduce you to my new Deputy, Captain Dave Sheridan." Introductions were made all around the table. There were only a hand full of military enlisted personnel, a safety NCO, a Supply NCO and an Explosives & Ordinance Chief. The rest were again mostly engineers from the top three DoD prime contractors, and a couple of high ranking GS civilians from the Air Force Weapons lab at Kirkland AFB in New Mexico.

After the introductions, Dave was given a status briefing on operations at the test site. Excavation for the silos was complete and the base foundation was being formed that would be ready for concrete in a week or so. The silo was to be a half scale model of an operational Peacekeeper (MX) Silo. Dave would be in charge of installing the rebar caging, the electromagnetic shielding and the classified concrete mix. The silo would look like the real thing. However, all the components that went into hardening a silo for an overhead airburst were amazingly similar to the configuration one needs to build a vertical torsional wave generator. The rebar cage would spiral around the silo like a huge coil. Its spiral shape and spacing was explained away as necessary for handling compressive shockwaves through torsional dissipation. Also, the spiral rings would dissipate electromagnetic effects in a nuclear blast.

The backfill material used around the silo would be layered and compacted thus giving the site a huge volume of constant density matter for generating and amplifying the wave.

The concrete mix would not be your average batch of 4,000 pounds per square inch strength used as generic driveway concrete. It would be five times stronger with a classified concoction of over twenty added mixtures, plasticizers, including aggregate of stainless steel ball bearings, slag, and tungsten needle filaments of various sizes. The concrete was specifically designed to compress, twist, and torque after a simulated nuclear air burst overhead without cracking and failure.

To generate the simulated nuclear shockwave, over six million pounds of conventional high explosives (iramite 360) would be detonated in a radial pattern laid out over the silo. The explosives would be mixed in cement trucks, poured in slabs, then overlain with explosive primer detonation cord, and cushioned with a one foot layer of Styrofoam prior to being buried under twenty-five feet of constant density desert playa covering over six acres.

The silo would be connected to a command bunker with over five hundred channels of buried instrumentation cable located six miles away. In theory, the blast would densify the nearly 45,000 tons of playa and send a torsional wave down the tube amplifying it with the rebar cage and concrete mixture.

The construction of the silo was on schedule and on budget, a rarity in the R&D world. Even though the Delta G Program Office had deep pockets, it was always good to meet cost, schedule, and performance milestones. This kept scrutiny to a minimum and having to answer a shitload of dumb questions from the brass and congressional oversight committees. Instrumentation transducers and cabling were in place. All that needed to be done now was back fill the cable trenches, place the concrete closure on the silo, and commence pouring the explosives, finishing by capping the complex with the playa overburden.

However, when all is going well, Murphy's Law has a tendency to kick in, that is, if it can happen it will. In this case, it included a couple of ancillary laws, too; *Mother Nature can be a Bitch and Shit Happens.*

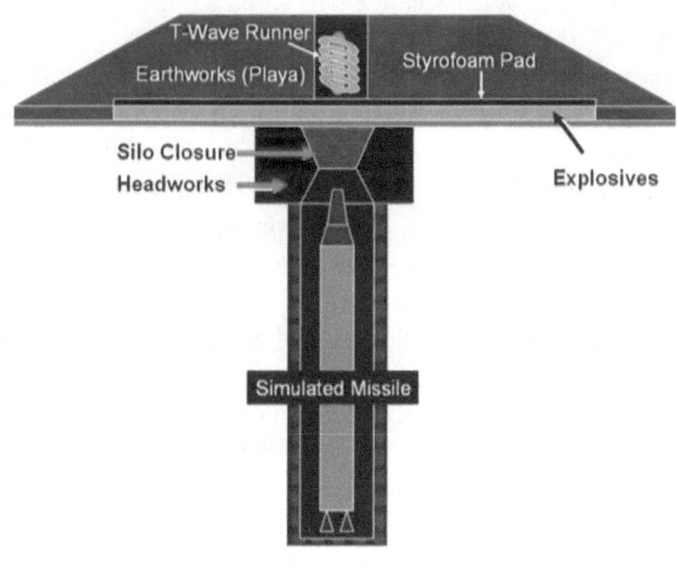

CHAPTER 24
Burning Sands

A funny thing about deserts, rainwater doesn't soak in very fast or very well. That was evident the winter of 1987 when a torrential rainstorm along the east side of the Gila Mountains caused a two foot wall of water to rush down the mountain side and onto the test site. The flash flood filled the silo with water and the cable trenches with silt. What's worse was when the mud, muck and silt dried as hard as concrete.

After months of rework and millions more in tax dollars, the Super Hard Silo High Explosive Simulation Test (HEST) was nearly ready. The T-wave runner was in place above the silo headworks encased in a beryllium launch tube surrounded by the near constant density playa, or dirt, compacted to military specifications. It was affectionately known by the Corps of Engineers Waterways Experiment Station as Mil-Spec dirt. However, it is actually composed of prehistoric lake bed sediment of microscopic animals, the precursor of oolitic limestone (the same material the pyramids are made with) and silica or sand.

But on a sunny spring day in 1988, again, Murphy's Law kicked in. Murphy was now two for two. However, it resulted from a human made oversight, not Mother Nature. True, Mother Nature can be a bitch, but humankind can also be a stupid bastard.

Being less than a dozen miles from the Mexican border, the signs surrounding the one hundred square mile complex read: "PELIGRO Area de Explosivos Mantengase Afuera" which meant "DANGER Explosives Area Keep Out." On this particular day they were very pertinent. A dozer operator was putting the finishing touches on the earthworks atop the silo by grading and compacting the playa berm, when he noticed a strange burning odor. Since all radio communications were banned anywhere near the six million pounds of explosives sitting a few feet below him, his only option was to jump out of his cab, run like hell, and wave his hands for everyone to get off the berm.

He ran for nearly a mile in desert heat before a security guard met him to see what the commotion was all about. Panting and hacking on dust he blurted out in Spanish, "Peligro, Peligro, Explosivos Quemante". It took a second for it to register, but the guard immediately broke radio silence, "BMO One, BMO One, this is Condor two with a priority emergency message". He didn't waste any time waiting for a response from Lieutenant Colonel Johnson. "We have an emergency situation on the silo. Evacuate the silo area immediately. Repeat, evacuate the silo immediately. The explosives are burning. Hit the sirens." Just then every vehicle siren on the complex was activated as well as a klaxon on the PA system.

Dave and Johnson were in an instrumentation calibration and planning meeting when they heard the radio transmission. Johnson said, "Get everyone the hell out of there. Dave call BMO HQ, then Yuma MCAS, run the checklist. I'm going out there."

They were located more than six miles from the silo outside the blast zone. Dave got out the Emergency Disaster Prep Checklist. It had phone numbers and procedures to perform in the event of an emergency. But it sure didn't cover the unexpected, that being six million pounds of explosives that were cooking under several acres of dirt.

Johnson hit the siren and barreled down the access road at breakneck speed. He had to give the rent-a-cops credit. They were showing some balls and driving up to the excavation. Men were hopping in the back of pickup trucks and hauling ass. Johnson met the pickup coming the other way. It slowed down enough for the EOD chief to yell over. "We've got all men accounted for. They're in these three vehicles. We've got to haul ass. That thing can blow any second. I'll explain at the CP." He too didn't wait for a response from Johnson, but tore off down the road. Johnson turned around and followed them. When they skidded to a halt at the ECP, the chief got out and ran up to Johnson.

"Colonel, we've got something burning underground. I saw smoke coming up out of one of the PVC cable risers. I don't know if we have an electrical fire but the explosives are on fire for sure. I've smelled iramite burning before."

Johnson said, "Okay, set up a perimeter. Don't let anyone closer than this five mile point. Are you sure you've got everyone accounted for?"

"Yes, sir, I've got the entry control log here. Eight men in. Eight men out including the dozer operator."

"Captain Sheridan is running the checklist and making notifications. All we can do is pray for a low order burn. With only half the overburden placed, I'm not sure what a high order detonation would do."

The chief replied, "On a day like today with the low hanging clouds and a temperature inversion we'd blow that dozer to Barstow and kill anything within ten miles."

Johnson said, "Okay, double the perimeter distance. Evacuate the ECP back to the administrative area behind the outcropping. I've got some calls to make."

Dave met Johnson on the front steps, "I've contacted the BMO Office. The exec took the call. General Powell is in the air via C-21 on his way up to Vandenberg. He'll try to contact him. Yuma Marine Corps Air Station (MCAS) is alerted. Their crash team and disaster response teams are en route. They'll be here in a half hour. Don't know what a few fire trucks are going to do but they're on their way. The word is out on the streets already. The MPs at Yuma were monitoring Condor's radio call and called to see what was up and if they can help. I told them to get a chopper up to patrol the southern perimeter and look for illegals and keep anyone off El Camino Del Diablo."

Johnson said, "Belay the chopper. If it blows, it will knock anything out of the air within ten miles. I want to keep this as low key as we can until we have a chance to access the situation further. We have no life threatening issues to contend with for now. We've pulled back enough. Let's keep it that way. However, for PR sake contact the Sheriff and Border Patrol if they haven't heard about it yet. I want an ECP back at the Mohawk Canal. I don't want a bunch of sightseers getting their eardrums broke."

Dave said, "I understand and concur. Did you want me to contact Delta G in D.C. or should we let General Powell to do that?"

"Let's get our ducks in a row and find out what's going on first." Just then Debbie ran out, "The general is on the phone, Colonel. I told him you were right outside."

Johnson ran into his office and grabbed the phone, "Yes, sir, we have an underground fire apparently burning the explosives. No high order detonations at this time. Our EOD chief saw and smelled smoke coming up from an instrument cable riser. Yes, sir, we are pulled back and all personnel accounted for. No, sir, those are low or no voltage cables. Yes, all six million pounds with det cord are in place. We've contacted the locals. No, we have not been in touch with D.C. Yes, sir, I'll talk to the MCAS commander and inform him you are en route. He'll have a chopper on the ramp for you, I'm sure. Yes, sir, I'll keep you informed when we can determine more. It is too dangerous to approach for a look." Just then Dave picked up a marker and wrote on the dry erase board: Need aerial infrared recon from satellite and/or F-4s, treat like underground coal fire. Johnson glanced over as he was finishing his conversation with the general and gave a thumbs-up. "My deputy here recommends that we get some F-4s up for an aerial infrared recon survey. They are fast burners and will not present a hazard for long. If I recall, they have a squadron at Luke. We need a bird's eye view." Johnson paused for a few minutes, and then gave Dave another thumbs-up.

There wasn't much you could do but sit back and wait as millions of pounds of explosives smoldered under the hot Arizona sun. Johnson got word that General Powell's plane had just touched down at Yuma MCAS.

The Huey's blades were spinning as he leapt into the chopper for its twenty mile hop across the Gila Mountains to the test site. The general had the pilot patch him into the MCAS Command Post commander, "This is General Powell. I appreciate your help on this matter, Ted. I need for you to get a hold of the wing commander at Luke AFB. I want him to coordinate an infrared aerial survey of the silo area. Give him the exact coordinates and he'll make it happen under my authority. Tell him I need those photos on-site in two hours and then updated photo sets every two hours after that. Take no excuses. They can do it. If he has to call in resources from Nellis, tell him to do it. I'm the on-scene commander. Thanks, Ted, BMO One, out."

He next had the pilot switch to the Test Site frequency, "BMO Two, BMO Two, this is BMO One over." This caused some initial confusion as Johnson's call sign had been BMO One until his boss showed up. Dave responded as BMO Two, "This is BMO Two. Who's calling?" "This is General Powell. I'm about ten minutes out. Have your staff ready for a SIT brief. We'll land on the road near the Admin trailers. Clear the road." Dave responded, "Roger, sir." He ran out to Johnson and handed him the brick, "Powell is ten minutes out. He thought I was you. I'm clearing the road for the chopper."

They could hear the chopper approach from the west. As it was just about to land it suddenly veered to the south and made a high speed pass towards the silo. Johnson said, "He's going to make a flyby. That's why they get an extra $110 in flight pay per month I guess. The chopper made one quick orbit at about a hundred feet and then returned back to the admin area. It set up for a landing about a hundred yards off, kicking up a hell of a dust cloud. As it turned out, the landing was more dangerous than the flyby. As the chopper hung about fifty feet in the air it became enveloped in the sand and dust. The chopper pilot aborted. Dave got on the radio, "BMO One, this is Two. We're going to hit that road with the fire hose and soak that dust down. Give us ten minutes." The pilot responded, "Roger, thanks for the assist. We had a total brownout. Will stand by." The chopper orbited about a mile to the east as one of the fire trucks sprayed the road down with the mister. After about five minutes the chopper returned and made a perfect landing.

Before Powell hopped out into the mud in his dress blues he gave an order to have the chopper return to MCAS and develop the 35 mm film from the copilot's personal camera. He said, "I don't care if you have to land that thing at a drug store parking lot, just get them prints developed and back here ASAP."

Powell walked into the conference room. "Johnson, what's the situation?" Johnson gave the general as much information as they had, which wasn't much. The good news was that the Kirkland AFB Weapons Lab people were on the phone with the chief and told him as long as the explosives were only burning, there was only a slight chance of a high-order detonation. The explosives needed a shock detonator like a blasting cap to initiate an explosion.

Powell turned to Dave, "Captain Sheridan, take a note, I owe that chopper pilot a bottle of scotch. The crew volunteered to do that flyby. It wasn't my idea. The copilot had his 35 mm Nikon with him. We shot a roll of twenty-four before we landed. I don't know if there will be anything to see on it, but we did verify smoke coming out of a white pipe located about here," as he pointed to a blueprint of the site layout on the wall.

Dave told the general, "That's one of the instrumentation cable conduits running down to the closure lid. The cables are not powered so we don't understand how they could start an electrical fire."

Just then Debbie walked in, "Sirs, I just got off the phone with the explosive manufacturer. They have a theory on what started the fire." She was excited and nervous, but all eyes were on her now, "They seem to think that when the explosives are mixed, batched and then poured like concrete into slabs, the process of hardening or setting up is much like that of concrete or plaster of Paris, it generates heat. When we started putting the soil layer on top of the Styrofoam cushioning, the heat had nowhere to escape, built up, melted the foam and is now burning the iramite. They said the only thing that can be done is to let it burn itself out. They don't think it will high-order either but don't recommend anyone go near the place. They said to treat it like an underground coal seam fire."

The general thanked her for her valuable input. "F-4s from Luke will be flying overhead in a few minutes, giving us an infra-red picture. We can tell the extent of the burn after we see the film. Now, if you will excuse me I have to get rid of some coffee.

Colonel, Captain, I'd like to talk to you outside." On his way to the Porta John, General Powell gave them both an earful.

"How the hell are we going to explain this one? We've had two major 'ah shits' on this shot already. The visibility on this program is blown. We've got maybe, one more chance with this thing then I'm pulling the plug. I'm starting to get the feeling that something or someone doesn't want this shot to go off. Watch your backs, gentlemen."

The general kicked a trash can and said, "Shit, it's going to be hard to argue against the Navy's proposal now. It is a simple plan, no explosives, and relatively cheap if it works, based on densification of seawater. When this fire is out and if it doesn't literally blow up in our faces, I want you two to get back in there, re-pack it, re-instrument it, and do the shot. We've got a ten billion dollar T-wave runner sitting in a dirt pile on a shitload of smoldering explosives. We've got another billion or so in equipment and manpower riding on this one right up there. Do you understand me?" Powell was pointing to the full Moon that was coming up over the horizon. Dave and Johnson knew the general was really pissed off and didn't ask any stupid questions. The only thing they could say was, "Yes, sir." When Powell closed the door to the Porta John, Johnson looked at Dave and said, "Was that some kind of threat? Watch our backs for what? What Navy proposal? What's the Moon got to do with all of this?" Feeling like a third grader again, Dave just shrugged his shoulders and shook his head.

With the general still in the can, the F-4 Phantom reconnaissance jet screamed in from the east and made a low level pass over the complex. It waved its wings as it circled around. The general came out of the Porta John zipping his fly. "Damn, he's actually early. Must have used the afterburner all the way from Luke. He's got to be running on fumes." Just then a Marine Corps Major ran up to the General and handed him a brick. "Sir, the F-4 pilot wants to talk to the man in charge down here." The general said, "That'd be me." He grabbed the brick and keyed the mike, "Roger, Red Baron, this is Major General Powell, request you make your photo run north to south over the dirt mound about six clicks south of the trailer complex you just flew over. You can't miss it. It has a big yellow bulldozer on top of it. Do you see it?" The pilot replied, "Affirmative, sir. I've got enough fuel to make three passes at five hundred foot intervals. I'll then afterburner it back to the base. We'll have the photos developed ASAP and choppered back to you." The general replied, "Negative on the chopper. Have them find something faster, and prepare for another pass in two hours. I want to monitor the rate of burn." The pilot acknowledged and then made his three passes. The first was a slow pass. The F-4 had its big flaps hanging down and that created its trademark and eerie whistling noise as it flew over the complex. The pilot toggled the cameras on and off as he flew over the mound. His other two passes where higher and faster. The F-4 hit its afterburners and left its famous dual trail of sooty black exhaust plumes as it climbed over the mountains to the northeast on its way back to Luke near Phoenix.

When the plane landed, it taxied directly to the hangar where it was towed inside. Photo technicians quickly removed the film canisters and rushed them to the photo lab. They developed two copies in less than twenty minutes. One set was sent to the photo interpreters at Base Intel. The other set was packaged inside an empty flare canister with its parachute folded with a shock cord looped around it. They sent it out to the flight line and handed the canister to a Navy A-6 Intruder pilot sitting with his cockpit open and engines at idle. He closed the canopy, taxied onto the runway, hit full throttle and was turning to the southwest before his wheels were even in the gear bay. This crisis was turning into a bona fide joint service operation. The A-6 made it back over to the test complex in only twenty minutes. He slowed the plane down and put it in a classic Navy landing configuration. The pilot slid the canopy back and he tossed the canister out. The chute opened as expected and it landed within a hundred yards of the complex. One of the firemen ran out to retrieve it and brought it into the conference room.

General Powell removed the photos and rolled them out on the conference room table. "These are great photos." The infrared photos clearly showed a hot spot under the mound on its southeast corner. Powell said, "The only thing we can do is let this thing burn itself out. It could take days. We'll monitor the fire every two hours with a recon pass. It's been three hours since the fire started, or was detected, and it looks like from the infrared that over a quarter of the explosives is involved. Johnson and Sheridan clear this room. We need to discuss some classified repercussions of this incident."

After everyone left the room Powell asked, "We've got to get that T-wave runner out of there. If that thing detonates in an uncontrolled blast, it will be destroyed. Also, I'm not sure what the heat is doing to warp those protruding vanes. We have no spares in the pipeline. The Navy has the only other two in existence. We can't send anyone out to retrieve it. It took two seventy-five ton cranes to lift and pivot it in place. Hell, the cranes aren't even on-site anymore. They are now being used to build the hospital addition in Yuma."

Just then Dave's Civil Engineering brain kicked in, "Sir, we have the technology." Powell glared sharply at Dave, "Don't be a cute smart ass with the Bionic Man crap. What technology?"

Dave laid out his harebrained scheme, "The *Nautilus* is at Dreamland. We can call her down here and she can extract the T-wave runner. She can hook on to the whole drill pipe case and yank her up through the guide tube just like a shell extraction. She can do that from 20,000 feet to stay clear of any blast. It could be done in the middle of the night. We don't have to worry about air space or onlookers. We've got this whole valley cleared. I volunteer to hook the cable up."

Powell looked at Dave and said, "Damn brilliant, but we'll have to act fast. You'll also need another set of hands. I'll help you."

"Not to be out done," Johnson said, "I hope my wife enjoys spending my retirement. Count me in."

Powell sounding a little more relieved replied, "Now that we've got a plan to literally pull the plug on this program without it blowing up, we've got to get cracking. Captain Sheridan, you are coming with me to Dreamland. Johnson, you stay here and keep the lid on things."

The pun was intended to relieve the tension some. But it also drove home a point that Johnson was on the bubble.

Johnson found it comfortable in the back of the Ford Bronco and being a gentleman, gave Debbie the couch in his office. At 0530 in the morning the sun came up and the results of the final pass were in. By now about half the explosives was consumed with a little cooling in the southwest corner. However, the center or core was getting hotter.

After the chopper landed back at MCAS, Dave and the general raced into base operations. The base commander offered to fly Powell up to Nellis in a Navy F-18. Powell respectfully declined. "Thanks for the offer, but by the time I suit up, we'd be halfway there in my C-21. Besides I need to drag along my trusty side kick here," as he pointed to Dave. He didn't mention to the commander that he was actually flying a hundred miles beyond Nellis and his Navy pilot wouldn't be cleared into Dreamland because of lack of clearance. Dave and the general boarded the C-21 Lear jet and were wheels up at 0700 from Yuma MCAS VFR direct to Dreamland. The general was going to work the operation personally from that end.

General Powell had fielded most of the calls from the Pentagon and the Delta G Office while in the air. He didn't have much time for chit chat with Dave. Not that there was much sleep, but again, Dave followed his grandfather's advice and more importantly, the general's insistence that they try to get some rest.

Johnson, on the other hand, was busy talking and handling the locals. By 0800 in the morning the press was sitting out at the Mohawk Canal demanding a statement. Johnson had prepared one, ran it by the general and then drove out to present it. It was simple, to the point and factual. "The USAF Ballistic Missile Office is conducting high explosives testing on a half scale missile silo in the valley approximately fifteen miles to the south. We've had an underground fire involving the instrumentation cabling. The high explosives are in no danger of detonating. However, we are being prudent, and evacuated the site. All personnel are accounted for and safe. We will wait for it to burn itself out. We will have another statement at 1300 this afternoon. Please direct all of your questions through either the MCAS or BMO public affairs office."

A half hour later, the C-21 landed at Dreamland with a vehicle waiting to pick them up. Dave was surprised when it roared off with them past the flight line hangars and off the runway end onto a dry lake kicking up dust as it accelerated on the baked hard pan. After a few miles, the vehicle slowed as it reached the other side of the dry lake and began a slow climb over and around a rocky knoll. Powell was speaking into a headset and in a threatening voice was yelling into it, "I don't give a rat's ass Dukes, either let us in or crank up your thirty millimeters because we're here." At that instant the Suburban hit the brakes and skidded to a dusty stop. As the dust cloud rose, it curled and flattened out in a strange anvil shape. The dust couldn't rise any higher. That's when Dave suddenly realized that they were under the belly of the *Nautilus*. Hovering in the canyon in front of them was the magnificent vessel. It was blending in perfectly with the hills in the background. The retro-projection showed the blue sky above. The hugeness of the craft actually played into its natural camouflage. A human's brain just couldn't register a craft this huge, so the mind makes it blend in as part of the landscape. Being a mile wide, it dominated the landscape and became simply another hillside.

Admiral Dukes was standing on the cablevator about a hundred feet in front of him. Dave could make out the cables and railing.

Powell hopped out of the Suburban. "Come on Sheridan. Close your mouth, we're going for a ride."

As they approached the platform, Dukes said in protest, "Powell, this is highly irregular and in violation of a half dozen protocols. This ship is in dry dock. Over half my crew is on leave. We're being retrofitted. We can't simply pull anchor, soar on down to Yuma, and go pull your cork. You're, with all due respect, out of your mind."

To this Powell shot back, "You're getting too cautious in your old age, Scott. Where's your sense of adventure? Besides, this is a rescue mission. The Mayday has been sent and you are the cavalry. You are the only one that can save a ten billion dollar T-wave runner. This mission isn't any more risky than you plucking shells out of some cornfield."

As the lift was being pulled up into the *Nautilus*, Dukes replied. "If you need the Calvary call the Army, we are not ready for a launch."

Powell said, "Okay, I'll put it in nautical terms, you're the Carpathia," referring to the ship that rescued survivors of the Titanic.

With this, Dukes rubbed his white beard and said, "Okay, Captain Smith, we'll go save your ass. But women and children first."

Dave looked down. They were several hundred feet above the Suburban and he could look up into the hangar bay. Once on board, they were whisked off to the bridge in a new mode of inter-ship transportation. A small dirigible like device lifted them and propelled them up to the bridge a thousand feet above them. It was fairly luxurious, including leather seating, ornate detailing with mahogany inlay and carpet.

Powell was truly impressed, "My, my Admiral, they have given you quite a few more toys to play with since I was in command of her."

Dukes' pride button and ego switch were now pushed and stroked. "Yes, she does have a few more capabilities from the old analog days. We have plenty of helium, why not use the lift and propulsion technology we enjoy so much on a much smaller scale to traverse our own vessel? It sure beats the clunky old mechanical elevators and childish golf carts we used to use. Not only does it free up space and reduce maintenance, but it gives us true three dimensional mobility in our own ship. As you can see, we have passenger versions and utility pods. They also can be used as life boats if needed."

Dave remarked, "Ingenious. It looks as though you've learned a few things from the Greys and are starting to think more spatially."

Dukes replied, "Very perceptive of you, Captain. Welcome back and welcome aboard. I think you will appreciate many of the modifications we are making."

A few minutes later, the Aireopod, as it was called, docked with the bridge. Over the docking port hung a bronze sign. Dukes pointed to it and said, "These docking stations are located strategically throughout the ship. Naturally, the bridge is the central hub. It is in effect as the sign says, 'Grand Central Station', minus the graffiti and prostitutes, of course."

Just then Dave couldn't resist. He'd bit his tongue long enough. He'd been brought up here for a reason. What was it? "Excuse me, Admiral, what is your status? Are you able to get her up?"

Dukes smiled and said, "Sorry, Dave. That sounds kind of personal. But yes, she is airworthy for your purposes. I'm not too worried about the technical challenges of this mission. I'm more worried about security and logistics. As I said, half my crew is on leave. While I can fly this beautiful lady with literally one finger, it leaves me absolutely no margin for error."

Dave continued, "Then sir, with all due respect. I do feel that General Powell is correct. We need your help and you can provide it. I have a lot of respect for you. I know that you do not engage in inner service rivalries. Also, with all due respect sir, we're not here to kiss your butt to save our butts."

The admiral kicked back in his crew chair, "Brilliant move, Powell, bringing the kid here along to act as your mouthpiece and integrator. I, too, have a lot of respect for you, my young Captain. I realize the value of your test shot, too. This will be a valuable data point. It is true we have always had inner service rivalries. Amazing isn't it? We're trying to communicate with the Greys to demonstrate our civility and intelligence, yet the Navy and Air Force are distrustful of each other. So, let's evolve and get down to business and get serious."

"Okay, General Powell," the admiral proposed, "I will bring the *Nautilus* down to Yuma. I'll pull your T-wave runner and bring it back here for checkout and recalibration. I'll even install a dummy or prototype billet in its place to keep the local crews unaware that we even pulled the T-wave runner.

"It is true, General, the Navy is working on a proposal to the Delta G Office for an ocean based wave generator process. Believe it or not, we don't even have to blow anything up to generate the wave. The dolphins will be happy to hear that, I'm sure." Dukes continued, "To tell you the truth, we could use your T-wave runner in one of our future shots. It would put us ahead of the curve.

So if things don't work out down there and you can't get the shot off, we want dibs on the T-wave runner. If you do have a successful launch, we want your support for the Navy proposal with no arguments and oh, by the way, we want your experts, too." Dukes turned to Dave and asked, "How's Florida sound to you?"

Powell knew he was over a barrel. Chances were that with the flood and now, the fire, the Navy had the upper hand in any future shots. He replied, "Deal. You help us with this shot, and I'll concede and support your proposal." With a handshake, the deal was set.

"Have a seat, gentlemen. Lieutenant Holly Perkins, prepare for departure. EDT Noon."

"Aye, aye, sir. Launch in T-minus three minutes. Propulsion is on line. Retro-projection on line. Hydrogen generator is set to 60 percent. Ready for ballast release and mooring line release on your orders, sir."

Powell said, "You, sly ol' son of bitch. You were prepared to come to the rescue all along."

Dukes grinned, "Sir, what are friends for?"

Dukes then touched a couple of areas on his monitor, acknowledged and said, "Roger, Lieutenant. Push off."

Just then a klaxon alarm sounded and a computer voice came over the PA. "Rapid departure procedures in effect; repeat, rapid departure procedures are in effect. Rapid ascent in T-minus 90 seconds."

Dave wasn't familiar with this checklist procedure or maneuver from his three month stay on the ship. Dukes turned back to them and said, "We are going to make an emergency ascent. If you think about it, we aren't too different from a submarine making an emergency ascent. We are blowing ballast and increasing our buoyancy. We will actually pull a whole half G. That ought to make you Air Force types get a buzz in your shorts. We will be at 100,000 feet in about twenty minutes. Your ears may pop some. Our pressurization system is calibrated to 12,000 feet."

Just then came a frantic female voice on the intercom, "Abort! Abort! Abort!"

The computer shut down the ascent procedure with forty -seven seconds on the clock. Dukes asked calmly, "What's wrong Anne? Why the abort?"

Anne replied, "I'm in the middle of an RV experiment. I've got the tanks full. It will slosh for sure."

Powell asked incredulously, "She aborted the launch, because she's afraid of a little water sloshing out of her tub? Doesn't our good doctor know how to use a mop?"

Dukes replied, "Au contraire, my good general. That is some very special water."

Dukes replied to Anne, "Sorry, Anne, I wasn't aware you had an experiment in progress. Will you be ready to go in one five minutes?"

Anne replied in a milder tone, "Roger that, reset to T-minus one fiver minutes. I'll be to the bridge in ten."

Dave was looking forward to seeing Anne again. It was amazing how many times their paths had crossed.

Powell asked, "Does that special water have anything to do with your sea-based wave generation process?" Dave was wondering the same thing, but didn't want to ask the question. However, he was surprised at the answer.

"General, if I told you I'd have to shoot you both!" Once again, Dave and Powell didn't see the humor in this response.

Anne hopped out of the Aireopod and strode over to greet General Powell and Dave. "Good morning, gentlemen. It is nice to see you both. Admiral, I apologize, I should have entered the lab status into the daily event log. The lab is now secure."

The lieutenant spoke up, "We are ready to initiate at T-minus forty-seven seconds on your mark sir."

Dukes said, "Hold on to your seats. On my mark clear the hold, and mute the audio. Mark".

The lieutenant touched the middle of her screen three times on the red flashing abort bar, and hit the mute icon. A clock on the admiral's screen flashed forty-seven seconds. He said, "Pity, I never did learn the words to the Air Force's Wild Blue Yonder song."

Dave said, "Well, sir, it was written by an Army guy anyway, named Robert MacArthur Crawford."

Just then, Lieutenant Perkins started singing,

"Minds of men fashioned this crate of thunder,
Sending it high into the blue;
Hands of God bless the world that's under;
How they flew, God only knew!
Souls of crew dreaming of skies to conquer
Without wings, ever to soar!
With Greys before and shells galore. Hey!
Nothing can stop the Delta G Force!

Sorry, sir, that's your crew's take on revising the second verse. I thought it was appropriate."

Dukes smiled, "That it is perfectly okay, Lieutenant. You have a lovely voice."

A few seconds later, everyone's stomach was light as a feather as they were pushed down into their chairs. Dave could see the altimeter click off numbers by the hundreds as he watched the video on a side monitor showing the dry lake below them shrink away. He couldn't help but notice and take a mental note of some strange spiral markings arcing away from the runway on Groom Lake. In the business Dave was in now, it was often better to observe than to comment. This was one of those times.

Dukes turned back to his passengers, "Sorry, I forgot to tell you to fasten your seat belts. We are about to engage our ion drive for lateral acceleration. We will be at 180 knots in about 30 seconds."

Dave watched the navigation display. He was very familiar with the air charts in this part of the country. After all he learned to fly Cessnas here north of Las Vegas. The *Nautilus* was heading south over the Nevada Test Site. The plot looked like it was going around the west side of Mount Charleston, following Death Valley on through China Lake Naval Weapons Training Center. It continued southward in California through Fort Irwin, and then on down over the Sultan Sea before turning back to the east over the Yuma Proving Grounds where it finally turned southeast along the Gila Mountains to the silo test site. They were not taking any chances.

Even though the ship had stealth technology, retro-projection, and could shut down or jam every radar emitter in the western hemisphere. It was best to play it safe and overfly unpopulated areas.

Dukes said, "This route will take us a little over three hours to reach the site. The plan is to get in place, hover, wait for the fire to burn out and then perform the extraction.

"I suggest you both go get a shower and some breakfast. I'll call you back a half hour out. Anne, would you escort our crew mates to the lounge?"

Powell was no dummy and offered a suggestion, "I know my way around the ship. I'm going to hit the shower and get some of this grit off of me. Why don't you two go get a cup of coffee and breakfast?" Dave appreciated the general's chivalry. He was looking forward to some one-on-one time with Anne.

Once in the lounge, Dave asked, "Isn't it amazing how our paths continue to cross? It's not like I can take your number and call you up for a date sometime."

Anne said, "I know. I've thought of you often, too. It's just that I get busy. I'm sure it's the same with you."

Dave sighed, "Yes, I am a hopeless romantic, but I'm a workaholic, too. I'm married to my career. Once we've been exposed to the secrets of the universe, it would be kind of hard for either of us to go back to a regular nine to five, even if I ever did decide to get out."

Anne said, "Yes, I agree. We do have a special bond, David. This is no exaggeration, but we both share a vision."

Dave laughed and said, "Yes, I know. Yours is worth a cool million. Mine is just a little bit different, but it ain't worth squat."

Anne batted her eyes, "Your vision is forever etched in glass, digitized, and is now being crunched by the Cray, too. By the way, we are closer to deciphering the meaning of yours. You were dead on when you circled the smaller skull and crossbones indicating Little Skull Mountain over a year before the Air Force decided to dig the tunnels out there."

Changing the subject back from work, Anne said, "Once I get done with this extraction, I'm going to Cape Kennedy. I'll be working with Delta G there doing some work on space borne

T-wave detection technology. I'll be land based and finally have a life, so to speak. I think there is a job there for you, if you want it." Dave replied, "I think Dukes has something in mind in Florida for me after the Yuma shot. Let's see where things go from there. But for now, it has been a long day. I need a shower, but I better make it a cold one." Anne smiled.

Dave had just finished getting dressed into a crew coverall and was lacing his boots when the PA crackled with Perkins's voice, "General Powell and Captain Sheridan to the bridge, please.

Powell and Dave arrived on the Aireopod with Anne. Perkins turned from her console and said, "We are a half hour out. Admiral Dukes is in the hangar bay. He's going over the extraction with Chief Eldon. This is going to be a tricky one. We have to splice some cable together. Most of our extractions are no higher than 10,000 feet. We're going up to 15,000 just in case that little bonfire down there decides to high order on us."

The general asked Perkins where the com panel was. He needed to coordinate a few things and wanted a status from Johnson about the fire. He sat down at the terminal, but couldn't make heads or tails of it.

Dave learned a few things in his six month tour on the ship. He came over and punched up the Yuma Site on the console. "General, this is an open land line, not secure. But Lieutenant Colonel Johnson should be with you in a minute."

Powell replied, "Thanks, Captain. It's been five years since I sat in that chair. This is what they call a real glass cockpit, all CRT screens. Literally all push button, fly by the wire technology. Yes, Colonel. We are en route. We should be there by 1500 hours. What is the status there?"

Johnson told Powell that the fire was about two thirds burned. Smoke was now coming up the pressure transducer shaft. In other words, the T-wave runner launch tube was becoming a chimney for heat and smoke from the fire below. Hopefully, it wasn't too hot to damage it. Even though it was solid beryllium and could withstand the heat, it was thin in spots, and could become warped.

Powell understood the situation, "Roger, understand. We will be on-site soon. We'll set things up for around 1600. In the meantime, I would suggest you tell your people to clear the area and back off to the canal. The fire is now getting some oxygen and may still high order. If it does, it could blow debris onto the admin complex. The winds could blow toxic smoke over the complex, too."

Johnson understood the drill. Powell was looking to clear the area. Even though the ship would be nearly invisible to the naked eye at 15,000 feet with the retro-projection technology, he was taking no chances. Everyone would be at least fifteen miles away. Powell's next call was to the Yuma MACAS commander. "Ted, I need for you to put a NOTAM (Notices to Airmen) out. I want airspace cleared for twenty miles around that area. I don't care what excuse you use. Tell them that Marine One is landing with the president. Just keep aircraft clear of this area for the next twenty- four hours. Thanks."

Powell told Perkins, "We'll be clear in a half hour."

Perkins responded, "That's great, it will be 1600 hours, on time. Sun angels will be optimal. One thing we cannot control is our shadow tracking across the ground. We have limited ability with the retro-projection system to simulate the Sun's appearance. But it is nowhere near its luminosity. Right now we are over the Sultan Sea at 102,000 feet. Here is our shadow projection." There was a triangle shaped pattern superimposed on the moving map display. Even though it was relatively small, it was perceptible. Flying over mostly unpopulated land, military installations, and now the Sultan Sea cut down on the chances of anyone noticing their shadow.

Just then Dukes arrived back from the hangar bay. "We've got one more problem, Admiral. The outside humidity and air temperature at this altitude are unfavorable to daylight navigation. Our ion propulsion will present a reverse contrail. We will literally punch a hole in these high altitude clouds by pulling the moisture out of them."

The admiral understood the significance of that, "I understand. That is what got Gary Powers' U2 blown out of the sky by a Russian SAM-2 back in '60. His high altitude reconnaissance plane made a wake in the high cirrus clouds. They got a visual lock, then a radar lock, then missile lock, and then kaboom. They got close enough to damage the tail of the aircraft to where he had to eject."

Perkins maneuvered the *Nautilus* east over the Colorado River and then south through the Proving Grounds, north of Yuma. She brought the ship in such that the shadow was tracking along the tops of mountain ridges. The few seconds it took to cross I-10 caused her to hold her breath. She tried to time it between most of the traffic. And if someone did notice a brief shadow on the ground, they'd chalk it up to clouds or an airplane. But at this height the shadow was still two hundred yards wide.

"General, we are now directly over the site. I've lowered our altitude to 40,000 feet until we get a verification of zero air traffic in the vicinity. Shadow is now a quarter mile wide almost directly below us. Retro-projection must be working fairly well. Nothing is on CNN with all those reporters sitting about twenty miles out."

Dukes said, "Okay, Lieutenant. Bring her down slowly five hundred feet per minute descent. Bring her down to one five thousand."

She replied, "Aye, aye, one five thousand. Wind is not a factor at this time, but it is marginal. Steady from two four zero degrees at five fiver knots."

Dukes replied, "Good, we're going to need a stable platform to lower the gondola with our two Air Force comrades on the surface. The gondola is actually a four man mini-submarine we borrowed from the Navy. It was almost off the shelf technology. Why not? It did the job. It was rugged, environmentally controlled, and had power and communications, and landing skids. It just has never been used in the ocean yet. All the extractions so far have been dry. We have a half dozen submerged shells located and suspect more will be found."

Lieutenant Perkins got up from the console and was replaced by the chief. She had not stood up in over four hours. "Sorry, gentlemen, nature calls. The ship is now in station keeping mode. I've got the infrared and telephoto cameras on this monitor. You can now monitor the silo fire real time from here. It looks like it is dying out. I'm going down to the laser room after I head to the bathroom. We can shoot a laser tomography scan through the smoke to take measurements of the T-wave runner. We can compare these dimensions to the CAD drawing and see if there is any warpage on the vanes."

Powell said, "That's a great idea, Lieutenant, but that beryllium will reflect 99.9 percent of the laser energy. You might not get a return."

Perkins replied, "I'm counting on the soot and dust build up on the T-wave runner to reflect the laser. That should help give us good readings."

Dukes couldn't resist a dig at Powell, "These young people are always thinking, aren't they? They do have sharp quick minds, do they not?"

A few minutes later, over the intercom, Perkins announced that she was in the laser lab. "I'm calibrating the laser pulse for the distance and smoke. Chief, I need you to nudge her two meters to the east." Dave was amazed that they could control and position a ship of this size to within less than ten feet.

Eldon touched a few buttons on his CRT and then moved a track ball on the console. "Aye, aye, Lieutenant. Two to the east. Be advised the wind is picking up some with gusts. I'm sending air movement Doppler interrogation signals out to the southwest in order to predict the gusts so that we can compensate. Our station keeping probable error is plus or minus half a meter. This should make the lifting sling attachment possible without too much trouble."

Perkins replied, "Confirmed EP (Error of Probability), half meter. Keep her steady as you can, Chief. I'm going to take a five minute low power laser tomography shot of the T-wave runner. On my mark....five...four...three...two...one...mark. Just then, a laser beam shot down from the ship down to the center of the mound and hit the T-wave runner. Then the unexpected happened, the laser light reflected off the T-wave runner and burst out into a fan like pattern spinning around at about one revolution per second at about a 62.5 degree angle upwards."

Dukes asked a little under his breath, "What the hell was that, Lieutenant?"

"I don't know, Admiral. Somehow the T-wave runner is amplifying my pulse and shooting it back as a rotating beacon."

Just then Dave asked, "What frequency are you using? You may be interfacing with the T-wave runner amplification vanes on the launch tube. That thing is designed to amplify T-waves. It might be doing it with the laser energy, too."

She acknowledged, "Shutting down the laser now. But it will take a minute to power down. Chief, move her off center, three meters to the north."

The chief moved the track ball. "Laser is off target."

Powell couldn't resist his turn for a dig now, "Well, so much for that idea. I think we need to suit up and get down there before it starts getting dark. I don't want to be down there with flashlights fumbling around in the dark. We'd stick out like a sore thumb if some idiot from the *National Enquirer* is camped out on top of one of these peaks around here hoping to get the shot of the month of a huge fire ball."

Dukes replied, "Roger that. You three head on down to Hangar Bay Four. I'll meet you in a few minutes. Chief, get us back over silo center. Keep her there. I think it is safe to descend to 5K. There's not much left of the explosives down there to high order. By the time we get centered, it should be completely safe. You will both be suited up with the Gondola prepped and the extraction rigging lowered. Nevertheless, I insist you use PPE with full Scott Air Packs."

Dave and Powell reached the hangar bay below. Another one of the crew already had their equipment laid out. The PPE (personal protective equipment) included a full-hooded coverall with gloves and self-contained breathing tanks and mask.

The chief explained the equipment and the extraction procedures. "Sirs, after you are down there on the surface. We are going to lower the extraction cable. It is a three-point hoisting system suspended from three independent hoists located about a thousand feet apart from three different bays. This will give the T-wave runner some stability when we pull it up. Even on a ship this size, pulling a thirty ton T-wave runner out of the dirt from 15,000 feet can cause some interesting stresses and balancing issues. When you get down there, it will be very difficult for you to manhandle the three strands of three miles of cabling that I will have sent down for the extraction. Even though it is thin walled carbon-composite fiber (CCF) cabling, it still will weigh several tons. Be careful once it starts swinging since it will have a huge amount of momentum, so get out of its way fast. The cable that I'm sending down will have a standard lifting lug and hook on the end. Your job is to wrap the sling around the T-wave runner several times and then crisscross it under itself. That way when you hook it over the lifting lug and I start to pull, it will tighten on itself. Be sure not to drape it over any sharp edges such as the vanes. Keep it wrapped around the inner core. This way the sling won't be cut and snap, so it should pull straight up and out of the corrugated tube. Once I've got her up here and secured, I'll send down the dummy T-wave runner to use as a decoy when the mound is excavated after the all clear is given. There is a tool box in the gondola, along with sledge, bolt cutters, pry bar, power saw, you name it, it's there. I'm an Eagle Scout. We never send anyone down without the tools. Be prepared, right? Any questions gentlemen?"

Dave and Powell finished suiting up and were placed in the gondola. The hatch was closed and they were lifted out over the bay and lowered down. On the headset on the way down Dave asked, "This might be a dumb ass question, but what is keeping anyone from seeing us being lowered down? We don't have a retro-projection system?"

To this the chief simply replied, "Nothing gentleman, the gondola is painted camouflage brown. You have a small optical footprint from a few miles away. The cables are only a half inch in diameter and invisible from two miles. So, unless someone is stupid enough to be camped out within a few miles of the silo you are essentially invisible. Those news crews at the canal are over twenty miles away. Even with the best telephotos they can't see you. Does that reassure you, Captain?"

"Yeah, Chief Eldon. You gave me a warm fuzzy. Talk to you when we reach the deck."

"Roger that, Captain. Just remember to keep your hands clear of the red handle overhead."

"So much for the warm fuzzy, Chief. What does the red handle do?"

"Captain, that's the emergency cable cutter guillotine charge. If you pull that, you'll drop like a proverbially rock"

"Thanks for the heads up. Anything else I shouldn't hang on to?" Dave asked sarcastically."

It took twenty minutes, but eventually the gondola reached the surface on the mound. Powell spun the hatch handle and exited the gondola. They were between the dozer and the T-wave runner access shaft. Dave hopped out right behind. They took the hoisting sling off the gondola and dragged it the hundred feet over to the shaft. It was hot. The sling was heavy. They were working up a sweat now.

"Powell, this is Dukes. The fire is about eighty-five percent out. Still showing smoke in the shaft. However, the temperature is only 130°. You should be able to get that sling wrapped around the T-wave runner a couple of times."

"Roger that. We need to get this done before we dehydrate and drop over from heat exhaustion. Dave, you take the left side. I'll take the right. Let's drag it over the shaft and let it hang down the hole. You rotate to the left with your end. I'll walk in the opposite direction. I think we can tie it up in a nice half hitch."

Dave thought to himself, "Damn, I always hated doing knots in Scouts."

The little dance they performed worked. The sling was wrapped tightly around the T-wave runner's inner core.

Perkins was on the headset now, "Gentlemen, heads up. The hoist is now one hundred fifty feet directly overhead. Descending at ten feet per second. We have some oscillation east to west, about three feet. Suggest you each lift the sling over your head, one on each side of the shaft. We will swing the hoist underneath and capture the sling just like a carrier landing. Once we've shagged the sling, drop to the deck, just in case we miss."

Dave and Powell complied. The sling weighed about a hundred pounds. Holding it over their heads was physically draining. They timed it perfectly. The hook swung in place and captured the sling.

"Okay, gentlemen, hop back in the gondola. We're going to put some tension on the rigging. Wouldn't want anything to snap and take your heads off."

Powell replied, "Thanks for the advice. Will comply."

The chief twisted a knob on his console. A digital gauge started to register the tension, "10,000, 20,000, 40,000 psi. She's lifting up now. Well within safety margin. She's clear of the shaft walls. Up 10, up 20. She's clear of the shaft. Tension is steady at 40,000 psi. Picking up some sway. Within tolerance. I'm bringing her up now. Gentlemen, stand by, this will take about a half an hour."

General Powell acknowledged, "Roger that, Chief. But I'd trade you this nice tool box down here for a cold beer right now. We didn't put any water in this damn thing"

It was 1600 hours now. Dave and Powell had been on the deck for nearly three hours now. The heat was rising off the mound from the fire below. "Gentlemen, I couldn't find any Carlsberg beer, but we are sending water down ahead of the hoist with the dummy T-wave runner. Suggest you take a break until then. Sit in the shade of the gondola. The hoist is on its way down now. You'll need all your wits and strength to manhandle this into the shaft. A thirty ton dead weight is no easy task to line up with a shaft only having two feet of clear space on either side. There is no margin for error. We can't afford to get that thing wedged in the shaft."

As promised the hoist arrived a few minutes later. It stopped about a hundred feet off the deck. Suspended below it was a nylon rope with an ice chest. They grabbed at it a couple of times and cut the rope grabbing the chest. Dave had never been so thirsty in his life. They went back over to the gondola, got inside, and cracked open a bottle of Gatorade each. "This is almost as good as sex," Powell said.

After they got their thirst and electrolytes back in sync, they hustled back over to the shaft. The dummy T-wave runner was swinging back and forth a couple of feet. They had two guide cables attached to the dummy. Dave spoke into his headset. "Down two. Left one."

He was shocked by the response. "We can control the vertical to within inches. The horizontal will be up to you. We will keep it centered as much as possible. You are going to have to give it the lateral tension to guide her in the hole."

Dave understood. He'd been around construction and crane rigging for years. The iron workers and riggers made it look easy though. Dave took the guide cable and tugged on it as the hoist swung out away from him. Even though the dummy weighed thirty tons, he did slow it down to a wiggle. "Down two more. We're centered over the shaft. Down one…down point fiver. Okay, we've cleared the rim. Steady as you can. General tug to the north, keep her straight. Keep her from spinning to the right. Down point fiver. Okay, down two…two more…we're halfway there. Give me three feet. Keep the cable clear underneath. Down two more….we're within four feet of contact. We are off center by one. Pull, General. We need her centered. Good. Down another two. Ready for contact. Now lower at slowest possible speed. Ready. Contact, all stop."

Dave let go of the guide rope and unhooked the hoist. He lost his balance and fell backwards on his butt. He looked up and grinned, "Now, General, that was better than sex. Can't get any closer than that. If it ain't perfect, I'll be up here with the recovery crew rigging it with the crane for extraction for the rebuild. I can explain any shift as thermal expansion or think of some other excuse. It's getting late. It's nearly 1730 hours. Let's get out of here."

Dukes replied, "Good work, gentlemen. We'll have you up in a half hour after we pull the hoisting cables back in. Hate to get you tangled up in the rigging."

CHAPTER 25
Gondola Ride

Just then a klaxon alarm rang on the ship. Perkins yelled into the microphone, "Admiral, we've got incoming, three fast burners out of the south. Range two zero miles inbound at five thousand."

"What the hell! This is restricted air space. Who the hell is that?"

Perkins replied, "Not who, but what? Computer IFF (identification friend or foe) says that these are three Grey ships, our friends. They are subsonic, but they will be here in two minutes."

Powell asked, "What the hell is going on? Get us up there. Get ready to bug out."

Dukes replied, "Negative. No time. Pull the cutter handle. We'll return later to get you."

"No way in hell. You might not get back in time. I'm not going to explain to the world how a Navy submersible crash landed on an Air Force missile test silo at a Marine core gunnery range. Start pulling us up now, damn it."

Perkins cut in. "Greys have altered course. They have started their standard spiral approach for landing. They must think there is something here worth looking at."

Powell said, "Damn it. We had no one to man the tactical display console. We missed their approach altogether. Yes, they are a curious bunch, just like kittens and dolphins. They get to poke their nose in where it doesn't belong. That laser burst must have tipped them off. It will take them 10 or 15 minutes to perform their landing spiral. That should give you time to pull us up."

Dave was dumbfounded. Powell and Dukes had seen this maneuver before. Dave knew a little about the Greys, but contact with them was very, very limited and sparse. Only a few of the top Delta G Team had ever met with a Grey.

Dave's mind flashed back to the strange spiral pattern on Groom Lake. It made sense, if the Greys truly do think in nonlinear exponential ways. They couldn't even comprehend of a nice three mile long straight runway, let alone land on it. The spiral landing track was there for a reason, their use.

Dave said, "I think they are here for a flyby. There is no track or dry lake for them to land."

Powell said, "You're wrong, Captain. They'll keep tightening their spiral until they can set it down on a dime if they have to."

Perkins said, "You are correct General, they are tightening their approach now. They should be over the silo in about five bands or fifteen minutes. We can extract you. Chief, speed her up. Get them up here ASAP."

"Aye, aye, ma'am, they're on their way up."

"We're pulling some G's down here now. Hope the hoist can take the heat." Dave said.

Powell asked, "Can we move with the hoist rigging slung underneath? We can drop the hoist rigging in the next valley over and then recover it later, if needed."

Dukes replied, "We can move with the rigging, but not until the gondola is up inside and secure. There are too many safety overrides for the human-rated system. Don't recommend dropping the rigging next door. Fifteen miles of cable dropping to the ground is going to make a hell of a spaghetti mess and a large dust cloud, too. It will be very noticeable. We'll just have to go low and slow to the east. Let the wind drift us until the hoist can clear the mountain range in ten miles. The Greys should ignore us. They've already been all over this ship. They are interested in whatever caused the laser flash below. They won't be visible to the MCAS radar or ground personnel. They have better retro-projection than we do."

Perkins responded, "I think you are wrong, Admiral. One's broken formation. It is coming straight in now. Five thousand feet, four hundred knots from the south. Holy shit, sir. It's going to hit the cable hoist. Their sensors wouldn't detect it. Brace yourselves, gentlemen. It can't miss the cables. Their ship is two hundred feet wide. It's going to hit at least one of the four cables. Impact in fifteen seconds."

The Greys were targeting the center of the complex. Dave did the mental math and hoped that they were off the center line of the ship enough to be the one that they did miss. That would give them a few feet to spare since they were about two thousand feet higher than the hoist below.

Suddenly there was a swooshing noise and then a loud twang as the furthest cable to the west was cut. The *Nautilus* shuddered under the unexpected tension and strain. The chief barely escaped getting crushed and swept out of the hangar bay as the hoisting mechanism from the bay was ripped from its overhead mounts and pulled through the hatch way. The cable swung and whipped madly in mid air. Dave felt the gondola lurch. The broken cable had whipped around their support cable.

The chief hit the panic button and stopped the gondola cable reel before it would get tangled and snapped.

After a couple of times trying to contact the gondola, Dukes swiveled in his chair and yelled back to Perkins, "Are they okay? Did it sever their cable?"

"No, sir, camera confirms that they are still with us. Number two cable was hit and severed. It has pulled the hoist mechanism out of the bay. That hoist cable is now tangled up in the gondola cable. It also severed the com cable running alongside the gondola hoist cable. The number one and three cables now have all the weight of the T-wave runner. They are holding. Nothing has hit the ground. The ship is in a mild harmonic bounce. No casualties in the bay. Waiting for ship diagnostics and critical system reports."

Dukes said, "Excellent damage control report, Lieutenant. What's the status on the Greys' ship? Did it crash?"

"Negative, Admiral. It has re-entered the spiral pattern and is now accelerating. They are climbing now and expanding their arc. Looks like they are preparing for departure."

"Good, Lieutenant. Keep me advised. Chief, how are things down there?

"Sir, we're not really damaged other than the bridge crane is down and blocking the number one bay. The bay doors are jammed open with some damage to the hangar flooring. But this harmonic swing is getting worse. We've got several tons of cable, structural steel, and the gondola hung a half mile below us, not to mention the aerodynamic drag. For some reason, the pendulum motion cannot be compensated for fast enough. There is a lag in the ion propulsion drive. We're in danger of the drive system over compensating. I've got to shut things down and go on manual until things settle down on their own or we are in danger of shaking ourselves apart."

"Roger that, Chief Eldon. Shut her down. Prepare for emergency ascent and drift mode."

The chief replied, "Sir, we cannot make ascent. The gondola umbilical is damaged. They have no oxygen, or heat for that matter. If we climb higher than 20,000 feet, it will kill them. Also, I don't think we can get the bay doors to close and seal a hundred percent. We won't be able to keep the ship pressurized."

"I understand, Chief. Can we clear the Mohawk Mountains to the east and lower the ship down so they can get out?"

"Yes, sir, barely. The gondola is 2,400 feet below us. That will put them 500 feet over the tops. We can put her in drift mode there."

Lieutenant Perkins got up from her console and ran over to the ion propulsion drive monitoring station. There were a series of alarms and warning messages flashing on the screen. Just then one of the IPD technicians called into the bridge, "Admiral, the port shell is offline. We've had feedback and a surge in the switch gear chamber. There was a minor explosion in the port shell manifold and power cable. The fire is out now. However, the switch gear is burned and welded in the open position. It will take an hour to repair. Lateral Two Propulsion is offline and this is causing the lag in compensation."

Perkins cleared the alarms and shut down the klaxons. "Sir, we are now dead in the air. Altitude is holding. However, we are drifting to the northeast."

Perkins gave a wind status, "Winds from two four zero at six zero knots. We'll be over the Mohawks in twenty minutes. On this track, with current winds, this will put us over Phoenix in two and a half hours. Sir, we've got another problem, the cable backlash did take out several rows of retro-projection triodes. It has caused massive circuit failures. We are totally visible from the east side. It will take hours to reset the circuits and replacement of the triodes is impossible. There is nothing out here but desert so we're safe for now. However, when we drift over the mountains, we'll be visible to motorists on I-8."

Dukes replied calmly, "Very good, Lieutenant. Hopefully, it will be dark by then."

"Murphy's law is a son of a bitch. Okay, Lieutenant, now I've got some calls to make."

Meanwhile, hanging a half mile below them, Powell and Sheridan were trying to figure out what had just happened.

"Captain, do you have any bright ideas? I'm fresh out. Not that I'd ever use one, but it would be nice if they'd send down a couple of parachutes right now."

Dave said, "I don't even think there are any on the ship to send down."

"I can barely make out the bay hatch above us. It looks like one of the other hoisting cables is tangled around ours. We have no power. No communications. I'm sure they are trying to figure things out from their end. Maybe they'll wait until dark and lower the entire ship. We could simply hop out and walk away. It'll be dark in less than an hour."

Dukes asked the Chief if they could send an Aireopod down to rescue the men trapped below them. "No, sir. We could never maneuver the Aireopod that precisely especially in these winds and gusts. There is no way to safely transfer them even if we could get close. Our best bet is to descend. Let the gondola touch ground and have them make an emergency egress." Just then Perkins spoke up, "Decent is not an option. We are approaching the Mohawk Mountains. We'd plow them into the rocks at sixty mph. It would kill them. Also, it will be dark as soon as the sun goes down behind the Gila mountain range behind us. No time to put together an aerial rescue."

Dukes considered his options, "Only two things we can do, Chief Eldon. One, we pull them in somehow. Or two, we get our propulsion on line so we can maneuver and stop this drift. The chief replied, "Pulling them in is risky, sir. There is no way to untangle that Gordian knot below us. If we start pulling on one cable we'll snap the other. The only real option is the ion drive."

From the propulsion chamber, Sergeant Peter Benneway, the IPD Tech, called the bridge, "Admiral, we can fix the drive and switch gear. It is just a matter of time. We have the spare parts. What we don't have we can machine or have the Laser Powder Deposition machine make for us. We need to torch cut the old relays out and splice in new. This is going to take two to three hours, sir."

Dukes ran through the worst case scenario through his head. Another option was to sacrifice the men either by cutting the cable or do an emergency ascent up to 100,000 feet. At least dying from oxygen starvation and freezing was way more merciful a death than the frantic free fall from a half mile. Option four would be to say the hell with it all and blow the lid off of the Delta G Program, the aliens, the secrets to the universe, and then do it in style with slow barrel roll as they passed over Phoenix Sky Harbor Airport in their mile wide UFO. Option five was that he could ride it out at 20,000 feet and hope they could glide over Phoenix without being seen in the dark. He knew he could shut down air traffic and radar detection with a flick of the switch. At 17,500 feet, the men below could survive. It would be cold, dark, and the lack of oxygen might get to them. Just then he remembered, "Chief, how much air do you think they have in their Scott Air packs. We could gain some altitude if they put on their breathing masks."

"Good idea, sir, I forgot about those. They probably have for- ty -five minutes of air. My concern would be if they have the wits about them to put them on when we pop up. I figure they could withstand 25,000 feet with the masks. Those coveralls won't pro- vide much heat. But it wouldn't be much worse than a World War II bomber crew if they can stay warm. It might buy us some time to get our propulsion online." Option five was on the table.

Just then Perkins piped in, "Sir, whatever we are going to do, we better do fast. We are now losing altitude. The sun is going down behind the Gila range behind us. The temperature is dropping. We'll drop a thousand feet for every three degrees in temperature drop. Also since the ion drive is offline, we are picking up some moisture and condensation on the outer skin. That's affecting our neutral buoyancy. We've got ten minutes before the gondola smashes into the ridge line ahead."

Dukes said, "Get somebody to ballast control, now! Get ready to dump ballast on my command." The *Nautilus* had two 100,000 gallon water tanks, at each end of the ship. In emergencies, which this surely was, the tanks could be dumped to give positive buoyancy. They could also be used to trim and balance the ship in the event it came out of level.

Meanwhile in the gondola below, Dave and Powell were trying to figure out some options of their own. But they came up with a big fat zero. They knew their fate rested with the crew above. The gondola had a huge Plexiglas domed window in front of them. However, the gondola was facing west. Dave said, "Helluva way to go, but it sure is a beautiful sunset." They were oblivious to the mountain range looming in the east.

Powell said, "We ain't going nowhere yet, son. Dukes and I go way back. He'll get us out of this mess. I understand why he's not pulling us in. But why in the hell doesn't he stop this thing and just settle us to the ground?"

Dave replied, "Maybe they will. Maybe they have to set things up. Maybe they are going to set down in the valley to the southeast. It's flat and smooth out there. I'm sure he has his reasons."

The chief said, "Sir, we have a problem with the ballast tanks. The water in them is nearly boiling. That Grey flyby must have affected the water somehow. The tanks are building pressure and venting He3. They'll handle the pressure, but we can't dump that hot water into the open atmosphere. It will flash into steam. That may cause an explosion we can't deal with."

This time Dukes' frustration showed, "Shit, Chief, if we can't dump ballast, we're going to plow into that mountain, too."

Perkins looked at the NAV monitor and did her own mental math, no time to program the computer, with all the variables and parameters. Just like Spock, she spat out the data and facts. "Sir, I figure we're going to have a few hundred feet to spare with the gondola below. We'll be passing two miles north of Mohawk Peak in about seven minutes. It's at 2,777 feet, the highest peak in the range. We are at 5,625 AGL. The gondola is at 2,800 feet AGL now. Our descent rate is 100 feet per minute with a fifty knot ground speed. This will give us at least 2,100 feet. I only hope the next highest peak isn't anywhere close to that and we cross at a low point in the range."

Dukes said, "That's cutting it mighty close, Lieutenant. They've got to be shitting their pants by about now down there. Give me a run down on the next obstacle and an ETA until we are over populated areas. Chief, figure out a way to cool that water in the ballast tanks. Give me a status on the IPD."

Just then Anne came across on the intercom from her lab, "Admiral, I know you have your hands full up there, but I thought you ought to know. The MIST tanks are hyper-activated. They are vibrating like crazy." Just then, the water bottle on Perkins's console started to bubble and fizz like someone had shaken a pop bottle."

Anne said, "I'm pretty certain that someone is hitting us with a MASER."

Dukes said, "If the water on the ship is boiling and giving off helium, then why are we still alive? Humans are 50 to 60 percent water."

Anne replied, "Sir, the MASER is resonating at a frequency not of water, but of the frequency of algae DNA."

Dukes said, "Anne, that makes sense; there is algae growth in the ballast tanks. We were supposed to flush them and put ionized water in them as part of our refitting. We never got that chance. And I'll bet the lieutenant's bottled water isn't so pure. The government buys that stuff by the bulk, low bid, and stores them in warehouses for months at a time. I'll bet there are algae in there, too."

Perkins replied, "Yes, sir, especially this one. It's been sitting at my console for a couple of days now."

Dukes looked at his watch, "This is all well and interesting.

But it doesn't solve the immediate problem at hand. We are about to make an unscheduled landing in Phoenix if we can't figure out how to cool the tanks."

Sergeant Benneway offered a suggestion, "Admiral, we don't have to dump the water. Let's find something else to dump. We can start throwing things overboard." Chief Eldon replied, "We appreciate your input, Sergeant. However, that only works in the movies. We need to jettison about a fifth of our weight. We don't having anything on this ship other than the water ballast that comes close to that weight."

Perkins started a countdown to their approach to the mountains. "Sir, Mohawk Range in T-minus three minutes. Descent rate is now at 150 feet per minute. We are going to clear the ridge line. We will be approximately ten miles south of I-8, paralleling it but still over unpopulated areas. Terrain isn't a factor for next eighty miles. Wind is now northeast at 45 knots, slowing. We'll pass over I-8 just west of Gila Bend in approximately one hour."

"Thank you, Lieutenant. Please punch up Dreamland Control on SATCOM channel three." Perkins ran back to the com panel and dialed in the appropriate frequency.

"Dreamland control, Dreamland Control, this is *DGA Nautilus*, Pan-pan, Pan-pan, Pan-pan, do you copy?"

Almost immediately there was a reply, "This is Dreamland Control, go *Nautilus*. What is the nature of your situation?"

The radio call of pan-pan means that there is an emergency on board a vessel but that, for the time being, there is no immediate danger to anyone's life or to the vessel itself. Dukes didn't want to send out a Mayday yet, which meant that there is imminent danger to life or to the continued viability of the vessel itself. He didn't want to cause a panic and commotion just yet. Besides, there wasn't much anyone could do for them just now anyway.

"Roger, we have a serious situation. We are adrift ten miles west southwest of Dateland, Arizona at 5,000 feet AGL. The ion drive is out. Retro-projection is also out on the starboard side. We've had Grey activity in the vicinity. I think they accidentally hit and severed one of our hoisting cables. We have two men stranded in a suspended gondola 2,000 feet below us. Our hoisting mechanism is INOP. We cannot make emergency ascent. Ballast tanks are INOP at this time. We are neutrally buoyant. However, we are descending at 150 feet per minute due to thermal effects of dropping OAT (outside air temperature). We are drifting to the east northeast at 45 knots. Do you copy Dreamland Control?"

Dreamland control responded again immediately, "Roger, *Nautilus*, understand. We're notifying Delta G HQ. Is there anything we can do for you at this time?"

Dukes had a flash of inspiration, "Affirmative, I want some military activity out on the Luke Gunnery Range. Tell them to light up the night sky with flares and tracers, anything available. I want some plausible explanation if someone starts reporting UFOs. Also, maybe we can divert some attention and eyeballs in the opposite direction, using a classic magician's trick, misdirection. If we have to put her down, I'm going to shoot for Luke Auxiliary Field one or six. If not one of these, I will be forced to put her down at Gila Bend Auxiliary Airfield before crossing I-8 and entering population zones. Clear and evacuate that airfield. I'm not sure how controllable the ship will be. After that, start back tracking that MASER burst and see if you can extrapolate and track the Greys' approach vector. Train the satellites on this area. Get me some top cover. I don't need to be buzzed by any more curious Greys."

Anne was excited as she exited the Aireopod on the Bridge and ran up to the admiral, "Sir, I just passed the ZPE lab. We have several tanks of liquid helium. We can use those to cool the ballast."

"What about it, Chief? Anyway we can cool the tanks with the liquid helium? That stuff is pretty volatile in itself when you throw it on water. Even though it is inert, when you dump super cold liquid into near boiling water, the expansion ratio is phenomenal."

The chief replied, "Admiral, we can hook up a quick heat exchanger by running some piping through the ballast tanks and vent the liquid helium through the pipes. The liquid helium will never come in direct contact with the water. I think we can rig something in a half hour or so. Good idea, Dr. Ahrens. I think this will work. It would take hours for those tanks too cool enough by themselves. We're essentially throwing in a giant ice cube. We could use some help down here, Doctor. Could you please come down here?"

Anne replied, "Definitely. I'll be down in a few minutes."

Perkins continued her countdown, "Admiral, we'll be over the Mohawk ridgeline in thirty seconds. The sun has set at 1945 hours, fifteen minutes ago. It will be fully dark at 2000 hours. Sorry sir, no pun intended, but we are now literally in the twilight zone. The good news is we have a haze and high level cirrus clouds above us. We will not mask any stars. We should blend into the backdrop and present no silhouette. Retro-projection is still working on all but starboard side. We should not be visible from the Interstate."

The chief gave a status on the IPD, "Sir, our IPD techs have just about repaired the drive. They are bypassing the breakers and safety overrides, but we should have lateral thrust in about fifteen minutes."

Dukes replied, "Good work. Hope we don't need the fail-safes. Understand, no choice at this time."

Anne, Chief Eldon, and Sergeant Benneway met in the ZPE lab. The liquid helium was stored in two insulated one hundred gallon Dewars. The Dewar was invented by the Scottish scientist James Dewar in his pursuit of creating an absolute zero environment. In 1892 he produced the first Dewar flask, which we generally call a Thermos, and in 1898 he became the first person to liquefy helium at -254° Celsius, only 19 degrees Celsius from absolute zero!

The Dewars were easily transported to the ballast tanks using the Aireopods. The challenge would be building a heat exchanger. The chief called up the schematic of the ballast chamber on his terminal. They were in luck. Since the tanks were considered hard points on the ship, they were used as structural anchors or foundations for the airframe. The huge tanks were crisscrossed with structural tubing. It was a matter of tapping into this maze of tubing to convey the liquid helium. As luck would have it, the tubing was invar (low expansion alloy that gets its name from "invariable" because it will not react to thermal expansion). On a ship this size the last thing you wanted to worry about were the effects of thermal expansion from flying twenty miles up to landing on a desert dry lake. The invar structural elements have favorable magnetic properties as well. The ballast tanks were Kevlar wrapped Pyrex glass. They were very lightweight yet strong.

The chief was busy drilling a one inch hole in the side of one of the six inch diameter structural tubes and then clamped a saddle valve across the hole. It didn't have to be perfect or even a hundred percent leak proof. All he needed to do was get enough helium in the pipe for it to cool the tanks. While Anne was retrieving cryogenic hosing from the ZPE lab, Sergeant Benneway was stripping the infrared optics telescope lab of hosing as well. What they were building was a plumbers' nightmare. The chief had devised a manifold from the hosing and connections to feed into the tanks. He had to traverse the width of the ship several times to accomplish this with a max speed of only twenty mph; the Aireopods were painfully slow in a crisis.

After forty-five minutes, the chief finally contacted the bridge, "Admiral, we are preparing to cool the ballast tanks. Ready on your orders, sir."

"Thanks for coming through for me, Chief. We've stabilized at 4,400 feet AGL. The OAT has stabilized at eighty degrees. We are now twenty miles west of Gila Bend. We can see the city lights now."

Dave and Powell were beginning to wonder what was going on now. Powell said, "I think Dukes is going to put us down out here at one of the Gunnery Range Auxiliary fields. He's been bringing us in on a shallow glide slope for nearly an hour now. I'm sure that's his plan. I used to strafe and bomb the hell out of this chunk of real estate back in my F-4 days as a young fighter jock. There's plenty of open space out here in the Sonoran Desert. He must have a crew on the ground standing by."

Up above, Dukes gave the order, "Chief, we will need to do this simultaneously on both tanks. Are you and Sergeant Benneway in position?"

"Affirmative, Admiral. Ready on your mark."

"Very well, gentlemen, on my mark open the Dewar valves. At the first sign of trouble shut them down. Lieutenant, give me a status on the tank temperature and pressure."

Perkins replied, "H_2O in tanks at two four zero, superheated. Pressure in both is at thirty psi or two atmospheres and venting."

"Gentlemen, you are cleared to open valves now."

Both Eldon and Benneway turned the globe valve levers at the same time. The pressure hoses tightened up. Some hissing and screeching noises occurred but both the saddle valves were doing their job. The tubes were filling with liquid helium.

Perkins read off the temperature, "Sir, the temperature is dropping. Now at two ten, subcritical. Dropping at ten degrees per minute. We can dump ballast safely at 140 degrees and 1.25 atmospheres. At this rate that should be in about eight minutes. That will put us fifteen miles west southwest of Gila Bend still over the desert. We should have lateral IPD on line by then, too."

Just then the radar alarm went off, "Sir, there are two bogies inbound from the southeast. They are inbound to the range." Everyone thought, "Oh, shit, not again."

Just then the SATCOM came to life, "*DGA Nautilus, DGA Nautilus*, this is Dreamland Control. Do you copy?"

"This is *Nautilus*, roger, go"

"*Nautilus*, be advised we have two A-10 tank busters in bound from the southeast out of Fort Huachuca. They will be dropping flares and lighting up targets with their Vulcan Gatling guns. They will be about ten miles in front of your position in ten minutes."

Dukes replied, "Roger, Dreamland. Thanks for the assist. We will be dropping 70 percent ballast in approximately five minutes, making an emergency ascent to 20,000 feet, and turning due south contingent on later propulsion coming on line."

"Chief, how is propulsion coming with IPD? It will take five minutes to amp up the capacitors." The chief replied, "We're shunting power to the capacitor bank now. Current is steady and holding. Capacitors are charging. You should have lateral IPD on your command in four minutes."

Just then Perkins said, "Sir, recommend we dump ballast at the same time that we accelerate to the south. That will swing the gondola out of the water dump stream. We didn't consider what effect if any dumping 70,000 gallons of water below us was going to do to the men below. We usually dump at above 15,000 feet and the water falls as rain. We're dumping close to the ground and were going to leave a trail in the desert."

Dukes replied, "Understand, Lieutenant. Good advice on the maneuver. Our piddle path will just have to be explained as a strange anomaly. Hopefully, most will evaporate or soak in by the morning. How's the temp and pressure doing?"

"Temp is now 160, pressure 1.4 atmospheres. We'll be marginal, but we can start the ballast dump countdown now at T-1 minute on your mark sir. All personnel are clear of the ballast tank area."

"Start the countdown now." Perkins flipped up protective cover on her console and then pulled the toggle. The klaxon alarm sounded with the same warnings on the PA for rapid ascent.

"Kill the noise, Lieutenant. Everyone hold on to something. We are about to pull 2.2Gs."

At T-minus ten seconds huge flapper doors opened below the ship and water started pouring out. The IPD kicked in as the triodes heated and ionized the air on the southern leading edge. The resulting pressure divergence in air densities slowly turned the ship to the south as it started to rise.

A half mile below, Powell and Sheridan heard the water hit them as they swung to the north. "Holy shit, Dave, they are climbing and accelerating. Whether we like it or not, we're climbing. They are making an emergency ascent that will kill us. We can't breathe at above 15,000 feet. Quick get the masks on. We're going to be unconscious in a few minutes if we don't do it now." Dave and Powell struggled to reach behind their seats against the Gs to pull on their Scott Air Pack masks.

As they strapped on their masks, the whole sky in front of their Plexiglas bubble lit up. Flares were going off a few miles behind them, lighting up the desert floor below. A few seconds later the sky was filled with two eerie red arches raining fire on the desert below. The A-10s were spitting out 20 millimeter tracer rounds the size of coke bottles at 3,000 rounds per minute. The resulting sparks and explosions from impact looked like a fourth of July celebration.

Dukes glanced at the camera monitors and saw the awesome display of fire power off to their right covering their maneuver as they climbed out and to the south. The only question now was. What now? They were sure in a hurry to get nowhere fast. Heading south would take them back over the Sonoran desert, away from population, towards Mexico. Now what? It would buy them time to figure out how to hoist the gondola up.

"*DGA Nautilus*, *DGA Nautilus*, Dreamland Control. Control, go. We've successfully dumped ballast and are now under power heading south, now at 7,000 feet and climbing."

"Roger, *Nautilus*. We've had a chance to have someone look at your situation and might have a way to recover the gondola. Please standby. We are patching you into Delta G."

Dukes replied, "Roger, appreciate the help. Standing by."

Dukes was surprised to hear Dr. Rapp on the other end of the SATCOM, "Admiral, we have an 85 percent solution for recovering the gondola without compromising your cover."

Dukes always thought Rapp was a Mr. Spock wannabe, too. "Dr. Rapp, it sounds as though you have thought this out. What is your plan?"

"Please patch this conversation on to your ships intercom. We have a limited amount of time to explain to everyone. We need your crew to hear this."

Dukes glanced at Perkins and gave her a nod. She patched the SATCOM link into the ships intercom.

Dukes gave his crew a heads up, "Attention all hands, attention all hands. Standby to receive audio transmissions from Delta G on SATCOM."

Rapp relied, "Thank you, Admiral. We propose you rendezvous with the Tethered Radar Aerostat balloon at Fort Huachuca."

Dukes asked, "What balloon? Please explain."

Rapp replied, "Call up file Delta G TRADEWIND. Password is 'Cerro Cubabi. It is case sensitive. It stands for Tethered Radar Aerostat Detection Experiment With Integrated Nautilus Detection."

Dukes replied, "Cute, but how is a radar blimp going to help us."

Perkins called up the file on the holo-projection table. A navigation globe appeared not too different from the projection of the nautilus shell map she was used to viewing. However, a set of crosshairs zeroed in on a set of coordinates highlighted in red, 31.72° N by 112.80° W Cerro Cubabi.

Dukes said, "The projection is up and running. Get on with this. I've got two men that may be dying as we speak. We are at 15,000 feet and climbing to 20. I hope they have their Scott Air Pack masks on. The gondola is swinging pretty fiercely right now, and we are pulling 1.5 Gs."

Rapp replied calmly, "Sir, hold your altitude at 17,000. This plan will save their lives. I am very confident. The tethered Aerostat balloon was put in place last year, ostensibly, to guard the Mexican border from low flying drug smugglers. It is in fact a Grey ship and Nautilus Shell Detection System. It is a 600,000 cubic foot semi-rigid dirigible tethered to a 15,000 foot cable winch. We're going to have you hover over this thing, settle the gondola on top of it, and then slowly lower your ship until the gondola is pushed up through and into the hangar bay. That Aerostat can handle a 3,400 pound payload and can easily hold the gondola."

Dukes said, "That is brilliant on paper, Doctor, but a very risky move. Not to mention, won't our guys at Fort Huachuca wonder what a mile wide UFO is doing humping their poor lil' ol' blimp?"

Rapp let out some nervous laughter, "Admiral, we have that covered. Delta G owns that blimp and the sky within two hundred miles down there. We'll also vector you in so that you're good retro-projection side is facing the Post."

During the discussion, Perkins took the initiative to level off at 17,000 and head the ship towards the Aerostat's coordinates.

Dukes let out a huge breath and said, "General Powell and Captain Sheridan have about 45 minutes of air at 15,000 feet. We cannot communicate with them. They have no idea what the rescue plan is. It has got to be getting quite cold in there, too."

Perkins anticipated the concern, "Sir, we are neutrally buoyant at 15,000 feet. OAT is 30° F. I had to vent helium from casks three and four. We are on a heading to Fort Huachuca. I'll need exact coordinates for the Aerostat. We can't light up the area with the search radar."

Dukes was impressed, "Very well, Lieutenant. What's our ETA?"

Perkins replied. "Distance is two hundred miles on a heading of 133 degrees, ETA forty minutes at 300 knots ground speed. Best possible speed. Winds are still out of northwest at 75 knots."

Dukes shot back to Rapp, "Okay, Doctor. You heard the lady. We're going to need pinpoint navigation."

Rapp replied, "No problem, sir. We can get you to the Aerostat tether point. However, the exact location will be dependent upon winds and direction at the time you arrive. With any luck, the Aerostat will be to the west of the post over some hills when you get there. You should be able to detect it via infrared when you are within three miles. Ready to copy coordinates of the tether point. They are 31° 29' 09" N 110° 17' 44" W."

Dukes replied, "We are on course. No luck on winds. They are out of the west. Now that we are on our way, it is time to fess up on this Delta G Post. Why was I not informed of this program? This falls within the *Nautilus'* coverage area."

Rapp replied, "N2K, Admiral. But now that the Greys are involved with your predicament, you've definitely have the need to know. Have Lieutenant Perkins zoom in on the coordinates on the holo-globe."

Perkins did as instructed. The crosshairs zeroed in on Cerro Cubabi. A note on the projection read "a highpoint just south of the US border near Sonotia and the lava fields." This point was about 150 miles to the west of Fort Huachuca, halfway back to Yuma.

Just then General Ahrens cut in on the SATCOM, "I've been monitoring your transmissions, gentlemen. I authorized the file disclosure. Now listen up. We've back tracked the trajectory of the Greys' ship that collided with you. The MASER burst came from near Cerro Cubabi. It was reflected off the lunar surface and beamed back to the Greys' vessel. They focused it and used it for propulsion somehow. We haven't cracked that code yet. The MASER did in fact react with the algae DNA and MIST particles. That caused hyper excitation of the surrounding water molecules that heated up the ballast tanks. We concur with your assessment that the Greys were attracted to the laser pulse and hit your hoist cable by accident. We have not heard from them since the incident. Believe me, gentlemen, when I say, that if they wanted that cable cut, they could have done it very easily, and in a much more subtle way.

"I advise you to read this file and share it with your crew, along with Powell and Sheridan when they are recovered. But for now, concentrate on your primary mission and mate with that Aerostat. Work with Rapp. He has my complete confidence and acts on my authority. Give my daughter my best. Ahrens out."

Dukes didn't have an argument or say in the matter now. Orders were orders. He was decisive in giving his own crew orders. Now was time to earn the big bucks.

"Bridge to crew, you heard the conversation. Make preparations to mate with Aerostat. Get the medical crash cart to the hangar bay. Get warm blankets and oxygen."

"Chief, the file up here has drawings on the Aerostat. I'm uploading them on the CAD terminal. See if our gondola will sit level on the top of the Aerostat. I am worried about sharp edges tearing the balloon."

"Lieutenant, concentrate on getting us there ASAP. But don't rush the final approach.

"Sergeant Benneway, get the vertical IPD on line. We can't descend other than by releasing helium. That is hardly precision flying.

"Anne, I want you to research this file and check out Cerro Cubabi. Once this situation is over, and no matter how it turns out, it looks like we are going to go shell hunting in Mexico. Investigate the MASER DNA and algae MIST link."

Fifteen minutes later the chief came back on line, "Sir, the Aerostat will handle the gondola. The landing skids should straddle it some and give us some lateral stability. There should be no sharp edges on the gondola skids. Recommend targeting the area one third of the way back from the front as the most stable area for center of gravity (CG) consideration. We should stay well clear of the Aerostat's tail. Also Admiral, there will be a point when the tension on the entangled cable is zero. When this happens, we will cut it and winch it out of the way. We will keep the original gondola cable attached as a safety line all the way down as we descend. We can't use their reel winch to assist in lifting it into the bay. The Aerostat will be at its maximum reel length. It will be up to our flying skills to essentially land on top of it. The good news is that we have a bay hatchway that is 300 feet by 300 feet, plenty of room for error laterally. The bad news is that vertical movement is iffy. I doubt if we can get vertical IPD on line. There is too much damage to the capacitors. We will have to do it the old fashioned way and vent helium. We can only go down, not up."

"Admiral, more good news. Satellite weather photos show we've got some scattered cloud cover at 8,000 feet near the tether point. That will help mask us."

"Good, Lieutenant,, crank up the infrared. I don't want any surprises. Get some spotlights down there to the bay, too. I don't want to be look-ing for them with a flashlight. But, if we have to, I want that capabil-ity too."

Down below in the gondola, panic hadn't quite kicked in yet. Powell didn't want to come across as a chicken shit to his younger officer. And the same was true for Dave. He was planning on going out as a professional, not a whimpering cry baby.

They both had their masks on, but Powell turned to Dave and said, "We've stopped our ascent. We've got to be below 20,000 feet or we'd be dead by now. Your water bottle is not freezing, so it is above freezing in here. I think they just gained altitude to get above terrain and out of sight. They have something up their sleeves. I can feel it. Hang in there, Dave."

Dave replied, "Well, sir, I have all the confidence in the world with Admiral Dukes. He's not going to drop us like a rock. He is buying us time. But if things don't work out, I've got a few thoughts I need to jot down. I know those flight suits, you Zoomies always wear are full of pens and pencils. Can I borrow one? I need to write my folks a note or two and amend my will."

Powell had been there and done that, flying combat missions. He handed Dave a pen and a Maglite. Dave blew on his hands to warm them and started to write.

Perkins swiveled in her crew chair, "Sir, we are now ten minutes out. I've got the cameras on. SATNAV has us on track for the tether point. I'm bringing her in around the downwind side. Dr. Rapp, do you have an exact elevation of the Aerostat?"

Rapp replied a few seconds later, "Lieutenant, the Aerostat is 14,875 feet plus or minus twenty-five."

"Roger on the altitude, 14 point 875. Gondola is 2,815 feet below to top of its hatch. We are at 17,000 plus or minus 50 feet. Sir, I'm going to need to use the radar altimeter to get vertical. It has a small footprint."

"Fire up the radar altimeter, Lieutenant. But it looks like we are coming in low. Be prepared to adjust."

"Yes, sir, we are about seven hundred feet too low. We need to dump more ballast. Calculating now."

Perkins read from her terminal. "Sir, we need to dump another 12,500 gallons. That will get us within one hundred feet. I'd rather come in high than low. It is more precise to vent helium than dump ballast."

"Agreed, Lieutenant. Are we clear to dump? Nothing below us?"

"Confirmed clear, sir. Dumping now."

A few seconds later the gondola was shook by another blast of water. "Captain, they're dumping ballast. We're climbing again. Hang on."

Perkins yelled, "Bull's-eye, Admiral. We are neutrally buoyant at 17,800 feet. Now eight minutes out inbound. Slowing to twenty-five knots. I want the swinging to stop on the gondola. Infrared should be in range in four minutes. Sir, I can make out the Aerostat, dead ahead five miles, one thousand feet below. We'll have to descend two hundred feet to mate. Lateral stability no factor."

"Bring her in slowly, Lieutenant. No need to tell you we get one shot at this."

In the back of her mind Perkins thought, "Yeah, right, Admiral. No pressure here."

"Winds steady 230 at 78, range two miles. Slowing to ten knots."

When she slowed down the ship, the nose pitched up. This caused the number four bay to be about 150 feet higher than anticipated. Perkins remained calm. "Compensating for negative lift and CG shift due to reduced drag. We are under control. Venting cask nine and ten Nose is lowering. Now in level flight. Slowing to five knots. Anticipating attitude change, compensating. Range now one thousand yards. Gondola is still on track for intercept down the centerline. Slight thirty foot side drift, adjusting. Venting twelve and fifteen casks. Nose climbing now. Range five hundred. Venting aft casks twenty-two and twenty-four. Now level. Gondola in a center line oscillation, plus or minus thirty feet. Now all stop. I'm letting her drift."

Dave had been bounced around for over an hour now. This swinging now gave him vertigo and motion sickness. He ripped off the oxygen mask and vomited on the floor. Just like in a school lunch room, when one tosses their cookies, others follow. Powell ripped of his masked and puked, too. Now at 15,000 feet and puking, he got dizzy and passed out. Powell wasn't much better off trying to get his mask back on to help Dave. Both men now fell unconscious.

"Admiral, we're going to lose infrared (IR) visual in a minute. The Aerostat will be passing below the camera located on our leading edge. I need an Aireopod up and over the bay to give me visual cues. They are going to have to light it up with the search lights to see it."

"Chief, get on it". The chief hopped in the Aireopod with a handheld million candle power spotlight and a blow torch. He hovered over the back center of the bay to get a look at the Aerostat below and ahead of the ship. He turned on the spotlight to where he thought the Aerostat should be. He hoped it would reach out the half mile below them to mark it. No luck it was still out of range of the spotlight. "Lieutenant, use the radar altimeter to ping the Aerostat as she slides under us. Give me range and altitude."

The radar altimeter was located forward of Bay Four and should be able to pick up on the object passing below them as if it were solid ground. The search radar would be useless this close in just like the IR camera

"Good idea, Chief. The radar altimeter is active. Now reading AGL. No hits yet on Aerostat. Wait a sec. There it is, radar altimeter now reading 2,700. Shit, too low. Venting center casks sixteen through twenty, full blow. Now midway between leading edge and bay four. Drift rate one hundred feet per minute. We're lifting 150 feet per minute. Hitting reverse IPD now. Should make the glide slope now. Chief Eldon, it should be about 300 feet ahead and 2,800 feet below. Do you see it yet?"

Just then the spotlight caught something reflecting back. "Just about missed it, Lieutenant. Damn, that's a small target from a half mile below."

Perkins replied, "We're dead stop now. Can you see the gondola? It should be one hundred feet above the balloon and descending. It's about a fourth the size of the balloon."

"Negative, no contact. I can see the entangled cable."

"Okay, Chief, we're on target. I'm blowing cask ten. This should settle us down. Watch for slack on the cable."

"Okay, Lieutenant, we've hit something. Cables going slack." Just then Benneway called in, "Ma'am, you should have infrared back. I went to the access hatch and cranked it down and to the aft."

"Thanks, Sergeant, your aim was dead on. Aerostat is now in view on IR. The gondola is sitting on it too far back on the tail. I'm punching us back twenty feet. She is sitting off to the left a few feet listing. We need to bring her up fast before she slides off. Clear the hatch. We're going to drop like a rock. Blowing casks eighty through one hundred."

The ship did drop like a rock and Perkins fought the lateral movement all the way down. The *Nautilus* wanted to drop like a feather, rocking back and forth. Fortunately, the number four bay was under the CG and did not move very much relative to the Aerostat.

"Now dropping five hundred feet per minute, contact with hoist cable in one minute." As the ship descended, it got closer to the entangled cable

The chief said, "Benneway, when I cut the hoist cable, reel it in fast and watch for the backlash." As the gondola cable became slack, the entangled cable began to tighten up. It was now or never. The chief reached out of the Aireopod door with the lit torch and severed the entangled cable. It snapped back. Benneway reeled it in and out of the way. Now all they had to worry about was the gondola slipping off the back of the Aerostat.

As far as Perkins was concerned, now it was an emergency landing she had practiced dozens of times with vertical IPD inoperative. She had always landed safely but on the icecap with a hundred mile margin of error. Now she had to hit a bull's-eye again. The computers were now calculating the venting protocol to speed the decent. They opened four more casks and increased the sink rate. The ship was dropping like a runaway elevator. She couldn't risk dumping ballast now to stop the sink rate until the last second because the water might knock the gondola off the Aerostat. She'd half to wait until about two hundred feet. At the 250 foot mark, she hit the ballast dump for a precalculated amount of time to stop the decent rate. The ship slowed as the Aerostat and gondola started to fill the view in the hangar bay.

"You got her, Lieutenant. Nice flying." Then the Aerostat appeared to move back and forth and bob slightly as it came through the hatchway doors. It was free floating and subject to the winds and tether cable tension. With some fancy flying of his own, the chief used the Aireopod to loop another cable through the gondola skids and attach it to the hoist. At the same time Sergeant Benneway cut the old cable. This wasn't going to be pretty but they snagged the gondola. They needed to get clear of the Aerostat now.

"Admiral, we have them."

"Outstanding. Close the bay doors and blow remaining ballast. Let's clear this area." With these words, everyone breathed a sigh of relief.

"Lieutenant, you've got the bridge. I'm heading down there." When Dukes arrived they had already hoisted and swung the gondola over the hangar landing zone and were cranking its hatch open.

Anne was first inside, "They are alive but unconscious. Get me oxygen."

Dukes handed her two small tanks of oxygen and she placed the masks on their faces. Just then Dave woke up and kicked back. His eyes were huge as he gulped for air. Powell instinctively grabbed for the mask and inhaled deeply. Their color returned as warm blankets were tossed into the gondola and Anne wrapped them around the men. In his dazed state Dave handed Anne a note pad he had been scribbling on. She glanced at it and then put it in her pocket. Smiling, she held his hand. Now, she knew things were going to be all right.

The *Nautilus* wasted no time in blowing the rest of her ballast and shooting up to its safe altitude of 100K. With the damaged IPD and retro-projection system it made a VFR direct course back to Dreamland. During transit, it was determined that the best place for Dave and Powell to warm up their bodies from their mild hypothermia was in the RV chambers. Anne had them transported there. She didn't waste time wiring them up and left the lights on. Instead of the saline solution, the MIST particles were used. They would vibrate and synthesize the feeling of warm water on their bodies to bring their core temperatures up.

Anne also had ulterior motives in using the RV Chamber. She wasn't sure what the near death experience would do to enhance RV reception, nor the men's weakened state. She was adding another data point to her experiments. One thing was sure, the chamber would not hurt them and something useful might come from it.

Both men were still a little dizzy and a little groggy. Chief Eldon and Sergeant Benneway stripped off their clothes and helped the men down into the pools. Both men laid there and relaxed as the MIST particles enveloped them. Even though no fancy equipment was hooked up to them, Dave and Powell both had RV experiences. After about an hour, Dave asked for a tablet and pencil to write down his thoughts. Powell did the same. It was surprising how closely both men's RV sketches were. Dave's looked like this.

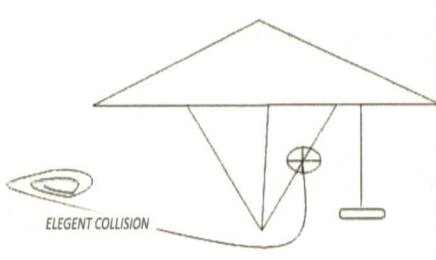

ELEGENT COLLISION

The sketches clearly depicted the Greys' ship colliding with one of the hoist cables. General Powell's even showed damage to the *Nautilus* and the cable entanglement. However, they also each made a note at the bottom of their sketches. Dave's read, "Elegant Collision". Powell's read simply "Reserve". Anne thought this was odd, but at least there were no number puzzles that could provide an infinite amount of possibilities. Dave and Powell really didn't recollect much more than what

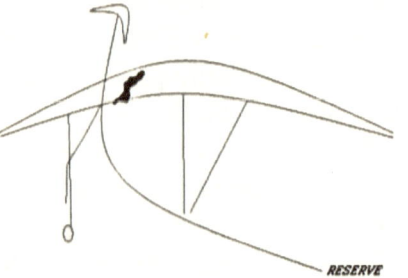

RESERVE

they sketched. Anne would input the words into the Cray and let it crunch on any interpretations based upon the day's activities.

As soon as Dave and Powell warmed up, they dressed in some comfortable coveralls and went with Anne to the canteen to get something to eat. It was after midnight. The men were starving.

The *Nautilus* did not encounter any difficulties on its flight back to Dreamland. Before it even landed in the valley to the north of Groom Lake, the maintenance and logistics personnel were busy ordering or manufacturing replacement parts for the retro-projection system, hangar crane, and the ion propulsion drive systems. The ship would continue with its modification and upgrade as originally scheduled. Meanwhile, the crew was debriefed and surprisingly, no one was chastised for the "Rescue Mission from Hell". As a matter of fact, the crew was commended for their ingenuity and inventiveness in the face of adversity. There were a few calls from concerned citizens with strange lights in the sky, but nothing that couldn't be explained from military exercises, flares, and gunnery practice out on the ranges.

At the debrief, it was learned that there were actually three Aerostat radar balloons in operation: one at Fort Huachuca, a second one just south of the Yuma MCAS, and a third in the Florida Keys. They had recently been built and put online with a lookdown radar platform to ostensibly detect drug smugglers flying low level. However, as Delta G assets, they were there to look over an area of interest called Cerro Cubabi and in the N2K case of Cudjoe Key, Florida. These were very active areas for the Greys. They were also points near or on the planetary grid. The Aerostats also had some very sophisticated Delta G MASER equipment on board. The Arizona pair had detected a TW generator somewhere nearby. They also did a halfway decent job of tracking the Greys' spiral flight path in and out of the BMO Test Site.

When Anne heard this, she had more data to enter into the Cray's algorithm. What popped out was very interesting. There was a place near Cerro Cubabi known as the Pinacates Biosphere Reserve, clearly a direct hit on Powell's RV sketch. Within this reserve was a volcanic crater known as El Elegante, a bull's-eye again with Dave's RV sketch.

Anne's research on the area included the following information from the NASA archives:

The Pinacates region of Mexico's Sonoran Desert is one of the most unique and striking landscapes in North America. Located just a few miles south of the Mexico-Arizona border, this volcanic field originated with the rifting of the Gulf of California millions of years ago, but the features seen today (volcanic peaks, lava flows, cinder cones and collapsed craters) formed in the late Pleistocene period (2 million to 11,000 years ago). The volcanic range is surrounded by one of North America's largest dune fields, Gran Desierto.

The natural history of the region includes thousands of years of human occupation; it is the aboriginal home-land of the O'odham tribe, also known as the Papago. The region also served as an early training site for Apollo astronauts in the 1960s.

Anne thought to herself, what else was NASA doing out here other than testing moon buggies? The file also referenced another strange place in Mexico a few hundred miles to the southeast near Ceballos.

> *In 1970, a faulty American Athena missile fired from the White Sands Missile Base in nearby New Mexico went off course inexplicably and crashed into the mysterious desert region known as "The Dead Zone." Within this zone of silence, radio and TV signals fail to travel through the air, creating a type of dark zone. The missile traveled fifty percent further than the fuel would account for, as if it was pulled into this area. The region is called, the Mar de Tetys, or The Sea of Thetys, because at one time, millions of years ago, the area lay at the bottom of an ocean.*

Unfortunately Dave couldn't stay more than a few days at Dreamland. The doctors gave him and Powell a clean bill of health. The very least Powell could do was fly him back down to Yuma in the C-21 and let him finish the TW-shot. Dave would have to let the Delta G Team at Dreamland figure out where the Greys had come from, their purpose, if any, of clipping the cable and if there were any shells buried near Cerro Cubabi.

Dave now had his plate full at the Yuma Test Site. He was trying to figure out what to do with five acres of military specification certified and calibrated dirt and then dispose of the ashes of six million pounds of iramite high explosives. Dave also had to negotiate with the Teamsters Union and the UAW to authorize triple overtime for the crews to work the mound. The budget was shot to hell on this one now anyway, so what's a few million more. Besides the USAF would be stimulating the local economy, as most of the crew went out the next day and bought new pickup trucks or boats to run on Lake Havasu. It is amazing what throwing a little cash around can do, no bitching, no griping. Even the press was content now and left them alone. Hell, if the union guys thought it was safe to work the mound, then everything was under control. No story here.

The mound was scraped and removed in less than two days. When they got down to the Styrofoam layer, it was put in dumpster trucks and hauled to a burn pit. The explosives were now five acres of charred briquettes eight inches thick. It actually had some commercial value as fertilizer. It still had plenty of nitrates in it. Without much paperwork, the EPA authorized its release, and the local farmers used it on their lettuce crops. Dave saw the Pentagon's strokes in that masterpiece.

The heat from the fire didn't damage the silo or headworks. It did scorch the concrete a bit, but it was grit blasted and coated with grout and an epoxy clear coat. The coatings were double checked for material compatibility.

The instrumentation cabling was replaced and the process of remixing and pouring the iramite began all over again within two weeks, an amazing feat. But this time, the six million pounds of explosives were allowed to set up and harden fully prior to placing on roofing felt and then Styrofoam layers on top of them. The Mil-Spec dirt was placed in eight inch lifts graded and compacted. In all, thirty-two layers were placed that resulted in an eight acre mound over twenty feet thick. Several of the union guys had invested some of their paychecks into the explosive manufacturer's stock. They claimed it paid off better than a weekend trip to Vegas.

Once everything was in place the countdown checklist was checked and double checked. The real T-wave runner was brought back in. It was the same dimensions as the Little Skull Mountain T-wave runner. It was lowered through a three foot corrugated casing to rest on the silo lid below. It was explained that the original one was damaged by the fire and unreliable as part of the instrumentation package to measure the forces, heat, EMP effects, and shockwave overpressure effects on the silo lid from the simulated nuclear shock.

On shot day, the countdown proceeded very smoothly. The Moon was directly overhead. Since the Moon has no magnetic field it was used to aim the torsional tangential wave to the left side giving it a gravity assist sling shot towards Saturn as well as intersecting the newly discovered lunar T-wave to tune it. The T-wave runner was expected to reach velocities of nearly ten times the speed of light. The space borne wave detectors now were a few million miles further out into space. Dave inserted his key into the fire control center and turned it at the exact same time Johnson turned his in the adjoining trailer. Ninety seconds later six million pounds of explosives sent a plume of dirt and dust 10,000 feet into the air. The shockwave rattled the windows in the control trailers. The T-wave runner was nowhere to be found while a perfect mile wide smoke ring rose 20,000 feet into the desert sky. A dust cloud blew over the Gila Mountains to the west and actually rained non-radioactive fallout down on Baja California a hundred miles away. Clearly another successful launch. Since there were no side lobes involved with the vertical wave generation, Anne was not involved with this test. They were still trying to crack the code and figure out what she saw back in Nevada.

At the Program Review meeting held at Dreamland the following month, Powell was ecstatic. They had successfully tracked the T-wave runner outbound. It followed a curved trajectory, spiraling around the Moon for a sling shot back towards Saturn. However, the spiral shape as always was open ended and the thing could have ended up anywhere.

Dave was informed that he was to head to Florida next week and help the Delta G Program down there for the next couple of years. Vertical silo testing was no longer a viable option for generating T-waves. Again politics, not technical merit had shut down the program. Besides, the Navy had been proposing a method to generate TWs using nothing but seawater. No nukes and no explosives. Was Dave right in his suspicions? Did they actually base their findings on Krakatau and the nuclear shots at Bikini atoll and use the rapid changing density of seawater to come up with that idea?

Dave departed from Dreamland with newly promoted Lieutenant Colonel Boop and his brand new C-130 D. He and his crew were on loan to NASA. Their NASA flight suits along with a shiny white Hercules with the famous NASA meatball logo painted on its tail would allow them access to far more places in the world than a USAF desert camouflaged military aircraft. Especially, if you told a host country that you were there studying global climate change, pollution, or some other touchy feely subject of the day. The C-130 was fitted out with the latest in satellite navigation and had extended range and payload capability. It was brimming from end to end with electronic detection hardware, infrared, and MASER technology.

On the nose was painted the name "Rosalind's Reward." In 1952, Rosalind Franklin had produced perhaps the most famous X-ray image on Earth, an image of the DNA molecule. This led James Watson and Francis Crick to pro-claim that they had found the secret of life in *Nature* magazine in 1953. They claimed that DNA is made up of two polynucleo-tide chains that encode the genetic information for all liv-ing things. The consequences were immeasurable. Unfortu-nately, Rosalind died of ovarian cancer at the age of 37 in 1957 a few years before Watson and Crick were awarded the Noble prize. She essentially was shafted by the two because they did not acknowl-edge her contribution in their earlier work. Boop always did have a weakness for the underdog.

The C-130 and crew made a slight detour on its way to Hous-ton to pick up Drs. Ahrens, Rapp, and Timken on their way to the Cape. They used their NASA cover to do some survey work at the Pinacates Biosphere Reserve, south of the border near Yuma. The big white C-130 spent hours flying a search pattern looking for the source of the TW-generator (a shell). The MASER had an effective penetration depth of about a hundred feet under dry sand. Hopefully, it was buried under the sand dunes somewhere. The C-130 orbited around a suspected site and blasted it with MASER energy. The MASER reflection was bounced back up into the *Nau-tilus* a 100,000 feet above them. The MASER wave was then shot into the shell on the *Nautilus* and then amplified and sent to the Moon where it was inverted and returned to the C-130. The three second delay combined with the MASER clock time dilation effect gave enough time and data for the Cray supercomputer to compute the TW-generators exact location. It lit up the T-wave generator like a bra strap under a funhouse black light. It was in fact buried in 110 feet of sand just south of Cerro Cubabi in the Sand Dunes, not an impossible excavation. But surely a costly one with some visibility risk to it. The way that the NASA survey would be written would make it appear that this place looked like a ripe place to do some oil exploration in the future.

As it turns out, this site excavation proved to be the Rosetta Stone of all shell excavations. What was found was a totally intact Grey Shell pod. Three large shells were found surrounding and partially embedded inside a perfect sphere of mercury. The shells were spaced 137.5 degrees apart around the mercury sphere. The sphere was hollow and had an outer diameter of 20.22 feet, and an inner diameter of 12.49 feet. There were three null sites of less than four inches in diameter located at the opposite 137.5 degree locations where small probes could be inserted to view the inside cavity. If anything touched the mercury at any other location it would be repulsed violently. The inner cavity appeared to be an empty crew compartment with holographic projections appearing of seemingly random fractals and patterns. There was nothing else in the cavity; however, it was fully lit, and had an atmospheric pressure of fifteen psi of a breathable, oxygen-nitrogen combination. There were no moving parts, but the air inside was in constant motion. The shell was either abandoned by the Greys, or left intentionally for us to explore and analyze.

What amazed the Delta G Team was that once the sand was excavated around the shell pod, it floated in space. It could be moved or tugged by pushing on the shells, but again reacted violently when the mercury was touched.

The *Nautilus* had no trouble pulling it up into its massive cargo bay.

CHAPTER 26
Homestead, FL

Dave didn't mind the transfer down to Florida. It would give him a chance to be closer to Anne at the Cape and besides the Navy had the ball now and they were the team to be on. His cover would be to work as an engineering officer at Homestead AFB in the Civil Engineering Plans and Programs Branch.

Experiments were underway at various locations in the Caribbean to harness torsional wave energy. It turns out there really was something to the Bermuda Triangle myth. The 100,000 foot overview briefing mentioned that torsional waves were generated due to rapid changes in the density of massive amounts of seawater. The electromagnetic forces from the Gulf Stream passing over mineral-bearing silica, along with variations in salinity, and temperature deltas produced thermoclines like no other place on Earth. As had been shown in the Nevada desert, rapid density changes of the desert playa and talc on a smaller scale resulted in huge torsional waves. While the density changes off of Bimini were not nearly as fast as a nuclear detonation, the deltas were much greater because of thousands of square miles of ocean and huge volumes of water. This energy could be directed and focused by regulating the Gulf Stream temperature, salinity, and mineral content.

The Navy's proposal was really pretty simple. The concept was to let nature generate a torsional wave, with maybe a little coaxing and nudge from us humans. Off the southeast coast of Florida there was evidence of torsional wave activity in the past. The MASER detector had detected residual T-waves. From the amplitude and strength, they appeared to have been generated every decade or so in conjunction with the solar max.

We knew that there was a shell located off the west coast of Bimini less than a hundred miles east of Miami. It is in about three hundred feet of water and is embedded in the coral rock. This one will be time-consuming and expensive to extract. It sits on one of the hubs of the planetary energy grid, so eloquently mapped out by Mr. Bruce Cathie in the mid-1950s.

What could be any simpler than using nothing more than seawater? Why would the Greys be interested in this part of the world? What is so special about this area, the Gulf Stream? It is an area where very warm ocean currents from the Gulf meet the deep cold waters of the Atlantic Ocean. It is an area where the density of the seawater makes relatively rapid changes. There are few other places in the world like it.

According to Navy calculations, the thermocline trigger was so sensitive that it could be set off by only one tenth of a degree rise in temperature. How do you regulate the Gulf Stream temperature? Simple, the Navy proposed to pump it full of nuclear reactor cooling water.

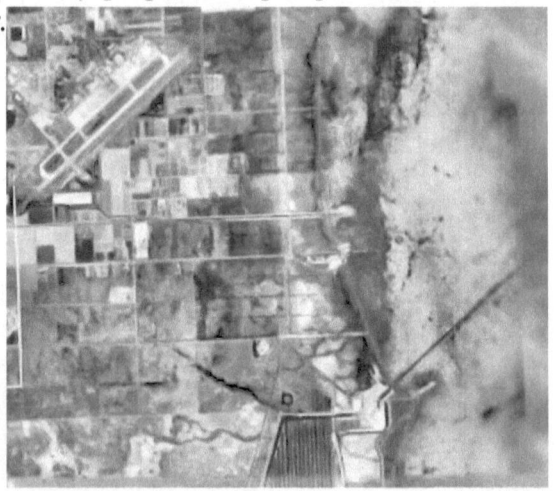

Has anyone ever wondered what the irony is of there being a nuclear power plant at the apex of the Bermuda Triangle? There is one. It is known as Turkey Point Nuclear Power Plant. It is located just a few miles southeast of Homestead AFB on the southern shore of Biscayne Bay just above the Keys. It has miles and miles of cooling channels running exactly north and south that eventually dump the reactor cooling water through the barge channel into Biscayne Bay. Any reason that the barge channel runs parallel with Homestead AFB's primary runway is coincidental. Or is it?

As was discussed earlier, gravity waves have torsional wave constituents. Torsional waves are actually spiral by nature. What other force of nature on this planet consists of a spiral form of energy? Hurricanes!

The details would have to wait until he received his Beyond Top Secret briefing, but thermocline physics basically goes like this. Temperature affects the density by changing the spacing between water molecules in a given volume of water. As temperature increases, water molecules get more energetic or vibrate more. They tend to spread out so as not to bump into each other. Thus, increases in temperature decrease the density of seawater. On the other hand, as we learned about the formation of ice in Greenland, decreases in temperature increase the density of seawater. Seawater density and temperature are said to have an inverse relationship; that is, as one goes up, the other goes down.

Salinity, the amount of salt dissolved in seawater, affects density by adding mass to a given volume of seawater. As more and more salt is dissolved in a particular volume of water (as water evaporates or ice forms leaving the salts behind), the density of seawater increases. Thus, increases in salinity cause increases in density. Similarly, decreases in salinity, caused by the addition of freshwater (i.e. rain, snow, ice melt, river outflow) or seawater with a lower salinity, causes decreases in the density of seawater. Salinity and density are said to have a positive relationship; as one goes up the other goes up.

Both temperature and salinity affect the density of seawater and both may change at the same time. Any given combination of temperature and salinity may produce the same density. Typically, temperatures we may encounter in the oceans range from -2 to 28 degrees Celsius (except near hydrothermal vents or in inland seas, where temperatures may be higher). Salinity typically ranges between 28 to 41 parts per thousand (ppt), although at the mouths of rivers and in surface waters of the polar oceans in spring, salinity will be much lower. Recall that the highest salinity given here occurs in the uppermost extension of the Red Sea. The average salinity usually quoted by oceanographers is 35 ppt.

The maximum density of water is 1 gram per cubic centimeter

(g/cm³) at 4°Celius. At a salinity of 35 ppt, the density of seawater at 4°C is 1.0278 g/cm³. While this does not seem like a
big difference, it's enough to move tremendous amounts of water.
The average density for seawater is between 1.024 to 1.028 g/cm³.
Again, while these differences may not seem large, these minute
differences multiply when you're talking about trillions of tons of
water.

What does this have to do with the so called Bermuda Triangle,
Homestead AFB, and Turkey Point? As mentioned earlier, temperature and salinity affect the density of seawater. Evaporation
and precipitation, which differ in various regions of the ocean, are
the principal factors that influence salinity. Heat exchange, driven
by the seasonal cycle of the Earth's movement about the sun, also
influences the density of seawater. As a result of these factors, a
world ocean develops a layered structure made up of water masses
of different density.

Lighter, less dense layers of water float on heavier, denser
pockets of water. The end result is an ocean that varies in density
both vertically and horizontally. Thus, rapid changes in seawater
density across horizontal scales form what are known as fronts.
These fronts exist at the interface between any two water masses
with distinct different densities. The most common fronts occur
where deep water masses are formed, but fronts may be present as a
result of wind-driven up welling and down welling of ocean water,
or where eddies form, precisely where the Gulf Stream meets the
Atlantic Ocean. Tidal surges from tropical storms and hurricanes
also rapidly change the density of the ocean in this locality. This
rapid change in density of trillions of gallons of seawater is what
produces the torsional waves that warp time and space.

Following his month long stay at the Pentagon, and now armed
with this information, Dave headed home to Ohio for leave and to
visit with his folks. It was a week before Christmas. He had managed to squirrel away quite a few bucks with flight pay, hazardous
duty pay, and just the fact that there was no place to spend your
pay check a hundred miles north of the Arctic Circle.

Dave did some rationalization. I'm heading to Florida. I need
a new car. While visiting his brother, Dan, in Columbus, they

decided to do some test driving. He had always wanted a Mustang GT convertible. This would be the perfect Florida car. There was six inches of snow on the ground now in Ohio. Convertibles weren't a major seller this time of year. The salesman had to literally dig the Candy Apple Red convertible from the back of the lot for Dave and his brother to give it a spin. The five-speed 5.0 liter growled with power as they lurched out of the lot. Dave stalled it a couple of times until he got used to the sensitive clutch. He turned a corner into a subdivision, down shifted, let off the clutch and gave it a little gas. The high torque and light weight backend resulted in a neck snapping 360 degree donut on a patch of ice. The nose of the GT came to rest about four inches from a mail box. Talk about your major pucker factor. He took a mental note for the need to add the pucker factor into the torsional wave calculation algorithm.

Dave wanted the car badly. He knew the car would sit on the lot until spring thaw. He negotiated a sweet deal and signed the paperwork.

CHAPTER 27
Flying in an Ink Bottle

Dave reported to the Base Civil Engineer at Homestead AFB in January 1989 and soon established himself as a knowledgeable, competent, engineer and respected leader. He rented a nice condo just before you entered Florida State Road A1A south to the Keys. After freezing his ass off in the Arctic and literally choking on desert dust, the tropics looked mighty appealing.

Dave had learned to fly Cessnas back in Las Vegas and had gotten his private pilot's license and was now enjoying his newly acquired skills and hobby in the skies of south Florida. He had flown out of Homestead General Aviation Airport dozens of times and enjoyed taking family and friends for sightseeing trips to the Keys or Gulf Coast.

As a member of the Delta G Team, he was a little more sensitive to the nature of the Bermuda Triangle. He had never encountered any difficulties in any of his flights. He had enjoyed a few beers now and then with some fellow pilots as well as some of the F-16 fighter pilots at the Officers' Club. A third of the stories heard could be chalked up to the beer. Another third of the stories could be chalked up to over active imaginations. The last third could only be chalked up as bizarre and weird.

Even the multimillion dollar fighter aircraft were subject to the strange forces of the Triangle. One famous case was that of Sting 27. Sting 27 was the call sign of a supersonic Phantom II-E fighter jet that disappeared after taking off from Homestead AFB on a training flight on September 10, 1971. It was piloted by Captain Richard Romero with his back seater, Lieutenant Norm Northrop from the 307th Tactical Fighter Squadron at Homestead.

It disappeared mysteriously and suddenly on a training flight southeast of Homestead AFB. Up until it disappeared, it was under constant radar tracking and communications. The weather was perfect. It called for 12,000 feet of broken cloud cover and an overcast at 25,000 feet, visibility 7 miles, at a warm 78 degrees and winds of only 2 knots.

They took off at a few minutes after 0800 and headed for a position forty miles south of Miami. They were told to change frequency a few minutes later and contact air traffic control for radar flight following during the maneuvering portion of the mission. At 0807 this contact was made and placed the Phantom at twenty-five miles south of Homestead AFB. One minute later Sting 27 started its supersonic run. The pilot headed southeast zigzagging 30 degrees left to right and then straightening out towards the end of his route. He then throttled back to subsonic speed. Eight minutes later, Sting 27 was seventy miles from Homestead. During a right turn, the pilot responded to a clearance request for 17,000 feet. The mission was already almost over. This course was maintained except for some slight maneuvering turns.

At 0816 another Phantom in the area, Sting 26, piloted by Lieutenant Axel Reardon contacted Sting 27, wishing to coordinate their positions to maintain the proper distance for their maneuvers. Sting 27 reported himself at 14,000 feet. One minute later Sting 27 requested a voice check. The following is extracted from the incident investigation transcript:

> *STING 27: "How are we coming over?"*

> *STING 26: "Loud and clear."*

Air Traffic Control did not hear the conversation between the planes, but did notice Sting 27's radar signature getting weaker.

> *ATC: "Sting 27, your SIF feature is fading. We're having trouble identifying you. Is that you at the boundary of Alpha six?"*

> *STING 27: "Roger, I am in a port turn at this time."*

Radar confirmed this turn. Sting 27 turned left to a northerly heading then right again as it executed its flight plan. During the right turn, radar contact was lost at 0822. The position was eighty-two nautical miles southeast of Homestead AFB.

Several stations including Homestead AFB tower; Miami Center, FAA Reader Facility; Scepter Control, ADC Radar Facility; and Image Control attempted, but could no longer raise Sting 27. Another Phantom, Sting 28, was ordered to contact the lost flight.

> *STING 28: "Sting 27, Sting 27, this is Sting 28, do you copy?"... "Come in two seven. Over."*

Several calls went unanswered.

ATC vectored Sting 28 to the last position of Sting 27. In five minutes he was over the spot, and began an "S" pattern search of the area at 5,000 feet.

Two more Phantoms Sting 29 and Sting 30 entered the search area. Sting 29 had dropped down to fifteen hundred1 feet to get a closer look at an area of disturbance in the ocean and then banked their F-4 and reported something strange.

> *STING 29: "Yeah, the water is discolored. It's an area of water discoloration. It is oblong in shape, with its axis running north-south. It's approximately 100 by 200 feet."*
>
> *STING 30: "That's Roger. The southern tip appears to be below the surface. The northern end appears to be above it. It's oblong in shape, running north-south."* Confirmed Sting 30, circling at a much higher altitude.

As STING 29 pulled out, he noticed the Coast Guard Cutter, *Steadfast* five miles to the south. He called them on Guard frequency. "We have a spot up here. It's five miles north. Maintain heading. You can't miss it. Is that a roger?" Running along at full speed, the *Steadfast* signaled an affirmative.

STING 29 roared over the ship and headed to base due to low fuel. However, this oblong shape, whatever it was, had disappeared by the time *Steadfast* got there only ten minutes later, and proved elusive throughout the entire search. Clearly this wasn't a fuel sheen. That would have been floating on the surface, not above and below.

The search expanded to take in the entire area of the Gulf Stream as far as Grand Bahamas Island, taking into consideration its drift. The Navy, Coast Guard and Air Force searched for four days nearly 60,000 square miles without any wreckage or trace ever being found.

The Navy even probed the suspected area of ocean with sonar from the 20th of September to the 23rd. After crisscrossing a five square mile track deemed the most probable, the results were a flat negative and search operations were finally halted. Other odd things regarding this disappearance involve the accident report itself. The Air Force does not and will not release conclusion or investigative material, not even opinions. They release the Summary findings, History of Flight and other relevant, though less classified, data on the airplane and pilots and crew.

In this incident even the standard questionnaire, with its many boxes where the clerk types in routine stuff like names and location, has the answer in the box marked Type of Accident cut out. Usually the answer is Missing/Unknown and therefore does not require censoring. The paragraph after Sting 27 disappeared from radar is even blacked out. This paragraph might hold the key to solving this mystery.

Also another strange fact is that the back of the report holds a map that was unedited. It is a chart of Sting 27's track line. Several notes marked key points in its flight path. One interesting note reads "suspected point of impact" before radar contact is even lost. Impact with what? Since the Air Force even edited their standard file sheet, there is absolutely no way to even approach an official opinion on this incident.

Dave's own encounter with the triangle happened on the evening of February 12, 1989, on a return flight back to Homestead General Aviation Airport from Lake Wales, Florida. He had flown up there in the afternoon with a friend, Ryan Harrison, to pick up a purebred cocker spaniel puppy from a breeder farm. Dave knew it would be dark after their departure. Weather was not a factor, calm winds, broken clouds at 7,000 feet and overcast at 12,000 feet and a visibility of 5 miles. Dave filed his flight plan, topped off the plane, and then loaded the puppy in its carrier case and strapped him in the back seat. Dave and Ryan took off at about 2200 and headed south. After leveling off at 3,500 feet he dialed in the La Belle VHF omni directional range NAV Aid on the NAV Radio. He wanted to stay plenty below any clouds that were reported at a few thousand feet above him since he was not instrument rated. He flew this leg of the flight with no difficulties. After passing over the VOR station, he reset the VOR needle to a heading of 156 degrees from the station for his 60 mile flight on down to Homestead.

They were heading out over the Great Cypress swamp and then on over the Everglades. It was pitch dark out and Dave had passed over the last roadway with any lights ten miles back. The overcast above him hid the Moon and any stars. With no highway or housing lights there were no visual references outside. There was no horizon. It was like flying around in an ink bottle. The glow of the instrument panel was reassuring and he scanned his instruments in the sequence drilled into him by his flight instructor. He had to trust his instruments. He was now flying in IFR conditions. He couldn't fly higher to search for city lights due to the cloud cover overhead. He kept his eyes glued to the artificial horizon and the VOR needle. All the instruments were in the green. If he lost the engine, there was no place to put her down. There was nothing, but alligators and saw grass below them for miles on end.

His knuckles were getting white now and the good ol' pucker factor was off the scale. However, he had to remain calm for his passenger's sake. He dialed in the Pahokee VOR on the second NAV Radio to get a side bearing and checked his sectional chart to see where the two bearings intersected. Well, at least he was on course and didn't have to contact Miami Flight Following yet for a radar fix. Besides he wasn't lost. He knew exactly where he was. He just had to guard against getting vertigo and putting the plane in a death spiral. He had gotten vertigo a couple of times before in his helicopter flights out to the missile field, so he knew this was a definite possibility. Time to concentrate. With visibility of only five miles in all directions, this didn't mean squat when there was nothing to see. Not one light was visible outside. Dave avoided staring out the windscreen ahead of him. He turned back to check on the puppy. It was sound asleep and oblivious. Chit chat with Ryan was tense. He could tell that Dave was a little stressed out and also knew Dave was not an instrument-rated pilot.

Just then, in his peripheral vision a strange blue glow began to envelope the plane's wing tips. The propeller tip also began to glow iridescent blue. Both Dave and Ryan gave each other a strange glance as they heard a strange hissing noise in their headsets rising and falling in a rhythmic tone. To reassure his passenger, Dave removed his headset and motioned him to do the same. Above the engine noise Dave yelled, "St. Elmo's fire."

Ryan nodded in understanding and proceeded to look out the right window. Dave had heard about St. Elmo's fire before. It is a mixture of gas and plasma caused by ionization of the air molecules in a highly charged atmosphere producing a faint glow easily visible in low-light conditions.

Dave continued to reassure Ryan, who was getting a little nervous, "You know this light show is a pretty rare treat. St. Elmo's fire is actually considered by sailors to be a good omen. It tends to occur in the dissipating stages of severe thunderstorms when the most violent surface winds and seas are abating. Heck, even Charles Darwin, Magellan, and even Christopher Columbus reported seeing the phenomena atop their ships' masts and rigging. Don't worry, the avionics is grounded and we are not going to blow up." "Hopefully," he muttered to himself.

However, the strange thing was, there were no thunderstorms anywhere within sight. The blue glow was in stark contrast to the dim red glow of the instrument panel in the cockpit. He was beginning to wonder if some rouge MIST particles had come by to haunt him, or better yet, lead him home.

The glow of St. Elmo's fire off the prop along with the noise from the engine became almost hypnotic. It was then that Dave then had a sensory moment. He was thinking of Anne and was going to invite her down for a visit. He remembered what she taught him on remote viewing. If there ever was a time when he needed a view of the horizon, it was now. He scanned his instruments one more time and then went through the mind prep. He could tell Anne was thinking of him and was worried. He concentrated on what the horizon should look like from 15,000 feet. He should be able to see the lights of Miami off to the southeast. What else would be out here to home in on and get a visual bearing? Time to trust his instruments, but remote viewing even more. He felt like Luke Skywalker, trusting the Force. Only this time it was, "Dave trust your remote viewing sense." He put his mind at 15,000 feet, 40 miles ahead. What was out there? Just then in his mind was a beautiful sight. Dade-Collier Airport glowed on the horizon. This was a practice strip that the airlines used for touch and goes out in the middle of the Everglades along Alligator Alley. It was originally slated to become Miami International but again the environmentalists shut the project down. He concentrated on following this glow on the horizon. The closer he got the fainter the glow. This didn't make sense. He should be able to see the runway lights by now. Nada. Nothing. Only the faint green glow off of the concrete runway. When he was directly overhead the runway disappeared. Where the hell did it go? Just then a few miles ahead he could make out a few lights that were moving east to west. A few minutes later auto taillights and headlights could be seen moving along the highway known as Alligator Alley. He was quite relieved as this put him back in VFR mode.

As the Cessna crossed over Alligator Alley, he made a gentle left turn to follow it until it crossed Krome Avenue, the main north-south roadway, on the eastern edge of the Glades. He then followed it south until he could see the airport beacon light at Homestead. He set up for a landing pattern and made a perfect landing. Ryan was much relieved, and so was the puppy. Dave never could explain the strange green glow of the Dade-Collier runway. Especially when he later learned the airport had been closed for the week, down for maintenance for a relighting project. The runway lights were inoperative according to a published Notice to Airman.

CHAPTER 28
Forces of Nature?

The control rods at Turkey Point Nuclear Power Plant were pulled out slowly, thus, increasing the neutron bombardment in the cooling pool. The water glowed an iridescent blue. This bluish light is caused by charged particles that are traveling through water at a very high speed which causes a shockwave to form. This shockwave is similar to the sonic boom caused when a jet exceeds the speed of sound in air. In the case of breaking the sound barrier, a wall of sound is formed in the shape of a pointed cone with the jet's nose located at the tip. This wall of sound results in a sonic boom. A similar situation occurs for the charged particle in water, but instead of a wall of sound, it is a wall of light resulting in a blue glow known as the Cerenkov radiation effect.

The core temperature rose as predicted and the cooling pumps kicked in and circulated fresh water through the heat exchanger tubing. After picking up and absorbing an enormous amount of heat, the cooling water was then discharged into the miles of parallel cooling canals located south of the plant. After a few hours, the lukewarm water flowing through these canals generated a huge Telluric Current. The Navy Card Sound Facility then tuned the current and further amplified it. It was then discharged through the oolite coral cut at a 36 degree angle out though the barge canal to Biscayne Bay and into the northerly flowing Gulf Stream current.

On this day, Thursday, August 20, 1992, tides were exactly right, the temperature was right, the humidity fell within the required 2 percent tolerance, the barometric pressure was falling, and the Telluric current was at the proper amperage and frequency. It was a perfect day to attempt to flip the thermocline and generate a torsional wave twenty-five miles off the south Florida coast. The Gulf Stream was pumping warm water northeastwardly along the Keys and mixing it with the cold Atlantic Ocean near Bimini. All parameters were in the green. A window like this would not come along again for another three months.

The submarine USS Alabama was submerged off the coast at 18 26.57° N by 76.80° W on the edge of the continental shelf near Great Abaco Island in the Bahamas. It was providing data back to the Delta G Blue Lab located in the old Saturn V testing facilities out in the Everglades south of Homestead. They were monitoring the thermocline conditions. The two tenths of a degree rise in the Gulf Stream temperature would be unnoticeable to the average boater or swimmer on the beach. But along with the outflow of fresh water from the cooling canals and its associated telluric current; it was enough to change the density, salinity, and electropotential of this part of the ocean. The thermocline was about to flip. A trillion gallons of seawater were about to change density in about five seconds.

The USS Alabama called the countdown of the expected flip, "Five…four…three…two…one…foxtrot…foxtrot…foxtrot," which indicated the flip had occurred. The sonar and instrument buoys were registering the density change. The gravimeters imbedded in the sea floor were registering a rapid change. The meters definitely showed the telltale signs of a spiral torsional wave being generated. A small vortex of ocean current and then a water spout formed within a hundred yards of the expected location.

Everyone clapped and shook hands as the first seaborne torsional wave was successfully made. The Navy would have a chip in this game after all. Nobody thought ahead far enough to figure out one thing: *how to shut the process down*. In theory, nature would balance the ocean and the thermocline would dissipate and the torsional wave would die out.

However, unbeknownst to the Delta G Blue Team was the formation of an even bigger low pressure system off to the southeast. Tropical Storm Andrew had just been named and was five hundred miles southeast of the Bahamas. And as they mentioned on the Weather Channel, "not a factor at this time."

Friday morning, a day later, the torsional wave was still spinning. It had reduced its strength by ninety percent, but it was still there. There was nothing visible on the ocean surface. The thin air was there, but the vortex was clear. Not enough humidity to compress into a cloud or visible funnel.

The Navy dispatched a destroyer to keep the area clear, claiming a jet had crashed in the area as a cover story. In a few hours, Andrew would be upgraded to hurricane status and looking for warm water and low pressure to feed its thermal engine. It only had to look a few hundred miles. The torsional wave drew Andrew in like a leaf swirling down a drain.

CHAPTER 29
Castles in the Sky

On Friday evening after the successful test off Bimini, Dave went back to his office at the Base Engineering Complex to wrap up some long overdue paperwork. He had just pulled into the parking lot when his beeper went off. It was the Base Command Post calling. A base-wide recall had been initiated. It was Dave's job to man the Command Post as a senior member of the Base Battle Staff. As the chief engineer on the installation, he had nearly four years on station. Major Enhoff, the new base civil engineer (BCE), had only been on base less than a month. It was now Dave's job to get him up to speed as quickly as possible. He would also advise the base commander and flying wing commander on engineering matters, and keep the Base Damage Control Center (DCS) advised. Dave showed his line badge to the guard manning the Command Post and proceeded over to his assigned console. He picked up his phone and began calling personnel on the recall roster.

The base commander came in and informed his staff that Tropical Storm Andrew was now five hundred miles east-southeast turning westward towards south Florida. He wanted to get the base prepared for the season's first tropical weather.

Dave pulled out a notebook from under the desk. It was the Base Hurricane Plan. He had actually written much of it himself. It included a checklist of activities and procedures that needed to be accomplished. It included the obvious and common sense things such as securing loose objects, filling generator tanks, giving them a test run, and taping up windows. But it also included hundreds of other items that required the base fire department, security police forces, and engineering staff to accomplish.

Since the threat of an imminent storm was minimal at this time and it was Friday evening, he set things in motion and put most of his staff on telephone standby. No one was really too worried about this storm. It had just about dissipated the day before due to unfavorable wind shear conditions. The battle staff was allowed to go home for the evening and would reconvene Saturday morning.

It was a long day and he was exhausted from the dual Delta G Test Site and the Command Post duties. After midnight, Dave drove home to his condo, where he broke out the expensive whiskey and fixed himself a seven and seven. The La-Z-Boy recliner felt like a corner of heaven as he fell asleep watching the Weather Channel.

He woke up Saturday to the smell of the automatic coffee pot brewing. His eyes adjusted to the set left on all night. Andrew was now a Cat I Hurricane. The phone rang at about the same time his pager went off. He was getting simultaneous calls from both the Base Command Post and the Delta G Office. He answered the phone.

"Captain Sheridan?" the voice on the other end asked.

"Yes," replied Sheridan.

"This call is to inform you that a base-wide recall and checklist Charlie is now in effect. Please implement your portion of the pyramid recall and report to the Command Post ASAP."

Checklist Charlie was the base emergency preparedness checklist leading up to possible evacuation of the base. It was 0800 and Andrew was now four hundred miles due east and inbound. The strike probability was for landfall on the Florida coast.

Dave called the half dozen officers who worked for him and repeated the recall order to each of them. He then phoned the Delta G Office at Card Sound. Lieutenant Andrea Brotskey answered the phone, "Captain, you are needed here right away. We've got a situation out here you need to be aware of."

He replied, "Lieutenant, I've been called back to the Command Post. Andrew is now a hurricane; we need to prepare the base and make plans for a possible evacuation. Can this wait?"

The lieutenant responded, "No, sir, I don't think so. The Pentagon is on the line with Drs. Timken and Rapp down here. There is also a lot of commotion and radio traffic."

Dave was a little irritated, "You mean they are actually worried about us in D.C. now that a hurricane is heading our way. That's considerate of them. Tell Timken and Rapp to turn on the Weather Channel. It will tell us more about where and when Andrew is going to make landfall and at what strength."

The lieutenant on the other end of the line got a little indignant, "Captain, you are dead wrong. Rapp and Timken can tell you when, where, and how bad Andrew is going to be to the hour, to the exact lat and long, as well as its projected speed. The Cray has it all figured out."

Just then Rapp picked up the phone on the other end, "Captain, get your butt out here, Andrew is being drawn into the residual TW."

Dave's jaw dropped. The fact that Rapp had violated security on an open line didn't shock him as much as the fact that Andrew was being pulled towards the residual torsional wave still spinning off the coast.

As Dave turned off of SR A1A and onto Card Sound Road the Mustang GT accelerated. He had rarely had her up over ninety but today the telephone poles were flying past at over one hundred thirty. The Mustang, being light in the back end, was starting to get a bit squirrelly. The convertible top started to sound like it was going to be ripped off. He wondered what this thing would really do. He still had some gas pedal left and wasn't anywhere near red lining the tachometer. As he approached the turn off to the Navy Card Sound Facility, he backed off on the accelerator. Dr. Rapp was waiting for him and waved him through the security gate. At about the same time, a Blackhawk chopper was landing on the pad. Dave couldn't mistake the cute set of buns climbing out of the back. He knew it was Anne. A crewman was helping her with several aluminum cases.

Rapp said, "I'm impressed Captain, you actually beat the chopper out here from the base."

Dave replied, "You said to get my butt out here ASAP. What's this about the TW still spinning off the coast and this hurricane being sucked into it?"

Rapp opened the door for Anne and Dave as the crewman dropped the cases in the lobby. "Not now, Captain, I'll bring you up to speed in a few minutes. The Cray is crunching some final numbers."

Dr. Timken met the group in the lobby. "Good to see you again, Dr. Ahrens. Thanks for bringing the equipment on such short notice."

Dave gave a smile to Anne, "When did you get the word of all this? I didn't know you were on base."

As they walked toward the briefing room, Anne replied, "I wasn't. I just flew down here from the Cape. I had to transfer some equipment over at the base onto the Customs chopper."

He had suspected that Anne had been involved at the Cape with the space based Delta G Program Office, but was now sure of it.

Dr. Rapp flipped on the overhead projector showing a satellite photo of the Caribbean and Florida east coast. Overlaid on the satellite image was the location and coordinates for the TW test location off Bimini and the current location of the eye of Hurricane Andrew. A dashed line connected the two.

"Ladies and gentlemen, we have less than forty-eight hours before this site is under about fifteen feet of water and most of Dade County is flattened by Andrew." In the room were Dr. Timken, Anne, Dave, Lieutenant Brotskey, Brooke Wilson, the Turkey Point Nuclear plant manager, Captain Morgan Sillence, the Naval detachment commander, and Colonel Butt, the base commander. Dave thought it was strange that Butt would be here instead of the Command Post on base, but he knew the battle staff was just in the process of getting up to speed and the base commander always made a fashionable late appearance anyway.

Since this was technically a Navy operation out here, Sillence responded first. "What do you mean we're going to be under fifteen feet of water? Andrew is four hundred miles out and barely a CAT I hurricane. What makes you think it is going to make a bee line for us and take us out?"

Rapp replied as he turned off the overhead. He picked up his trusty piece of chalk and started to draw on the board. "The TW is still spinning out in the Gulf Stream contrary to all expectations. As you well know, a TW is only stable if it is coupled to another torsional wave somewhere in the universe. Either we've established a stable TW linked to our space based generator, which I doubt, or we have linked in with one of the world's largest sources of torsional energy, a hurricane."

Just then Anne jumped in the conversation, "I can tell you for a fact that the orbital TW detectors aren't picking up a thing. Right now they are in Lagrange Point Two on the opposite side of the planet and are picking up no anomalies."

Rapp drew an Earth-Moon diagram and plotted the five Lagrange points between the Earth's and Moon's orbit. Lagrange points are imaginary points in space where objects sent there will stay put. A French-Italian mathematician named Joseph-Louis Lagrange, born in 1736, discovered their existence during his study of planetary physics. Lagrange believed that in a two-body system, such as the Earth and Moon, there would be five points nearby where an object could be sent and remain in place. He theorized that at certain points, the gravity of two bodies would cancel out one another and halt the motion of the spacecraft, keeping it in one spot. He was correct.

Rapp continued plotting things on the board. "You say the Lagrange point is stable now. Then there is another source of torsional energy other than the TW that we set off and Andrew. The TW we set off hasn't moved from its original location more than a mile or so. Andrew is moving towards it. This means there is another TW source somewhere west of the Bimini TW Site that is anchoring it. The Cray computer is now crunching the numbers based upon the forces required to keep the TW spinning and the rate of approach of Andrew. We'll have a location in a few minutes. But I have my own hunch where it is located. Anne, can you and Lieutenant Brotskey set up your equipment? The Cray coordinates are going to be approximate and within a mile or so radius. If I'm right and the Cray is right, we have another shell located within a few miles of us."

Dave chimed in. "If that's the case, why haven't we ever

detected it? Besides, we aren't anywhere near any of the plotted shells. Major Boop and his crew pulled one from the jungles of Puerto Rico a few months ago. That was hundreds of miles away."

Timken spoke up. "As you well know, my good friend, modern man hasn't been the only one to run across these shells. Other past civilizations have found and moved these shells all over the globe. This may be the case here."

Anne and Lieutenant Brotskey started opening up the cases and pulling out the assorted electronic gear. "Damn it. I forgot the connection cable. A million dollars' worth of microwave detection equipment and I can't even plug it into the wall."

Dave walked over and lent a hand. "You just need standard wall power 110 V AC?"

"No, the adapter cable had a twelve volt, five amp DC transformer built in."

Dave said, "Wait right here. I think I can help you out." He ran out to the Mustang and got his overnight bag and brought it in. He pulled out his electric razor and started to read the placard on the charger. Anne exclaimed, "I don't think your razor has enough juice to power up my system."

Dave just grinned and said, "No, but the recharger is twelve volt five amp, presto!"

Anne couldn't help but laugh, "Dave, you are amazing."

Timken smiled and said, "You did it again, comrade Captain."

Dave pulled out his Swiss pocketknife and cut the cable.

Anne was ahead of him this time and was unscrewing the case to the detector. "Here, screw down the wires on these two leads."

Just then a Navy enlisted man walked in and handed Captain Sillence a stack of computer print outs. Sillence thanked him and pushed them over to Rapp, "Here are your Cray results." Rapp flipped through the fan fold printout and concentrated on a line near the end. Dave watched Rapp's expression as he went over to a wall map of south Florida. His fingers ran horizontally from left to right as he glanced to the top of the map to get a longitude reading.

Rapp simply said, "Our good friend, Ed Leedskalnin, has cracked the code indeed."

Colonel Butt said, "What are you talking about? Who the hell is this Ed guy and what code did he break?"

As a relatively long time resident of Homestead, Florida, Dave knew who he was.

Dave smiled, too, and turned to Rapp, "You've got to be shitting me."

Rapp grabbed his chalk and wrote the numbers 25° 30' 02" N - 80° 26' 40" W along with 82° 22' 07" N - 82° 22' 07" W on the board.

Butt's jaw dropped. As a pilot he recognized the lower set of coordinates as being only a few miles due west of the base. He murmured half under his breath, "That's not possible, is it?

Rapp sighed, "Yes, sir. It is. It appears we have located two shells. One lies along FL SR A1A, just north of Homestead. The other link is 6,105 kilometers due north in Canada."

Dave went over to the map on the wall and put his finger on it. I was just here a couple of weeks ago with my brother, Glenn. I'll be damned, the Coral Castle."

Timken asked one of the Navy enlisted men to run into town and get any information he could on the Coral Castle, such as pamphlets, tourist info, books at the library and bring them back ASAP.

Anne looked puzzled. "Isn't that a castle some eccentric built using huge blocks of coral rock? He was supposed to have discovered the secrets of how the pyramids were built and used it to levitate the blocks in place."

Dave replied, "Yes, it's one of the most popular tourist attractions down here. It's one of those mysterious places that defy explanation.

Butt jumped out of his seat, "This is all well and good, gentlemen, but what does this shell have to do with Andrew? Is it really pulling it in? If so, what can we do about it?"

Rapp said, "No, Colonel. I don't think we can stop it short of setting off a tactical nuke fifty miles to the north. I doubt that is going to happen. We can only prepare for it and evacuate. If I'm correct, that shell is embedded in the oolite coral rock that was deposited in south Florida over 100,000 years ago. Even if we knew exactly where it was, we couldn't excavate it in time to make any difference."

Butt headed for the door. On the way out he said, "I don't want to hear any wisecrack about the only thing to do is bend over and kiss your Butt goodbye. I heard enough of that in my SAC days. I've got people to take care of and a base to evacuate. You can contact me at the Command Post."

Sunday morning at the Command Post everything was running fairly smoothly. Checklists were being completed. In less than thirty hours Hurricane Andrew had gone from a CAT 1 minimal storm to a monster of a CAT 5. It defied all predictions and computer modeling that showed it should weaken and veer to the north. It had been tracking on a due west course for nearly a day now and had not deviated more than a few miles from the 25° 30' latitude.

The decision to evacuate the base had been made. All nonessential personnel and dependents would evacuate. Safe havens would be established at Patrick AFB up near the Cape, MacDill AFB near Tampa as well as both Eglin and Tyndall AFB in the Florida Panhandle. There would only be a cadre left behind of about 150 personnel, including security police, fire department, and base civil engineering personnel, as well as the battle staff.

Colonel Butts directed Dave to contact the National Hurricane Center directly to get a prognosis on wind speed and tidal surge. He talked to Dr. Bob Sheets, the director of the center. He told Dave flat out that the winds might not kill you all, but the tidal surge will be fifteen to twenty feet. It didn't take long for Dave to do the math. The centerline of the runway was seven feet above sea level. He made the recommendation to the base commander to evacuate the cadre NLT 1700 hours. That would give a twelve hour window from the expected land fall at around 0500 hours in the morning. But just where to evacuate to was not in the checklist. All of Dade County east of I-95 was an evacuation zone.

Someone had mentioned to Sheridan that there was a brand new Army Reserve building that was just built west of the Miami Zoo. It was well inland and should have enough room to shelter the cadre. Butt ordered Dave and Captain Sandie Bender to

drive up there to check it out. They ran downstairs to the CE staff
car and rolled westward out of the base. They had the siren and
flashing lights on as they weaved in and out of traffic until they
turned north up Naranja Road. It took an hour and a half to get
up there. The facility was brand new and included a high bay and
gymnasium that could easily accommodate the cadre. Dave talked to the Reserve Center commander, Lieutenant Colonel Richard Zanowick and gave him a heads up that the cadre would be
arriving after 1700. He said he would make arrangements and get
things ready. A few families had started to show up even though
it had not been officially recognized as a hurricane shelter. Dave
was confident the concrete and brick block construction would be
adequate to weather the storm. It also was a help to know that the
center was twenty-two feet above sea level.

It was now noon. Dave and Sandie were out of radio range
with the base. The telephone lines were all clogged. They didn't
have as much traffic heading back south to contend with. As they
turned eastward on SW 288th Street toward the base, they radioed
in to the Command Post that the center was acceptable as a shelter for the cadre and that Lieutenant Colonel Zanowick would be
expecting them.

As they approached the west gate Dave saw a pair of F-16
fighter jets climbing out at full afterburner. The base was in the
process of evacuating its three fighter squadrons of aircraft. They
would be going to safe havens in Georgia and South Carolina.

Dave was getting a little worried about Anne. She was still out
at the Card Sound Facility getting things ready for the Coral Castle
survey. The equipment required calibration. Her request to have
Colonel Boop fly down with the C-130 to do an aerial survey was
predictably declined. Trying to explain to people why a C-130
was orbiting less than three miles at the end of your only runway
while trying to evacuate an entire base was a hard sell. Besides,
the C-130 was down for routine maintenance anyway and couldn't
be operational for several hours. So Anne was tasked to get a non-
conspicuous van and tote her equipment up to the Coral Castle.
There were two problems with this scenario. First, renting a moving van or truck was impossible. There were a quarter million

people evacuating the Keys and south Dade County. There wasn't a van or truck available for hundreds of miles. Second, she would have to take her readings virtually on top of the Castle. The good news here was that there wouldn't be too many tourists around to ask questions today. Since Anne, Rapp and Timken were the only ones left at the Delta G Facility, it was their job to secure the place and its valuable equipment as much as possible. Captain Sillence and his crew had bugged out an hour or two earlier to secure their homes and evacuate north.

Anne tried Dave's beeper, but the phone lines were busy. There was a hotline to the Command Post that she picked up and used. Butt answered on the other end. "I'm kind of busy bugging out right now, Anne, but what can I do for you? Sure, I can get a crew van down to you shortly. It has a gas generator and 110 V DC for your power source. On second thought, I'll find and commandeer you an RV with a generator. It would be a little less conspicuous. Could you meet the vehicle at the McDonald's at junction of A1A and Card Sound Road? I don't want my people caught on that road with all the traffic pouring out of the Keys."

Anne agreed and tossed her equipment in the back of a Navy pickup. After shredding and burning the classified information, they turned out the lights and secured the facility. Timken wondered aloud what would be left, if anything, when they returned.

The three of them hopped in a white Navy pickup and merged into the bumper to bumper traffic on Card Sound Road. At this rate it would take them hours to reach the McDonald's. They could almost walk it faster. Rapp actually got out and walked back down the access road saying he forgot something. He came back by them peddling a shiny red ten speed. "I'll meet you in a couple hours. I'll buy you a Happy Meal." They, too, didn't want the poor airmen waiting for hours if they had families of their own to take care of.

It was a hot sunny afternoon. The traffic was moving, but barely. Luckily they had air conditioning and plenty of gas. Anne was getting worried about the million dollars' worth of electronics in this pickup. It was baking back there in the south Florida sun.

An hour or so later, a Winnebago had pulled into the McDonald's parking lot around 1400. It pulled around back. Two airmen got out. Dr. Timken peddled over to them. "I'm Dr. Timken. I believe Colonel Butts sent you out here with this for us. I have to admit this is a bit much for our needs."

One of the airman said, "All we know is that the colonel ordered us to go find an RV with a generator at the base campground and hot wire it if necessary and then bring it down here. Something about some general's daughter needed to be evacuated out of the Keys. Must be nice to have friends in high places."

Timken turned around and saw the white pickup truck down the road about a quarter mile. "There's your ride back to the base, gentlemen. They should be up here in about fifteen minutes. Not quite a fair trade. A nice Winnebago for a Navy pickup truck, but what are you going to do?"

The pickup pulled into the McDonald's. One of the airmen handed Anne a large envelope and a handheld radio with a recharger. Colonel Butts was no dummy. He was looking out for his own ass by taking care of General Ahrens' daughter. The envelope contained a list of base frequencies, phone numbers, and also a map to the reserve building in Kendal near the zoo for the Team to meet up with later.

The airmen helped transfer the heavy equipment out of the pickup and into the Winnebago. The equipment just barely fit through the door. Patience was wearing thin when one of the airmen suggested it would be faster if they just busted out a side window in the Winnebago.

The two airmen were smart enough not to ask any questions about the equipment. They figured the truck came from the Card Sound Facility and that's all they needed to know. They hopped in the pickup and drove out over the back parking lot and disappeared behind some hedges. They had taken a shortcut cross country back towards the base.

Anne, Rapp, and Timken hopped in the Winnebago and stared at each other. Anne asked, "Either one of you ever drive one of these land yachts?"

Rapp shrugged his shoulders and said, "It can't be all that complicated. Half the Canadian population over sixty knows how to drive one of these." He climbed behind the wheel and they headed up A1A.

The traffic was not too bad on the west side of I-95. As a matter of fact the west side of I-95 wasn't declared an evacuation zone even though the "Big One" was barreling towards them at twenty mph. It was now around 1500 hours. The Winnebago pulled into a parking lot across the street from the Coral Castle. Rapp was pouring over the tourist info and books the Navy enlisted man had given him. Anne and Timken were busy setting up, connecting, and calibrating their sensor equipment.

Anne booted up the terminal and inserted a floppy disk. This equipment had a two man encryption key, both she and Timken logged on.

Rapp rubbed his chin and said, "This Ed guy had things pretty much figured out. He claimed he could see energy fields and beads of light surrounding objects and figured a way to focus the magnetic fields around all matter in such a way to levitate objects. That's how he supposedly moved these thirty ton chunks of coral rock. He supposedly built this place as a dedication to his fiancé that jilted him. His sweet sixteen as he called her. He spent twenty years of his life from 1920 to 1940 doing this. Nobody really knew how he built the place. It was always fenced in and shielded from public view. Some people saw him move the blocks with ropes and pulleys. Other claimed to have seen blocks of coral tethered like kid's balloons. In my mind it is physically impossible for one man to build such a structure with levers and pulleys. Just like the pyramids, the fit of the joints between blocks is so tight you couldn't slip a butter knife between them. He even built a nine ton coral block swinging door so precisely balanced you can open it with one finger. The layout of the Castle also has an astrological theme to it."

Anne and Timken had things pretty much set up. Now came the tricky part. They would have to place three hardwired sensors around the perimeter of the Castle and string the wire across a busy street. How would they explain that trick?

Rapp continued with his reading, "This is interesting. Edward Leedskalnin stated that all forms of existence are made up of three components: North and South Poles and neutral particles of matter. He claimed to have 'rediscovered the laws of weight, measurement, and leverage' and claimed that these laws 'involved the relationship of the Earth to celestial alignments'. This is downright weird, too. The center of the Castle has a one piece spiral staircase carved in it that descends to a basement refrigerator. Why do I have a feeling that his spiral staircase is more than an access to his wine cellar? Too much of a coincidence here. I'll bet you that staircase amplified and focused the torsional waves coming out of the complex."

Anne said, "We'll see. If that's the case, then we should be able to verify that there is in fact a TW generator here on the premises. We can do that without the triangulation sensors in place. All I have to do is use the antenna to sense for microwave photon packets. We should be able to detect the side lobes from here. Also the Kirlian effect will be amplified in the presence of a TW generator. I have the camera and film to perform those tests but from what you just read about beads of light. I think it is safe to say good ol' Ed hid a shell in his basement."

Timken strung the antenna cable outside the Winnebago and walked it down the parking lot for about a hundred feet. He threw a cable up over a cable TV line running down the street careful not to hit the power line. He picked up the lead and ran across the street with it. He tossed it over a billboard and pulled it taut up off the road before anyone had a chance to run over it. One passerby did ask what he was up to. He simply replied he was setting up a HAM radio base station here to help with the evacuation. That satisfied the curious onlooker and he drove on. This emboldened Timken. He went back inside the Winnebago and got the three triangulation sensors. Then he walked back across the street to the Castle. There were hundreds of vehicles racing up A1A that were too busy getting out of town to care what some nut case scientist was doing placing three small parabolic dish antennas on the walls of the Coral Castle. Besides, if anyone asked he had a cover story. A HAM radio base station. He was pretty proud of himself.

Once the dishes were in place with the microwave photon prisms, it was a relatively simple process of letting the software do its number crunching. It became a waiting game now.

It was now about 1600 hours on Sunday afternoon, August 23, 1992. According to the radio, Andrew was now a strong CAT 5 with a central pressure of 922 millibars barreling westward at 16 mph near Eleuthera in the Bahamas. Its maximum sustained wind speed was an incredible 175 miles per hour with gusts over 200. There wasn't a structure in south Florida that could survive that. Mobile homes would start to disintegrate at 90 mph and houses at about 120. Perhaps a bank vault would survive 175 mph. People didn't understand simple physics. The forces on a structure quadruple with a doubling of the wind speed.

Anne watched the computer screen as rows and rows of numbers scrolled past her. She glanced out the window of the Winnebago and watched the procession of people migrate up A1A. For the most part it was an orderly flow. Every once in a while some idiot would try to sneak across the busy intersection during a yellow and invariably cause grid lock. A few middle digits would be exchanged with not much else. "Damn," she said, "People have figured out this thing is going to be a killer and are starting to bug out even from the west side of I-95. I'm surprised they haven't made that a mandatory evacuation."

Timken replied, "It's too late now. They couldn't possibly evacuate all of Dade County. There is less than twelve hours to land fall. If you aren't smart enough to figure things out and get the hell out of here without some government official telling you to do so, then I guess they just chalk that up to survival of the fittest and evolution's natural selection process."

The numbers kept flying by on the computer screen. Anne began to doze off when all of a sudden an audible alarm went off and the printer started to spit out fanfolds. Timken and Rapp nearly ripped the sheet in half grabbing for it after the printing stopped. They both looked at the print out.

Rapp asked, "How do you say, holy shit in Russian? That place is saturated with residual microwaves and resonating at the DNA frequency. The Kirlian factor is off the scale. There has to be a shell there. The primary vector of the TW is in line with the Bimini TW event. We have confirmed that they are coupled. But why isn't the Bimini TW dying out…unless we activated a shell out there, too. The plot is also showing that it is linked to something to the north, coordinates 82° 22' N by 82° 22' W." Rapp did some mental calculations, "Hell, that puts the other end somewhere on Ellesmere Island, west of Thule. I thought we identified and pulled all the shells in that area of the world."

Timken brought everyone back to reality, "Okay, gang, let's unplug and haul ass. We have no chance of outrunning this thing. They will call for a curfew at dusk. I don't want to be within two hundred miles of this monster in this contraption. Let's meet up with the cadre at the evacuation site. We can contact Delta G in D.C. and give them the information to chew on. Spiral waves are attracting spiral energy. No chance of turning this event off. Andrew is going to come screaming over this intersection at 0500 in the morning just like the Cray said it would."

Anne picked up the handheld radio, "Charlie Papa one, Charlie Papa one; this is Delta Gulf."

Anne got an almost immediate response, "Roger, Delta Gulf, what's your status?"

Anne didn't want to say on an unsecured channel that they confirmed a shell that sat under the Coral Castle. She couched her remarks in a fashion Butt would understand. "We have secured the Naval Card Sound Facility, passing by Coral Castle on A1A en route to the Reserve Center. All is okay and confirmed Tango Whiskey is in place. Will have myself, plus two." She knew Tango Whiskey would keep anyone not familiar with the Delta G Program guessing about anything but torsional waves.

Sheridan was monitoring the radio transmission on his brick as he was driving with Sandie in the convoy out to the Reserve Center. It was good to hear Anne's voice. Sandie said, "Sounds like this place is going to get crowded. I've got a condo just down the street from the Reserve Center. I've got a few people coming over to my place tonight to ride this thing out. Want to come over? We can kick back, have a beer or two, turn on the Weather Channel and watch things from there. Besides, I'm on the third floor. At least we won't drown."

Dave replied, "That sounds like a good offer. I'll think about it."

The convoy was making good time. It consisted of about thirty vehicles including the base security police, fire department and engineers' heavy construction equipment on tractor trailer low boys. They brought a dozer, front end loaders, and forklifts. Several light-all carts and generator carts were included, too.

Timken pulled the Winnebago off of A1A and slowly made his way up north towards the Kendall-Tamiami Executive Airport. The area was buzzing with choppers and private planes. Coast Guard choppers were landing as well as a few Black Hawks from who knows where. Rapp thought out loud, "How about we go over there and pull some rank and trade up? We could use one of those Black Hawks to get us out of here and back up the Cape."

Anne said, "It is tempting. But they are going to need every chopper that they can get their hands on down here. Besides, we have the info we need. When this thing blows over, we'll need to be down here ASAP to take post readings and see what we can do to recover that shell. This is ground zero. I'm staying put."

Timken pulled the Winnebago into the Reserve Center parking lot. He didn't really know how to turn the thing off. Luckily it never stalled as the thing was hotwired. They just left it running figuring it would eventually run out of gas. They had beaten the convoy there.

They walked in the center and met a sergeant at the door. He had them sign a roster. Anne asked if she could speak to the commander. The sergeant took her back to the administrative area. Lieutenant Colonel Zanowick was on the phone complaining that they needed more cots. After a couple of minutes he hung up and came over to Anne, Rapp, and Timken. "Sergeant Thomas told me that you are up here from Card Sound. What can I do for you?"

"First of all thank you for the hospitality and safe haven. We have some very delicate and classified equipment out in the Winnebago; we would like to bring inside for safekeeping." Zanowick had heard the urban legends of super-secret communications capability that they had at Card Sound to be able to send radio waves through the Earth's mantle and core to have contact with the submarine fleet 100 percent of the time. He figured the equipment had something to do with that mission and was more than happy to accommodate his three guests. Little did he know that its real purpose was to tap into and amplify the telluric currents and ley lines that intersected directly under the antenna farm.

"If I could borrow your phone and call the Pentagon I'd appreciate it. As a matter of fact, I'll trade you. You might want to use this radio to contact Colonel Butts, the Air Base Commander. The last I heard, they were about twenty minutes out. Please tell him we arrived safely." Zanowick got up and told Anne to have a seat. He took the radio and made his call, "Colonel Butts, Colonel Butts, this is Lieutenant Colonel Zanowick, Commander of the Army Reserve Center, over"

Zanowick got an immediate response, "This is Colonel Butts. We are about ten minutes out. We have a cadre of 142 personnel, plus approximately 31 vehicles, five of which are tractor trailers with low-boys."

Zanowick replied, "We're ready for you, Colonel. I have troops ready to marshal you in. We've got an escort waiting for you at Quail Roost and 137th."

"Roger that, we're coming up on the intersection now. Thank you for your help. I will see you in a few minutes. My troops are instructed to follow you and your men's instructions. We'll stay out of the way as much as possible."

"You're no bother, Colonel. Be advised I have approximately sixty-five troops here, plus another twenty-five civilians."

"Thank you, Colonel Zanowick. We came self-sufficient, plenty of food and water, plus two hundred cots."

"*Thank you, sir.* You just solved one of my logistical problems. Zanowick out."

The convoy turned the corner north with an Army escort. It was like a parade. Kids came out of their houses to wave as the vehicles moved up 137th Avenue. As promised, Army troops were waiting and marshaled the vehicles into the parking lot. The convoy had arrived.

Dave pulled his pickup in behind Colonel Butts' staff car. Butts got out and started giving orders to his troops. "Captain Sheridan, have your Prime BEEF (Base Engineer Emergency Force) troops unload the cots, position the generators, and set up the water buffalos.

Keep them busy and have them help with whatever else that needs to be done around here."

Zanowick welcomed Butts to the Reserve Center and led him into his office. Anne was on the phone with D. C. when they walked in. She stood up as a matter of courtesy. With the phone cradled under her ear, she shook Butts hand. She said, "Nice to see you again, Colonel. I'm on hold trying to get through to the Program Office. It is Sunday evening and everyone is at home up there. I've got a better idea." She hung up the phone and then redialed another number. "Hello, Dad. Yes, I'm fine. I'm down here at Homestead. We've had some anomalies pop up with our recent testing that I had to check out with our portable equipment. We've confirmed there is a generator present. I need a favor. I'll be fine, Dad. I'm at an Army Reserve building well inland near the Miami Zoo. Colonel Butts is here with about 150 of his troops left over from the base. He is taking good care of me." Butts glanced over to her and gave her a wink and a nod. "We'll need a recovery team down here after this thing blows through. I can't get a hold of anyone at the Delta G Office. I need you to get a hold of them and explain the situation."

Butts thought, "It was a damn good thing to have a four star's daughter as your guest. That meant just like in the movies, the Calvary would be here first thing after the storm."

"Dad, there is a line here to use this phone. They all want to contact their families. I've got to go. I'll give you a call, if I still can in the morning. Love ya, Dad. Yeah, Dave Sheridan is here along with Drs. Rapp and Timken. Take care, bye." She handed the phone to Colonel Butts.

"Thanks, Dr. Ahrens. I need to contact Air Combat Command at Langley in Virginia. We are out of radio range with the wing commander at the Alert Facility on base. He has a dozen or so people riding out the storm there. I need to phone them, too."

"Zanowick, my troops are at your disposal. They can help you out with anything you need."

"Thank you, sir. We are pretty much set other than for the cots. Glad you brought a bunch. I just received another hurricane update at the top of the hour at 1800. We've got some good news.

Andrew has weakened a bit and it is now back down to a CAT 4. But the bad news is that it is heading straight for us. The tidal surge is expected to be twelve feet."

Butts replied, "Thanks, I'll let the guys know at the Alert Facility out on the flight line. They are hunkered down in the crew quarters on the second floor, hopefully, above the surge. Your buds, the Army Corps of Engineers, tell us it was built to withstand a CAT 5. I hope to hell that they are right."

Sheridan walked over to Rapp and Timken. They were trying to figure out how to unfold their cots. Dave could hear Timken murmuring a few Russian swear words under his breath. Two of the smartest men on the planet Earth and they couldn't unfold a government-issued sleeping cot. Dave helped the men out. He took the opportunity to ask them about the TW generator that they located at the Coral Castle. "How'd you figure that out? The Cray Computer couldn't have figured that out all by itself."

Timken replied, "I've always suspected that there was some underlying truth to Leedskalnin's claim to have discovered the secrets to the pyramids and levitation. However, we were too busy with our own experiments off the coast to look into it. But when the TW kept spinning out there, one of two things had to have occurred. Either we had linked in with a shell somewhere out in space or we had tapped into one here on Earth. Since the orbital detectors at the Lagrange Point 2 were registering nothing, that meant we had tapped into a terrestrial shell. All the ones we had recovered were not active. I used the Cray to ping the known shells we haven't yet recovered. They too, were not showing any activity. We had Colonel Boop fly down yesterday and orbit the Bimini TW Site. He lit the place up with the MASER and detected the TW had a slight parabolic arch back to the west. It was like following a rainbow back to the pot of gold. And of course, Boop couldn't aim the MASER into a populated area. So we just used the Cray to do the number crunching to back track the other end of the arch. It did not totally surprise me it that it ended up to be the Coral Castle." Dave just shook his head in amazement.

It was now about 1900. Sheridan approached Colonel Butts, "Sir, I'd like to respectfully request permission to leave the facility and head over to Captain Bender's residence less than a mile down the road. I'd like to help her secure her place. That will also free up a couple of cots here. Besides, you have more than enough help here. We're stepping on each other's toes."

Butts didn't have to give it much thought. "Sure Captain, on one condition."

Dave replied "Yes, sir. What do you want me to do?"

Butts pointed down the hall, "You take Dr. Ahrens with you. This is no place for her. Besides, if this place gets blown away we'll have someone alive with the information on the TW generator."

Butts was half kidding, but Dave immediately said, "Will do, sir."

He went down to Zanowick's office and extended the invitation to Anne. Anne didn't hesitate either and accepted the offer.

Sheridan smiled and said, "I'll tell Sandie that she has another houseguest."

Sandie's roommate, Mary, pulled up out front. The four of them hopped in her Jeep Cherokee and drove up to the condo complex in the Hammocks of Southwest Miami suburbs. They had a brick with them; however, no charger. They would use it to keep in touch with the Center down the road.

Mary turned on the Weather Channel and offered Dave and Anne a wine cooler. There were a couple of other people that Sandie had invited over. There was a young second lieutenant and his wife, Captain Mike Stebbins, and a neighbor who was a nurse. Both Anne and Dave enjoyed the company and the ability to relax after three days of hell. Here they could let their hair down, get out of there sweaty fatigues, take a shower, and sip on wine coolers, while watching Andrew bare down on them via the Weather Channel. It was surreal. A curfew was now in effect and the highways cleared at 2100 hrs.

Dave used Sandie's phone to call his folks back in Ohio. He wanted to reassure his mom and dad that he was well inland, hi and dry, at a friend's home in Kendall. After all, he was a structural engineer and wouldn't ride out the storm in anything but a bunker. Dave had noticed walking up the three flights of stairs that the condo's concrete construction was pretty stout. He felt this thing should be able to handle a CAT 4. Besides they were ten miles inland. He also reassured his mom that the hurricane would start to wind down when it made landfall. His dad wished him luck and told him to be careful.

They broke out a game of Trivial Pursuit to pass the time. Dave was enjoying himself and the company of Anne. At around midnight, one of the outer bands of Andrew had made it on shore. A nasty thunderstorm lit up the sky. Andrew was still a CAT 4 with 150 mile per hour winds now. The eye had just passed over the Berry Islands about 110 miles due east. It was moving west at about twenty mph. Preliminary news reports from the Bahamas showed very little damage and no fatalities giving everyone a false sense of security.

At about 0200 on Monday morning, things really began to pick up. The winds were bending the huge ficus trees over. Outside the condo the winds were gusting to ninety mph. During lightning strikes, Dave could see the nasty, low hanging, fast moving clouds from his third floor perch. Dave helped Sandie put more duct tape over the windows. They moved the sectional couch against the patio doors and leaned mattresses against the bedroom windows. Dave did a radio check at the Reserve Center. They had moved everyone out of the high-bay and gymnasium into the smaller offices and hallways. There was too much of a danger that the roof was going to be ripped off. They had lost telephone contact to the Alert Facility on base.

Brian Norcross, the local weatherman for Channel 4 News, was begging people to get indoors and hunker down. This was going to be the big one everyone worried about hitting Miami. The Doppler radar had blown off the TV station roof. So now Dade County was effectively blind. A half hour later the power went out. Dave could see out the window several aqua blue green flashes to the east as power transformers were hit with lightning or blown over.

At about 0400, the huge ficus trees were no longer outside the condo. The winds had ripped them out of the ground and blew them over the condo. The sliding glass patio doors were actually bending inward an inch or two and water was spraying in through the gaps. This was getting dangerous. It was still an hour or two before the eye wall was scheduled to hit them. Dave was worried about the windows blowing in. There wasn't enough duct tape in the world to hold back these forces.

Anne was a pretty strong woman, but still came over to the edge of the couch where Dave was sitting and squeezed his hand. The winds were now howling and things began to bang off the side of the building. Anne said to Dave, "People are dying out there tonight, aren't they? Andrew will flatten this place and we've still got another hour before the worst of it hits."

Just then a loud bang was heard in the back bedroom. Sandie rushed over to see what had happened. As she ran down the short hallway to the bedroom, another loud pop was heard. The wooden door frame from the back bedroom had blown past her. In the glow of the Maglites, Sandie was now being pushed back down the hall by the bedroom door that had been blown off its hinges. She dove into the living room as the door pivoted around her and ricocheted around in the kitchen. The rush of air then blew the roof off the condo. It sounded like a machine gun was going off as the rafters were split and ripped upward. The sheet rock ceiling disappeared into oblivion. Dave felt his ears pop and as if someone had lobbed a hand grenade in the room. Everyone had hit the floor by now. Sandie was yelling for everyone to head towards the front bathroom. All seven of them were now crawling towards the bathroom. Insulation was being blown around the room. Water was pouring in. Dave was getting rug burns on his knees as he followed Anne through the bathroom door. The lieutenant dove on his wife in the tub. Sandie, Mary, and Mike Stebbins were already in there sitting with their backs to the concrete outside wall. Dave flung himself in and closed the door. Sandie's small kitten was clinging to the shower curtain going nuts. She hadn't had him declawed yet.

Water started to spray in under the door. There was a tremendous amount of crashing noises on the other side of the door. The wind howled like a jet engine at full throttle. The vent pipe from the bathroom was vibrating behind the wall like a guitar string as the wind whipped it back and forth.

Mike Stebbins was somewhat of a Jesus freak. He asked out loud what everyone thought God's role in all of this was. The young lieutenant looked at him incredulously and put it very simply. "Well, Captain, sir, to put it bluntly, I'd have to say he must be pretty fucking pissed about now." That sort of broke the tension as everyone got a chuckle out of that reply. Dave made a mental note, "This young man is going places if we get out of this alive."

He looked at his watch. It was now 0530 in the morning. This was the peak of it now. They could feel the concrete slab vibrate and undulate under them. The sheetrock walls were bending and bowing with every gust of wind. Dave and Anne held onto each other as they sat on the soaked tile floor.

CHAPTER 30
Andrew's Aftermath

After about an hour of this torture, things began to die down. It was about 0630. Dave opened the bathroom door. There was enough sunlight to make out the mess in the living room. The roof was completely gone. Furniture was tipped over and insulation blown everywhere. Dave could see the dark grey clouds streaking overhead. The rain had stopped but there was a light drizzle. Dave cautioned everyone that they might be in the eye of Andrew and things could worsen in a matter of a few minutes. Sandie walked over and grabbed the brick that they had left outside on the counter. She tried to raise anyone at the center with no luck.

Dave grabbed the AM radio and turned the tuning dial, nothing. All the transmitting antennas must be down. They walked over to the patio doors. They were cracked but not blown in. The tape held. As the sun was coming up in the east, they couldn't believe their eyes. The dozen or so three story condo buildings surrounding them were all missing huge sections of roof. Most of the windows were blown out. Some had furniture and mattresses sticking out of them. There was not a tree or bush standing. Insulation was blowing in the breeze like a pink and yellow blizzard. Sandie opened the front door. The metal door frame was bent and it took some effort. They all went out onto the breezeway. Several neighbors were out and about checking on each other. Fortunately, no one was hurt in this complex. But everyone living on the third floor had similar stories.

The parking lot was a mess. A large garbage dumpster had bounced around the lot and smashed several cars. Several cars were turned over and the smell of gasoline reeked. Tree limbs were everywhere. It would take hours to clear the lot just to get out to the road and who only knows what shape that was in.

A neighbor had a radio tuned into Miami. They were claiming downtown Miami had survived a direct hit and somehow managed to dodge the bullet with very little damage. However, reports were that south Dade had suffered extensive damage. They could not get accurate reports as the weather was still too dicey to get choppers up.

Dave changed back into his fatigues and contemplated walking down to the Reserve Center, but instead decided to clear the parking lot and get Sandie's Jeep free. He figured it could go cross country and over things if necessary. They could also use it to get back to the base if need be.

It was now about 0800. The chain saws were now firing up. People were tying tree limbs to vehicle bumpers and clearing the parking lot. Dozens of sirens were heard off to the west. A metro Dade cruiser was going down the main street and turned into the complex. Dave walked over to him. The officer asked, "Any casualties or injuries in this complex?" Dave replied, "None that we know of. How bad is it out there? Have you heard anything about the base?" The officer replied that things were really bad the further south you went. Kendall-Tamiami Airport was flattened and there were several fatalities in the Country Walk subdivision a couple miles to the south. He also said that the Zoo was totally destroyed. He didn't know anything about the base. He said that the road to the Reserve Center was fairly open but didn't know what shape it was in. He said that Sandie's Jeep should be able to make it. He got on the radio and told the dispatcher that the complex was clear. He had to take another call, so he raced out of the complex and on down the road.

At about 0930 Dave, Anne, Sandie, Mike and the young Lieutenant Devin, hopped into the Jeep to attempt to make their way back to the Reserve Center. Mary and the lieutenant's wife were taken care of by a neighbor that lived on the second floor where it was relatively dry and intact. Devin kissed his wife goodbye. She teared up a little; she knew that he had no choice but to go.

Sandie wove in and around the trees and downed power lines.

She ran through yards and over debris as they raced down 137th. Her biggest worry was getting a flat tire running over all the debris. There were millions of shingles on the road. Luckily the roofing nails were not long enough to puncture the thick tires. However, they did stick to the tires like fly paper and beat the fender wells to death.

They reached the Reserve Center in about fifteen minutes. Zanowick told them that the base personnel had loaded up the convoy and headed back to the base. The Reserve Center had most of its roof missing. Gravel had blown out most of the vehicle windows in the parking lot. But miraculously, no one was hurt as everyone had ridden Andrew out in the smaller side rooms and offices.

Zanowick told them that the convoy followed the same route back. They had taken the huge D-9 dozer off the low-boy rig and were using it to plow a path back to the base. They had left around 0745 and thus had a two hour head start.

Anne found Rapp and Timken in the back parking lot removing sheet metal debris from around what was left of the Winnebago. Rapp said, "She was too big and bulky to get around down here in all this debris anyway. Do you think Colonel Zanowick can spare one of his vehicles to get us back up to the Cape?"

Anne shook her head, "I don't even want to ask. These people are going to need every resource they can get their hands on down here. Colonel Zanowick and his troops are about to become the Calvary and need every horse they can get their hands on."

Zanowick overheard the conversation and out of chivalry he did the next best thing. He gave Anne the keys to his own pickup truck and pointed to it. Luckily, it was in fairly decent shape up against the building. "I've got no family down here to worry about right now. They evacuated up north to Orlando. Take my truck and haul your equipment and yourselves up to the Cape. I'm going to be very busy down here and won't need it. I've got my own Humvee. This is my wife's phone number. When you get to a working phone, call her and let her know I'm all right. She'll come over to the Cape and get my truck later. Now hurry and get out of here before the roads get clogged with pain-in-the-ass sightseers and emergency vehicles."

Anne gave him a hug and wished him Godspeed. Rapp and Timken wasted no time loading the equipment. Anne gave Dave an even bigger hug and kissed him goodbye. "We're going up to the Delta G Office at the Cape. They've got deep pockets and connections. We're going to send you help ASAP. Here's where you can get hold of me." as she handed him a note. On it, she had written, "I love you, too."

Dave was dumbfounded. He watched her peel out of the parking lot with a lump in his throat.

Sandie brought him back to his senses, "Hop in Dave, we're heading to the base." Dave held on to the roll bar as Sandie gunned her Cherokee down 137th. Dave could see the dozer tracks in the pavement as it made the corner at Quail Roost. He could also see where it was used to clear the road of debris in several places. People were out checking on each other and clearing the roads. The damage was unbelievable. It looked like someone had dropped a nuke on this place. Thousands of homes were missing their roofs or worse, flattened all together. There was not a tree standing, as far as the eye could see. When they drove past the Kendall-Tamiami Airport hangers, they were flattened and planes strewn all over the place. A half mile on down the road the subdivision of Country Walk was flattened. There were several fire trucks and EMS vehicles sifting through the rubble. A Coast Guard chopper was landing across the road.

The jeep made its way down to I-95. There were no cops stopping them. There were no check points. It was every man for himself. It was Dodge City. Sandie avoided some downed Interstate road signs and accelerated on down the Interstate. Surprisingly, there was not much traffic up there. As she crested an overpass near the Cutler Ridge Mall, the view to the south took their breaths away. They could see the five or six miles to the base from up there. It was a barren treeless landscape. What scared the hell out of them the most was that they could see straight through the large maintenance hangar on the flightline. It was missing most of its siding. As she exited the freeway and headed for the west gate, Sandie accelerated to over seventy mph.

You couldn't recognize the neighborhoods you were in. All the landmarks, traffic signals, and street signs were gone. And unfortunately, houses and buildings were gone, too. The mobile home park just outside the west gate was a twisted mound of sheet metal and smashed two by fours. If anyone had ridden it out there, they were surely dead.

They came upon two Security Police at the main gate. The gate was lying on its side. The SPs said. "Boy, are we glad to see all of you." They radioed the Command Post and let them know they were on base. "Ma'am, the CP is operating out of the back of the Commissary warehouse. That's the only thing big enough standing that has a reserve generator and running air conditioner for those of us left down here. They are expecting all of you. Also, would you please send someone out here with some ice?"

Sandie said, "Will do," as she drove onto the base. It smelled heavily of JP-4. They could see a huge dent and crease in one of the JP-4 jet fuel storage tanks. A fire truck and crew were over there working the problem. As she drove closer, she could see someone driving a wooden board into a pipe of gushing jet fuel to plug the leak, as one of the crash trucks was foaming the lake of fuel inside the containment dike. Dave shook his head in amazement, "One spark, and half the base would go up in a chain reaction inferno. Somebody's got some balls out there."

She pulled into the Commissary parking lot. The four of them got out of the Jeep as the BCE came up to them with a huge smile and a handshake. "Boy, are we glad to see you four all in one piece. Are your families okay?"

Dave replied, "Yes, sir. We had a close call with the roof being ripped off the tops of our heads. And Sandie's guardian angel earned triple time when her spare bedroom blew up in her face. We're okay though. How's the team? What can we do to help?"

Enhoff told his war story, too, "The wing commander, base commander and I had a close call, too. The alert hangar that we were in nearly flew apart. The damn roof picked up enough to pull the hangar doors off the trolley rails. That brand new, fifteen million dollar, four bay, alert hangar turned into a giant foosball machine. The doors smashed into the two F-16 hangar queens we couldn't fly out. After bouncing around in the bays and sloshing JP-4 all over the place, Andrew eventually spit them out onto the ramp. As the roof started to go, we had no place to run or hide. It was either get sucked up through the roof, drown in the tidal surge, or get burned up. So we compromised, and lashed ourselves to the middle landing of a stairwell. We were all scared shitless.

"We've got damage control teams out surveying the base now. The number one priority is plugging the leak in the JP-4 storage tank as you saw coming in. We've also got ordinance that needs to be secured. We also have four Security Police teams out securing any classified safes." Enhoff stated, "Power production is checking out the electrical grid and the status of standby generators. The Water and Waste Maintenance Shop is out trying to get the sanitary lift station pumps working. We are going to have to divert waste into the drainage canal for now or we're going to have shit everywhere the next time it rains. We have crews out clearing the roads. We're working on access to the flight line and main gate since this will be the life line down here with airlift coming in.

"We have a crew over at the Conference Center. It is relatively intact. We are going to use that as the Command Post as soon as we can get standby power up and communications. All the com towers are down." Enhoff declared, "We have just line of sight communications with our handheld bricks. Believe it or not, we have not had any contact with HQ Air Combat Command (ACC) at Langley or anywhere else. The combat commander (CC) is trying to raise someone on the Guard frequency 121.5 on a portable aircraft radio."

Just then one of the Security Police ran over to Enhoff. "Sir, the wing commander has got in touch with a Navy plane. They should be overhead in a minute or two. He wants you and your deputy at the conference center ASAP."

Enhoff said, "Dave, that would be you and me. Come on."

Dave and Enhoff entered the conference center. It was a brand new facility and was semi-hardened. It was a CORONA south location, where every year, every three and four star in the Air Force would come down to meet and play golf. It had top of the line communications capability, if there were power and operating antennas. The power generator was running, but they hadn't yet switched on the power to the facility. The roof was damaged and they needed to make sure there were no exposed wires that could start a fire.

The wing commander was outside the entrance way looking up and talking into his brick, "Roger, Navy. This is Colonel Best, the Base Wing Commander. We're in a world of hurt down here. We have 155 personnel down here on base. No casualties. We need for you to relay messages to our HQ at Langley. Do you copy?"

Just then, a Navy P-3 Orion aircraft came screaming in low over the base and started a thousand foot orbit around what was left of the base control tower.

Back on the radio the P-3 acknowledged. "Roger, sir. We have enough fuel to orbit for several hours. We'll relay your communications through Key West NAS to Langley and start working on an electronic patch to link you up. We have choppers on the way up from Key West with some com people on board that can help you out. Standby to copy a voice communication from the Air Combat Command CC."

Colonel Best acknowledged the P-3. A few minutes later the Orion crew called back, "This is a relay communications from ACC CC. We understand your situation. Video is being uplinked via Navy. We need for you to clear the runway of debris and do a FOD walk on the ramp. Will have Emergency Response Team and on-site by 0800 in the morning. Hang tight. Godspeed. Help is on the way. ACC CC out."

Best was a 5,000 hour fighter pilot with 125 combat missions in Nam. What he heard really pissed him off. "Damn it to hell, I don't mind the wait. I can understand that. They've got to get their shit together. What pisses me off is that we have to do a Foreign Object Damage (FOD) walk on the runway and ramp. Aren't those C-130 pilots combat rated? Can't those bastards earn their flight pay for just one lousy landing? Okay, Major, Captain, you heard the man, get some guys out on the runway and do a FOD sweep. Concentrate on the big stuff. Tell them not to sweat the small shit, roofing nails, pebbles, and crap like that. That C-130 can land on a dirt strip and its engines are mounted high. This is now a combat operation. Get it done by noon. Also, I want a handwritten status report every two hours on what is going on. Post it on the board. I want a situation board set up in the lobby. We need to start prioritizing things. You've also got my permission to raid the freezers at the Commissary to feed the troops here. Better get some cigarettes to the smokers or there will be a mutiny. The Commissary and Class Six Store are off limits to everyone but the NCOs and my officers. Just keep a list of what you take. That meat is going to go bad, so feed them well. No telling how long we'll be without power or a good meal before we have to resort to MREs. My guess is that it will be weeks if not months before we get power restored."

Enhoff gave Colonel Best a run down on what they were doing. A big problem was that there were no ignition keys in any of the vehicles, such as forklifts, and front end loaders. They were in a key box blown somewhere into the Everglades. There was a crash course going on at the base motor pool on how to hot wire vehicles.

"Dave, I need you to get the water buffalos out. We need to set up some showers and shit houses. We're going to have to live out of the warehouse until we can figure out quarters.

"Tom, we need perimeter security on the gates. This base is closed to the public and even nonessential military personnel and our own dependents. Relay a message to the P-3 to have all military stay put in their safe havens until we can secure and safe this base."

Best was a first rate commander. He knew how to take charge of a situation. Dave and Enhoff were inspired, saluted and marched off smartly.

CHAPTER 31
Oolite Balloons

The huge Army Chinook twin-rotored helicopter had taken off from Patrick Air Force Base Florida near the Cape in the early morning before sunrise on Thursday, August 27. On board were, Rapp, Timken, Anne and a half dozen Delta G Extraction Team members. The day before, there had been a huge argument and consternation at the HQ Delta G Office in the basement of the Pentagon. The argument for shell extraction at the Coral Castle was won. Anne remembered what Dave had once told her. The reason the Pentagon was shaped the way it was, was to deflect the blows so it wouldn't hurt as much when you got bounced around in there. He was right.

Anne, Rapp, and Timken had proven that there was a shell on the property, but where? It had to be underground somewhere. The logic being simple, since it was a public tourist attraction and no one had ever run across it. Besides, the shell was too big to disguise as a coffee table. The speculation was that Ed Leedskalnin had acquired a small shell somehow. He was a very clever man and had placed it below grade near his main quarters were he then built a coral rock spiral staircase above it. One of the arguments for extracting this particular shell was because it might actually be the key to the Greys' inertial damping and antigravity technology. It was suspected that the oolitic spiral staircase that Ed built had somehow concentrated and inverted torsional waves when coupled with electromagnetic fields.

The Delta G Team did determine how he carved and moved the big blocks of coral. He first laid out a grid pattern with copper cable over the coral bedrock. He then saturated the grid with

hydrochloric acid. The copper wire was energized as the hydrochloric acid dissolved the rock. The resulting magnetic field
accelerated the acid cutting process. He let the cable in essence
become a huge electro-spark discharge machine (EDM) eroding
the rock as it sliced them into cubes. He could do both horizontal
and vertical cuts. He then used the coral spiral stairway to aim
a torsional beam at the blocks. The billions of fossilized oolitic
spheres and marine spirals embedded in the blocks would vibrate
at their natural frequency; essentially changing its density to that
of helium-3. He then simply pulled the blocks around like a party
balloon. Little did Ed know that sixty years later, after an exhaustive search off the coast of Florida the reason why the shell could
not be detected was that the staircase deflected MASER Energy.
Ed had discovered shell stealth technology.

The Chinook landed about two miles to the south of the Coral
Castle in Homestead at the City Park. They didn't come empty
handed. They brought a load of ice, cots, tents, and MREs for a
tent city that was being set up by the Florida National Guard to
house the thousands of now homeless hurricane victims.

After they landed, they had two vehicles waiting for them.
They loaded up gear and then headed up Highway A1A to the
Coral Castle. It was very early in the morning and still under
official curfew. They parked around the back side of the Castle.
The extraction crew climbed the wall and rigged a rope ladder for
Anne, Timken, and Rapp to climb across.

There was no sign of the Coral Castle owners or employees on
the premises. Had they encountered anyone, they had permission
to approach the situation in two ways. Try bluffing them at first.
If that didn't work, they should bring them into the Delta G fold.

Their cover story, should they be challenged, was that they
were there to assess the damage for the governor of one of south
Florida's prime tourist attractions. Tourism was big business in
south Florida. Homestead would need to secure tourism dollars in
order to rebuild. It was a weak excuse. But down here the people
would buy it since the government response so far was lacking and
chaotic. Worry about the tourist industry and not the people; that
had a government bureaucratic ring of truth to it.

The extraction crew walked over to the spiral staircase that Ed had carved out of the coral rock and descended to what was known as Ed's underground refrigerator. It never made sense to anyone why Ed would take so much time and effort to carve a spiral staircase below grade. Especially when everyone knows you don't build a basement in south Florida. It had to have a more practical purpose than just a place to store milk and cheese. Sure enough, there were a few inches of standing water at the bottom of the stairs.

The extraction crew sized up their situation. The refrigerator was about ten feet square. They were looking for any indication that a shell might be buried below the stairs somehow. They anticipated the water, and had brought a couple portable sump pumps and generator with them and began pumping water out of the pit. As they did, they noticed water seeping up around the edges of the pit. This was a clear indication that the pit had a false floor. It was going to be difficult to keep up with the water flow.

It was going to be a problem lifting the spiral staircase that weighed several tons and then the false coral rock floor underneath without knowing how thick it was. They would need to call in the *Nautilus*. Bringing in a heavy crane to pick up a bunch of coral rocks could not be explained to the suffering public when other priorities existed. They would have to wait until after dark to lower the extraction cables and hardware down from the *Nautilus* to make the pick.

In the meantime, they did bring a six inch core drill for boring a hole through the false floor. They set it up and began drilling. The plan was to lower a camera through the hole to see what they were dealing with. Anne was worried that the noise of the generator and drill could be heard over the wall by the residents of the apartment complex only a hundred yards away. There appeared to be no one in them. But there was no electricity anywhere in south Dade County so there was no telling if anyone was camped out in them. Luckily, it only took a half hour to drill through the coral floor slab. It was only about two feet thick. At about 125 pounds per cubic foot, the coral slab would weigh about 25,000 pounds.

With all the billions of dollars' worth of equipment at their disposal, you still couldn't beat the simplicity of tying a string to a rock and lowering it through the hole to see how deep it was. One of the team members counted out twelve feet of string.

Two more holes were drilled in a triangular pattern. They would be used to place hoses to pump out the water. They calculated that the lower hidden chamber held about a thousand cubic feet of water, or about 1,300 gallons. Both pumps could clear the chamber in about twenty minutes, not counting the makeup rate from continuous seepage.

The team had noticed that the walls to the subterranean chamber tapered backwards slightly. This would make pulling the slab up much easier as the pit got a few inches wider towards the top. What was strange was that there were no lifting lugs or marks on the floor that gave any indication of how Ed had gotten the slab down here in the first place. He was a master Mason. The joints between the walls and floor were no more than a fraction of an inch.

As the water was pumped out, the camera was slowly lowered

into the first hole. It had a small light attached. As the camera was twisted around there was nothing to see for the first foot or two. Slowly, towards the middle of the chamber, a smooth curved surface could be seen protruding above the water. It got wider as the water was pumped out.

Anne said, "Hallelujah! It's here. I knew it." As everyone huddled around the closed circuit monitor, Rapp sketched on a notepad. He was trying to decipher what they were seeing. He drew a ten foot by ten foot cube with a spiral in the center. What he drew didn't quite match up with what they were seeing. As the water kept lowering, the drawing made more sense. The shell was sitting diagonally across the cube. The outer edge was tilted back about forty- five degrees.

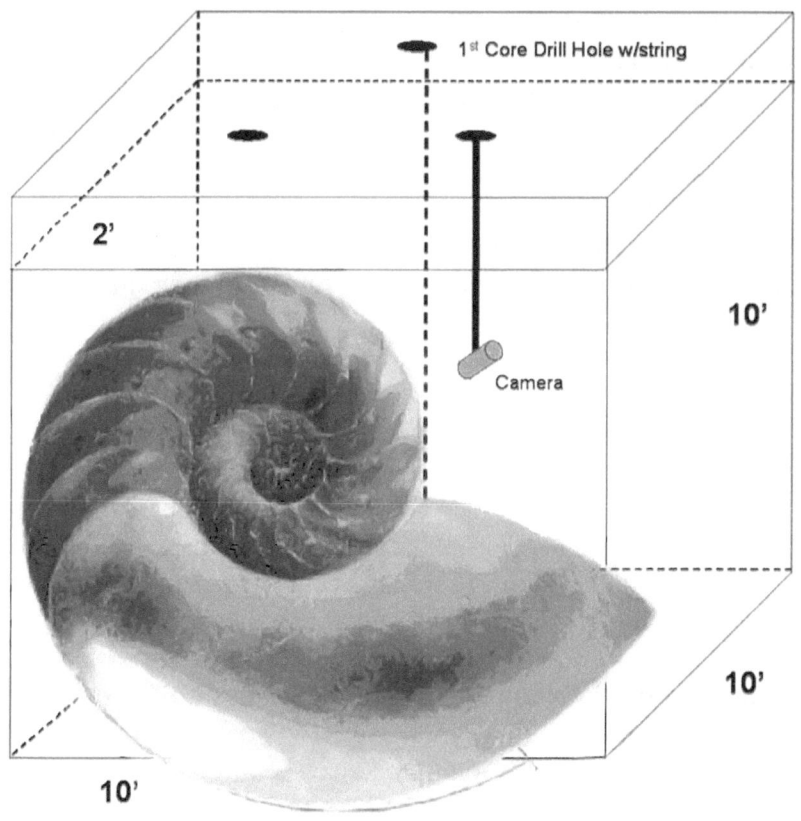

It took less time to drain the chamber than expected. They had not taken into account the volume that the shell was taking up. The pumps had no problem keeping up with the seepage. As the camera was moved from hole to hole, a better picture of what they were dealing with emerged.

Timken was the first to figure it out, "Damn, this shell is embedded in the coral rock floor by about three feet. I thought Ed had brought this thing with him. But it now looks like he found it here." Rapp replied, "That makes sense. He initially started out a few miles south of here in Florida City. For some unexplained reason. He picked up everything, including several flatbed trucks of coral, and moved up here to Homestead. It took him a couple of years to figure out where to look. But why would he only excavate three fourths of the shell? Also, he had a gold mine on his hands. Why not expose it to the entire world? He took this secret to the grave with him."

Ed died from malnutrition from stomach cancer in 1951, at the age of 64, without ever revealing his secret. The only apparent clue he left was a plaque found over his bed which read, "THE SECRET TO THE UNIVERSE IS 7129/6105195." The Delta G supercomputers still couldn't decipher what this meant.

Just then Rapp jumped up, "Hot damn! How far did the plot say the second shell was up north."

Rapp checked the printout again. "It reads 6,105.2 kilometers north of here, on Ellesmere Island, just west of Thule. Is that what Ed meant? Those numbers are actually an X, Y plot in meters distance east and then north from this location. I'm sure of it."

Anne said, "This only deepens the mystery behind this strange man. Come on, gents, the sun is coming up. Curfew will be over in ninety minutes. We need to gather our gear and get ready to bug out. We've got to figure out how to get that thing out of here. Jackhammers are too noisy. Plus, they would damage the shell. We need to run over to the base and figure this out." Anne was really deep down, looking for an excuse to go over and pop in on Dave. She hadn't heard from him since she left on Monday. She knew that he'd be busy and that there were no phones working down here anyway.

It only took a few minutes to clean things up and pack things away. After the last of the extraction crew climbed back over the wall, a group of kids had gathered around them. Anne asked were their parents were. They replied, "Up in the apartment complex next door." Just then, one of the kids' mothers walked briskly their way. "Josh, get back here. Leave those people alone." As the mother approached, she looked worn and ragged. She noticed the US Government license plates on the white pickup trucks. "What are you doing here? What are you looking for in there?"

Anne tried to explain using their cover story. She wasn't buying it. She tried a different tactic. "Ma'am, we're here looking for a crewman that fell out of that big helicopter that landed in the park early this morning. We think he hit somewhere in this compound. Would you please make sure your children stay out of the area? We'd hate for one of them to run across such a terrible sight. We're going to keep a crew here looking for him."

To the woman, this made more sense, "Good grief! We've got enough problems down here without our own government dropping bodies on us."

Just then a couple of men approached. "What's going on, Helen?"

The woman turned to her husband and said, "They are looking for some crewman that fell out of a chopper. They think he landed around here somewhere."

One man started asking a million questions and offered to have him and his buddies help them look. Anne thanked him, but politely told him they would not need their help. As a matter of fact, she was going to run out to the base and get more help. In the meantime, she offered the family an ice chest full of cold water. She told them to walk south a mile or two down to the tent city at Tom Harris Park where they could get hot food, a shower, and plenty of water. That appeased them as they thanked her. They went back upstairs to the apartment complex to tell their neighbors about the tent city being set up.

Anne felt bad for these people. She had also felt bad lying to them. But she also felt good about getting them down to the tent city where they could get some help. Without power or air conditioning it was going to be pushing ninety degrees today and would be miserable.

Anne and Rapp took off for the base. The rest of the crew stayed behind to keep an eye on things. They had handheld radios, but were not sure if they had enough range to reach the base five miles to the east.

On the way into the base, Rapp was deep in thought when all of sudden he keyed his radio, "Romeo, Romeo calling Tango, Tango, Copy."

Timken responded, "Tango here. Go"

"The answer to our problem is Charlie Alpha Charlie Oscar three, plus Hotel Charlie Lima, plus Hotel two Oscar. We'll work out the logistics. Over."

Timken knew exactly what Rapp was talking about and replied immediately. "Copy that and understand".

Anne turned to Rapp and asked, "What was that all about?"

Timken smiled and told her. "Actually Anne, it is pretty simple. The coral rock is nothing but calcium carbonate and can be dissolved with a strong acid. The shell's nickel, cobalt, and carbon composition is impervious to the acid. We can free the shell from the rock with a hydrochloric acid slurry. I'm sure of it." Thus the code name for the shell became Excalibur.

Anne stopped at the main gate. The SPs checked her orders and let her pass. Rapp and Anne couldn't believe their eyes. The devastation was total. There was not a building on base that hadn't been damaged or destroyed by the full force of Andrew. Even though it had been three days since the hurricane hit, it might just as well have been an hour afterwards. It had been three very hot days. Spoiled food from refrigerators and freezers blown out of base housing mixed with the acrid fumes from the spilled JP-4 fuel tank.

Several columns of black smoke rose on the horizon behind them as people were burning brush as they cleared streets and yards. Anne pulled up in front of the makeshift Command Post. Dave was outside talking to someone when Anne hopped out of the pickup. She never so badly wanted to hug someone in all of her life. Dave felt the same. But rules were rules, no PDA. The military had an acronym for anything and everything. PDA was Public Display of Affection when in uniform. Dave shook hands with the officer he was talking to and then rushed over to greet Anne. "What the devil are you two doing back down here? I thought you were up at Patrick." Anne threw the rulebook out the window and gave Dave a big hug and peck on the cheek. She was discrete, no one had noticed.

"Dave, we found the shell buried under a false floor at the Coral Castle. We need help extracting it."

Dave gave Rapp a disbelieving stare, "Anne, you've got to be kidding me. That's hardly on anyone's priority list down here right now. We are in combat survival mode."

Rapp was a little more forceful, "Damn it, Captain. We understand that and appreciate that. But nature may have dealt us a fortuitous opportunity. This particular shell may hold the secret to antigravity and torsional wave vectoring. This could be quite literally the path to the stars. Speaking of stars, I assure you, right now, in the basement of the Pentagon and under Cheyenne Mountain, there are quite a few stars working diligently trying to figure out how to pull off this extraction."

From what Dave knew about Delta G, he knew Rapp was correct. "Okay, I understand. How can I help?" Anne gave Dave a list of equipment that they would need: mostly hand tools, a few power tools, and some tarps. They also needed an excuse to keep people out of the Coral Castle, even the rightful owners and their employees. The chopper crew member story wasn't going to cut it. Besides, that kind of lie is self-perpetuating, inviting the press and other morbid curiosity seekers.

It was Dave that came up with an ingenious solution. It was from a problem that they were dealing with on the base now. "Dr. Rapp, I have the solution to keeping the nosy out. I'm having signs made up now, marking the locations of transformers that have blown down that contain carcinogenic PCBs in their cooling oil. I can load a non PCB transformer in your pickup. Just toss it down on the parking lot out there, tape off the area and then mark it with the danger signs that PCBs have been sprayed by the winds all over the Coral Castle. Then pose as a HazMat crew in there cleaning up the mess."

Rapp replied, "Simple, but ingenious. That will work. That will also explain the tanker truck we need to bring in with a few thousand gallons of concentrated hydrochloric acid."

Dave gave a half-assed laugh, "Well, as long as it doesn't cause cancer, feel free to have them haul it on down. What are you going to do with all that HCl?"

Rapp said. "We need it to dissolve the coral around the shell."

Unphased, Dave brought up a couple of points, "That's going to call for some heavy duty protective clothing. How about a few chemical warfare protective suits? We've got some experimental ones I've tried out, that should hold up to HCl. You're also going to need some soda ash or lime to neutralize the acid when you're done. We have plenty on base to contain HazMat spills. If you get the acid, I'll arrange for the rest."

Logistically, the Coral Castle extraction operation was easy to support from the base. It was straight out the west gate along Biscayne Boulevard, a little over four miles. Government vehicles running out there would not be given a second thought.

Anne asked if the base commander and wing commander should be apprised. Dave thought for a minute. "Not at this time. They've got enough on their hands. Besides your orders say enlist required support and resources from the base on a N2K basis, right?"

Anne said, "Dave with any luck, we'll have this thing ready to yank by this evening. We are going to bring in the *Nautilus* for the extraction at 0200. It is stationed out over the Everglades now and can be on station in a few minutes. We'll need to make sure there is no night flight activity in the vicinity during the extraction."

Dave said, "That shouldn't be a problem. There will be no nighttime arrivals until we establish a mobile ATC and get some airfield lighting operational. I don't know about transient air traffic though. The Aerostat at Cudjoe Key can help warn and keep traffic away from midtown Homestead. Give me a couple of hours to round things up. I'll bring the transformer and suits out myself. In the meantime can you do me a favor? I haven't had a chance to go check on my place. Could you run by? I've got a cat at home, too, if the place is still standing. Also, I haven't had a chance to call my folks to let them know I'm okay. Can you pass along that message for me? Do you remember how to get to my place, Anne?"

Anne replied, "Yes, I can find your bachelor pad. When did you get a cat?"

"Her name is K.C. Short for Kitty Cat. Lieutenant Brotskey talked me into taking care of one from a litter of kittens that we had found under a pallet of hazardous waste drums. They were about to become alligator food." Dave said, "As soon as things get back to normal, if and when that ever happens, I'll invite you up to my bachelor pad to show you my etchings."

Anne winked and said, "I'd like that. You have a date." He handed her the key to his place. She gave Dave a hug and another kiss and hopped in the truck with Rapp to head over to Dave's apartment. People were very resourceful when it came to clearing the roads. Anything and everything was used to plow and drag things out of the way. Three days after landfall, most of the main roadways had been cleared of debris. However, there were no traffic lights, but surprisingly the four way stop system worked fairly well. Blue tarps were starting to go up on roofs. Pickup trucks and rental vans were everywhere as people tried to pick things out of the rubble and salvage what was left.

Andrew had done nearly thirty billion dollars in damage in south Dade County. Over 120,000 homes were severely damaged and destroyed. To give it some sense of scale, a weatherman mentioned that three shopping malls and twenty-two McDonald's restaurants were destroyed.

At the gate to the apartment complex, Anne explained that she was there to check on a friend's place. She signed in and then one of the residents escorted her to Dave's place. They were taking no chances with looters down here. Everyone was locked and loaded.

At first glance, Dave's place didn't look too bad. However, when Anne opened the door, the appearance was deceiving. About a quarter of the roof was gone. What wasn't blown out the bedroom roof was drenched because of the rain soaking through the sheet rock ceiling. A lot of the ceiling had fallen in on the furniture. Again, insulation was everywhere. A couple of windows were shattered and the waterbed was leaking as glass shards had punctured it. There was no sign of the cat. Dave's bedroom closet contents were sucked up into the rafters. Anne figured the cat had climbed out of the broken window. But Rapp had heard a faint meow. He looked under the waterbed. All he could see up against the wall were fangs, claws and eyeballs. The cat hissed and arched its back. It wasn't coming out, and neither had the guts to go in after it. The water bed was too heavy to move. Anne found some dry cat food and threw it under the bed. She then lifted the lid on the toilet. She figured between the wet floor and toilet the cat wouldn't die of thirst. They did what they could.

Just then a neighbor came in and introduced himself. He was setting up a portable generator. He said he'd look after the cat and the place for Dave. Anne had to trust him and gave him the key. Dave had several firearms in the house and his neighbor took them next door for safekeeping. They draped some plastic over his entertainment center to keep the rainwater off. Mold was already starting to grow on the walls. The neighbor warned them not to open any refrigerator doors they run across. They couldn't handle the stench. Also, there was no running water anywhere. He gave Anne a word of advice. Any toilet they ran across, if it wasn't already used, had one good flush left in it. It had been hours, both Anne and Rapp took his advice. Sorry, K.C., but nature called.

Anne and Rapp hopped back in the pickup and headed back up A1A to the Coral Castle. The crew was still there. Timken was in the truck with the A/C running. The extraction crew where mostly ex Special Forces types and didn't mind the ninety degree heat and ninety percent humidity of south Florida. It was now around 11:00 AM. People were out and about putting plastic on their windows. One of the first response teams that Anne had seen had Charleston, South Carolina painted on the sides of their trucks. These people had gone through Hurricane Hugo a few years ago and knew what the people needed first, rolls of plastic and tarps. As Anne witnessed in Dave's apartment, what Hurricane Andrew didn't get, the tropical rains and humidity down here would eventually destroy.

Dave showed up around noon as promised. Anne told him about his place. He was relieved that he at least had something to go home to and appreciated his friend and neighbor looking after it. She still hadn't gotten a chance to phone his folks yet.

Dave pulled the blue tarp off the transformer he had placed in the back of the pickup. It was heavy but he had drained the non-PCB oil back at the base to make it light enough for a couple of troops to manhandle it on the truck, "You'll have to find your own oil to trash around the scene." He was sure the extraction crew could muster that. He knew they were very resourceful. As a matter of fact, there were transformers down all over the place; they could have rustled up a few of those, too. And perhaps they all really did have PCBs in them. Dave and one of the team members kicked the transformer off the back of the truck. It made a sickening thud as it hit the ground next to the coral block wall. Dave handed them some barricade tape and the danger signs he had made up. It now looked like a first class HazMat spill scene. One of the team had found an abandoned tractor trailer rig. He punched a hole in its diesel tank and drained it into some containers. He then poured it out around the transformer and splashed it on the wall to give it a more menacing look. Hopefully it would keep the curious away.

Now all they had to wait for was the HazMat truck from Kennedy with the acid. Timken had called in the order on one of their portable crypto sets. They had plenty of hydrochloric acid at the Cape. They wouldn't miss a few thousand gallons. They had plenty of other nasty chemicals up there, too, that they offered up. Dave handed the sergeant six canvas bags. They contained the latest aircrew chemical warfare suits including air breathing tanks. They would be a lot more flexible and versatile than the moon suits that NASA was planning on sending down. Now all that they needed to do was to wait until dark. The team was busy figuring out how to move the spiral staircase out of the way. Its center of gravity (CG) wasn't very easy to figure. They estimated it weighed about 12,000 pounds, an easy lift with the *Nautilus* cablevator.

By about four that afternoon, Timken received word that the

acid truck was caught in traffic about five miles north on A1A near the Cutler Ridge Mall. Dave grumbled, "Whoever told that driver to take that route should be stood up against the wall and shot. It is in serious danger of running out of fuel. Tell him to pull into the mall parking lot. I'll run up there with some diesel and escort him back down here."

Dave had one of the team drain the second diesel tank from the tractor trailer rig and put it in the barrel he had brought with him. He flipped on his emergency lights as he pulled out of the parking lot onto A1A. He didn't have to hit the siren. Most people moved out of his way. He managed to make fairly decent time and pulled into the mall parking lot. The NASA truck was drawing a crowd of curious onlookers. Most people figured it was a truckload of water and were looking to fill jugs. When they found out it was a HazMat truck, they lost interest quickly and moved on down the lot were the National Guard was passing out bags of ice.

The truck was huge, bigger than Dave had imagined. It looked like something NASA would put together. It had several huge tanks along with a system of pumps and vacuum chambers. Dave walked up to the cab, "Good afternoon, I'm here to escort you down the road about five miles. Can you make it on fuel if we don't have to stop? I've got a barrel of diesel. But I don't want to screw around with it if we don't have to."

The driver replied, "Yes, sir, I've got less than a quarter tank. We'll make it if I don't get bogged down in the traffic again. It took me nearly an hour and a half to go the last five miles."

Just then Dave saw a Metro Dade cruiser in the lot. He was watching over the crowd getting ice. Dave approached him, "Officer, we've got a Hazardous Material Spill down by the Coral Castle along A1A. We might need to block the highway. Can you help and provide me an escort on the way down there for this spill recovery truck?" The officer didn't have to think twice, given the choice of standing out in the hot heat and babysitting a bunch of people in line, or hopping in an air conditioned cruiser with sirens blazing and actually being able to do something worthwhile and productive. He got clearance from his supervisor and pulled out onto A1A to blaze the trail. Dave followed behind in the Base

Crash 1 vehicle with lights and sirens on. It worked, most people pulled to the side. When they were about fifteen minutes out, Dave gave Anne a heads up that they had a police escort.

The extraction crew went into show business mode and put on the chemical gear and put the barricade signs and gates up. Also, as luck would have it, there was a huge transformer bank on some primary power lines that ran along A1A here. It was decided to make those the culprit. The small transformer Dave brought out didn't have the visual impact that these huge overhead transformers did. The cover story was getting bigger and bolder now that the Metro Dade Police had been informed. On the positive side, this would give them even more legitimacy now that the Coral Castle was going to be contaminated with cancer-causing PCBs. Any cops cruising up and down A1A that evening would be aware of the situation and not stop to poke around. They told the police that the coral was very porous and could make the Castle unsuitable for public tours for years. By golly, it had to be saved, right? One of the team members climbed the tandem power pole to the transformer platform and started draining the coolant down the pole and into a drainage ditch along the road.

The mini-convoy arrived. The officer took one look at the crew donned in the chem gear and now regretted the trip. "Shit, this is very serious. What did I get myself into?" Dave made an excuse for the officer saying he better get back up to the mall parking lot. He had overheard on the radio that there was trouble back up there. In fact, there was. Fights were always breaking out in ice lines.

They were now set. They had the crew, the gear, and the truck. And luckily, so far, no Coral Castle personnel. It was 1700 now and the curfew would kick in at 1900 so it looked as if no one would show today.

Dave decided to stick around. Since he was the Delta G Integrations Officer, it was his primary task. He did mention to Colonel Butts before he left that he needed to deliver some equipment to the Coral Castle for an official government activity taking place there. Butts read the situation and told him good luck. The less he knew the better. He hated the debriefs that accompanied a Delta

G Team visit.

Dave had just been trained in the use of the new chem gear during the last base exercise. He gave the team some pointers and had them put talc powder on their wrists, shins, and other areas that rubbed up against the neoprene rubber material. He suggested it would be better to do the acid application in shifts of two. The oxygen tanks would last an hour but could be replenished easily from any fire department tanks. He would work the first shift with another team member. The plan was to flood the chamber with about six inches of HCl. The acid was the high strength 37 percent concentration, the strongest commercially available. It should dissolve the coral in no time. However, a deadly problem was that the fumes would fill the bottom of the pit. Visibility would also be an issue. It would be getting dark soon. The crew had brought lights, but they were not explosion proof. They would also need explosion proof fans from the base fire department. Luckily, Dave was the acting deputy fire chief now that he was running around in the Crash 1 vehicle. He got on the crash net and had the equipment run out to them. No questions asked.

With Dave suited up, the acid hose was snaked into one of the core drill holes. This part was a one man job. All he had to do was open the valve at the end of the hose and let it drain into the pit. His mask visor was fogging up in the humidity. Unfortunately, he couldn't take it off now to spit in it the way they taught him in SCUBA training.

It only took about fifteen minutes to put the HCl in the pit. Rapp figured that there were now a few hundred gallons of HCl eating away at the calcium carbonate. It reminded Dave of the baking soda and vinegar rockets or volcanoes he made as a kid. Only this stuff was 1,000 times nastier. He walked back to the lot and took off his mask. He was soaking in sweat. The chem suit was inhumanely hot. It is basically a rubberized wet suit with a charcoal filter layer. He took a huge swig of water and sat down. It was the next man's turn. After a couple of hours they placed the vacuum hose down the hole. They pumped the old acid out and then refilled the pit again with new. It was working. The floor was starting to dissolve. They would let this batch cook in the hole for two hours before pumping it out.

By now, it was 10:30 PM and plenty dark. It was eerily quiet with the curfew in effect. They did have a sheriff's car pull in once. But he had been briefed on the PCB cleanup operation and just dropped by to see if he could help and shoot the shit. Everyone was cordial and offered him a cold soda. He mentioned that the apartment complex was empty. It had been evacuated when they heard there were carcinogens in the ditch next door. The deputy told Dave, "It is amazing how rumors get started down here. We heard you were cleaning up the mess from someone falling out of a helicopter."

Dave laughed, "That'd be one helluva a big Bubba if we had to suck up his guts with this monster." Everyone got a good laugh at that one as the deputy climbed back in his cruiser and continued his patrol.

They decided to change out the acid one more time and let it set until the *Nautilus* showed up overhead. They were in luck. It was overcast. The *Nautilus* could hover at 5,000 feet, making things easier and quicker in using the cablevator.

They had enough HCl for three or four applications if need be. It was also decided to call in the *Nautilus* at midnight. It wasn't going to get any less quiet than now. It would also allow more time if the unexpected happened before sunrise.

The extraction team chief got on the crypto set and made the call. They would be overhead in only fifteen minutes. They had been hovering over the Everglades at 100,000 feet all day. They called this a combat approach.

The cablevator was lowered a mile below the *Nautilus*. There was a fairly brisk offshore breeze. However, the gyro-stabilized platform had no problem adjusting to the gusts with its thrusters. At the bottom of the lift, Chief Don Eldon hopped off and shook the extraction crew members' hands. He then walked over to Dave as they discussed the lift and pick of the staircase. "It is nice to see you again, Captain Sheridan. It will be good to work with you again, sir. We can lift the stairs and slab in two lifts and set them over here. We'll then set up for the shell pick. We've been studying the situation from topside. If that thing is buried in three feet of coral, it is going to take some persuasion and rocking to pull it free. We're going to need to take some pry bars and spud bars to break up the rock. Hopefully we can get the acid to leach in under the shell and start eating away from below. We've got some small diameter high strength carbon-composite fiber (CCF) cable. Wrap that cable around the bumper of the HazMat truck and see if she will budge. It should be like trying to pull a tractor out of a manure pile." Dave thought that was a little simplistic, but what the hell. The chief saved his neck once and he trusted him.

The extraction crew wasted no time in setting things up for the staircase pick. The *Nautilus* had fabricated a very elaborate cage that wrapped around the stairway. It provided bracing in every direction and automatically adjusted for CG shifts. As he stood on the cablevator lift platform and manipulated the twin joy sticks, Eldon said, "This is the easy one." The stairs lifted straight up with very little effort. The chief called up to the ship to move laterally twenty feet. He did not want to kick in the stabilizers. Even though they were quiet, they were not totally quiet. The crew disconnected the cage and proceeded over to the fully exposed slab. They dropped three expandable grappling hooks through the core holes. They sprung open underneath. They attached CCF cables to the hooks and connected them to the cablevator. This time Chief Eldon flew the cablevator platform. He applied tension to the cables as he held the lift exactly centered over the slab. This was precision flying. The slab started to rise.

However, it began to tip. The CG was not perfect and the self-leveling cable hoists kicked in. The slab leveled and came up smoothly. The chief had an inch or two to spare. Suddenly, a slight gust hit and swung the slab into a side wall. "Damn, there went the leave no trace." He couldn't just leave the owner a note and his insurance company info. The chief pulled the slab free and clear and again set it off to the side. The shell chamber was now fully exposed. A mist of HCl gas hung in the pit like a dragon's breath. The extraction crew again wasted no time. They dropped a fiberglass ladder down the hole. An aluminum ladder wouldn't have lasted twenty minutes. Two men went down the hole with the pry bars to loosen up the floor. Two other crew members dropped air ducting over the side and turned on the fans. The other two set up some lighting fixtures.

The floor of the pit was spongy now. They proceeded to break up the floor. It came apart fairly easily. The crew started wrapping the cable around the shell and looped it over a steel pipe laid at the edge of the pit wall. The CCF cable was then tied to the truck bumper. The truck driver gunned the engine as he inched forward. The cable tightened but the shell did not budge. The two men in the pit attempted to open a crack under the shell. However, they were getting exhausted and their air was running out. Chief Eldon had the smarts to tether them off before they went in. He lifted them out over the hole as Dave hit them with water from a hose from the truck to rinse them down. They were swung over and then disconnected. Anne and Rapp had water waiting for them. As they pulled off their chem gear the next crew was hoisted in. They proceeded to pound and pry some more. The floor broke up into bigger chunks. They were pulled out and the pit again flooded with the remaining HCl. The truck again tugged on the shell. This time it did move an inch or two. With every tug, more and more acid worked its way underneath it. It was just a matter of time, which they had plenty of. It was only 0230 in the morning.

Just then the chief came running over to Anne and Rapp. "We've got company." They thought he meant someone on the ground. He pointed to the air. A metro Dade chopper was working its way down A1A with its million candle power spot light lighting up the four lane thoroughfare checking for looters. He ordered the cablevator up and cleared the area. If they get curious and overfly the Castle they couldn't miss those cables.

Dave had flashbacks of the Yuma cable incident. The last thing they needed was a helicopter crashing into the CCF cables and crashing down on them in a huge fireball. It was a race now. Could the cablevator be raised above the five hundred foot altitude before the chopper swung it? It was going to be close.

Luckily the chopper was on the west side of the road. The lights were shut down on the pit and redirected to the ditch and transformer. The chopper circled the area as the cablevator cleared through its altitude. With just seconds to spare, the chopper moved in and hovered directly over the pit, as it illuminated the ditch the crew was working in. It circled the area a few more times and then flew on off to the south. It must have radioed in and found out about the HazMat cleanup operation.

The crew shook off this event and went back to work. The chief decided to hook up the CCF cables to the cablevator and give it a tug. It was now or never. The scene was getting too hot in more ways than one. The cable had a half million pound tension capacity. This was way beyond what was being hoisted. He gave the shell a good tug and it started to rock free. He gave it a second tug and a huge suction sound was heard as the shell broke free. It slowly lifted above the pit. Dave hosed off the shell the best he could. Chief Eldon made a command decision. He decided to take it on up while the *Nautilus* made a run to the north to clear the wall and dripped HCl onto the parking lot. Dave was out of water. The shell still had a pool of HCl inside as the chief raised it on up into the ship. The *Nautilus* crew laid plastic liner out on the deck as it was hoisted in and then lowered in place. The decontamination crew did their job to neutralize the acid and seal the shell.

Chief Eldon then descended again in the cablevator with a load of fly ash to dump in the pit. The crew raked the ash around as several loads were lowered into the pit. The pit was eventually filled about halfway up. Hopefully, it was totally neutralized. The slab was lifted back in place along with the staircase. The core drill holes were plugged. You would never know anything was moved other than a one foot gouge in the wall.

The *Nautilus* pulled the extraction crew up along with Anne, Rapp, and Timken. Following Ed's clues, the ship then made an immediate departure the 7,129 meters to the east to a point directly over the runway at the base and then turned north for the much longer 6,105,195 meter trek to Ellesmere Island. Major Boop and his C-130 crew were already on their way from the Cape. There had to be something up there to find and investigate. They simply followed the T-wave back to its source. If these coordinates were correct, then there was something to find within one square meter of the Earth's surface. That's about the size of a bathtub.

All that Dave could to at the moment was escort the HazMat

truck driver back on to the base where he offered him breakfast as the sun was rising. All in a day's work.

Dave's folks and brothers rented a truck and came down a week or so after the Hurricane to help him salvage what they could from his apartment. They couldn't believe the amount of damage. They camped out in the apartment overnight and then headed out the very next morning along with the cat.

Dave spent the next few months at Homestead as one of the disaster recovery team leads. He moved into a tent setup in a compound on base. He worked with the Army Corps of Engineers to safe the base and come up with a recovery plan. From time to time, Dave would drive up to north Dade or down to the Keys to use a phone to call Anne or his folks. Anne was now going to Wright-Patterson AFB near Dayton, Ohio.

He had a feeling that he was going to end up there, too. There had been a lot of activity at Wright-Pat following major discoveries the *Nautilus* had made on Ellesmere Island.

In late November, he drove down to the Naval Air Station at Key West to use the STU line and received a classified briefing on what they found up there. Massive deposits of Grey Matter were found imbedded in the bedrock fifty miles south of the DEW Line Site near Alert. Apparently, the Inuits had found some of it and sold it to Ed's mentor in the early 1920's. Ed then got a hold of some and used it with his shell to make it an antigravity device.

Homestead would eventually be rebuilt to some capacity. Turkey Point would be up and running in a couple of months. However, personnel and their families could not be left down there in that environment. Since money was no object, it was an easy thing to replace facilities, and move personnel.

A priority now was relocating the Delta G personnel. Half went to Nellis near Las Vegas. The other half went to Wright-Patterson. What little equipment that there was left at Card Sound had been crated up and sent to Ohio. Most of Dave's other friends on base ended up at HQ Air Combat Command in Virginia or Patrick AFB near Cape Kennedy.

Then just before Christmas 1992, Dave got his choice of assignments: out to Delta G at Dreamland, or up to Delta G Black at Wright-Patterson. Dave wanted to spend time with his folks and family. He also now had a chance to catch up with Anne. He didn't have to think twice about it. He packed what little he had left into the Mustang and headed up I-75 to Dayton. He wondered what was in store for him. The Delta G Program was in limbo as far as T-wave generation was concerned. He wanted back in the ball game.

Looking back on the Hurricane, Dave knew that very few Americans realized that the Turkey Point Nuclear Power Plant was the first structure hit by a CAT 5 hurricane. Andrew was only the second CAT 5 hurricane ever recorded to strike the US. Wind speeds topped 200 mph. This was one of the few times in nuclear power history that a reactor was actually scrammed due to a natural disaster. Only a handful knew that it wasn't in fact natural.

CHAPTER 32
WPAFB

It turns out that being a civil engineering officer in the United States Air Force gave Captain Sheridan access to some very interesting programs and facilities. Now that the Delta G Blue Facilities, Laboratories, and for that matter its personnel, were literally scattered by and to the winds, Wright-Patterson Air Force Base now became the safe haven to pick up the pieces and determine what went wrong to avoid it in the future. It was where work on the Grey Matter progressed.

Wright-Patterson has a rich history in aerospace research and development. It is also high on the list of UFO myth and legend from Hangar 18 to Project Blue Book.

There has long been rumored to be super-secret tunnel complexes, and for that matter, an entire underground flying saucer base under Wright-Patterson. These rumors went back as far as the Roswell incident that occurred in July 1947. Captain Sheridan knew from his time with the Delta G Program that what was found in the New Mexico high desert was in fact an alien craft. However, it did not resemble a flying saucer. As a matter of fact, what was found there were several pools of a mercury-like substance, a very dense liquid metal found northwest of the Cibola National Forest. Two shells were found in the hills between where the crew capsule was found and these pools of liquid metal, along a fifty mile path.

The craft was not shot down as rumored. It is doubtful that anything could have shot it down even if they tried. There was very little damage to the shells and the crew capsule. It simply fell from the sky and the alien occupants apparently died of massive impact trauma. They hit the Earth doing only a couple hundred miles per hour. This implied that they were falling at a terminal velocity slowed down by Earth's atmosphere in non-powered flight. The crew compartment had actually separated from the craft, but apparently too late. A thin metallic membrane had deployed as if it were a parachute (later classified as a type of Mylar). The liquid metal being more massive continued on its northwest trajectory where it impacted the ground in several pools and impact craters. An extensive recovery and cleanup ensued. Dave had to smile every time he read the "Official Description" of the incident.

> The original shell discovery, or Roswell incident, centers on an area northwest of Corona, NM near and in the Cibola National Forest. A Grey Torsional Wave Generator is still buried under a Native American mound shaped as a nautilus shell located at 34° 15' 48.58" N by 105° 58' 41.21" W.

> The Roswell ship was on a vector approach to this location when it crashed short of the intended landing zone (LZ). A line drawn from where the crew capsule and five (5) corpses that were found on the Foster Ranch (33° 56' 28.91" N by 105° 18' 29.74" W) to the LZ located at the Atkinson Flats crater (34° 15' 16.36" N by 105° 59' 21.04" W) passes over the T-wave generator. The Corona 1, 2, 3 objects were all located in an area in the northwest quadrant of the Cibola National Forest (34° 21' 10.28" N by 105° 56' 56.97"W). An exhaustive search of this area of New Mexico for additional material has had no results.

> The object is made of a highly compact diamond-like carbon material. It is several times denser than lead or depleted uranium. It is silver in color and about thirty feet in diameter. The material is an alloy called CoN-iC by scientists at WPAFB. It is a densified carbon, nickel, and cobalt formulation. Speculation is that the material comes from near the core of a massive planet or asteroid. It cannot be manufactured on Earth at the

present time. The heat and pressure necessary cannot be duplicated.

Early airborne radars encountered "strange" ground effect phenomena in this area. Two pipelines were built straddling the crew compartment recovery site by about eight miles. The pipelines converged at Kirkland AFB one hundred miles to the northwest. The pipelines were filled with distilled water and are used as a giant dowsing or divining rod to detect telluric currents, microwaves, and torsional waves emanating from the area. This was the first US attempt to detect gravitational waves.

Telluric current effects on pipelines have been observed for nearly half a century. Most telluric currents are produced by geomagnetic disturbances, although tidally-induced effects have also been reported. As well as pipelines, other systems such as power lines and phone cables are affected and these are just one class of technological system that is affected by geomagnetic disturbances.

Nowhere in the "Official Description" does it mention its spiral shape, the liquid metal pools, nor the fact that it can generate T-waves, or generate isotopes of helium.

The truth of the matter was that the craft and the corpses of alien beings were recovered and flown back to WPAFB back in 1947. They were stored in underground film storage vaults. Since film is highly explosive, containing nitrides, what better place to store the components than forty feet below grade, in a secure, cool, yet very accessible site. WPAFB was also perfect because a huge labyrinth of underground steam heating tunnels traversed virtually every facility and laboratory on base. This tunnel complex could be utilized, expanded, and above all easily secured. During World War II, an entire underground cold storage facility was constructed to freeze who knows what. The facility was built under the side of a hill and covered dozens of acres. Today, only a little used parking lot above it is all that can be found.

The hill on which Area B of Wright-Patterson Air Force Base

is built is very deceptive looking in its height. The bottom of the hill where the old Wright Field is located and now is the home of the US Air Force Museum is at an elevation of 790 feet above sea level. The top of the hill, on the eastern boundary, near the Building 620 avionics laboratory is at 980 feet above sea level. Thus, there is almost a 200 foot rise to the top of the hill or 20 stories to work within concealing underground facilities.

Another highly secure facility with a strange history is Building 470. Construction of the Nuclear Engineering Test Facility, Building 470, was started in 1956 on the side of this same hill in Area B. This was to support the nuclear powered aircraft propulsion program. Construction of the reactor continued despite cancellation of the nuclear propulsion project the next year. Somebody wanted it built for other reasons. When it was completed in 1960, the light water cooled test reactor was the Air Force's only research reactor and the seventh largest of its kind in the nation. It had a ten megawatt capacity and could accommodate a full scale jet engine. However, its internal facilities were not completed until 1965, when the Air Force Institute of Technology (AFIT) accepted operational control and safety responsibility for the reactor. The reactor's first nuclear chain reaction was achieved in April 1965. The reactor was used for a variety of projects, ranging from biomedical studies to solid-state electronics. It operated for the last time on June12, 1970 and then was decommissioned in June 1971. After the reactor material was removed, the entire reactor chamber was entombed in concrete.

However, it turns out that wasn't the only thing entombed in the complex. On a sunny summer day in 1958, a convoy of Air Force Security Police cordoned off the area around the reactor construction site. Several dozen SPs fanned out around the complex with orders to shoot to kill anyone approaching the site. Thirty minutes later, three deuce and a half ton military trucks climbed the hill from Building 18 with some strange cargo. The deuce and halves entered through the construction gate and another dozen men climbed out of the trucks. A crane then hoisted the crates from the trucks and lifted them down into the center of the one hundred foot circular foundation slab being poured. The crane lowered them into the cavity of a six foot thick rebar cage. Immediately after lowering the crates in place, a convoy of cement trucks kept coming through the base gate and proceeded slowly up the hill. Over a hundred truckloads of concrete were poured finishing well into the next morning.

What was so special about those crates? Urban legend has it that the bodies of the Roswell aliens were placed in them. Once the Air Force was done dissecting them, and experimenting with them, they simply had them buried in the foundation of this nuclear power plant. What better place could there possibly be to dispose of the bodies?

Dave's job would be to build another Beyond Top Secret (BTS) complex into the side of this same hill under Building 620. The addition to the Lair facility would be used to test torsional wave vectoring technology. Dave couldn't wait to get to Wright-Pat and get started. Torsional waves were real. They could be human made, focused, and directed; although humankind was currently having a little trouble with the directing and aiming at this time. Dave was proud to be part of the elite team solving theses secrets to the technology. As Spock would say, it was fascinating how a craft could navigate space and time with absolutely no moving parts. It was now understood that it was space and time that moved around the craft. The craft was just an island in the stream. Or simply put, a surfboard had no moving parts but could ride one hell of a wave.

CHAPTER 33
Urban Legend Under Wright-Patterson

On a cold Monday morning in January 1993, Major David Sheridan reported to the Aeronautical Systems Command (ASC) Commander at Wright-Patterson. There were only twenty-eight people on the entire base of over 20,000 cleared for the Project Delta G Program. All of them reported directly to Major General Charles Ahrens. He was ultimately responsible for security of the program, and he took it dead serious.

"Major David Sheridan reporting as ordered, sir." Dave was used to reporting to general officers by this time in his career. However, he was not too sure how to read this particular one.

"Have a seat, Dave. Welcome to Wright-Pat."

"Thank you, sir."

"Have you put all the pieces back together after Andrew? That must have been a hell of ride."

"Yes, sir, we're getting things organized."

Ahrens pulled his glasses off and held them in his clenched fist, "I'm not too thrilled with having my base overrun by a lot of Delta G types that are new to the game and the rules here. That event at Homestead has just about quadrupled my N2K footprint." Sheridan realized when you double the amount of people knowing about a program you exponentially increase security risks.

"But I guess that's all water under the bridge. Or should I say, water over the bridge in this case?" chided General Ahrens. "Don't worry. We'll put the program back together. Your cover while you are here will be as an engineering officer over at Base Civil Engineering. The BCE is cleared for Delta G clearance and will give you any resources needed and stay out of your way."

General Ahrens leaned forward, paused, and then leaned back in his chair. "By the way Major, on a personal note, my daughter is in town." He let that hang in the air for a few seconds. "She accepted a position at Wright State University. I understand you two hit it off very well in Greenland and that you took great care of her at Homestead during Hurricane Andrew. For that, I am eternally grateful. My wife, Barbara, and I would like to invite you over for dinner Friday at 1800. You are under no obligation, Major. However, should you accept, for all the tea in China, don't discuss some of the harrowing Arctic, Yuma, or Hurricane details in front of my wife. She has no idea about half the stuff Anne is up to. Don't worry. This isn't like a blind date. Anne will know that you are coming to dinner. To tell you the truth, she is very impressed with you. That means a lot to me."

Dave didn't have to think twice. He immediately replied, "General, I accept and look forward to Friday."

Ahrens smiled and then said, "Not that it matters, or even counts in the scheme of things, but I guess I'm giving you permission to date my daughter. I haven't had to have this conversation with a young man since she was a junior in high school." Ahrens leaned forward with his hands on his desk, and with a leer, made his point in a fatherly way. "Major, don't break my little girl's heart. I've got a hell of a lot more than a shotgun at my disposal and there are many worse places to send you than the North Pole. There is a nice little island out in the middle of the Indian Ocean not much bigger than the size of my desk. Get my drift? Treat her right."

The only thing Dave could say were two little words. He looked the general in the eye and said, "Yes, sir!"

The general stood up and continued, "Now that we settled that, let me take you on a little tour of our facilities. Keep an open mind, Captain. These facilities have been around for over forty years. We don't spend a lot of funds on upkeep and maintenance. We try to keep a low profile here. However, since you are going to be working over in CE now, it's going to be your job to upgrade our facilities. Think you can handle that?"

Dave was confidant, "Yes, sir, I've got plenty of experience building facilities and infrastructure for black programs. I've got contacts in firms that can keep their mouths shut. Also, it takes layer upon layer of cover stories. Nobody is going to work on or see the entire big picture."

General Ahrens responded coldly, "I'm glad you understand that, because I'm not going to show you the whole picture either."

Dave acknowledged, "Fair enough, sir."

The general punched up the intercom and called out to his receptionist, "Going to CC Call." That was a code to let her know he was going subterranean.

He had his executive officer, Darrin Schaudt, open one of the oak panels on a side wall. General Ahrens' office was a secure SCIF or Sensitive Compartmented Information Facility. It reminded Dave of Wayne Manor, just like Batman and Robin. Behind the panel was access to a secret tunnel at the bottom of the stairs eighty feet below his office. After they reached the bottom of the stairs General Ahrens said, "I know what you are thinking, but a Bat Pole would have been hard on the family jewels and an elevator is too noisy and maintenance intensive. Besides, we, military members, are supposed to be in good shape and have no problem running up and down eight flights of stairs."

The general and his exec took a couple of key cards out of their wallets. They simply looked like credit cards. Actually, they were Officer's Club cards coded for access to the vault complex. They were unimposing and innocent looking, if lost or stolen. They certainly did not say *Code Access for Secret Underground Vault Complex* anywhere on them.

The exec said, "Your card is waiting for you over at the O Club. However, the two-man policy is in effect. Every security door requires two cards swiped simultaneously at least ten feet apart to gain access. There are no sentries. However, there are cameras. Somebody somewhere is monitoring the hallways, vaults and tunnel complex."

General Ahrens smiled and said, "For heaven's sake, don't forget to pay your bar bill or they'll cancel your card and you won't get in."

The massive steel door opened in the alcove at the bottom of the stairs. Schaudt stated "The blast doors were salvaged from the old decommissioned Titan Silos." Dave thought they looked familiar. The old Strategic Air Command Shield had been painted over to reflect their new owner, Air Systems Command. The exec continued, "What you see in the way of facilities, infrastructure, and equipment is all commercial, off the shelf technologies. No need to draw attention to ourselves with custom built items."

General Ahrens added, "Yeah, it's kind of hard to get the lab rats that live down here into that mode. They watch way too much Sci-Fi. They always want to play with the latest state of the art crap or design and build exotic shit. We do have deep pockets, but we've got to keep a low profile. Fortunately, having this facility located at the Air Force Logistics Center Headquarters helps hide some of the operational costs and explain strange shipments into and out of the base."

Waiting on the other side of the door was another electric golf cart. Dave wondered who had the General Services Administration (GSA) contract to supply these to the Federal Government. They were making a fortune. Maybe they brought some down off the *Nautilus* after they refitted her with the Aireopods. The general said, "Just because I've got to put up with 110 stair steps doesn't mean I've got to walk the half mile to the Lair." The exec unplugged the cart from the charger and hopped into the driver's seat. The general climbed in next to him. Dave hopped in the back. The electric motor whined and echoed off the tunnel walls. The tunnel was ten feet wide by ten tall and ran several hundred feet before coming to an intersection. There were no directional signs anywhere, only several vault doors spaced every fifty feet apart or so. The ceiling was hung with insulated piping labeled Steam, N2, CO2, and what Dave assumed were electrical, com, and fiber optic conduits.

They made a left turn and proceeded down a shallow ramp. Dave noticed that there was some water seeping in through cracks along the walls and trickling into a gutter alongside the tunnel.

"Like I said Major, this place is forty years old. We spend

a lot of time and money on dewatering. Hope you're taking notes."

Dave thought to himself, "I'm the man who finds alien spacecraft and delivers them to Uncle Sam. Now they want me to fix a leaky basement."

Schaudt stopped the cart at the next door. Both he and the general got the cards out and slid them into the readers at the same time. The door lugs started pulling back and clanked. The exec then pulled on the door. The massive door pivoted on its hinges and opened back. He drove through to the other side. They continued for another quarter mile, again passing several vault doors along the way. They made a right turn and ran into a dead end.

"Okay, Major. This is the point of no return. You go any further and your life is changed forever. You will be a member of a select few that has come this far. The area behind this wall has been manned around the clock for the past forty years. Do you understand?"

Dave knew he had already passed the point of no return flying back from Greenland. "Yes, sir. I understand."

"Just like in the missile silos, the two man policy is in effect. The team down here has complete control over the Lair. They control who enters and leaves. You have a good sense of direction, Major. We didn't blindfold you to get you down here. We didn't have to slip you a drug or a Thule Blue Nose. We are exactly 100 feet below the Tower at Building 620, the Avionics Lab. This building sits on the highest point on the base. The space you'll see behind this wall was mucked out and dumped into the quarry pit across the river a few miles away. We had absolutely no problem getting rid of the spoils."

The exec picked up the phone on the concrete wall. Dave understood that they were inside the entrapment area. He was sure there was a camera trained on them, but couldn't see one. Schaudt pressed the key on a hand set and said "Exec one with Ace plus one. Ready to authenticate."

The sentry at the entry control point somewhere within the complex said "Please standby for authentication."

A few seconds later the exec was speaking into the handset, "Charlie, Charlie, Mike, Hotel, Delta, Gulf."

"Authentication confirmed." Just then Dave heard the sound of hydraulic motors kicking in. A placard lit up reading, "STAND CLEAR OF WALLS". The entire floor slab was being lowered. They descended about twenty feet and stopped.

The vault door in front of them opened. Dave was expecting to see the Bat Cave complete with Batmobile and Bat Reactor. What he saw was a little anticlimactic, just another tunnel. However, it was wider and taller. The tunnel was about 150 feet long. It only had four doors, two on both sides of the hall. The center of the isle had a rail system embedded into the concrete. Each vault door had a monorail hoist system protruding out over the tracks. The tracks ran up to the walls on both ends of the tunnel and suddenly stopped. They drove past the first set of doors and parked the cart just past the second set on the right. Both the exec and General Ahrens again reached for their cards and slid them into the slots simultaneously. Schaudt said, "You only have a one second margin of error to time this right or the sky cops will jack you up." Just then the door lugs kicked back and the door opened. Now is when Dave was awestruck. Sitting on the other side of the door was a high bay about four stories tall by 200 feet long and 150 feet wide. The walls were awash in a bluish white light emitted by the MIST particles suspended overhead. Sitting at the opposite end was the nautilus-shaped shell they had brought back from Greenland.

Dave knew better than to ask how they got it down here. However, the general did speak up, "I know you're wondering how we got this beast down here. I'd have to shoot you if I told you, he half kidded. Like I said, Major, N2K. We have our ways."

"Welcome to the Blue Room, Major. Very few people have ever ventured in here. Many of our prominent politicians and senior ranking military members have tried to pressure or bully their way down here. The President of the United States doesn't even know this place exists. There is an old story told within Delta G that Barry Goldwater, who was a U.S. Senator from

Arizona, a retired Air Force Reserve Brigadier General, and a pilot, tried to gain entrance to the Blue Room. At that time, General Curtis Emerson Lemay's answer was 'Hell no, you can't go there. I can't even go there, so don't ask me again.' So you see, Major, how seriously we take our secrecy and security here."

"Major, your job is to expand these facilities. Believe it or not, we are running out of room down here. With the Navy personnel and their experiments now moved up here from Homestead, we are going to need another 50,000 square feet added to the Dragon's Lair."

CHAPTER 34
Close Encounters

Friday the 13th came very quickly. Dave wasn't superstitious, but did have a new healthy respect for numbers and the calendar. He had been busy that week in-processing and finding an apartment. He had attended several briefings, and endured getting poked and prodded at the Wright-Patterson Medical Center. He spent the afternoon at the new mall just south of the base picking out a new wardrobe. Even though the dinner this evening was going to be a casual barbeque he wanted to make a good impression. Not so much for the general, but for Anne, his daughter. She hadn't ever seen him in anything other than his fatigues.

Dave pulled up to a large Tudor mansion and rang the doorbell. He had brought a bottle of Grey Goose. He had done a little research by asking the exec officer what he should bring to the party. The general liked a good martini. A valet escorted him to the living room where the Ahrens' were sitting. He shook the general's hand as he was introduced to his beautiful wife, Barbara. He could see immediately where Anne got her beauty, class, and poise. He turned around and heard the exquisite Long Island accent saying, "Hi, Dave, welcome to our home. It is very nice to see you again." Dave spun around and couldn't believe his eyes. This was the first time he had seen Anne in anything other than her blue jump suit. She literally had her hair down, too. It was brunette and down to the middle of her back. She was in a sundress, wearing makeup and jewelry. "Wow, was she a knockout," Dave could just think.

"Thank you," was all Dave could stammer out. Mrs. Ahrens made a suggestion, "Why don't you go out back and compare penguin stories, while your father and I get the steaks ready for the grill?" Anne smiled as she grabbed Dave's hand and said, "Mom, they don't have penguins in Greenland."

"My mistake, then what kind of critters do they have up there?"

Dave responded by saying, "You'd be surprised how much wildlife, plants, and beauty there is above the Arctic Circle."

The general smiled and gave Dave an opening, "Are you referring to my beautiful daughter here?"

Dave took the targeting opportunity, "You bet. She definitely lit up the place. That's hard to do with a place that's dark six months out of the year."

Anne blushed a little and said, "Come on out on the terrace. We better leave my dad alone while he beats the hell out of those steaks." Dave followed Anne outside.

She took the opportunity to pump up his ego, "You know, my dad really does like you. My mom hasn't really had a chance to figure you out, yet. Dad has been chasing away, or at least intimidating the hell out of my dates for years. But now I think my parents' grandkid clock has kicked into high gear. I think Mom has a bug in his ear about wanting to be a grandma sometime."

With this, Dave simply said, "Well, we all eventually succumb to Father Time as we saw in Greenland with the help of an atomic MASER clock. How do you feel about all this? What's your clock telling you?"

She cooed slightly, and in her theatrical southern twang replied, "Well sir, are you talking about my lil' ol' biological clock?"

Dave replied in his Rhett Butler imitation, "You assume correctly, Miss Ahrens, if a gentleman may inquire of such things."

Anne got serious for a minute or so, "Well, to tell you the truth, my hormones are raging and my biological clock is ticking madly. I've been all over the world and accomplished much in my career. I want to settle down and raise a family. But how do I meet the right guy, fall in love, tell him that I know the secrets to the universe; that I work with flying saucers, that I can talk with aliens, and oh, by the way, I have ESP, too?"

Dave had to smile and laugh a little, "I do see your predicament. I feel much the same way. This is a lonely life we lead. If I might not be too forward, maybe we've found each other. I've had more than a crush on you since we first met. We are both going to be here at Wright-Patterson for at least a few years. Why don't we see where things take us? I'd like to take you out to dinner tomorrow night."

Anne came over and gave him a hug and a peck on the cheek, "I'd like that very much."

"Very well, I know of a nice restaurant on the Ohio River overlooking Cincinnati. It's only an hour away. I can pick you up in the morning and we can make a day of touring the sites," Dave suggested.

"I have a few things to take care of in the morning, but how about noon?"

"You bet, you've got a date," Dave responded.

Anne smiled, "This is great. Let's not tell the folks just yet. Let's play this out this evening and see what they have up their sleeve. I'd hate to bust their bubble in trying to play matchmaker."

Just then General Ahrens came outside with a tray full of steaks, wearing his barbecue apron. It had four huge stars with the words underneath, "Guaranteed Four Star Quality Meals". The general had a sense of humor after all.

Their cover this time around was a lot more complicated and intricate than past assignments. Wright-Patterson was not some remote location in the middle of the desert, at the polar extreme, or nestled into a swamp. It was surrounded by a thriving metropolitan area just a few miles east of Dayton, Ohio. Dave would now be working with mostly non-cleared civilian contractors and the US Army Corps of Engineers. He was placed there as a civilian project engineer in charge of construction management for the multimillion dollar Avionics Laboratory Complex addition to Building 620. In this capacity, he had ingeniously worked in the needed Lair design requirements for dewatering wells, computer systems, HVAC and additional power requirements integrated into the construction project. The above ground work would be visible to the hundreds of scientists and engineers working in Building 620 without them knowing about the improvements of the Lair literally right beneath their feet.

The construction of additional basement space, as it was called, required the lab addition to be built by excavating it thirty-five feet into the side of a sandy hillside. The hillside was saturated with groundwater which would explain all the water pumps and dewatering wells that were installed to keep the entire Delta G Complex dry. General Ahrens would be happy about that one. Also, by strategically placing reinforcing steel, rebar, and new foundation walls adjacent to the Lair vaults and tunnel complex, it would be a simple matter to tie in the infrastructure once secured and enclosed. The tons and tons of structural steel involved would mask the steel brought in for the underground rail spur being built for the additional high-bay.

After about a year of construction, Dave had figured out or as engineers are fond of saying, reverse engineered, where and how this rail system under area B was constructed. The huge sixteen foot wide by sixteen foot tall tunnel ran all the way through the hill from under Bldg 620 to the north side of Area B down to and under the steam plant, a distance of over a mile. Dave had reached the end of the tunnel one day and saw a few chunks of coal sitting along the drain channels. He had a handheld GPS unit one day that he passed off as a survey unit. He read the coordinates 39° 47' 38.70" N by 84° 04' 40.66" W. He must have been near the surface for the GPS unit to work. Dave had figured that the entrance to the tunnel lay under the hundreds of tons of coal stockpiled near the steam plant. This made sense; the spoils and tailings for the tunnel were simply hauled off in rail cars under the coal ash.

On a bar napkin, he had calculated it would have taken several hundred rail hopper cars to haul away all of the spoils from the Lair complex. A typical train is maybe ninety cars long. That meant a shitload of rail traffic. He doubted that all that ended up in the quarry across the river from the base. Then a light bulb went off in his head. If you simply disguise and build all these tunnels as part of steam plant access tunnels, building foundations, underground utility shafts, or sewer lines then most of this super-secret complex could have been dug out under the cover of legitimate military construction projects, just what he was doing with the building addition he was working on. He thought to himself, "My, my good ol' Uncle Sam could be kind of resourceful when he had to be."

CHAPTER 35
Bells Going Off

Major David Sheridan finally got the nerve to ask Anne to marry him. He had set it up perfectly by making reservations at the Riverfront 360 Restaurant across the river from Cincinnati, where they had their first official date. That was a little less than a year ago.

The timing for the proposal had to be perfect. As the restaurant revolved it faced a beautiful fairytale clock tower in Goebel Park to the south. Dave pointed to it, got on his knee and said, "Anne, see that clock tower below? It is 7:15. The time is now. The place is here. I would like to spend the rest of my days with you. Will you marry me?"

Anne's face lit up. It is not like she did not expect the question. She knew Dave was a hopeless romantic. She said, "I would very much like to be Mrs. David Sheridan, from now to forever. We have all the time in the universe."

With that, Dave pulled the box with the ring from his jacket pocket and opened it. The ring had a heart shaped diamond embedded in a spiral band of gold. He slipped it on and said, "Anne, I love you very much. Together we'll reach the stars."

The June wedding was magnificent. General Ahrens pulled a lot of weight. Nothing was too good for his only daughter. Barbara Ahrens was in seventh heaven helping to organize her daughter's wedding. They went back home to New York and were married in St. Patrick's Cathedral. It was a military wedding with mess dress and arch-of-swords ceremony.

Dave's family from Ohio attended. Everyone was awestruck by the beauty and pageantry. Anne looked like a princess in her long flowing white gown. It was truly a Cinderella wedding, complete with a horse-drawn carriage from the Cathedral to the reception in the Waldorf Astoria Hotel. Traveling on the SST, they honeymooned in London, England.

CHAPTER 36
Twisting the Dragon's Tail

The summer of 1994 was very busy for the newlywed Sheridans. They set up house in a quaint little village north of Dayton and commuted to work together. Even though they were technically paid by the university and a private contractor, they were still working for the Delta G Program. They were doing pretty well for themselves living in suburbia. Anne had even gone back to school to get her theater degree and then directed and performed in plays in their new hometown. Dave was active at the Base Aero Club, getting his instrument rating. He was also involved in the Dayton Engineers Club. They both enjoyed their time near his parents and family about an hour north of them. They had in fact settled down, had roots now, and were working on a family.

Serving on the Delta G Program gave them both a unique perspective on life. It was amazing that it didn't jade them or let it all drive them both crazy with the secrets they carried. They were actually in awe at the order and structure to the universe. It was elegant yet complex in its design. One would think with all the science and gadgetry that they worked with, that it would have hardened their souls. It had just the opposite effect.

Anne's job as a professor of Bioinformatic Engineering at Wright State University allowed her to interact with some interesting subject matter experts from all over the world on everything from DNA, genetics, evolution, anthropology, geology, psychology, neurology, and even archeology.

Dave was now well connected and respected with the research laboratories and command structure at Wright-Pat. As a Civil Engineering Officer, he had free rein of the base. He had built quite a reputation on base of being able to take the tough problems and get things done.

A major discovery concerning evidence that comets contained antimatter had just been made. This was observed between July 16, and July 22, 1994 when the comet Shoemaker-Levy 9 collided with Jupiter. The comet broke up into small pieces and their impacts should not have been viewable from Earth. But that wasn't the case. Each of these pieces caused a huge explosion on Jupiter. One of the explosions was a hundred times brighter than the Sun. The energy output of the impacts is estimated to be about 200 million megatons of TNT or 1,000 times as powerful as the Hiroshima bomb. The plume of one of the explosions reached 5,000 miles into the sky. Its impact covered an area several times the size of the Earth. Delta G determined that nothing, but a matter/antimatter reaction could have caused that kind of explosion. This information also confirmed that the Tunguska event was indeed an antimatter event.

Anne was again busy monitoring the space borne T-wave detection equipment. When Shoemaker-Levy hit Jupiter, the T-wave detectors pegged off the scale. At the exact same moment, the rings of Saturn rippled registering an instantaneous reaction to the impact on Jupiter tens of millions of miles away, proving what was already known, that T-wave propagation was superluminal, faster than the speed of light. Thus, Delta G sent probes to Saturn to monitor the ring ripple effect and to map other T-waves passing within the solar system, providing valuable data to build and calibrate T-wave instrumentation and equipment.

By this time, Major Dave Sheridan had spent almost two years constructing the addition to the Delta G Complex under Building 620. Its construction was proceeding on schedule and under budget. However, some technical challenges were cropping up. To solve them, Dave made several visits down to the Lair. This was necessary because of utility tie-in requirements and to coordinate with Lair technicians concerning vibrations caused by normal construction activities. During these visits, he took the opportunity to learn a thing or two.

At one such meeting in 1996, he ran into Dr. Timken. Timken

assumed that as the Delta G integration officer, and the fact that he was General Ahrens's son-in-law, that Dave was privy to the workings and experiments in the Lair. At a break in the meeting, Dave sat down at a table next to him in the break room as he was sipping on a cup of coffee.

"You know, Major Sheridan, we've been down here twisting the dragon's tail for over a quarter century. We've learned quite a bit from these shells. You'd be surprised. The shell material is actually a densely packed tungsten carbide nickel and cobalt lattice. That has led to the discovery of buckyballs and nanoparticles. The shells dense construction made it very difficult to cut even with diamond drills since it is just as about as hard as diamonds. The highly reflective surface and heat absorption properties made it impossible to cut with lasers. It wasn't until recently that we developed a gamma knife that could actually make a dent. Gamma knives are now used for cancer treatment. Hell, we couldn't even X-ray the darn thing because nothing would even penetrate through just two or three spiral layers. Also, in a roundabout way, fiber optics was developed to enable us to snake a thin diameter probe down the dragon's throat to see what is in there. All that we found was that the shell continued to spiral in on itself at the same angle and rate down to at least twenty microns. That was as thin as we could make the Lucite fiber optic cable.

"Then we got inventive." Timken continued, "Somebody figured out that we could fire neutrons down the gullet. We knew they would ricochet off the walls and then bounce back if they ever hit anything solid in the center. Funny thing happened. The neutrons never bounced back. We did get some other strange particles back such as quarks and meson particles. But the cloud chamber results showed they had an opposite spin of normal matter. This damn thing inverts any radiation we send down it. Hell, we even had an accidental discovery. Those do happen in science every once in a while. One of our scientists was setting up a Doppler radar to shoot down its gizzard. He was setting the pulse when a loud pop came out of the wave guide. This thing eats radar waves. Shazaam! Stealth was born.

"By the way, Major, we've been making great progress on that shell we pulled off the Greenland icecap. It is a great generator of helium-3 and hydrogen-5 isotopes. It is proving invaluable in our Zero Point Energy and cold fusion experiments. Also, do you have any idea whatever happened to that piece you did manage to cut out of the shell with the diamond drill? Even though it was only a few inches in diameter, we are concerned that it may be causing some distortion or edge effects in our antigravity experiments. We were hoping to find it and attempt to patch the hole. We tried to patch the hole ourselves but we can never match the material. The patch work gets rejected just like a skin graft or an organ transplant. It is almost as if this material is alive and self-aware."

Dave responded a little defensively, "It's a long story Dr. Timken, but I never did find that disk. I put it in my parka pocket and haven't seen it since I showed it off to the Raven cockpit crew. It had a very sharp edge and tore a hole through my pocket. It must have dropped out in all the confusion of the crash and recovery. I don't think anybody had the opportunity to take it from me."

Actually, Dave was taken back a little with this entire discussion. He knew the Coral Castle shell had something to do with antigravity and had also heard rumors to the effect that it was this kind of shell that existed on the Moon. Since the Moon has no magnetic field, there are a lot more things that can be done experimentally up there without interference or force coupling complications. So he took a chance to pump Timken for some info. "Doctor, forgive me for asking a stupid question, but why don't you just perform your antigravity experiments on the shell we recovered from the Coral Castle? Obviously, it is tuned to provide torsional waves out of phase with the Earth's gravitational and electrical fields to provide your antigravity force vector."

Timken replied, "Well, Major, we normally would have. But that shell is not in the best of shape. It was after all, imbedded into the oolite coral rock for over 100,000 years. The Grey Matter 182 embedded in its core has reached much of its half-life. Even though it is stable, it is not perfectly stable. It also turns out the coral rock and its location on Earth was an integral part of the wave inverter. It was tied directly into the Earth's energy grid and massive central node located on Ellesmere. When we used the hydrochloric acid to etch away the oolite to recover the shell, we may have inadvertently changed the shells tuning capability. However, we may be in luck. With our MASER detection and mapping capability, we have located several shells near the Sphinx and pyramids in Egypt. These are embedded in limestone similar to the oolite coral rock in south Florida at the Coral Castle. The pyramids and Sphinx are built mainly of nummulitic limestone. If you don't know, nummulites are large cone-shaped shells with many chambers arranged in spiral order. These are fossilized in the rock much like the spherical algae based oolites are in the coral. We are working on the hypothesis that these embedded spirals and spherical shells somehow tune, amplify, and invert the torsional wave by putting an opposite spin on it.

"We have poured over Ed Leedskalnin's notes, as well as his European mentor. We're on the verge of cracking the code they figured out over fifty years ago. It has to do with the rock itself, the location on Earth, the so called, Bruce Cathie planetary energy grid, and electrical fields. The Egyptians, or more correctly, their predecessors by ten millennia, had figured it out, too," Timken concluded.

Dave played along and continued to bait the good doctor for even more information. Luckily, this time he didn't even have to trade shots of vodka with him. He dug a little deeper, "I'm not too familiar with the planetary energy grid concept. But it sounds like it matches up pretty well with the Keyhole satellite orbital node pattern. It did after all predict the location of shells in Florida and Egypt. By the way, how are we going to extract those Egyptian shells? We can't just go in and dig under the ancient wonders of the world."

"Correct, Major, there was an eighty percent correlation with the nodes. As you and your lovely wife know, several older shells have been shifted around or relocated on the globe due to glaciations, human discovery, and even plate tectonics on a smaller scale. And back to your thorny question, it is obvious that we will bring the lab in under the guise of an international archeological project using advanced MASER ground penetration radar or Madar.

"Besides, we have a pretty good indication of where exactly to dig. The shells are not inside or under the pyramids of Giza or the Sphinx. It turns out that the layout and construction of the pyramids are based upon the logarithmic spiral." Timken grabbed a napkin from the dispenser and pulled his trusty number two pencil out from his coat pocket. "Let me show you, my friend. The layout of the pyramids traces a spiral curve. If you overlay a logarithmic spiral through the center of all three Giza pyramids, two things become apparent. First, we find the center of the spiral is about 2,000 meters to the southeast inside a fig orchard. The other thing is that the spiral centroid or

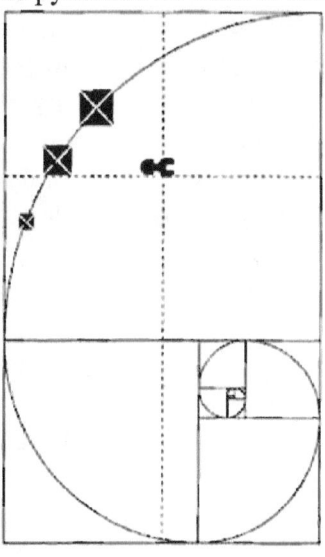

center of mass falls under the right shoulder of the Sphinx. We will excavate in the fig orchard."

Timken grabbed a second napkin and drew the pyramid. He then traced a spiral starting at the top and ending a little left of center. "Again if you trace a logarithmic spiral vertically through the pyramid, the burial chamber lies exactly in its center. And when you stop and think of it, the pyramids were built in a rising spiral method.

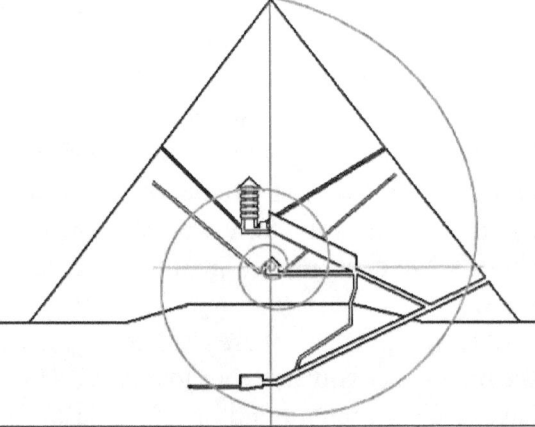

"Also, another interesting fact is that the large pyramid is at the center of the Earth's land mass above sea level. If you run a line along the north-south axis it passes through the maximum amount of land through Asia, Africa,

Europe, and Antarctica. Also, more than coincidently, the line running along the east-west axis is the maximum water covered parallel running through the African, Asian, and north American seas."

Timken picked up the napkins and gave them to Dave, "It is a funny thing, my good friend. It appears that the wave of the future, excuse the pun, is literally dependent upon digging up and understanding our past."

Timken changed the subject, "And speaking of digging up the past, I understand that we will be doing some excavation of our own here at Wright-Pat. Or should I say exhumation. It is a fact that advances in science and technology are ripe with regrets, what ifs, should haves, and could haves. I understand you are about to start digging a side drift tunnel from under the Avionics Lab back down the hill to under old Nuke Testing Facility in Building 470. It looks as though somebody has finally figured out that those aliens we buried in the foundation of that thing might have some scientific value that wasn't available in the late fifties. Humankind, in its arrogance, felt that they had dissected, inspected, X-rayed, electron microscoped, and even spectrographed the corpses and tissues of those beings to acquire all the knowledge that was available. Sort of like the attitude that persisted when the US patent office considered closing at the end of the last century because it was felt that the limits of all science and technology were known to civilization. One technology that wasn't available in the fifties was the understanding of DNA. We are going back to exhume those bodies from underneath the old reactor facility to conduct DNA experiments on them. It sounds kind of creepy, but welcome to the world of the grave diggers from below. Now with these disturbing parting words of wisdom, I must depart for my appointment. Good to see you again. I'm sure I'll continue to bump into you from time to time, down here in the Lair. Keep up the good work."

Dave thought to himself, "Damn, I've learned more in a ten minute conversation over a cup of coffee than I did in a year's worth of meetings and conferences. So much for being an Integration Officer was apparent that there was still way too much compartmentalization going on. No one, not even his wife, had mentioned a potential exhumation."

He also took a mental note. He was going to need to brush up on anthropology, world history, archeology, and DNA. He also wondered what geological feature lied on the opposite side of the globe than the pyramid. He bet there was something interesting there, too.

CHAPTER 37
Ice Scraper

Anne's work for the next several years depended upon her understanding and investigation of Earth geology and anthropology. Following up on her husband's work while on the *Nautilus*, she learned that over 70,000 years ago the ice began to accumulate, building upon itself. As it got thicker it began to spread as it moved southward at an astonishing rate of over a foot per day.

This glaciation period continued for over 10,000 years and then stopped suddenly. Then the cycle started all over again 40,000 years ago. The ice sheet accumulated another half mile in depth while it moved another 100 miles south. During this period, it eventually slowed and even retreated a little. Then only 20,000 years ago it spread out even further on its southern trek. The ice sheet literally built mountains in front of it as it scraped and eroded the bedrock. Over the millennia, this cycle of advance and retreat filled in ancient river valleys with hundreds of feet of till and altered the shape of a continent. In one cycle, the glacier dammed up one of the oldest rivers in the world creating a lake of over 7,000 square miles and 900 feet deep. One day it overflowed its western shoreline and cut a new channel 500 miles long to the southeast.

Within one of these glaciers was a spiral shell. It rode the ice flow as it moved southward until the ice sheet retreated only 10,000 years ago. This was at about the same time the Sphinx was being built in Egypt. Because of the shells extremely hard Tungsten Cobalt Nickel Carbide (WCoNiC) properties, it eventually worked its way up and to the front edge of the ice field, much as a splinter works its way out of the skin. This massive quarter million pound shell eventually deposited itself as it retreated and is now located on the edge of an escarpment buried under several hundred feet of erosion deposits and up against a soft chalk escarpment near where an ice dam had formed.

That shell is not located in Greenland or in Canada. It is located only a few miles from a small town in Southwestern Ohio called Peebles. The river that was dammed those millennia ago, was known as the Teays River where it flowed northward near present day Peebles, Ohio. The diversion channel that was carved out is now known as the Ohio River Valley. Delta G realized that the area around Peebles is indeed a very special and mystical place.

On August 14 and again on August 18, 2003, two sets of crop circles appeared in soybean fields near the Serpent Mound on Ohio State Route 73 near Locust Grove, Ohio, about five miles north of Peebles. One was located directly across the road from the main entrance to the mound. The other a few miles away near Hillsboro. The designs were identical and consisted of several markings. The smaller circles on the sides of the design measured twelve feet in diameter with the larger bottom circle measuring sixteen feet. The total design measured three hundred feet in diameter. The mound circle was discovered by the farmer less than twelve hours after he checked the field for flood damage. The Delta G Team took soil and crop samples to the lab at Peebles. Several universities also confirmed the findings, although not knowingly.

There were high concentrations of minerals in the western most circle of the designs, high radiation levels inside the designs, as well as higher electrical and magnetic fields than those outside the markings. Also, the MASER Energy creating them had a more profound effect on the soybeans than what typically occurs in wheat. The DNA was altered and the twist rate increased. Eureka! Evolution in an instant!

The Serpent Mound has always been a mysterious place. The mound is 1,200 feet long and about 5 feet high. It is made of soil and is formed in the shape of an uncoiling snake about to swallow an egg-shaped oval in its open mouth. The head of the serpent is aligned to the summer solstice sunset and the coils also may point to the winter solstice sunrise and the equinox sunrise.

It was never used for burials. Some have speculated that the vast earthwork was an offering to the gods. It certainly seems meant to be seen from above; the serpent is difficult to see from ground level. Visitors can climb a tower to see and appreciate its shape.

The coil of the serpent's tail is a common sacred symbol throughout the ancient world and often symbolizes the sacred forces of the Earth. It was thought that the mound-builders worshipped the Earth as a divine mother.

If only people really knew the meaning of the mound and the eons of history behind it. The Delta G archeologists and anthropologists have been working in the area for thirty years. The entire area around the mound was saturated with torsional energy.

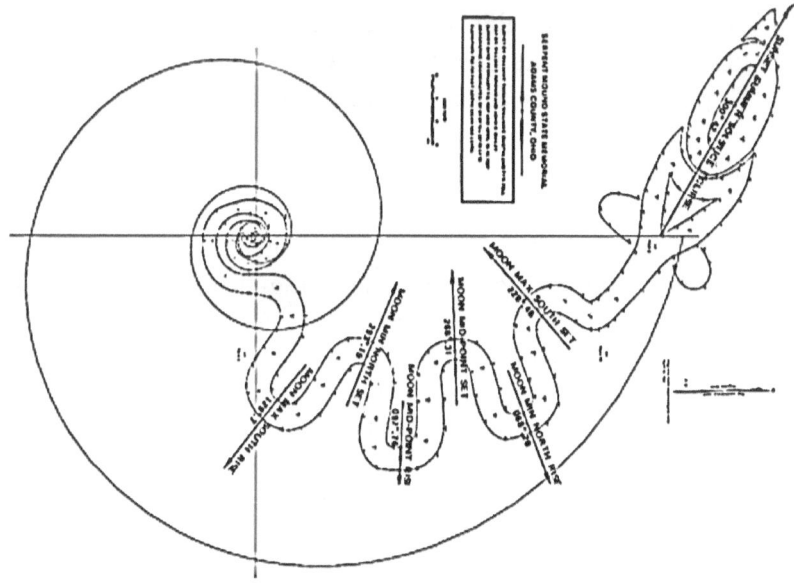

Anne had been an integral part of the Serpent Mound Analysis and Recovery Team (SMART). There was no question that a shell was located somewhere nearby. However, even the MASER could not detect it. It was buried deep. Even after twenty years of excavation (using a rock quarry operation as cover), the shell could not be found.

The mound was much, much older than given credit for by

conventional dating methods. The conventional wisdom was that it was built by the Native Americans about a thousand years ago. Carbon dating of charcoal and fire pits put the construction at around 1070 AD. The Delta G Team put the actual age of the original mound at over 8,000 years. The primitive civilizations that built them were not so primitive. They clearly understood the significance of the area. The cultures and tribes that came later understood the significance, too, such as the Fort Ancient Culture and the earlier Adenans. These later tribes, who inherited the land, simply maintained the mounds and its heritage, along with its lore and legends for eons. Then suddenly in the early 1600's, these maintainers died out. This has been attributed to possible inner tribal warfare from the Iroquois or Delaware until the Miami Tribe moved in around 1650.

The possible reason this area was selected for the mound was not known until satellite photos were available in the late 1960s. The Serpent Mound is actually located in an eroded meteorite impact crater. It lies largely in Adams County, with the northern part mostly in Highland County, except for a small northeast part in Pike County.

The crater is classified as a complex crater because it features a central uplift, a transition zone, and a ring-shaped trough in the outer part of the crater. Although eroded, the original rim diameter is estimated at five miles wide. It was a fairly shallow impact crater. It did not punch through to the magma below. There was no igneous rock exposed. Its age is estimated to be less than 320 million years.

The Delta G Team investigation led to some interesting findings at the Serpent Mound. The tip of the tail to its head is laid within a perfect logarithmic spiral. Also, the snake was not eating an egg as was previously thought. It was in fact a representation of a torsional wave generator gaining its energy from the remnants of the impact crater, shown as an oval, the egg, feeding into a shell, the coiled tail. From a Delta G perspective, it made sense. Even the alignment with the lunar solstice made sense, as TW detection equipment at Lagrange Point Two showed the T-wave deflected by the lunar shells.

However, even more bizarre was the fact that the Serpent Mound Impact Crater was located exactly halfway between the Egyptian pyramids at Giza and the South Pacific island of Rapa Iti on the great circle arc. Dave was correct in his earlier suspicions that there was something interesting on the opposite side of the Earth from the Great Pyramid of Khufu, the Pyramid of Khafre and the Pyramid of Menkaure.

Rapa Iti is a group of four uninhabited volcanic rocks protruding from the sea along with several submerged rocks, forming the southeastern end of the Austral Islands of French Polynesia. Rapa Iti is located at -27.917S, -143.433W. It is an exact opposite of the geological land centroid of the Egyptian pyramids at Giza. Interestingly, from orbit above this island's location, the hemisphere visible is almost 95 percent covered by water. This island is in fact the centroid of the Earth's ocean volume. It was also the spot on Earth least affected by tidal forces. It was also a great source of torsional energy and the location of a subterranean shell. As a matter of fact, there was talk with the Delta Blue Program Office to take Howard Hughes' old ship, *Glomar Explorer* out of mothballs again to go search for it.

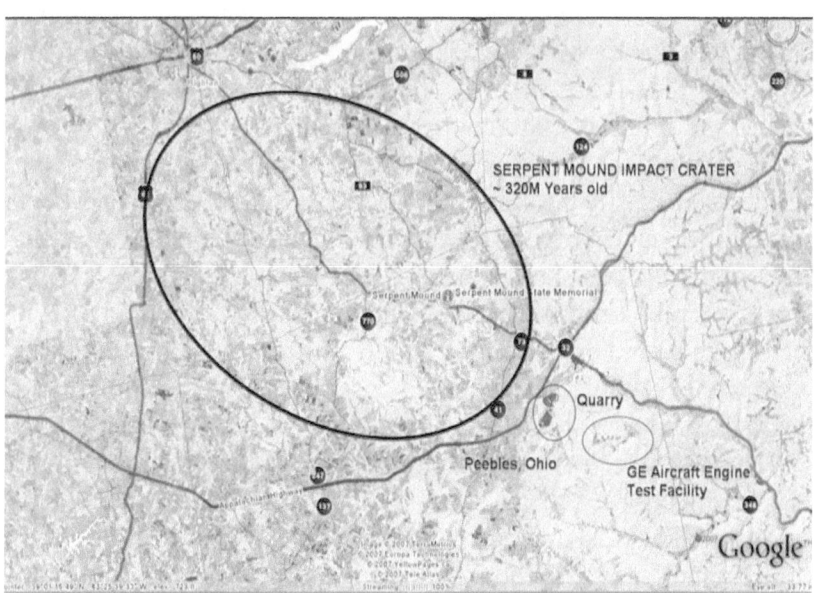

It became clear that the Delta G Program needed to establish a foothold in the foothills surrounding Peebles, the mound, and the torsional energy generator buried in the glacial till. Thus, it is no coincidence that a highly classified aircraft engine test center was established a few miles from the quarry near the town of Peebles. The impact crater held some secrets to be investigated. Whatever was feeding the shell was buried only a few hundred feet underground. Between the quarrying and tunneling being done at the engine facility a few trace nodules of GM 182 were found.

It was soon understood that conventional mining techniques would not work in the loose rock strata. To solve this problem, a tunnel boring machine was brought in. Dave noticed the Air Force logo on its side. However, it wasn't the one he used in Little Skull Mountain. He wondered what strange program this one came from. He'd investigate that mystery later. For the time being, it would be used to bore through the loose limestone and shale while the opening left behind was lined and reinforced.

While this excavation proceeded at Peebles, word finally came down to Dave in early January 2004 from Delta G Black to start construction of a half mile long tunnel from the Lair to under Building 470, the abandoned reactor facility. Although no official reason was stated, he knew from his off chance heads up conversation with Dr. Rapp, several years ago, the reason why. Delta G was going to finally exhume the alien bodies

Dave was becoming a mining and tunneling expert by now. He had essentially become the Delta G's tunnel rat. The body snatcher tunnel project, as it was affectionately called, was somewhat complicated. The dig would be through some loose sand, gravel and clay; not hard rock. The tunnel did not have to be all that big in diameter. So, Dave simply had large precast eight foot wide tunnel sections brought onto base as a part of a steam tunnel upgrade that he ran down the hill.

There were no official drawings or records of the entombment; just recollections and guesses. Ground penetrating radar from below would be used to easily find the voids. With any luck, they could tunnel under the foundation of Building 470 and cut into the foundation easily from below with saws and jack hammers.

Evidently, the Delta G Black Office had felt that the Grays would appreciate the turnover of the corpses of their dead crew members. There had been decades of discussion and arguments on this point. What if the Grays didn't understand the crew members were killed in an accident and we didn't kill them? Have we been able to communicate well enough with them to convey this fact? It was also not known what their feelings were regarding death. Some felt the touchy-feely liberal side of the Delta G Program had gone too far. The turnover was not necessary. Why quite literally dig up the past? Let sleeping dogs lie.

However, Dave could only salute smartly and get out his shovel. It only took a couple of months to put the steam line tunnel in that ran past Building 470. It was then a simple matter of digging a tunnel from a junction near the street to under the facility and line the tunnel with steel I-beams and wood lagging brought in from the Lair. This was going to be a temporary tunnel anyway. No need to make it permanent.

At a point nearly under the center of the reactor complex, a complication crept into the project. The earth they were hauling out was slightly radioactive and full of HazMats such as benzene and toluene. The earth was simply hauled back through the Lair complex and mixed with earth from a couple of environmental compliance and restoration cleanup projects on the base. This did slow things down a bit and required everyone to wear PPE. But once under the center of the complex, the radar penitrometer was brought in.

Sure enough, three large voids were found within a dozen feet of the tunnel. It was much easier than anticipated. There was no concrete to cut into at all. Since the crates were set on the gravel sub-base and not over any reinforcing steel, the crates or what was left of them were easily found from below.

No one knew what to expect or what kind of containers, if any, the Grays were placed in. For all anyone knew they were simply wrapped in sheets, or stuffed in drums, or encased in concrete. Dave was in the tunnel when the final exhumation took place. The bottom of the crates were relatively intact. They were about six feet cubed which made sense if they fit in the back of a two and a half ton truck. There was no ground water to worry about under the complex. The edge drains worked well. The gravel was slowly shoveled away and the crates were braced on I-beam supports on hydraulic lifts. A Sawzall cut around the bottom of the first crate and the crate contents lowered down on the jacks. General Ahrens and Dr. Rapp were watching the process on closed circuit TV back at the Lair.

Inside each of the crates were actually four small child size coffins. This was odd, since the Greys were known to be fairly tall creatures. However, it was apparent that this was obviously not a rush job to hide the evidence. Some thought, concern, and even a little compassion was put into their burial.

Each coffin was brought out of the tunnel, placed on a cart and then hauled by an electric golf cart up the hill to the Lair. Once the exhumation was complete Dave had the crew pull out of the tunnel carefully, backfilling it, and then a concrete wall was placed across the chamber. No one would ever know that they were under the facility.

At the Lair clean rooms, the forensic pathologists in their white lab coats would again dissect them, inspect them with electron tunneling microscopes, and also perform analysis on their DNA. The subject of the Greys' DNA had come up several times between Dave and Anne as pillow talk. She confided in him that with the limited contact, no DNA had ever been extracted or even left behind. The Greys never went to the bathroom in the presence of humans; they never so much as spit on the sidewalk, and since they didn't have any hair, they did not leave any follicles to perform DNA experiments on. In over fifty years of sporadic contact with the Greys, no human had ever come in physical contact with them, at least officially. They didn't communicate using pencil, paper, or even keyboard. They couldn't comprehend a handshake other than as a potential transfer of microbes. Any visual meetings were conducted through the protection of space suits, holographic projections, and telepathy. Anne wasn't even sure the Greys were aware that we had buried a few of their comrades under Building 470 over forty years ago.

CHAPTER 38

The Cow Jumped Over the Moon

Dave enjoyed the outdoors. He decided to take some time off between Christmas and New Year's and go down to his brother's farm near Lancaster, Ohio, to do some deer hunting. Doug Sheridan and his partner had been raising cattle on this farm for several years. They were all sitting around the fire place the evening before opening day, sipping on whiskey. The history of the farm was brought up. It was actually part of an original 640 acre section of land granted to a revolutionary war soldier as payment for his military service. As a matter of fact he was buried on a wooded hillside on the Amish farm next door. Dave had helped Doug and Tom clear the brush and fallen timber away from his tombstone and fix the small fence around the grave site.

The kitchen of Doug's farm house was actually built around the original log cabin from the early descendents of this man. Over the years, the house had eventually been added onto and in the process the cabin was enclosed within the two story farmhouse. After a few more sips of whiskey, Doug proceeded to tell Dave how the house was haunted. Both Dave and Tom had seen the spirit of Sarah, the wife of Jacob, the Revolutionary War soldier. She seemed to appear visually every Christmas Eve and made her appearance last week. She never appeared threatening and said nothing. She just stood at the end of the bed staring and then slowly faded away. However, other strange things happened all the time including movement of objects, strange noises, and cabinet doors opening and closing. One of the strangest events was when Doug found a child's toy on the stairs leading to the basement. It was one of those plastic Fisher-Price Snap-Lock Beads that have the various colored shapes that pop together. A string of a half dozen of them was laid out on the steps in a perfect straight line. There were no kids in the house and Doug had no idea where it had come from.

After a few more sips of whiskey and a few more ghost stories, Dave let a few things slip regarding UFOs and the Greys. No details, just that he had seen some strange things in Greenland, Nevada, Florida, and now Wright-Patterson and was now involved with Transitioning Advanced Technologies. Although Dave never really ever mentioned the true nature of his work to Doug, his brother knew enough to know that he was involved in some very strange technology. Everyone took another sip of Jack Daniels, and hummed the theme to Twilight Zone. Doug chalked his brother's war stories up to the family's hyperactive bullshit story telling gene. After all, the only difference between a war story and a fairy tale is, one starts out, 'Once upon a time…'; the other starts out with, 'This ain't no bullshit, but…'

Opening day of deer season was exactly five hundred days after the crop circles appeared near Peebles. Something fantastic was about to happen on this day. While Dave was sitting in a tree stand, his mind was literally a trillion miles away. The relaxed setting had unintentionally put him into an RV mode. He was sensing a shell hurtling through space passing through the rings of Saturn. Actually there were three shells clustered together with a shiny metal sphere in the center. As they spun around and around, he could see a strange blue glow projected behind the cluster. Dave suddenly felt a tingling sensation on his left shin and noticed a smell of ozone in the air around him. He had a flashback of when he and his sister, Deb, were nearly struck by lightning under the neighbors oak tree when he was eight. He had the same tingling of the neck hairs and ozone smell. He turned around in the tree stand to notice steam rising from the wheat field behind him. The sun was just coming up. He could make out the patterns of a crop circle in the hay field behind him. He climbed down from the tree stand and walked into the field. The smell of ozone was fainter now. But the morning frost was sizzling and popping on the winter wheat where it was bent down. Just then, he heard a large cracking noise and a thud as the ground shook beneath his feet. Something had just crashed through the trees a few hundred feet into the woods ahead of him. A few seconds later he heard a second, and then a third crash. At about the same time, the T-wave detectors in the Newtonian Satellite cluster at the Lagrange points were pegging off the scale at they sent triangulation data back to Cheyenne Mountain. The Hubble telescope was trained on the rings of Saturn which were shimmering and rippling slightly as the spiral density waves could be seen propagating in the direction of Earth.

Doug and Tom heard the crash in the woods from the farm house. They thought a plane had crashed in the woods. There was no explosion or fire. They ran from the farm house across the steaming field and into the woods yelling for Dave. They feared that whatever it was that landed in the woods might have come down on top of him.

Dave yelled back to them as he ran towards them in the middle of the field. He began limping as his left leg went numb. He knelt down on his right knee as a burning sensation shot up his left shin. He was wearing his mukluks he had brought back from Greenland and struggled to unlash them and rip them off his feet. As he grabbed for the laces he could see a round-shaped scorch mark on the outside skin of the mukluk and smelled the burning hair of the seal skin. He was frantic to get it off. His brother reached him and helped him remove it. As they tossed it aside the spot grew larger and then burst into a blue-green flame. All three stared at it in amazement. Doug asked questions in rapid fire succession, "What the hell is going on out here? Why is your boot on fire? Who made this crop circle? What landed in the woods behind you?" All questions Dave had no answers for.

After a few minutes, the flames went out on the mukluk. Dave poked at the boot with a tree branch. He pulled back on the seal skin liner to see what had caused the burning. "I'll be damned." Dave said, "That's the piece of shell I cut out with the diamond drill up in Greenland a few years ago. I thought it had fallen out of my pocket in all of the commotion. It must have cut a hole in my pocket and then fell down and caught between the linings of my mukluk." It was glowing red hot. "The material in the shell must resonate or generate some type of energy for other shells to home in on. Timken was correct. It is self-aware."

Doug and Tom just stared at Dave in disbelief.

The farm was very isolated and the woods were a good half mile from their nearest neighbor. Dave doubted any of the neighbors would have heard the crash. The three of them walked down the hill into the woods and jumped across a creek. Just on the other side was a cluster of three shells. One had just crashed through a two hundred year old oak tree and didn't appear to have a scratch on it. The other two were lying nearly side by side in a thick briar patch. All three were still steaming in the crisp winter morning air. These shells were much smaller than the one recovered in Greenland.

Dave asked, "Well, do you guys still think I'm full of shit? The family secret is out in the open now. I really do chase flying saucers for a living." Doug and Tom's jaws dropped as Dave bent down to put his mukluk back on. "It appears they are now chasing me."

Doug said, "I guess you can be thankful their aim is a little off. Whatever landed in the woods missed you by a couple hundred feet."

Dave said, "I don't think luck had anything to do with it. Somebody is trying to send me a message. I need to make a phone call."

On the way back to the house, they noticed more steam rising from the Amish farmer's pasture. They walked over to investigate. Just on the other side of the fence they saw the neighbor's cow down on its side with steam rising over it. As they got closer and walked around the other side, the sight just about turned all their stomachs. The cow's internal organs were laid out in front of them. It had been cut and gutted with surgical precision. Dave was just glad it wasn't him. He had heard of cattle mutilation before in connection with UFOs, but couldn't figure out the connection. He'd have to leave this one to the Delta G Team to figure out.

They ran into the house where Dave picked up his cell phone and waited for a signal. He dialed Wright-Pat. Rapp was on the other line. Neither were too concerned with a secure line at this point. "The detectors have pegged. Where are you? Big Blue is crunching the numbers now. We'll have a fix on the location in a

few minutes, but it is somewhere in southeast Ohio, pretty close."
Dave spoke up. "Power down the computers. Your fix is about
three miles southeast of Brittney, Ohio. The damn thing nearly
landed on top of me. It's a long story, but I think it homed in on
that piece of shell that I thought I'd lost back in Greenland.

"Get the recovery ship down here ASAP." Then he thought for
a minute, "Belay the recovery ship. I've got a better idea. This
one is accessible via land route. We'll need some lumber hauling
equipment down here." Dave thought that would be the perfect
cover. Doug had mentioned to his neighbors that they were about
to clear out some old growth trees: oaks, cherries and walnuts. A
furniture manufacture had flown over the farm, spotted the trees,
and made them an offer. They even came out to measure and mark
them. So having an army of lumber cutters show up in a day or
two wouldn't surprise the neighbors. Even a chopper flying overhead and circling could be explained away. Now, if he could only
explain to the Amish farmer what happened to his milk cow?

Dave spent the next couple of hours explaining to his brother
and partner what had just happened on their farm. Amazingly, they
took it all in stride. The only thing Doug asked to break the tension was, "Do you think I can write-off the crop loss on my taxes
next year? Can I put a claim into the Pentagon for post traumatic
shock and damage to my trees? Also, I don't know what we're
going to do about poor ol' Malen's milk cow?" Dave smiled and
said, "Don't worry. Both you and your neighbor will be very well
compensated."

The initial Delta G Extraction Team arrived at the farm in a
little over two hours after the call to Wright-Patterson. The Delta
G Program and team had been expanding for years. The initial
team included biologists and botanists to investigate the crop circle
and the dead bovine.

Dave knew there had to be a connection between the crop circle,
the shell, the dead cow, the burning boot, and the RV experience
he had just before the shell nearly landed on top of him. He felt
very little happened by chance or accident in nature as proven by
the now popular mathematical discipline known as chaos theory.
Coincidences are rare in nature. There is a reason for everything.

As integration officer, Dave had found and demonstrated that most fields of science were interrelated to each other by one degree or another.

Since all matter is self-aware of other matter, then outcomes can be predicted, foreseen, and linked to other events. The reason humans were so special was the fact that the brain could filter out this universal awareness and allow the individual to become self-aware or self-conscious. However, under certain circumstances and with certain individuals, this filtering capability can be tuned down or even turned off. The ability to filter out universal awareness is what allows humans to focus, think, anticipate, and calculate. Without this filter, one would go instantly insane. It would be like a trillion times worse than ADD without the ability to concentrate on a single thought for even a nanosecond. Dave suspected that when you die, the filter is turned off, and your internal energy or soul then becomes universally aware of all other matter, time, and space. In other words, you go to Heaven.

The lead biologist on the team was none other than Anne. She was after all, the Delta G Bioinformatics Engineer and this is where she shined. Her group was working on a theory regarding the so called cattle mutilation phenomena.

Anne gave Dave another hug and was relieved that he was okay. It was starting to look like the Greys were taking a personal interest in him.

Dave couldn't understand why she was so excited. He thought she might be excited because of her relief to see that he had dodged another bullet. He was genuinely hurt when the first words out of her mouth were, "Where is it? It's a fresh kill; only a few hours old, right?"

He replied, "Nice to see you, too, honey. I didn't bag the four-teen pointer to hang on the den wall. But I think you'll be happy with the trophy laying up there on the hill by the fence." She was chomping at the bit to dispatch her team to start dissecting and collecting samples from the dead cow.

It had been discovered early on that when Masers were used to search for shells, certain mosses and pond algae, and even cow manure were affected in the vicinity of the MASER shot. Even at low intensities, they started to smoke and burn.

The cows stomach lining, or hydrogel biofilm rumen, contained vast amounts of bacteria. It is filled with so many microbes that biologists refer to cows as mobile fermenters. Bacteria colonize the digestive tract of a calf soon after it is born. Within a few weeks the microorganisms have modified the chemistry inside the rumen, which soon becomes home to over thirty species of bacteria, forty species of protozoa and five species of yeast. Some of these bacteria are known as rumen spirochetes. Spirochetes are long and slender spiral shaped bacteria, usually only a fraction of a micron in diameter but 5 to 250 microns long. They are tightly coiled and look like miniature springs or cork screws. Again, another classic example of spirals in nature.

The Delta G biologists felt there was a definite link between the spiral-shaped bacteria, torsional waves, and microwaves. As a matter of fact, they thought that the Greys actually used one or more of the bacterium, such as the Treponema Byrantii, as a data archival storage media. After all, for an advanced civilization to store vast amounts of data for eons, what better media to store it on than encoding it on artificial DNA genomes of the modified bacteria of the host planet? The data is self-replicating insuring archival over thousands of generations and as long as the species survives. It is a rather ingenious storage medium. It's cheap and long lived. One bacteria strand can contain about a hundred base pairs of coding, or a simple English sentence. A shot glass full of this liquid can contain up to a billion bacteria, the potential capacity of such a memory system is enormous. A cow's rumen can contain up to forty gallons of biofilm providing terabits of storage capability.

The spirochetes can also tolerate high temperatures, desiccation, ultraviolet light and ionizing radiation doses 1,000 times higher than would be fatal to humans. What better storage medium to traverse the harshness of interstellar space than a bacterial data storage device?

Evidently, the Greys had perfected the process. But Dave still didn't know how to tell the Amish farmer next door that his cow was burned and cauterized from the inside out due to an alien torsional wave-guided gamma knife gene splicer, while trying to access data stored on the lining of its guts.

Just then, the light bulb went on over his head. He rushed over to Anne who was kneeling down over the cow, scraping the lining out of one of its stomachs. Dave just about lost his own watching this. After she was done, he grabbed her by the elbow, "Anne, I think we have another clue left by our little Grey friends in the farm house." He proceeded to tell her about the hauntings. This even got her more excited, "Dave, do you think they still have the plastic toy?" Dave replied, "I don't know. It scared the crap out of them. I didn't ask what they did with it."

Anne had her team put the sample she collected in a cooler and walked with Dave down to the farm house. Doug and Tom were on the porch sipping on coffee watching as a lumber truck pulled up the lane. Doug said, "Boy, you guys don't waste any time do you?"

Anne gave her brother-in-law a hug and said, "No, we are pretty resourceful."

Doug smiled at Anne and said, "I knew you were too smart for Dave. How'd you rope him into this?"

Anne replied, "It's a long story, Doug. I'll have to tell you it sometime. But for now, can you help us out? Dave mentioned the plastic snap-lock beads child's toy you found a couple weeks ago on your basement stairs. Do you still have it? We think it was left here by our alien friends. This didn't faze either Doug or Tom. They both stood there sipping on the coffee."

Tom said, "Well, it's like this. It was kind of creepy. It was as if some ghost put a snake on our stoop. It took us a long time before I decided to pick it up. I put it in a bag and was going to bury it. Sort of out of reverence to maybe one of Sarah's kids that had died very young and is supposedly buried somewhere on the farm. I haven't gotten around to burying it yet. It is down at the pole barn. Why? What's the significance of a child's toy in all this?"

Anne said, "I think they just laid the secret or key to their DNA and ability to communicate on your stoop." They walked down to the pole barn and Tom dumped the toy strand onto a workbench. It was a Fisher-Price Snap-Lock Bead toy with eight colored shapes strung together.

Anne asked, "Do you remember which stair step it was lying

across and in which direction it laid?"

Tom said, "Yeah. It was the third step from the bottom, lying with the blue ball at the left end. I had to step over it a couple of times while I went downstairs to the bathroom to pee. It gave me the willies."

Doug asked, "I see where you are going with all this. You think this represents some sort of code, for genetic sequencing. The toy is a gene and the position on the stair is where it falls in the DNA sequence. But that could be anything. The plastic pieces could represent any type of chemicals and the third stair could mean a position, but where on the DNA strand, and whose DNA strand?"

Anne said, "It runs in the family, Dave, doesn't it? If I'm right, the DNA is from a strand of bacteria in the dead cow out there. The gene is eight links long, and the position on the ladder is one fourth of the way up the ladder, if you count all twelve stairs. Also, there is probably some significance with the colors and shapes. There are too many combinations and possibilities for the human brain to compute. That's what we have IBM on the payroll for. Plus, the crop circle will also give us some clues."

A few minutes later a helicopter flew overhead taking photos. It then dropped a chute to the ground. Dr. Rapp ran out to pick it up. It was a tube filled with Polaroids of the crop circle.

Dave looked at them and then said, "This is a fairly simple layout. You know Anne, it might be a lot simpler than all that. Maybe we are reading too much into this. Maybe they are just trying to tell us, 'Hey, you dumb shits, why don't you just try pouring some of the gut juice you collected down a shell gullet and see what happens.' Hell's bells, we've discovered quite a bit, both accidentally and on purpose, with what these shells can do when you run stuff down their gullets."

Anne had to laugh, "Well, Dave, so much for the elegant bioinformatic engineering analysis I provided. But you just might be right. Sometimes simpler is better."

When Anne looked at the photos, her jaw dropped. The aerial photo showed a crop circle with a simple spiral and arrow pointing to the dead cow along with a single squiggly line followed by a double helix.

Anne said, "I see what you mean. But we're waiting until we get back to Wright-Patterson to try it."

Dave and Rapp blurted out simultaneously, "Agreed."

The extraction crew spent the rest of the afternoon clearing and dragging lumber from the woods to make room for a drag line to haul the shells across the creek bed. They had the lumber truck and dozer hooked up and ready to go. They brought a harness kit with them and hooked it up to the shell and dragged it up to the pasture.

Loading the shells on the truck worked out fairly smoothly. They even cut logs to stick out the back end as they were all wrapped up in tarps. Dave had one more unpleasant chore to perform before the truck pulled away. He had the extraction crew place the dead cow in the gravel lane leading up to the farm and supported it upright with two by fours. The idea was to accidentally hit the cow with the lumber truck on the way out of the farm. Hopefully being hit by an eighteen wheeler would mask any damage to the cow that happened from the MASER burst. Doug would then apologize profusely to the Amish farmer about accidentally having a tree fall across his fence allowing the cow to get out and then unfortunately getting run over by the lumber truck. Dave would pay for a new cow and even help bury this one. After a sickening thud and a bounce or two, the truck proceeded down the lane, out onto the country road and then up to I-70 for its trip back over to Wright-Patterson.

Dave made a command decision. After the circle was photographed and surveyed ten ways from Sunday, and after several samples of the wheat had been made, he had Doug run through the field several times with the tractor obliterating any sign of the crop circle. The farm was directly under the flight path to the Port Columbus and Lancaster Airports. It wouldn't take long before some curious pilot or passenger would notice it and call in the tabloids.

On one of the passes with the tractor, Doug suddenly stopped, flashed his lights, honked the horn and motioned for Dave and Dr. Rapp to come up to him. Beside the tractor along the wood line was a small crater about fifteen feet in diameter. Inside the crater was a pool of shiny liquid that looked like mercury. Dr. Rapp told

Doug and Dave to back off immediately. If it was mercury, it was highly toxic. Before Dave backed away from the crater, he glanced in the pit and couldn't believe what he saw.

This event quickly turned even more bizarre and complicated than just a dead cow and crop circle. So much for a simple extraction of three small scale shells, time to call in the big guns. The Delta G Team did bring a crypto set with them. He plugged it into the house phone jack and typed out the following message.

To:
Director, Delta G Black

Subj:
Status Report from Brittney, Ohio on 12-30-2004-1750L

Extraction of triple shell event was successful and all are in route to Lair.

Bovine biological samples recovered and are also in route to Lair.

The site is secure.

Need assistance from Delta G Black with recovery of fourth object. Object is one of our own T-wave runners found floating on material that appears to be liquid mercury pool located in crater on-site. The crater is approximately fifteen feet diameter and eight feet deep. It is located on north edge of the wheat field along the tree line.

Please advise. Standing by.

Regards,

David J. Sheridan, Major, USAF

Delta G Integration Officer

CHAPTER 39
In the Heart of It All

The State of Ohio boasts on their license plates, "OHIO, THE HEART OF IT ALL". However, most Buckeyes don't realize how much truth there is to this statement. Or to put it more correctly, Ohio is the start of it all; plus the new license plate's slogan, "OHIO, SO MUCH TO DISCOVER".

Anthropologists are still arguing whether the cradle of civilization began in Africa, Iran, or China. School books claim that Homo sapiens populated the Earth around ten thousand years ago and migrated out of Africa, up through Asia, then across the Bering Sea land bridge to Alaska, and then eventually migrated southward to populate the Americas.

Anne's Delta G Team was about to rewrite the text books and blow conventional wisdom out of the water with what was found at Peebles. Her latest thesis set out to expose and prove that 20,000 years ago there was an advanced civilization that occupied the American Midwest. It was centered on the headwaters of the now buried Teays River Valley in what is now southwestern Ohio. Her thesis included documented cases of the discovery of a race of giants that occupied the Ohio Valley. Examples are as follows:

Reference and credit:

A Tradition of Giants in the Ancient Ohio Valley
by Ross Hamilton

George W. Hill, M.D., dug out a skeleton "of unusual size" in a mound of Ashland County, Ohio. In 1879, a nine-foot, eight-inch skeleton was excavated from a mound near Brewersville, Indiana. (*Indianapolis News*, Nov 10, 1975)

"A skeleton which is reported to have been of enormous dimensions" was found in a clay coffin, with a sandstone slab containing hieroglyphics, during mound explorations by a Dr. Everhart near Zanesville, Ohio. (*American Antiquarian*, v3, 1880, pg. 61)

A mound near Toledo, Ohio, held twenty skeletons, seated and facing east with jaws and teeth "twice as large as those of present day people," and besides each was a large bowl with "curiously wrought hieroglyphic figures." (*Chicago Record*, October 24, 1895; cited by Ron G. Dobbins, *NEARA Journal*, v13, fall 1978)

Over the face of the country, throughout Ohio and the adjoining States, the extinct race of giant men...have written a mystic record of their existence in hieroglyphics perhaps uninterruptible...And this dead race of giants...who were they? (Lafcadio Hearn, Cincinnati Commercial, Cincinnati, Ohio, April 24, 1876)

Evidence for the occupation of this region before the appearance of the red man and the white race is to be found in almost every part of the county, as well as through the northwest generally. In removing the gravel bluffs, which are numerous and deep, for the construction and repair of roads, and in excavating cellars, hundreds of human skeletons, some of them of giant form, have been found. A citizen of Marion County estimates that there were about as many human skeletons in the knolls of Marion County as there are white inhabitants at present! (*The History of Marion County, Ohio* complied from past accounts, published in 1883)

In this issue there is an account of a mound which was evidently explored more thoroughly than most of those which have been known to exist here. "Saturday we were shown some interesting relics consisting of a queen conch shell, some isinglass (mica), and several peculiarly shaped pieces of slate which were found on the farm of Solomon Hill, Concord Township, Delaware County, Ohio. The mound is situated on the banks of a rocky stream. The nearest place where the queen conch shell is found is on the coast of Florida; the isinglass in New York State, and the slate in Vermont and Pennsylvania. Two human skeletons were also found in the mound, one about seven feet long, the other a child. The shell was found at the left cheek of the large skeleton. A piece of slate about one by six inches was under the chin. The slate was provided with two smooth holes, apparently for the purpose of tying it to its position. Another peculiarly shaped piece, with one hole, was on the chest, and another with some isinglass was on the left hand." (*The Delaware Herald* for September 25, 1879)

Anne's thesis was titled, *Eastward Migration of Advanced Civilizations*. The title was not immediately controversial. But the proof, research, and documentation within it was pretty much indisputable. That alone would make it highly controversial.

The thesis demonstrated how this advanced civilization traversed the Teays River system to where it meets the Mississippi near present day St. Louis. Keep in mind that glaciation has completely obliterated most of the evidence of this society's existence. The Teayans, as she called them, migrated down the Mississippi, around the Gulf of Mexico shoreline, and eventually populated the Yucatan and South America. They were the precursors to the Inca, Aztec, and Mayan civilizations. They then migrated throughout the Caribbean and then used the Gulf Stream and westerly trade winds to migrate eastward to Atlantis, the British Isles (Stonehenge), and later populated the Mediterranean becoming the Pre-Egyptian, and Pre-Babylonian cultures. They eventually reached the top of the world in Tibet about 17,500 years ago and started the Ramayna Empire.

Within the hundreds of pages, she would explain how these civilizations were much more advanced technologically than we currently give them credit for. Evidence of several large cities still exists in the deserts of India and Pakistan such as Mohenjodaro. Ancient Indian texts from this period tell of antigravity space ships called Vimanas and Astras. They even mentioned a battle with the Atlanteans and their Vailixi machines on the Moon.

The Dogon tribe in central Africa is another example. The Dogon are an ancient people of Mali in Northwestern Africa. They are thought to be the root human civilization. They currently inhabit one of the most inaccessible and inhospitable deserts south of Timbuktu south of the Niger River on the southern edge of the Sahara Desert. There are no paved roads, no electricity, no surface water and little contact with the outside world, the Dogon Territories in the Hombori Mountains have been called the end of the Earth. As Anne points out in her thesis, the name Timbuktu literally means a place almost at the other end of the world, not the beginning.

Studies by British anthropologist Robert Temple, have revealed a stunningly complex and sophisticated Dogon society. But what has amazed and mystified researchers most is the fact that the Dogon have a quite unusual and extensive knowledge of the star system Sirius. For centuries the Dogon believed as their most sacred religious tradition a body of knowledge of the star Sirius

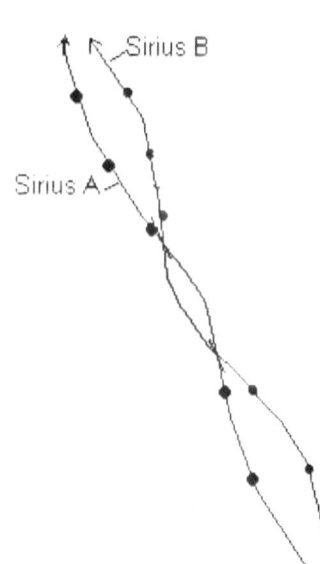

which should be impossible for any primitive tribe to know. They consider that the most important star in the sky is Sirius B, a small star that orbits the bright star Sirius. Sirius B is invisible to the unaided eye and was only photographed via telescope for the first time in 1970. Their ancient cave drawings show the helical rising of Sirius with the Sun and Sirius joined together. This is the same rate as the DNA twist. Their drawings also show the rings of Saturn and the four major moons of Jupiter as well as the elliptical orbit of the invisible star Sirius B around Sirius. They knew it was a heavy star, which it is now known to be far denser than Earth. They also knew that its elliptical orbit is completed once every fifty years, an event they celebrate at exactly the proper moment, even if only once or twice in a person's entire lifetime

Dogon legend has it that this information was given to them by a long-vanished people they call the little blue men.

The Great Flood that has been documented in several myths, legends, and religions of the world was actually the result of the glaciers damming the Teays River valley. This resulted in the formation of a huge inland sea over nine hundred feet deep. It eventually spilled over its western shore flooding the now Ohio River valley and carving a new five hundred mile channel to St. Louis.

It turns out most of the crop circles discovered on Earth occur near ancient ritual sites such as Stonehenge in England and now here in Ohio at the Serpent Mound near Peebles. A significant number of the crop circles found in North America were actually found in Ohio.

The Teayans knew the path to the stars and the secrets to torsional energy. The Serpent Mound was not so much a ritual site as it was a symbol of respect for torsional wave energy. As a matter of fact, most of these sites are also peppered with petroglyphs or pottery shards depicting spirals.

Consider this: the story of Adam and Eve is based upon fact and science. Indirectly, the snake did impart the sum of all knowledge unto humans. That mound symbolizes it right here near Peebles, Ohio. Thus the Garden of Eden was in the Buckeye state, not Ancient Babylonia or the Jungles of Africa. Humankind was literally pushed out of Eden by the hand of God, as an ice sheet covering half a continent and the rising waters of Lake Tight.

Think of it. What animal has the ability to coil into a spiral, to undulate in a wave pattern, and when mating, can wrap around each other in a double helictical pattern representing the DNA molecule? Additionally, snake toxins have some of the most complex mixture of enzymes and proteins.

We are now just starting to study snakes using DNA techniques. But we have already found a few surprises. Preliminary results indicate that the vipers are not the most recent of the snakes, but instead diverged from much, much earlier forms.

From fossil and DNA studies, it appears that snakes underwent a rapid radiation in their initial burst of evolution, with a number of different lifestyles appearing at once and then developing independently and in parallel afterwards. There quite literally could have been a snake in the grass when hit by a MASER blast over twenty million years ago.

The intent of the Delta G Program Office was to gradually sensitize the world population to the idea that aliens existed and that the Earth was not the center of the universe in terms of intelligence, not even close. But how do you tell the world population that the aliens have been visiting Earth for perhaps millions of years, and that they are only now noticing us; that we humans, occupy it, with some sort of fascination and curiosity?

Part of Anne's new position as Bioinformatics Engineering Professor at Wright State University was to expose the world to new revolutionary Earth-shattering concepts and ideas such as the retro-migration of advanced civilizations from the North American continent and into the Mediterranean. This very concept in itself would be highly controversial, let alone any discussion of their alien connections. It would fly in the face of conventional wisdom and knowledge. Entire cultures and governments took pride in the fact that they were the cradle of civilization, such as the Egyptians, Romans, Greeks, Africans, Babylonians, and even Chinese.

In Phase I of the thesis concept, the Delta G Program, through Anne's doctorate thesis, was about to expose the retro-civilization theory. As soon as that idea took off and gradually established itself as a somewhat valid scientific theory, then the Phase II plan would expose the world to the concept of torsional waves. Finally, Phase III involved the discovery and exposure of the Peebles shell, the unified field theory solved and the concept of interstellar beings. The public would be invited in on its discovery and excavation. This would be the next Reality TV.

By this time it was hoped the legitimate governments of the world would have a twenty-year head start on reverse engineering and analyzing the several dozen shells already recovered from all over the world. The technologies behind the shells would be closely guarded long after the concepts have been exposed. These technologies would have much too devastating an impact on world economies and governments. The protection of civil society and governments was a top priority. Too much knowledge at the wrong time and in the wrong hands could be a very dangerous thing. The old adage that knowledge equals power and that absolute power corrupts absolutely was true.

Dave and Anne were only a couple people in a select group that understood that the power of the Giza pyramids actually resided on the opposite side of the globe, four small islands protruding just above the surface near coordinates 27° 54' S by 143° 30' W near Bass Islands.

Both Dave and Anne had spent the last twenty years of their lives preparing and being groomed to be part of this awesome responsibility. As Integration Officer, Dave was personally familiar with the shells, their potential, and their threats.

He was keenly aware of the threat the rogue T-wave runner possessed as it shot through the Earth at the apogee of its expanding logarithmical retro-time spiral as it once again accelerated towards deep space. Its first encounter with its host planet was only a mere eighty years ago. The second would be 160, the third 320, and so on. Eventually, it would target and hit near the cradle of civilization almost 12,000 years ago near present day Peebles, OH. It had to be stopped, destroyed or redirected somehow.

CHAPTER 40
A Shot of Spirochete

This time, the *Nautilus* floated stationary over the second most remote place on planet earth, the South Pole. This particular experiment had been planned in excruciating detail. However, should anything go wrong, biologically that is, the super cold atmosphere at 110,000 feet above the South Pole would hopefully keep any mutated bacteria from spreading. Also, the hole in the ozone layer actually helped. The Sun's UV energy would also zap anything that might escape should the one in five million chances go wrong. Even though the odds were extreme, they weren't exactly zero either. After all, someone wins the Lotto every week.

Dave rode this experiment out back at the Lair and watched on a video feed as his wife was now preparing to concoct the elixir. One beaker contained a few billion strands of Treponema byrantii bacteria that had been freeze dried at Wright-Patterson. It was about to be mixed with a beaker of warm deuterium. Deuterium, or more commonly known as heavy water, was selected as the rehydration media as well as the carrier for the bacteria as it was poured down the gullet of the shell. Interestingly enough, deuterium was predicted in 1926 by Walter Russell, using his spiral periodic table. Also, as far as anyone new, this particular shell reacted neutrally to any deuterium or hydrogen-3 element. Also, pure deuterium had no impurities, heavy metals, or minerals in it to skew the data. However, the viscosity was a little higher than distilled water. Hopefully it would flow to the shell's center, and not get bogged down with surface tension problems. One other important factor was that the deuterium would act as a moderator or inhibiter in cell growth and also inhibit any DNA mutations via mitosis. In effect, it was to act as a safety valve and give some time to abort the experiment.

The idea to use deuterium resulted from the recent autopsy results of the Greys that Anne participated in. They showed some starling and yet interesting DNA results. First of all, their DNA was more closely aligned to a bovine than a human, and not reptilian as expected. This made sense since their skin was more akin to the dolphin family than any reptile. The second surprise was that their DNA was deuterium based. Anne and the Team also assumed that their body mass was composed of deuterium similar to humans that were 72 percent water. The Greys' bodies were severely dehydrated yet well preserved in the embalming fluid. Their DNA was extracted from their bones.

DNA contains hydrogen in the nitrogenous bases and in the deoxyribose sugars. In fact, the DNA molecule takes the shape of a double helix because of hydrogen bonds between the nitrogenous bases that are across from each other. When heavy water is introduced into a cell, deuterium atoms gradually replace hydrogen atoms in DNA molecules. The bonds between the deuterium atoms are stronger than the original hydrogen bonds; this has the effect of the DNA molecules becoming more rigid. The mitotic process is heavily dependent on the hydrogen bonds of DNA, so any alteration of this will adversely affect mitosis. For example, DNA replication requires the double helix to uncoil and when deuterium is incorporated in DNA, it makes it harder to uncoil because of the increased rigidity. Or if the DNA does replicate, deuterium oxide can still affect mitosis. When the DNA begins to coil into chromosomes, the deuterium oxide causes the chromosome to become shortened and thickened. The effect is also felt in the cytoplasm, which becomes more rigid due to the increased viscosity of heavy water and again makes cellular division all the more difficult to take place. Very importantly, heavy water is unique among all anti-mitotic agents in that it works on many stages of mitosis, unlike most others which act specifically on only one stage of mitosis.

The planet that the Greys came from was obviously based upon hydrogen-3, so it made sense in more ways than one, to try pouring the bacteria down a shell's gullet with heavy water as the medium.

If everything went right, some sort of feedback should be registered. It was sort of like booting up a PC, or loading the operating system on a computer. But in this case, there was no GUI, or graphical user interface. The lab was sealed and could be jettisoned in an instant if things started to go haywire. The valve from the deuterium beaker was turned robotically from the control room. The heavy water flowed into the beaker containing the bovine bacteria. They were mixed together in a slow mechanical oscillation machine. The contents were heated to a temperature of 104.5, the temperature of a healthy milk cow. Dave thought to himself, "Damn, the witch doctors might have been onto something. There could actually be some ring of truth in the ability to read entrails."

The camcorders began recording, along with every other sensor and electronic measuring device known to man trained on the gullet opening. After an hour of warming and stirring, the elixir was poured down the gullet. It was funneled down to as far as the surgical tubing would go. After all, there was no need for the fluid to be wasted on wetting the inside surface of the shell. The surgical tubing was pulled out when all of the fluid had drained into the shell.

At first nothing happened. In contrast, when the hydrogen gas was accidentally exposed to one of the shells by the cutting torch, the resulting helium reaction was almost instantaneous. No one knew what to expect with pouring this concoction down the shell. It was known that shells worked well submerged underwater to produce helium-3. However, the heavy water should make this fusion process less likely. Hopefully, no explosive gasses or compounds would be generated. That was considered when limiting the experiment to only a liter of fluid. If this thing belched, hopefully it wouldn't be an explosive one.

After a few minutes, a high pitch screech was heard followed by a flash of red light. The light was a laser burst and the noise had a familiar ring to it. The sensors and instruments had registered the visual and audio signals and the Cray was busy crunching the data.

Just then an alarm sounded in the RV lab. The MIST tanks were again overheating and vibrating. The MIST particles started to fly out of the containment vessel and gathered in midair in the central part of the ship in the landing bay. There were trillions of them but they were swarming like mad hornets. Everyone was awestruck. The MIST particles had always been autonomous and nonthreatening. They were now a swarm that started to spin and flatten out. The resulting disk was only a few MIST particles thick but covered the entire width of the landing bay. The disk started to spin at a constant rate and then began to wobble up and down. Dr. Rapp was the first to figure that the wobble left and right had a period proportional to the wobble front and back that was exactly 0.618 to 1, the Golden Ratio. The disk took on more detail as it began to spin. It was an exact replica of the rings of Saturn with gaps and spacing and coloring. The oscillation must have represented the rings wobbling cycle of over several million years.

Just then the shell made another burst of light and another high pitched screech. They did not isolate the shell from sound or noise. Thus, even the laser flashes made their way through to the control room window and reflected off the structural members of the ship until they illuminated the disk. The acoustic waves caused the MIST particles to vibrate and shimmer in the bath of the laser light. The crew couldn't believe their eyes; they were witnessing the projection of a laser disk. Although they couldn't tell what the information was saying, everyone agreed that the disk was playing digital signals. It was a simple stream of zeros and ones, on and offs, or in this case light, no-light. Anyway you read it; it was a digital signal with trillions of bits of information. Dr. Rapp speculated that the MIST particles were in communication with the shell. The ordering of the particles was an exact match of the bacterial data strands within the gullet. They had been aligned in a string of code coiled in the disk. It would take years, maybe even decades to crack the code on this data stream. But at least it was data. The experiment was a tremendous success. As with the DNA extraction on the Greys a generation later, perhaps the next generation of scientists would decipher the signal from the shell.

Anne and Dave appreciated the irony of this discovery. It was made from the intestines of an Amish farmer's cow. The Amish are averse to any technology which they feel weakens the family structure. The conveniences that the rest of us take for granted such as electricity, television, automobiles, telephones and tractors are considered to be a temptation that could cause vanity, create inequality, or lead the Amish away from their close knit community. Little did Doug and Tom's neighbor realize it, but his cow's intestines just expanded the community to include beings from other stars.

CHAPTER 41
Negative Feedback

While Anne was busy dissecting aliens, experimenting with their DNA, and preparing her retro migration thesis, Dave was again busy working the graveyard shift. At 0300, the witching hour, on May 15, 1995, a train derailment was staged to close down Kauffman Avenue running parallel to the CSX railroad tracks adjacent to the Area B steam plant on Wright-Patterson AFB. The staged derailment occurred as the switch engine tuned out onto the main line. The switch engine and two box cars full of ordinance derailed when the switch failed. This particular switch is not used that often and failed due to a faulty tie down, or at least that was the cover story. It was a convenient and compelling excuse to evacuate all personnel from that side of the base.

A C-5 transport plane had just arrived an hour before from Thule AFB Greenland and off loaded shell number twelve at the hot pad in Area C, four miles away. Shell twelve, just like shell six, was an oversized shell fifteen feet in diameter. After removing it from the plane, it was loaded onto a flat car, tarped, and then transported by rail to the steam plant siding in Area B along with several hopper cars full of coal.

Brad Detwiler was the steam plant engineer; one of twenty-eight. He had explicit instructions and a very tight timetable. He was told to remove over a hundred tons of coal out of the storage pit to expose the access portal concealing the rail line and tunnel leading to the Delta G Lair Complex under Building 620.

Most of the twenty-eight were on-site that evening, the Base Civil Engineer (BCE), Base Commander, General Ahrens (ASC Commander), Security Police Commander, and the Delta G Support Team. This was a big event. The staged derailment ensured total evacuation and plenty of room for Brad to work alone for a couple of hours with the front end loader to remove the coal. He was about a half an hour behind schedule. Colonel Dick Caprella, the BCE, knew how to operate a dozer and helped him remove the coal.

By 0400 the doors were exposed. They had not been opened for over ten years since shell number six had been transported to the underground lab.

Caprella and Detwiler put a chain around the rusted handles of the massive steel and concrete double doors. They attached the other end to the front end loader and gently pulled. The doors opened and locked into place exposing the rail tunnel behind them. It was now a simple matter of dropping in two rail extensions to fill the short gap. A special tunnel sled with small diameter rail wheels was pulled out into the pit. The front end loader had a special lifting rig with a spreader bar attached to it. Detwiler lifted it up and over the tarped shell. Colonels Caprella and Sheridan connected the lifting lugs. Detwiler picked the shell clear of the rail car and pivoted it onto the tunnel sled. A clamping mechanism secured the 15,000 pound shell in place. It was now a simple matter of throwing the switch and the cable system pulled the sled up into the tunnel. Once inside, the doors were shut. Detwiler and Caprella spent the next hour and a half pushing and dumping coal back into the storage pit, once again concealing the entrance. The Explosives Ordinance Disposal Team had removed the real ordinance and secured the site. All this took place before the sun came up.

The shell made its slow one mile trek up the slight incline to the Lair. The Delta G Laboratory was fully operational and running at a hundred percent. The linear accelerator, lasers, X-ray machine, and neutron guns were powered up, ready to slice, dice, and probe the next generation shell.

As the shell made it to the end of the tunnel, an overhead crane hoist lifted it off the sled and swung it over to a holding fixture. The overhead monorail trolley then pulled the shell into the newly constructed test chamber. The shell was slowly turned onto its side facing the inner wall.

As the holding fixture began to swing downward, a loud piercing screech was suddenly heard. A flash of blue light lit up the room. A klaxon alarm sounded and the room was immediately evacuated. The same thing was happening in the adjacent chamber with shell number six. As the two shells now faced each other end-to-end, the wall between them dissolved into thin air. The air was being sucked out of the room and the ceiling was in danger of collapse. Anything loose in the room was sucked into either of the two shells. This was another one of those rare events in science. No one had ever lined two shells up end to end before. Something was happening. Just like when you put two speakers facing each other. Some type of nuclear feedback was initiated. The shells had gone supercritical. A torsional wave was generated that was stripping the concrete off the ceilings and floors, exposing red hot reinforcing steel. The monorail beams overhead were melting and bending. The fire sprinkler system went off and halon fire extinguishers discharged.

Dave grabbed the joystick from the hoist and started the winch, nothing. There was no power in the room. Light was being bent 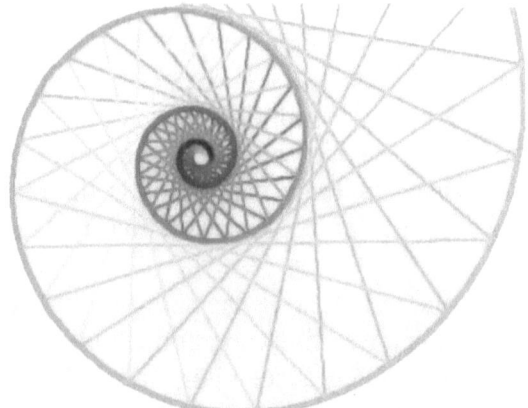 and sucked into the torsional wave. The trolley car was still in the connecting tunnel. Dave opened the high bay door. The air was rushing into the void from the tunnel. The trolley car started to move. It picked up momentum and started to roll toward the shell. It hit the shell with enough force to knock it out of alignment with the adjacent shell. Another flash of red light this time as things settled down. Timken picked himself up off the floor and asked, "What the hell just happened?"

Dave replied "I think we just accidentally hit a criticality point between these two shells. The nuclear material from one shell fed into the other and set up a feedback loop. The resulting annihilation of matter set off a torsional wave. Could it be that simple? Simply a left hand shell placed next to a right hand shell that sets up a feedback loop. If so, this accidental discovery that damn near killed us, might be the breakthrough we were looking for. Isn't that funny?"

Further analysis pointed out some simple geometry. Torsional feedback and resonance reaches a supercritical stage when projected tangential to the inner surface and is reflected off the opposite wall.

CHAPTER 42

Left Hand Not Knowing What the Right Hand is Doing

Like so many of nature's secrets, they are simple to understand once discovered. As the famous scientist, Isaac Newton once said, "this was indeed an eureka moment." Controlling torsional waves was literally as simple as knowing your left hand from your right. It was ironic that the super-secret, paranoid, compartmentalization of science, truth, and knowledge, had just about buried (literally) the secrets of interstellar space travel forever.

General Ahrens shook Dave's hand and said, "The left hand needs to know what the right hand is doing for all things to be right in the world. It will take the world another fifty years to trust each other enough to expose this technology. Delta G will need to be around to spread the seeds of this knowledge, to culti-vate the technology, to enlighten, and to educate. Entire cultures, religions, societies, and governments are going to be turned end-on-end. Entire branches of science such as Biomathematics, Bio-informatics, Spirology, Asymmetrical Science, and now Torsional Wave Mechanics will be taught in schools throughout the world. Unlike the space race, and even the space station, there is tremen-dous potential for international cooperation to put all the pieces together. The UN is an obsolete, bigoted, and corrupt organization and cannot be trusted with the knowledge. The world will have to start over in terms of cooperative forums. Each country is sover-eign and yet about to expand their culture, their knowledge, and their curiosity to the stars. A half a century is but a grain of sand in the scale of time loaded in the Cosmos hourglass."

The general was right. The secrets of T-wave vectoring tech-nology would not last long. Preparing the human race for interstellar travel was going to take some effort. The gap between the haves and the have-nots was about to widen exponentially. Thus, only a handful of countries in the world had the knowledge and the resources to attempt interstellar travel. However, in time the simple nature of this technology would make any nation on Earth capable of traveling the stars. The tapping of this knowledge, power, and energy had the potential to evolve humankind, or make them extinct in an instant. As another famous Isaac, once wrote, "It is change, continuing change, inevitable change that is the dominant factor in society today. No sensible decision can be made any longer without taking into account not only the world as it is, but the world as it will be," by Sir Isaac Asimov, the famous science fiction writer.

Even though the knowledge of the Greys had ended World War II, it started a technological race and eventually the Cold War. Governments gathered, held close, and even fought over alien technology. Several skirmishes since 1947 were the result of discovering and recovering alien technology.

For example, the Falkland Island war was caused by the Argentinean's claim to a shell and a Grey ship that was discovered in the early 1980's on St. George's Island at coordinates 51° 47' 02.05" S by 58° 29' 27.54" W in a secret underground base left by the Nazis. The Argentineans were not privy to the Delta G Program at the time and did not understand the implications of what they had discovered.

The Germans had actually discovered the Grey ship back in 1938. The ship used a mercury disc rotated at several hundred thousand rpm to generate a torsional wave. They attempted to reverse engineer and build a duplicate with the Japanese towards the end of the war.

A map from a Spanish book called *Is Hitler Alive?* shows the route of the U-859 as it passed alongside South Georgia Island, east of the Falkland Islands. She was one of a select number of U-boats to join the *Monsun Gruppe* or Monsoon Group, which operated in the Far East alongside the Imperial Japanese Navy.

Declassified Nazi records show that on April 4, 1944 at 4:40 a.m. the German submarine U-859 left on a mysterious mission carrying sixty-seven men and thirty-three tons of mercury sealed in glass bottles in watertight tin crates.

The sub was sunk six months later on its way to Japan, twenty-three miles west of Penang Malaysia in 160 feet of water by a British submarine. Most of the crew along with the scientists and plans to build the ship perished. One survivor on his death bed about thirty years later told about the mercury cargo and top secret nature of the voyage. Divers checked out his story and found the mercury.

In 1972 a total of twelve tons of mercury were recovered from the U-859 and brought into Singapore. The West German Embassy claimed ownership of the mercury. The Receiver of the Wreck took possession of the mercury, and the High Court of Singapore ruled that "the German state has never ceased to exist despite Germany's unconditional surrender in 1945 and whatever was the property of the German State, unless it was captured and taken away by one of the Allied Powers, still remains the property of the German State..." They clearly intended Germany to recover any and all alien technology from the wreck.

Dave understood now more than ever why even the president of the United States was not privy to the Delta G secrets. This was above and beyond politics. After all, a sovereign nation's secrets were based upon N2K, and presidents didn't have a need-to-know. This was evident when President Bill Clinton was being impeached. If he had known about the Delta G Program, it would have been on CNN if for no other reason to disrupt and divert attention from the impeachment proceedings.

CHAPTER 43
The Sacred List of the Realm

Up to this date in 2004, over two dozen shells had been recovered from all over the world. Many had been found near impact crater sites, magnetic anomalies, or extremely remote locations with diverse ecologies. There were several more that had been located but were inaccessible do to location, depth under water, encasement in rock, buried in sediment, under sand dunes, buried in glacial till, or near population centers.

The Delta G Program Office had spent decades trying to replicate how the Greys generated T-waves. Their efforts were often complicated, expensive, and involved time dependent physical changes of massive amounts of terrestrial matter. The Greys had come up with a simpler, natural, and an "at will" methodology to traverse the galaxy, not dependent on the rapid densification of matter. They simply used the periodic table to their advantage to transmute matter and amplify and steer the resulting T-waves.

As Integration Officer, Dave insisted on learning as much as he could about each shell and its history. Drs. Rapp and Timken were very helpful in this regard and prepared a highly classified list called *The Realm*. Within this document, each shell was listed in its order of discovery and had been given a code name. This name gave the shell some personality instead of just a bureaucratic number.

Dave studied the list in detail and set out to integrate information from the other Delta G Program Offices worldwide. It was time to fire up the Joint Worldwide Intelligence Communications System (JWICS) and start mining the data streams. He soon discovered that it was not just a case of other program offices hording information or keeping things compartmentalized on purpose, but more times than not, they held information that they did not know was relevant to other programs and discoveries.

The Peebles Shell would eventually be excavated. As such, it had to have an earth shattering, profound and insightful name as this one would be the first shell exposed to the world community. The name Peebles just would not cut it. Since it was buried under hundreds of feet of glacial till and would drastically shift and shape the world's views well into the future it would be called Glacial Change.

Dave and Anne spent the next three years back at Area 51 in Nevada. Now that torsional waves could be generated, directed, and throttled, it was a relatively simple matter to build a craft around this technology to traverse the universe.

The shell recovered from the Coral Castle was sacrificed to learn its inner secrets and workings. That shell had been nick-named Excalibur, after the fabled sword that King Arthur pulled from the rock. The original Excalibur had some apparent links to DNA and serpents. Legends do sometimes have some basis in truth.

> *"Then they heard Cadwr Earl of Cornwall being summoned, and saw him rise with Arthur's sword in his hand, with a design of two serpents on the golden hilt; when the sword was unsheathed what was seen from the mouths of the two serpents was like two flames of fire, so dreadful that it was not easy for anyone to look."*
>
> —From *The Mabinogion*, translated by Jeffrey Gantz.

As had been speculated by the Delta G nuclear physicists at Dreamland, the Zero Point Energy source was based upon the Grey Matter 182 element at the center of the shell. Dissection of the shell was first attempted by bisecting it down the middle. The damn thing just couldn't be cut straight down the middle, either mechanically with diamond impregnated wire saw, electro-discharge machining, gamma knives or even high power laser. When the gamma knife cut in closer towards the center the power would grow weaker and always move off center. The diamond wire cutter would always bind and snap. It was if it had a mind of its own and was aware of the probing.

Finally, chemical milling was tried. The three percent tungsten content of the shell worked to some advantage. A peroxide based dissolving solution was developed. The shell was laid on its side and was dissolved a few microns at a time by using a pool of peroxide floating atop a mercury bath. The peroxide's chemical affinity for the tungsten component in the shell was all it took to break down its microstructure. As the shell's outer layer was dissolved away, the Grey Matter eventually fell away and sank down through the mercury while everything else floated and was skimmed off. The Grey Matter 182 pellet was only about one ten thousandths of an inch in diameter, but amazingly it weighed over two pounds. It was so dense, in fact, that the gravitational fields of the neutrons and protons overpowered the nuclear binding energy causing a mini singularity. The event horizon of this singularity was a fusion machine that spun off torsional waves and fused hydrogen to helium-3. With this particular shell, it was tuned to produce an antigravity wave that was amplified as it twisted out of the shell. Objects or matter that had a corresponding Grey Matter 182 core would be rendered weightless. This was the case with the coral rock and limestone. As had been discovered from the search on Elsmere Island, that Ed Leedskalnin had in fact acquired a pellet of GM 182 through his mentor.

We think his mentor got it from a treasure trove located inside or under the Rosslyn Chapel in Scotland. This is another interesting place on earth. It is a very intricate fifteenth century church filled with intricate carvings and so named, a library in stone. Just about every surface of the church is covered with these carvings. Both the church and carvings are made of the same type oolitic limestone of the pyramids. Inside the hollow core of one of the most intricate and famous carvings called the Apprentice Pillar, Delta G found several tons of GM 182.

The Apprentice Pillar gets its name from a legend dating from the eighteenth century, which involves a master mason in charge of the stonework in the chapel and his young apprentice. According to the legend, the master mason does not believe that the apprentice can perform the complicated task of carving the column, without seeing the original which formed the inspiration for the design. The master mason travels to see the original himself, but upon his return is enraged to find that the upstart apprentice has completed the column anyway. In a fit of jealous anger, the mason takes up his mallet and strikes the apprentice on the head, killing him. As punishment for his crime, the master mason's face is carved into the opposite corner to forever gaze upon his apprentice's pillar.

The pillar consists of two intertwined spirals from floor to ceiling. At the base are eight dragons tail to tail. At the top are thirteen angels surrounding the pillar. This not only represents the DNA sequence, but also acknowledges the golden ratio.

How Ed's mentor got the GM 182 out of the chapel is a mystery, but Ed simply had to place it under any object he wanted to lift and then used the aluminum door as an on-off switch to shield the T-waves from the shell in his basement to levitate the object to the desired location.

Mercury was also becoming a much sought after commodity in the Delta G business. It was pure luck that the Nevada Test Site had huge reserves of cinnabar, one of the primary minerals containing mercury metal. After all, the front gate of the Nevada Test Site, including home of its industrial complex and administrative facilities, is located in Mercury, Nevada. It wasn't named that way after a thermometer or because it was hot in the Nevada desert. It was named after the metal that was mined and manufactured there long before the Atomic Energy Commission or DOE took over the land.

As it turns out, the most efficient and effective way to produce a torsional wave runner for interstellar travel is simply make it out of a sphere of pure mercury, with a core of Grey Matter 182 at its center.

Buried in 110 feet of sand just south of Cerro Cubabi in the Sand Dunes, the intact Elegante shell and mercury sphere became invaluable in studying how Grey technology and T-runners work. It was accidently discovered when placing a He3 compressed hose line through one of the four inch diameter null points of the sphere that would expand it like a balloon or bubble to enable access to the inner core of the Greys' Crew capsule. Just recessed seating areas in the inner mercury-lined wall and holographic projections of what appeared to be fractal patterns. There were no crew survival gear, water, and or waste lines. They appeared to have total control over the shells transmutation capability and navigation technology.

This also produces one heck of an electrical battery that lasts eons to be used for powering the ship. Mercury has some very strange and peculiar properties in its own right. It is very dense with a specific gravity 13.6 times that of water. The mercury will protect the inner sphere from radiation and also prevent breathing atmosphere or other gases from escaping from within. This is especially true with the very small molecules of helium-3 that like to permeate through just about anything. The mercury is also self-healing in the event of micrometeorite punctures. The surface is ten times more reflective to microwaves, torsional waves and photons than the beryllium units that earthlings manufactured. This interstellar ship involves very few moving parts to wear out with no seams to crack or rupture. The electrovoltic potential between the mercury and GM 182 would heat the sphere above its freezing point of -34F and it could be spun to keep it shaded at a relatively low temp of 600°F to prevent boiling when near stellar objects. On entering the atmosphere, mercury also ionizes fairly easily to provide a thermobaric insulator.

Guidance used an ingenious gyroscope that used huge spinning disks of mercury weighing hundreds of tons. These disks would be spun up to 20,000 rpm and would be up to twenty feet in diameter. The resulting centripetal force would result in two very important physical phenomena. First, it would form the disks of mercury into a parabolic shape. Secondly and more interestingly, just like in the early days of the Manhattan project where we used centrifuges to enrich uranium, the spinning mercury would accelerate molecules so that particles of different masses are physically separated in a gradient along its radius of rotation. What is separated is in fact Grey Matter-182. The resulting torsional wave that is generated then becomes amplified and focused by the parabolic shape. Just like with criticality in the fission process, a critical mass is accomplished between the GM-182 being produced and the target sphere of GM-182 in the focal point of the parabola and becomes self-sustaining and controllable. This concept is then coupled with three adjacent shells aligned along the x, y, and z axis to both propel and steer the sphere.

Building the sphere would just be a matter of time and money. The only question now was where to point the darn thing? That answer came on a sunny day in the plains of San Agustin, west of Socorro, New Mexico near Kirtland Air Force Base. This is home to the Very Large Array (VLA) radio telescope, part of the National-al Radio Astronomy Observatory, one of the most powerful radio telescopes in the world. The VLA consists of two dozen eighty-two foot radio dishes that can be moved on tracks to cover an area as large as twenty by twenty miles. The antennas are linked together to form a single image of the radio source being studied.

The Delta G Office really had nothing to do with the VLA as they assumed the Greys did not use radio waves to communicate. They used directed MASERs. Delta G also assumed that any communications would involve complex multiplexing frequencies in a code impossible to decipher. Thus, they were surprised when the Greys rung our doorbell again. This time in an unmistakable tone of two overlapping frequencies detected chirping in the 3,820 MHz and 6,180 MHz range. Each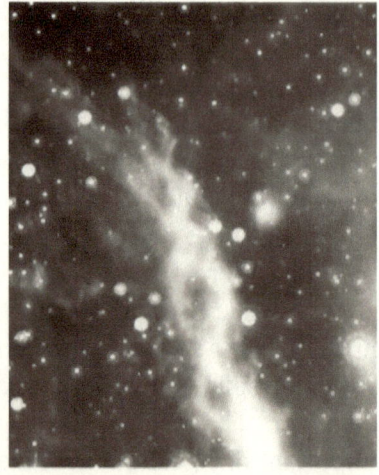
chirp was first 1.4 seconds long followed by another, then another at 2.8 seconds, then one at 4.2 seconds and another dozen or so chirps each progressively longer in length. The Greys had no idea of what our time measurement scale was, so they could not use timing in their signal. However. this sequence was independent of time with each progressive build on top of the other. The pattern

was unmistakably a Fibonacci sequence of ten chirps of exponential length. The frequencies were not random either. 382 GHz and 618 GHZ were the exact proportions for the DNA sequencing overlap. And the most amazing thing of all was the direction from where it came. The direction of the signal came from galactic longitude 0.064 and galactic latitude of 0.68 degrees near the center of our Milky Way Galaxy. The VLA had the good sense to contact the Pentagon to crosscheck with any space-related experiments or signals. The Delta G Office got wind and classified the detection as BTS (Beyond Top Secret). Now every DoD and NASA telescope were pointed in the direction of this signal and what they found there was truly stunning.

They found a double helix-shaped nebula of two intertwining strands wrapped around each other of the exact proportions to the DNA molecule. The nebula was approximately eighty light years in length, and situated only three hundred light years away from the massive black hole at the center of the Milky Way. Most nebulae are either spiral galaxies full of stars or formless amorphous conglomerations of dust and gas. What was found indicated a high degree of order. The magnetic field in that part of the galaxy is 1,000 times that of the Earth's. The magnetic flux somehow formed a torsional wave that propagated through the nebula cloud. This could not be a random event. Thus it was proven there is a direct link between DNA, magnetic fields, and torsional waves.

The frequency detected fell well within the microwave range (3,000 to 30,000 MHz). Microwave ovens operate at a standard frequency of 2,450 MHz. In interacting with matter, microwave radiation acts to produce molecular rotation and torsion, which manifests itself through heat. Thus again microwaves twist the matter of the universe

Although no one technically figured out the exact meaning of Anne's sketch she had made a decade ago, it was clear that her RV vision was mostly on the mark. The T-wave runner had arrived at the coordinates she specified. It had ridden the torsional wave and slung around the Sun using its magnetic field.

It was clear now that the Greys were pointing in this direction. Although the shells in their own way where interesting and shed light on many mysteries of how the universe worked including Earth's own anthropological and biological evolutional and history, it was truly the discovery, collection and eventual understanding of the GM 182 within them that became the focus of Delta G now.

Now that Delta G had cracked the code on how to communicate with the Greys using the rings of Saturn to read the ripples in space and time they would provide the blueprints used to build the ship to the stars.

Using a triple arrangement of the shells at Dreamland to generate a T-wave to launch, and steer a mercury orb to Lagrange Point 2 made it possible to collect enough material there to construct a space habitat that supported a crew of eighteen.

Also, the huge deposits of GM 182 and mercury left on the Moon by the Greys for us to use would insure enough material to get us to the DNA nebula. Another triplex set of shells near the lunar spiral crater on the dark side would be used to launch the first manned T-wave runner.

Chapter 44

Mercury Rising on the Moon

The lunar surface proved to be a very effective launch pad for T-wave runners. There was very little magnetic field to distort and interfere with wave propagation. What little fields that did exist were stable and predictable and easily dealt with. There wasn't any atmosphere to worry about so aerodynamics was not a factor and no shockwaves to contend with. The gravitational force on the Moon is one sixth of that of Earth's, allowing for more mercury and rotational energy that could be transferred to the mercury rotors. This important factor also allows for more GM 182 per volume of space within the runner. Spinning up to 200 tons of mercury to 20,000 rpm would require huge amounts of energy on Earth. Not to mention the environmental concerns if everything flew apart in a catalytic explosion.

Smaller wave runners had been built on earth based upon the earlier beryllium reflective corkscrew design using methods to rapidly densify huge volumes of adjacent

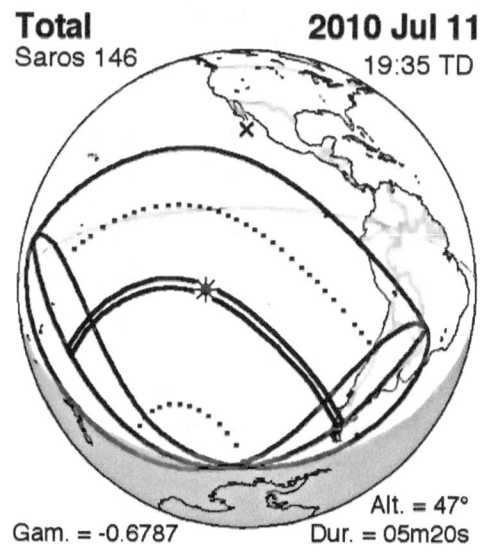

Total
Saros 146

2010 Jul 11
19:35 TD

Gam. = -0.6787

Alt. = 47°
Dur. = 05m20s

materials, such as playa, talc, sea water, and ice. Now that the secrets of the original Roswell shells had finally been cracked, it was now known that simply using three shells pointed at 137.5 degree angles to each other can easily steer and bend the waves. The waves could also be focused and amplified via a parabolic spinning mercury pools. T-waves could be completely blocked or attenuated using a simple block of aluminum. This meant that a relatively large six-manned T-wave runner could now be built very safely with predictable and controllable results with only ten percent of the number of parts as a space shuttle. As a matter of fact, steering was simply a matter of using Distant Viewing to tell the runner where you want to go via mind control. The rpm of the spinning mercury and relative position of the shells bends the T-wave in the direction you want to travel.

It turns out crew environmental controls and life support were no problem either. The transmutation ability of the shells produced all the oxygen and drinking water needed. Food was still a bit of a problem as the shells were tuned to the Grey's DNA and metabolism. The crew still had to rely on good ol' MREs.

Over two billion dollars were spent in the mid-eighties to construct SLC-6 on Vandenberg AFB to launch space shuttles. Although they never launched any, the control facilities proved invaluable in monitoring and coordinating T-wave runner launches on the Moon. Dave looked at the chronograph on the wall of launch control center. It read 07-11-10 0005 Zulu or Greenwich Time. It was just after midnight, a half hour till launch.

Anne gave Dave a glance and a wink as she peered up over her bioinformatics console. As the mission control director, Dave was monitoring the status of the launch facilities. On the big board on the right quadrant of the control room was a projection of the solar eclipse that was about to occur over the Southern Pacific.

The MASER satellites station in halo orbits at L1 and L2 were focused on the coordinates: -29.979063156584917,-148.8654327392578 in the South Pacific just a few miles southwest of Rapa Iti Island. These coordinates were the exact opposite side of the globe as the pyramids of Giza.

Colonel Boop snugged up his chest harness and then reached

up overhead to flip on the cabin camera. Although there were few moving parts in the actual wave runner, there were a zillion components that could go wrong with life support, communications, navigation, instrumentation, and telemetry. These thoughts weighed in heavily on the very first superluminal human to be sent outside the solar system on a test run of sorts. Instrumentation from six previous unmanned runners showed the launch procedures to be well within the norms for human survival. Hopefully the fidelity of these test runners was adequate to cover ninety-nine percent of the expected. It was the other one percent that earned Colonel Boop is hazardous duty pay.

Anne clicked in over the com set, "BP and HR within tolerance Colonel, enjoy the ride." "Thank you, Doctor Sheridan, I'll send you a post card. If Einstein is correct, the US Post Office will postdate it before I even lift off."

Compared to the early rocket launches in their cumbersome space suits and helmets, Colonel Boop actually looked relaxed in his tab shirt and running shorts. The safety philosophy had shifted some for this launch. It was felt, if things went to hell in a hand basket, a hundred pounds of Buck Rogers spacesuit ain't going to save your ass; might as well be comfortable.

Anne clicked in again, "Cabin air seventy-two, body core ninety-nine and outside lunar surface temp above the boiling point of water up there at Reiner Gamma crater. How do you feel?" Boop replied coolly, "A-OK, Doctor."

Dave then broke in. "Break, Break this is the launch director, T-minus 15 minutes, all status lights green. On my mark activate the rotor core. Three, two, one, mark." Just then Boop touched a key pad and 6,000 volts of electricity charged through a magnetic superconducting core in the center of the ship. This started the mercury pool to start rotating, slow at first, but like a locomotive picking up speed and momentum quickly. Since that was the only manual thing Boop had to do prior to the computers and automation kicking in, he cranked up the volume in the cabin to the old 70's hit, *Moon Shadow*, by Cat Stevens.

Dave responded to the music piping in over his headset coolly, "Nice choice, and very fitting. Can you crank her down a notch

for a status report? Lunar shadow is approaching French Polynesia and will be over Rapa Iti as advertised. T-waves are merging
on the island as projected, awaiting amplification affect."

Boop clicked his mike twice in acknowledgement. The solar
eclipse would scarcely be noticed by 99.99 percent of the Earth's
population as it was almost entirely over the South Pacific. However, little did they know its ramification. This was a very rare
event when the Sun, Earth, and Moon aligned nearly perfectly
with the Sun directly over the Giza plain in Egypt, the centroid
for land mass and the Moon over the centroid of Earth's sea mass
opposite Giza. The T-waves will project from the spinning mercury generator in the wave runner and then hit 99.99 percent water
centered at Rapa Iti lagoon, amplify them through the Earth's core,
bounce back from the base of the Giza pyramid and then reflect
back to Reiner Gamma crater where they get focused within the
spinning mercury to strike the target pellet of GM-182. Sounds
simple enough, but can a human be sent out to near the center of
the Milky Way riding a torsional wave and then be slung shot back
by swinging around a massive black hole to then hit a pinpoint
orbit around the Moon? As in the early rocket days, it worked for
the monkeys.

At T-minus five minutes Colonel Boop again snugged up his
five point harness and neck brace. Even though test shots showed
no vibration or perceptible acceleration to the test articles and
chimps, NASA and old pilots were set in their ways. Boop continued through his checklist strapped to his knee board. Most were
toggle switch throws to turn on cameras and sensors. The computer would do ninety-nine percent of the work on this one. Earlier test shots via remote viewing had set the shell gimbals for their
departure trajectory. If all else failed, Boop was to put himself in
a RV state and vector the ship back to the moon base.

At T-minus one minute the mercury was spinning at 18,500
rpm. The aluminum shutter was still closed over the parabolic
beryllium mirror focused upon the GM-182 pellet suspended
by the ununpentium 115 rods overhead. The aluminum shutter
blocked the T-waves from reaching the shells until the very last
microsecond when the Eclipse reached its maximum. Dave did

his green board status check with all of his launch team. Everything checked out A-OK.

At T-minus 10 seconds the rpm were at the required 20,000 rotations and the traditional countdown crackled over the PA system. When finally the long anticipated word "launch" was reached, there was a collective "Oh, wow!!" in the control room. The T-runner glowed yellow green for a few moments, hovered over the launch site, and then spun out of sight in an instant. What awestruck Dave while viewing the launch site monitors was the swirling dust cloud shaped like a boomerang spinning up off the lunar surface. "Hot damn," Dave thought, "this is déjà vu", as he fondly remembered his experience on the ice cap that fateful day twenty-five years ago.

The List of the Realm

ID	NAME	LOCATION
1	Corona 1, 2 and 3	Corona, NM

COORDINATES
Location of Grey Crew remains @ 33° 56' 28.91" N by 105° 18' 29.74"W Three shells located @ 34° 21' 10.28" N by 105° 56' 56.97"W Debris found @ Atkinson Flats crater near 34° 15' 16.36" N by 105° 59' 21.04"W

DISCOVERY

AGE	Unknown

EXTRACTION: Originally extracted and shipped to WPAFB 1947

PHYSICAL PROPERTIES: All appear same

Weight:	1,357 lbs.	DIAMETER	5 .43 feet
MATL		MASER FREQ: 96 GHz	

UNIQUE CHARACTERISTICS:

The temperature inside these shells decreases at a constant rate of 1.618 degrees K per 0.2 wraps of the spiral and is unaffected by outside ambient conditions.

Shells found to amplify telluric currents

DISPOSITION: Currently located at Dreamland Delta G Labs – Area 53

COMMENTS:

The original shell discovery, or Roswell incident, centers on an area northwest of Corona, NM near and in the Cibola National Forest. A Grey Torsional Wave Generator is still buried under a Native American mound shaped as a nautilus shell located at 34° 15' 48.58" N by 105° 58' 41.21"W.

The Roswell ship was on a spiral vector approach to this location when it crashed short of the intended landing zone (LZ). A line drawn from where the crew capsule and five corpses that were found on the Foster Ranch (33° 56' 28.91" N by 105° 18' 29.74"W) to the LZ located at the Atkinson Flats crater (34° 15' 16.36" N by 105° 59' 21.04"W) passes over the T-wave generator. The Corona 1, 2, 3 shells were all located in an area in the northwest quadrant of the Cibola National Forest (34° 21' 10.28" N by 105° 56' 56.97"W). An exhaustive search of this area of New Mexico for additional shells has had no results.

Early airborne radars encountered "strange" ground effect phenomena in this area. Two pipelines were built straddling the crew compartment recovery site by about eight miles. The pipeline converged at Kirkland AFB one hundred miles to the northwest. The pipelines were filled with distilled water and were used as a giant dowsing or divining rod to detect microwave and torsional waves emanating from the area. This was the first US attempt to detect gravitational waves. The phenomena known as the telluric current effect is common on long metallic objects, such as transmission lines and pipelines.

Telluric current effects on pipelines have been observed for nearly half a century. The first extensive investigation of telluric currents was made in the Midwest US by Gideon and coworkers for the American Gas Association. Construction for the Alaska pipeline in the high latitude region noted for enhanced telluric current activity prompted further investigations. Subsequently, other high latitude pipelines were shown to be affected and reports of telluric current effects were also obtained for pipelines in New Zealand, Africa and Germany, as well as on the seafloor. Most telluric currents are produced by geomagnetic disturbances, although tidally-induced effects have also been reported. As well as pipelines, other systems such as power lines and phone cables are affected and these are just one class of technological system that is affected by geomagnetic disturbances.

ID	NAME	LOCATION
2	Narwhal	Greenland

COORDINATES
66° 15' N 37° 33' W

DISCOVERY

AGE	<12,000 years

EXTRACTION: US Navy and Danish Coast Guard removal from ice flow

PHYSICAL PROPERTIES

Weight:	4,225 lbs.	DIAMETER	8 feet
MATL	WgCCoNi	MASER FREQ	22GHz

UNIQUE CHARACTERISTICS:
Appears to affect the human dream state and unconscious state. Enhances Distant Viewing (DV)

DISPOSITION:
DISPOSITION: Currently located aboard the Delta G Airship Nautilus as a helium generator and DV experimentation

COMMENTS:

This was called the Narwhal Pod due to the fact that a shell was found in a fjord on the east coast of Greenland in an iceberg surrounded by dozens of narwhals swimming in a clockwise orbit around the iceberg.

This shell precipitated the building of the Airship fleet and the Icecap DYE Sites. From the earlier findings of the three shells from the Roswell incident, it was believed that others may be present on the icecap.

The spiral shaped tusks of the narwhals detected the T-waves emitted from shells. The purpose of the tusk has been the subject of much debate by marine biologists. Early theories thought that the tusks were used just to pierce the ice covering of the narwhal's Arctic Sea habitat. However, nature is much more complicated than that. The tusks are in fact to be a T-wave sensory organ. Electron micrographs of tusks revealed tens of millions of tiny, deep tubules extending from the tusk's surface, apparently connecting to the narwhal's nervous system. While such tubules are present in the teeth of many species, they do not typically extend to the surface of healthy teeth. The narwhal has the ability to detect subtle changes in pressure, temperature, salinity, and possibly other environmental information. Precursors to T-wave generation in the ocean.

Narwhals have also been found in great numbers near the Tunguska event exit location south of Greenland in the North Atlantic. This is much further south than their normal habitat.

Medieval Europeans believed narwhal tusks to be the horns from the legendary unicorn. These tusks were considered to have magic powers. Vikings and other northern traders were able to sell them for many times their weight in gold. The horns were used to make cups that were thought to negate any poison that may have been slipped into the drink. During the sixteenth century, Queen Elizabeth received a carved and bejeweled narwhal tusk for $10,000,000 (the cost of a large castle) which she used as a scepter. Also, churches would put small chunks of narwhal tusk in the holy water to help speed along miracle cures for ailing churchgoers.

ID	NAME		LOCATION
3	Rainbow		Meyrin, Switzerland
COORDINATES			
46° 14' 07" N 6° 02' 35" E			
DISCOVERY			
AGE		<12,000 years	
EXTRACTION:			
PHYSICAL PROPERTIES:			
Weight:	4,225 lbs.	DIAMETER	8 feet
MATL:		MASER FREQ	
UNIQUE CHARACTERISTICS:			
Bends and focuses gravitational waves. Acts as a gravimetric lens			
DISPOSITION:			
DISPOSITION: This shell is still in place			
COMMENTS:			

Named in deference to the spiral beginning of the yellow brick road in the Wizard of Oz. Also known as Regenbygen. Excavation of this shell started in 1979. Orbital shifts, oscillations, and abnormalities across western Europe were thought to be caused by the large gravimetric effects of the Alps. However, after careful and precise instrumentation and plotting of tangential vectoring lines, an exact location and cause was determined to lie buried under the Alpine valley near the town of Meyrin, Switzerland. This valley at the western edge of Lake Geneva is filled with glacial till from the retreating Rhone glacier from 12,000 years ago. The shell location was verified by gravimetric mapping and then tapped via exploratory drilling in 1981.

Location of the CERN particle accelerator labs was based upon the location of this shell.

ID	NAME	LOCATION
4	Tupilak 1, 2, 3	DYE-3 Greenland Icecap

COORDINATES
65° 10' 57" N 43° 49' 10" W

DISCOVERY
AGE
EXTRACTION:
PHYSICAL PROPERTIES:

Weight:		DIAMETER	
MATL:		MASER FREQ	

UNIQUE CHARACTERISTICS:
DISPOSITION:
COMMENTS:

These three shells were found surrounding a semispherical shaped lake that formed on the Greenland Icecap after a close encounter event on June 6, 1985.

ID	NAME		LOCATION	
5	Elegante		Cerro Cubabi, Mexico	
COORDINATES				
31.72° N by 112.80° W				
DISCOVERY				
AGE				
EXTRACTION:				
PHYSICAL PROPERTIES:				
Weight:		DIAMETER		
DISPOSITION:				
UNIQUE CHARACTERISTICS:				
DISPOSITION:				
COMMENTS:				

Buried in 110 feet of sand just south of Cerro Cubabi in the Sand Dunes. This intact shell and mercury sphere became invaluable in studying how Grey technology and T-runners work. It was accidently discovered that placing a He3 compressed hose line through one of the four inch diameter null points expands the mercury sphere to enable access to the inner core of the Greys' Crew capsule. There were absolutely no moving parts. Just recessed seating areas in the inner mercury lined wall and holographic projects of what appeared to be fractal patterns. There were no crew survival gear, water, and or waste lines. They appeared to have total control over the shells transmutation capability and navigation technology.

ID	NAME	LOCATION
6	Tenoumer	Mauritania, Northwest Africa

COORDINATES
22° 55' 02.92" N 10° 24' 25.72" W

DISCOVERY	
AGE	~1,000,000 yrs.

EXTRACTION:

PHYSICAL PROPERTIES:			
Weight:		DIAMETER	
MATL:		MASER FREQ:	

UNIQUE CHARACTERISTICS:

DISPOSITION:

COMMENTS:

The Dogon tribe knew, in the 1940's that Lake Bosumtwi was formed by a meteor impact and they described it in great detail, including the direction and angle of entry of the meteor. Modern geologists, however, did not even seriously speculate that the lake was formed by a meteor impact until 1979, largely because it is situated in a dense jungle forest that limited access to the lake. (See http://omzg.sscc.ru/impact/ab33.html). The debate went back and forth for years as to whether or not the lake was formed by an impact until recent evidence positively confirmed its meteor origins dated to 1.07 million years. This shell was found at the bottom of the lake in 1982. This shell has strange magnetic properties that oscillate between poles at a frequency of 7253.6281 days, the period of conjunction between Earth, Saturn, and Jupiter.

ID	NAME		LOCATION
7	Anaconda		Machu Picchu, Peru
COORDINATES			
13° 9' 23" S, 72° 32' 34" W.			
DISCOVERY			
AGE		~10,000 years	
EXTRACTION:			
PHYSICAL PROPERTIES:			
Weight:		DIAMETER	
MATL:		MASER FREQ:	
UNIQUE CHARACTERISTICS:			
DISPOSITION:			
COMMENTS:			

This shell location was actually mentioned in the ancient Vedic literature of India in a poem called the Mahabharata, a poem of vast length and complexity. The actual location is, however, very close to Machu Picchu, Peru several thousand miles away.

It describes a heated spinning mercury engine that generates force fields to propel occupants across the heavens. The documents preserved with this shell also led to the development at Dreamland of the Magnetic Field Design (MFD) magnetic plasma vortex field, which disrupts or neutralizes the effects of gravity on mass within proximity, reducing the weight of the aircraft by 89 percent, and making it able to outperform and outmaneuver any craft. Like other high performance aircraft, the maneuvers are limited to the ability of the crew to withstand G forces. But inside the TR-3B the G forces are also reduced by 89 percent. Thus, the crew of the TR-3B can perform a 40G maneuver with the crew feeling 4.2 Gs.

Charged particles of the plasma don't just spin uniformly around the ring, but they tend to take up a synchronized, tightly pitched, helical motion as they move around the ring. This can be understood in a general way as follows: the charged particles moving around the ring act as a current that in turn sets up a magnetic field around the ring. It is a well-known fact that electrons (or ions) tend to move in a helical fashion around magnetic field lines. Although it is a highly complex interaction, it only requires a small leap of faith to believe that the end result of these interactions between the moving charged particles (current) and associated magnetic fields results in the helical motion described above. In other words, the charged particles end up moving in very much the same pattern as the current on a wire tightly wound around a toroidal core.

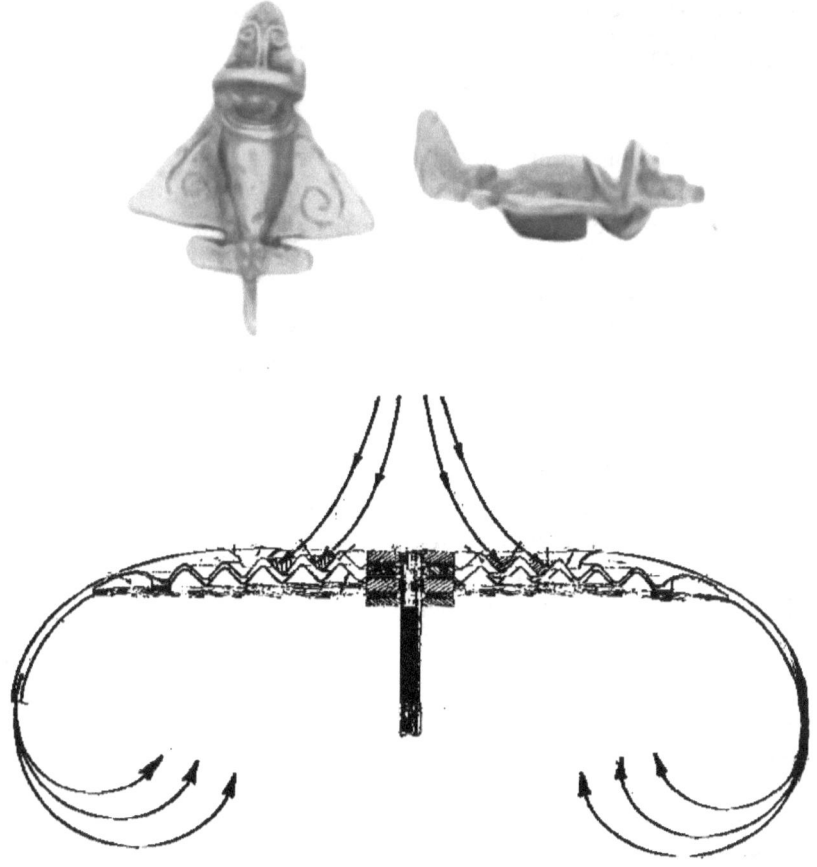

ID	NAME	LOCATION
8	Coanda	Falkland Islands
COORDINATES		
51° 47' 02.05" S 58° 29' 27.54" W		
DISCOVERY		
AGE	EXTRACTION:	
PHYSICAL PROPERTIES:		
Weight:	MATL:	DIAMETER	MASER FREQ:
UNIQUE CHARACTERISTICS:		
DISPOSITION:		
COMMENTS:		

The real reason behind the Falkland Islands War.

A map from a Spanish book called *Is Hitler Alive?* with the route of the Führer's convoy showing it passed alongside South Georgia Island, where later a secret underground base was the focus of a secret battle during the Falkland Islands War.

On April 4, 1944 at 4:40 a.m. the German submarine U-859 left on a mysterious mission carrying sixty-seven men and thirty-three tons of mercury sealed in glass bottles in watertight tin crates. The sub was sunk by a British submarine and most of the crew died. One survivor on his death bed about thirty years later told about the expensive cargo and some divers checked out his story and found the mercury. For what purpose was this mercury to be used? And where were they trying to take it? (Apparently mercury is theoretically usable as a fuel source for certain forms of aerospace propulsion. –Branton Files)

From the Samarangana Sutradhara:

"Strong and durable must the body of the Vimana be made, like a great flying bird of light material. Inside, one must put the mercury engine with its iron heating apparatus underneath it. By means of the power latent in the mercury which sets the driving whirlwind in motion, a man sitting inside may travel a great distance into the sky. The movements of the Vimana are such that it can vertically ascend, vertically descend, and move slanting forwards and backwards. With the help of the machines humans can fly into the air and heavenly beings can come down to Earth."

As a propulsion device, the vaporized form of mercury can be used in a meson particle accelerator. It was proposed by G. Landis in 1989 to allow accelerated mercury atoms to coalesce into droplets en route. In 1996, Bishop proposed the Starseed Launcher accelerator. By ganging many thousands of these devices together, several grams per second can be fired in nearly continuous, collimated matter beams, at speeds from a few meters per second to some fraction of light speed. The receiver on board the spacecraft may be as simple as a pusher plate or may incorporate particle ionization and magnetic mirroring (Singer 1980).

The requirement for a dense material moving at relativistic speeds would explain the use of mercury plasma (heavy ions). If the plasma really spins at 50,000 rpm and the mercury ions are also moving in a tight pitched spiral, then the individual ions would be moving probably hundreds, perhaps thousands of times faster than the bulk plasma spin, in order to execute their screw-thread motions. It is quite conceivable that the ions could be accelerated to relativistic speeds in this manner. I am guessing that you would probably want to strip the free electrons from the plasma, making a positively charged plasma, since the free electrons would tend to counter rotate and reduce the efficiency of the antigravity device.

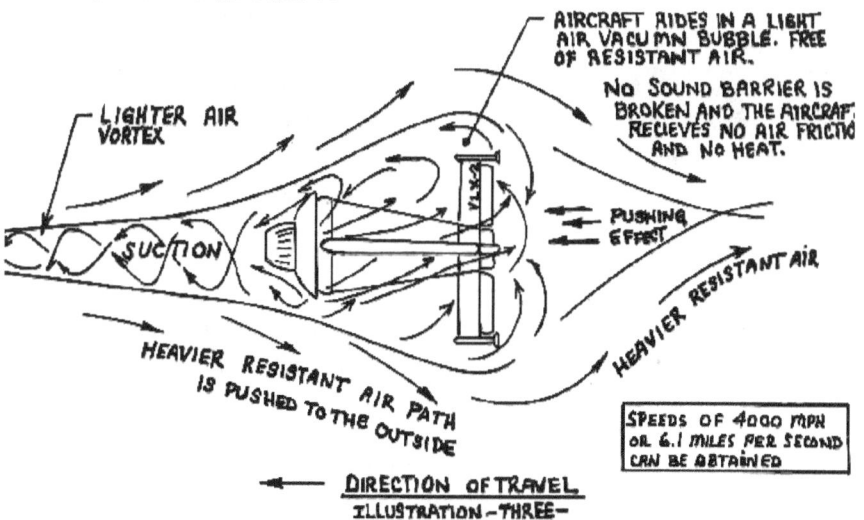

THE AIR VEHICLE PRODUCES A HORIZONTAL VORTEX AHEAD OF THE AIRCRAFT WHICH SUCKS THE VEHICLE INTO IT. THE SPINNING VORTEX CUTS THRU THE MORE RESISTANT AIR AHEAD OF THE AIRCRAFT AND SEPARATES THE HEAVIER AIR WITH THE LIGHTER AIR, WHEREBY CREATING A VACUMN AREA FOR WHICH IT SITS IN. A PUSHING EFFECT FROM THE REAR, HELPS ACCELERATE THE AIRCRAFT.

AIRCRAFT RIDES IN A LIGHT AIR VACUMN BUBBLE, FREE OF RESISTANT AIR.

NO SOUND BARRIER IS BROKEN AND THE AIRCRAF RECIEVES NO AIR FRICTIO AND NO HEAT.

LIGHTER AIR VORTEX

SUCTION

PUSHING EFFECT

HEAVIER RESISTANT AIR

HEAVIER RESISTANT AIR PATH IS PUSHED TO THE OUTSIDE

SPEEDS OF 4000 MPH OR 6.1 MILES PER SECOND CAN BE OBTAINED

DIRECTION OF TRAVEL
ILLUSTRATION -THREE-

ID	NAME	LOCATION
9	Vimanas and Astras	Mount Kailash, India

COORDINATES
31° 04' 05.57" N 81° 19' 06.26" E

DISCOVERY

AGE

EXTRACTION:

PHYSICAL PROPERTIES:

Weight:		DIAMETER	
MATL:		MASER FREQ:	

UNIQUE CHARACTERISTICS:

DISPOSITION:

COMMENTS:

Most Sacred Place in Asia, where three religions meet, Hindu, Buddhism, Bon (Tibetan Vajrayana Buddhism). The Union of Opposites. The Bon Spiral, Ying and Yang

A closer look at the Dropa Stones, the Lolladoff Plate, as well as the use of mercury in devices found near the Mount Kailash, India shells led to a detailed investigation by the Soviet Delta G scientists. They discovered ancient instruments that they suspect were used in navigating the Greys' vehicles in caves in Turkestan and the Gobi Desert. These devices were hemispherical objects made of aluminum ceramic glass with a cone-shape protrusion. X-rays showed a drop of mercury inside. To date they are still figuring out how they worked, but they appear to link the brains RV receptors with the ships directional controls.

The Lolladoff Plate was discovered in Nepal, and appears to show a hovering disk-shaped object in the center of a spiral and a small being, resembling an alien, beside it. The disk also seems to represent the evo-

lutionary process from reptiles to mammals. There was some controversy as to whether the plate was a hoax. However, the Chinese are in possession of 760 Dropa Disks.

ID	NAME	LOCATION
10	Mercury 1, 2 & 3	10 miles southeast of Lancaster, OH
COORDINATES		
CLASSIFIED BTS		
DISCOVERY		
AGE		
EXTRACTION:		
PHYSICAL PROPERTIES:		

Weight:		DIAMETER	
MATL:		MASER FREQ:	

UNIQUE CHARACTERISTICS:
DISPOSITION:
COMMENTS:

Greys intercept and return Wave Runner #1 encased in Mercury Metal Sphere

ID	NAME		LOCATION
11	Orient Express		Tunguska , Siberia
COORDINATES			
60° 53' 23.92" N 101° 55' 07.75 E			
DISCOVERY			
AGE			
EXTRACTION:			
PHYSICAL PROPERTIES:			
Weight:		DIAMETER	
MATL:		MASER FREQ:	
UNIQUE CHARACTERISTICS:			
DISPOSITION: Star City, Soviet Union			
COMMENTS:			

Unsuccessful attempt by Greys to intercept Wave Runner #1 that is on a time reversal recurring spiral trajectory. The Russians actually found this shell in 1968 and pulled them from the forest using a Chinook helicopter captured intact during the Vietnam conflict. The Russians also discovered vast amounts of mercury spread across the area. This single shell or uni-pod arrangement implies that the Greys have an alternate navigation and steering technology than the triple shell arrangement. The shell was found sixty miles from the center of the blast event and imply that it was jettisoned prior to the impact.

ID	NAME	LOCATION
12	St. Paul	St. Paul Island, AK, Bearing Sea
COORDINATES		
57° 09' 25" N 170° 16' 23" W		
DISCOVERY		
AGE		
EXTRACTION:		
DISCOVERY DATE		
Weight:	DIAMETER	
MATL:	MASER FREQ:	
UNIQUE CHARACTERISTICS:		
DISPOSITION:		
COMMENTS:		

This shell was discovered in the 1960's during the lead up to the cold war. Gravimetric mapping was underway to improve ICBM Guidance and accuracy. A large gravimetric anomaly was discovered here. The Russians also detected the anomaly and sent a Spetsnaz team in to investigate. They were discovered by recon overflights which led to a tense diplomatic incident. They were captured and eventually released. The Navy Seabees excavated a large rock quarry here for road building material and runway sub-base material. The shell was too heavy to transport by plane or get out to a ship. This shell led to the design and construction of the *US Airship, Golden Phi*, in reference to the spiral shape object to be extracted. The shell was lifted out of the pit and then transported to an awaiting cargo ship. The *Golden Phi* was the precursor to other lighter than airships used to extract shells worldwide.

This shell also had a coating of ununpentium 115 applied at three points just inside its opening.

ID	NAME	LOCATION
13	Eclipse	Diego Garcia, Indian Ocean

COORDINATES
7° 16' 8" S 72° 21' 55" E

DISCOVERY
AGE
EXTRACTION:
PHYSICAL PROPERTIES:

Weight:		DIAMETER	
MATL:		MASER FREQ:	

UNIQUE CHARACTERISTICS:
DISPOSITION:
COMMENTS:

ID	NAME	LOCATION
14	Kerguelen 1	South Indian Ocean

COORDINATES
49° 20' 25.42" S 69° 03' 29.77" E

DISCOVERY
AGE
EXTRACTION:
PHYSICAL PROPERTIES:

Weight:		DIAMETER	
MATL:		MASER FREQ:	

UNIQUE CHARACTERISTICS:
DISPOSITION:
COMMENTS:

Fabled location of Lemuria, now on the submersed Kerguelen Plateau. Both shells appeared linked via magnetic lines of force. T-waves bisect the straight line path (not great circle) between both shells.

ID	NAME		LOCATION
15	Niamh		Northern Quebec
COORDINATES			
58.28 N 76.80 W			
DISCOVERY			
AGE			
EXTRACTION:			
PHYSICAL PROPERTIES:			
Weight:		DIAMETER	
MATL:		MASER FREQ:	
UNIQUE CHARACTERISTICS:			
DISPOSITION:			
COMMENTS:			

Named in honor of the Lady of the Lake Protector and keeper of Excalibur. This shell has some unique elemental transmutation properties. It is truly the philosopher's stone and can convert silver, lead, and mercury to gold. Much like what was discovered with earlier shells that convert or fuse hydrogen into helium, this particular one can convert heavy metals into pure gold. This was accidentally discovered after extraction onto the *Nautilus* when a roll of solder was left on a cart located within the shells event horizon (the radius of the shell opening) overnight. The lead and silver solder was turned to pure gold in less than eight hours.

ID	NAME	LOCATION
16	Boyne Valley	Ireland

COORDINATES
53° 34' 47" N 6° 36' 43" W

DISCOVERY

AGE

EXTRACTION:

PHYSICAL PROPERTIES:

Weight:		DIAMETER	
MATL:		MASER FREQ:	

UNIQUE CHARACTERISTICS:

DISPOSITION:

COMMENTS:

Deep within the innermost chamber of the Newgrange passage tomb in Ireland's Boyne Valley, 6,000 years old, older than the Egyptian Pyramids, this evocative spiral stands eternal watch over the burial place of the high kings.

The Hill of Tara is where the ancient Irish kings settled their kingdom (actually, there is not much to see in Tara nowadays, but the site is inspiring), located nearby are: Monasterboice with its High Crosses, the Mellifont Abbey, and many other interesting things.

Newgrange is the most important of three pre-Celtic funerary monuments, and was built approximately 5,000 years ago, therefore being older than the Egyptian pyramids at Giza. It covers an area equal to 4,000 square meters and is located on top of a hill. When arriving there, you almost have the impression of seeing a starship landed in a field, due to its circular shape. The tumulus is surrounded by a stone circle.

The entrance is pretty spectacular due to the shining white quartz stones forming the wall. Quartz was not mined locally but in southern Ireland and this implied a long trip by boat. A gigantic stone with spiral engravings is located there as well.

The white stone facing is made of quartz and was reconstructed from the fallen stones found on-site. In the sun it glistens like studded glass and to the ancients it must have looked like magic.

They risked their lives to bring these stones from sources many weeks away by dugout canoe.

This stone is famous. On the left hand side you can see one of only three known examples of the tri-spiral.

The second example is in the passageway that leads up into the darkness under the mound. It's on the left hand side.

And the third example is in the small chamber at the end of the passage, facing back towards the door. Though the main chamber can hold two dozen, this last chamber could only fit one or two people. Long ago, perhaps, the high priestess would stand here and pour sacred water on the tri-spiral as she waited in absolute darkness on Winter Solstice Morning.

Double and triple spirals:

The triple spiral is found carved on the stones. This particular spiral is said to represent the threefold Goddess and the cycles of life. Another similar triple spiral called the triskele, was used in Europe as well as in the Americas by the Hopi Tribe. This spiral represents the cycles of life within the threefold, or the three spheres of the material world, such as land, sky and sea.

The double spirals are everywhere. They have that same sort of non-linear placement that seems to be trying to say something, but not loud enough for our modern ears.

Charles Ross and his experiment where he arranged a lens in front of a wooden plank, so that it focused the Sun's rays on the plank and burned a track on the wood. Each day he put a new piece of wood in this holder and after 366 consecutive days he plotted out the pattern the Sun's rays had burned into the planks. He found the resulting shape was a perfect double spiral.

ID	NAME		LOCATION
17	Excalibur		Homestead, Florida
COORDINATES			
25° 30' 00" N 80° 26' 39" W			
DISCOVERY			
AGE		EXTRACTION:	
PHYSICAL PROPERTIES:			
Weight:	MATL:	DIAMETER	MASER FREQ:
UNIQUE CHARACTERISTICS:			
DISPOSITION:			
COMMENTS:			

ID	NAME		LOCATION
18	Michelevka		Siberia SW of Lake Baikal
COORDINATES			
52° 31' 43.82" N 103° 09' 54.68" E			
DISCOVERY			
AGE		EXTRACTION:	
PHYSICAL PROPERTIES:			
Weight:	MATL:	DIAM:	MASER FREQ:
UNIQUE CHARACTERISTICS:			
DISPOSITION:			
COMMENTS:			

ID	NAME	LOCATION
19	Darwin	Galapagos

COORDINATES
0° 14' 43.28" S 90° 50' 47.65"

DISCOVERY

AGE

EXTRACTION:

PHYSICAL PROPERTIES:

Weight:		DIAMETER	
MATL:		MASER FREQ:	

UNIQUE CHARACTERISTICS:

DISPOSITION:

COMMENTS:

This spiral shell was found in a crater that was thought to be a volcanic cinder cone. This shell has some unique DNA and/or genetic splicing technology associated with it. This could explain some of the biodiversity that famed biologist Charles Darwin noted.

ID	NAME	LOCATION
20	Tasman	Near Derwent River in Tasmania's Jordan River Basin near the town of Brighton

COORDINATES
42o 42' 25" S 147o 15' 28"E

DISCOVERY

AGE

EXTRACTION:

PHYSICAL PROPERTIES:

Weight:		DIAMETER	
MATL:		MASER FREQ:	

UNIQUE CHARACTERISTICS:

DISPOSITION:

COMMENTS:

ID	NAME	LOCATION
21	Pine Gap	Australia
COORDINATES		
23.799° S 133.737° E		
DISCOVERY		
AGE		
EXTRACTION:		
PHYSICAL PROPERTIES:		
Weight:	DIAMETER	
MATL:	MASER FREQ:	
UNIQUE CHARACTERISTICS:		
DISPOSITION:		
COMMENTS:		

Named after Pine Gap, Ohio, the back entrance to Peebles Test Facility. Pine gap and Peebles are linked via T-wave that travels through the earth. The two shells located at these two sites communicate with each other instantaneously. These shells have been used to test the t-wave modulation capability.

ID	NAME	LOCATION
22	Dolce	Dolce, NM
COORDINATES		
36° 59' 00"" N 107° 00' 18"" W		
DISCOVERY		
AGE		
EXTRACTION:		
PHYSICAL PROPERTIES:		

Weight:		DIAMETER	
MATL:		MASER FREQ:	

UNIQUE CHARACTERISTICS:
DISPOSITION:
COMMENTS:

A series of earthquakes in 1966 brought out interest in scientists and geologists in this area. This shell was actually discovered due to the high incidence of ball lightning seen in this area. T-waves generated in this area are closely attuned to the hydrogen plasma frequency. Cameras mounted on the mesa triangulated the direction of flow along telluric lines of force and centered on an underground cavern complex. Several tri-pods of shells were discovered in these caves.

ID	NAME	LOCATION
23	Berner's Heath	Five Miles southeast of Lakenheath AB, UK

COORDINATES

52° 21' 15.24" N 0° 38' 12.42" E

DISCOVERY

AGE

EXTRACTION:

PHYSICAL PROPERTIES:

Weight:		DIAMETER	
MATL:		MASER FREQ:	

UNIQUE CHARACTERISTICS:

DISPOSITION:

COMMENTS:

ID	NAME	LOCATION
24	Dreamland Express	Denver, CO

COORDINATES
39° 51' 30" N 104° 40' 23"

DISCOVERY

AGE

EXTRACTION:

PHYSICAL PROPERTIES:

Weight:		DIAMETER	
MATL:		MASER FREQ:	

UNIQUE CHARACTERISTICS:

DISPOSITION:

COMMENTS:

This shell was used as a part of a large diameter photon accelerator under Denver International airport.

It was named after the John Denver song to confuse with Area 51.

A series of earthquakes 1963 to 1966 lead to a geologic investigation of fault lines in this area. This shell was extracted with the use of a large tunnel boring machine through buried volcanic talc at a depth of six hundred feet. This particular shell has an interesting effect on photons, visible light, and UV that enter around its leading edge. The light is converted to laser energy.

ID	NAME	LOCATION
25	Unicorn	Under the Sphinx, Cairo Egypt

COORDINATES
29° 58' 30" N 31° 08' 15" E

DISCOVERY
AGE
EXTRACTION:
PHYSICAL PROPERTIES:

Weight:		DIAMETER	
MATL:		MASER FREQ:	

UNIQUE CHARACTERISTICS:
DISPOSITION:
COMMENTS:

Phenomenal Healing Powers of this Shell. Cures cancer. The spiral horn of the unicorn is like the helix of life and can send healing energy into any time and any place.

According to Edgar Cayce, a famous psychic, the opening to the Halls of Records, which hold the history of the Earth, will be found in the right shoulder of the Sphinx. This has been clearly marked geometrically. Looking at the figure below, if you bisect the golden mean rectangle that fits around the spiral that runs through the centers of the three pyramids on the Giza plateau; the line passes exactly through the headdress of the Sphinx. Also, a line extended from the southern face of the middle pyramid and the line that bisects the golden mean rectangle, forms a cross that marks a very specific spot on the right shoulder of the Sphinx.

The Unicorn shell was actually located a hundred feet below a fig orchard southeast of the Sphinx and the center of the spiral.

Richard Hoagland states that the Arab name for the Sphinx means "The End of the End connected to the Beginning of the Beginning". This is definitely a "timeline. One of the meanings of the Sphinx is a time cycle from the beginning of Leo to the end of Pisces, the age we are in and the beginning of Aquarius.

When the Sphinx was built some 12,000 years ago, in the Age of Leo, it faced almost due east, where the equinox point was in the Age of Leo. In the New Age of Aquarius, the Sphinx will be facing the zodiac signs in the sky, 180 degrees rotated from its original position and now facing Aquarius.

PYRAMIDS
OF GIZA

SPHINX

Center of Spiral
Location of 'Unicorn' Shell

ID	NAME	LOCATION
26	Glacial Change	Peebles, OH

COORDINATES
38° 56' 53" N 83° 21' 33"

DISCOVERY

AGE

EXTRACTION:

PHYSICAL PROPERTIES:

Weight:		DIAMETER	
MATL:		MASER FREQ:	

UNIQUE CHARACTERISTICS:

DISPOSITION:

COMMENTS:

ID	NAME	LOCATION
27	Big Blue Marble	Rapa Iti (South-central Pacific)

COORDINATES
38° 56' 53" N

DISCOVERY

AGE	Carbon dating of organic matter packed within the shell dates back 650,000 years

EXTRACTION:	

PHYSICAL PROPERTIES:	High beryllium content and slightly radioactive.

Weight:		DIAMETER:	MATL:

MASER FREQ:	Variable with complex wave form

UNIQUE CHARACTERISTICS:
Acts as a T-wave amplifier and lens

DISPOSITION:

COMMENTS:

Rapa Iti is a group of four uninhabited volcanic rocks protruding from the sea (and several submerged rocks), forming the southeastern end of the Austral Islands of French Polynesia. Rapa Iti is located at -27.917, -143.433. The closest island is Rapa Iti, seventy-five kilometers. further northwest, but separated from it by an ocean depth of 4,000 meters. The rocks are part of the municipality of Rapa. The significance of this location is that it is the exact opposite side of the earth from Giza, Egypt. This is also the exact centroid for oceanic mass. When viewed from space over this location very little land mass can be seen only on the edges of the Earth's horizon. From here it is truly water, water everywhere but not a drop to drink. Nearly 99 percent of the Pacific ocean is viewable from space over this location.

The ocean captures t-waves like a fishbowl lens and then they are focused through the shell on Rapa Iti through the Earth where they meet under the Great Sphinx. These T-waves have great healing power or life force.

ID	NAME	LOCATION
28	Athena	Near where the boarders of the Mexican states of Durango, Chihuahua, and Coahuila meet

COORDINATES
26° 42' 16" N 103° 37' 54" W

DISCOVERY	
AGE	>1,000,000 years
EXTRACTION:	NASA in cooperation with Mexican Military
PHYSICAL PROPERTIES:	This shell had significant portion of silver in its material make up, ~ 3%

Weight:		DIAMETER	
MATL:	AqWcNi	MASER FREQ:	

UNIQUE CHARACTERISTICS:
Absorbs radar and radio energy

DISPOSITION:

COMMENTS:

"THE DEAD ZONE"

Near Caballos in Durango State is the Area 51 of Mexico. This area is called "The Dead Zone" because a group of oil company workers searching for drilling sites found that no radio or TV communication could be transmitted here. Also called Mar de Tetys, electromagnetic waves are blamed for the anomaly. Multicolored balls of light, alien-like creatures, and the apparition of a tall fair-haired man have been reportedly seen here.

In 1970 a faulty American Athena missile fired from the White Sands

Missile Base in nearby New Mexico went off course inexplicably and crashed into the mysterious desert region and made the world aware of the unique and apparently unusual properties of the area. Subsequently a team of U.S. Air Force investigators, with Mexican Government approval, journeyed to the crash site and made an unexpected discovery. Within an unspecified and sometimes shifting area within the zone, radio signals fail to travel through the air, creating a type of dark zone. No television, radio, short wave, microwave, or satellite signals seem to penetrate this zone. The name, Zone of Silence, was quickly adopted, and researchers began flocking to the remote location shortly thereafter.

It turns out there may be some natural anomaly associated with the region. High levels of magnetite have been discovered there, and scientists have also found that the area is a hot bed for meteorite activity, raising speculation that there may be some unusual magnetic properties associated with the minerals in the chalky soil. Researchers have been trying to determine whether magnetic ore is naturally occurring or is the product of contamination from thousands or millions of years of meteorite bombardment. And if the high-magnetic properties are a result of natural causes, could this be the reason that so many iron-rich objects from space find their way to this remote spot on Earth?

NASA immediately knew something was drawing the missile to the area. First of all, the missile accelerated in this direction when all propulsion was spent. Second, the Athena made course corrections involving spiral curves before it crashed at the coordinates shown above. The investigation of this area eventually lead to the discovery of a shell buried eighty-five feet below a dry lake bed. The exact location was determined using magnetic and gravimetric mapping, as well as telluric current mapping and ground penetrating radar.

Experimentation of this shell in the mid-1970s eventually led to stealth technology.

ABOUT THE AUTHOR

David Crawford spent nearly fifteen years as an engineering officer in the United States Air Force in the 1980s and 1990s. In that time he had a very exciting, challenging, and "unique" career. He was instrumental in developing and testing several advanced aerospace technologies. Assignments included everything from Ballistic Missile Engineering (including upgrading guidance and targeting hardware), Nuclear Shock and Blast testing, Sub-terranean Engineering (tunnel boring machines), and currently advanced propulsion. He worked near and on super-secret military installations at the Nevada Test Site (Area 51–Dreamland, S-4, and Little Skull Mountain), and the Yuma Proving Grounds. He's been literally to the top of the world where he was involved with research on gravitational anomalies and detecting gravity waves. He was Chief Engineer at Homestead AFB, Florida; one of the apexes of the Bermuda Triangle, before, during, and after Hurricane Andrew destroyed the base in 1992. He then went to Wright-Patterson Air Force Base in Ohio, as Project Engineer, to build an addition to the Avionics Lab, Building 620, straddling the supposed secret tunnel complexes under the base. He is now an engineer working with advanced technology at Wright-Pat. His book leaves you wondering what this former military engineer really knows. Which parts are truly scientific and which are pure fantasy?

www.ingramcontent.com/pod-product-compliance
Lightning Source LLC
Chambersburg PA
CBHW020458260626
47156CB00006B/1774